PAPER CHASE

WILLIAM GARNER

GRAFTON BOOKS

A Division of the Collins Publishing Group

LONDON GLASGOW
TORONTO SYDNEY AUCKLAND

Grafton Books
A Division of the Collins Publishing Group
8 Grafton Street, London W1X 3LA

Published by Grafton Books 1988

British Library Cataloguing in Publication Data

Garner, William
  Paper chase.
  I. Title
  823'.914[F]

ISBN 0-246-13334-1

Printed in Great Britain by
Hartnolls Ltd, Bodmin, Cornwall

Extract from the poem 'A Bedtime Story' from *Crow* by Ted
Hughes is reproduced by kind permission of Faber & Faber Ltd.

To the sisterhood of man,
all journalists who put conscience first,
and, as always, my wife

My gratitude to Dr C. J. Hinds, Director of the Intensive Care Unit at St Bartholomew's Hospital, London, for his patient medical guidance and precious time. Any corner-cutting is mine, not his.

The hospital and intensive care unit in my novel are products of my imagination and are not intended to resemble any actual hospital at Redhill.

MILNE: No matter how imperfect things are, if you've got a free press, everything is correctable, and without it everything is concealable.

RUTH: I'm with you on the free press, it's the newspapers I can't stand.

TOM STOPPARD
Night and Day

News is what someone, somewhere doesn't want published. All the rest is advertising.

1st VISCOUNT ROTHERMERE
Oral Tradition

SIX DEAD, NINE MAIMED IN KIDDY HORROR VILLAGE

Nick got back in his car for the last time, the usual draining away of energy now that the adrenalin had stopped running. Pure luck that he'd happened to be in the area, on his way back from covering the Lincoln rape trial verdict when news desk called him on the radio phone. Hey, ace, nip across country, grab us some juicies before the pack gets off its arse.

It would be a full-page splash. A sizeable chunk of Phantom had dropped in for tea at Nethercott Stoney just as the kids were going home from school. SIX DEAD, NINE MAIMED IN KIDDY HORROR CRASH. From *Globe* man-on-the-spot Nick Brooke in grief-stunned slaughter village.

Cheap and nasty, sure, but he didn't set the style, just filed his copy.

By the time the rest of the mob began flocking in, the whole scene still cluttered with emergency vehicles, the fuzz had turned a bit nasty too. The TV crews took most of the heat: great, serve 'em bloody right, acting as if they owned the place. Still plenty of superficial action, shovel squads, smoke wisping above shattered rooftops, but the two body bags, featherweight as packets of potato crisps, had already left for the morgue. So had the small fleet of ambulances taking the rest of the kids to hospital. No chance of getting near the wreckage out in the fields. The military minders had swarmed out like bugs from the woodwork.

No sweat. By that time he'd already inputted his last wodge, signed off the freelance photographer they'd sent him from Oxford, headed for home. First in, first out; *Globe* style.

The chopper, a USAF machine of some kind or other, had been at three thousand feet, destination Fairford if that local copper had known what he was talking about.

The Phantom had been returning to base from a low-level attack exercise, contour hugging at treetops plus one somewhere in Wales, where the natives hadn't enough clout to tell the military to get stuffed.

Somewhere over Gloucestershire the Yank pilot made one last run, unauthorised, scaring the hell out of cows, horses and the people at some big pot's farm. That local Plod, the only one willing to talk, pity his inspector had turned up so fast to switch him off, said the farm manager, hadn't even got as far as the telephone to call Upper Heyford when it happened.

By then the pilot must have known he'd be for the chop when the complaints started to pour in, had abandoned his hell-raising and used boost to give himself quick penetration of the cloud base, broken but not much more than two thousand feet. Saw this red glow, the copper said; looked like he was on fire, but Nick's guess was he'd flared his afterburner.

Anyway, must have taken out the chopper at around five hundred miles an hour. Eyewitnesses said there'd been an explosion, but any bird hitting another bird at five hundred plus was going to be an explosion in its own right.

Not that it made much difference one way or another to the poor bastards whose remains, together with a few million quids worth of metal, had ploughed the fields and scattered. Snappy phrase, pity he couldn't use it. Bad taste, Tim Bryce would say; horrible bad taste, Nick.

Bad taste! Tim Bryce, editor of the pits-plumbing *Globe*, arbiter of taste! Jesus!

He picked up his Excell to give Sarah a call. She expected it these days, ever since they'd switched over to the radio phones. If he didn't ring her, she'd like as not call him. She worried.

'Nick?'

He could hear Emma in the background. 'Is it daddy? Is it daddy, mummy?'

'Hi!' he'd said. 'Heard the news? Give you one guess where I am.'

'Oh, Nick!' Instant shock-horror. 'How awful! Just wait a bit, darling, daddy will talk to you in a minute.' Little Emm loved the idea of the pocketphone.

'And here's me thinking you'd be home any minute. Oh, Nick, you do get some stinking jobs. It must have been awful.' Poor old Ess, the original bleeding heart.

'It's a job, Ess.' They had this one regularly. He was too tired to have it again.

'So you'll be home when you're home. Tonight, though?'

'Do my best, but I'm not sure yet.' Not breaking his neck for a late scratch meal and Emma out of bed every five minutes if she heard him arrive. Rather take his time, do himself a bit well on his exies.

'Back when I'm back. Don't wait up, okay? See you.'

Only when he'd rung off did he realise he hadn't said goodnight to Emma. This bloody job! Screwed you up more than you realised, but how else could you earn so many crispies?

Bloody cold outside, people talking of snow before Christmas. So what? Engine running, car getting fuggy warm. Always have an overnight bag in the back along with the shovel, bag of grit and stuff in case you got bogged down, snowed up, whatever. You picked up a few tricks if you were as old a hand as Nick Brooke.

Still, no intention of getting bogged down, least of all in Nethercott bloody Stoney, where the sexiest news was the local vegetable show except when half an F-111 came through the rooftops. Okay, his own bed, keep old Ess happy, but a meal and a bottle first.

He nosed his way out of the village, feeling the reaction now the excitement was over. Feeling a bit bad about those poor bloody kids, feeling a bit bad about little Emm.

PART ONE

I

GLOBE MAN-ON-SPOT ON SPOT

Sarah drove all the way back from Dorking still thinking about Nick. Something was bothering him, had been bothering him for two days now. The more he denied it, the more certain she was.

Aggressive, cocksure, nearly always engaged in one of the great editorial dogfights that were part of the *Globe*'s way of life, he normally made sure she should be the first to know all about it. If a trouble shared was a trouble halved, Nick could be generous to a fault.

Not this time. This time all the signs were there but he would discuss nothing, insisted there was nothing to discuss. Nick subdued and evasive was a new experience, something she didn't seem able to handle. Thirty-five years old, married, a daughter of eight and failed, as yet, to get the hang of that kind of wisdom.

Good at feeling, though: for herself, for Nick, for Emma. Only you couldn't say that you were good at something that was part of you like it or not. You could be good at history because you'd done it at university well enough for them to give you a degree in it. No degrees for feelings, any more than there were for life, and they were an awful lot harder than history.

If they gave degrees in life, Nick would have walked it. Had it all off pat. Maybe rather too pat; high marks without ever actually advancing the subject.

'You know me,' he'd said when he told her she was going to marry him. 'Old Nick Brooke, good at people, good at life. Sarah Purdy? Just good at exams. Exams aren't real life, Ess. You need me to look after you, not fit to be out on your own.'

Ess for Sarah.

Shy, timid Sarah. Father a regular army colonel dead when she was still a child. Mother now a pillar of genteelly middle-class society in the cathedral town of Wells. The central tenet of Mum's philosophy: men know best.

Little Sarah Purdy, privately educated until daddy died. After that, with all kinds of maternal misgivings, committed to the state system. Even then it had been an all-girls school, where she disappeared almost without trace for several years, devoted to gerbils and romantic poets like Keats and Shelley.

Large, boisterous girls, good at sports, and vivid, self-aware girls who daubed on lipstick before meeting boys on the way home from school, had patronised her and thought her a bit wet. Everyone, Sarah included, was more than a bit surprised when, in her late teens, she became a quietly impressive performer in the school swimming team and, with three good A-levels, chose to read history at clever, faintly raffish Sussex instead of Oxbridge or some earnest provincial university.

At Sussex she was no longer patronised, no longer anything except, perhaps, a bit of a prig, a bit of a swot. Certainly not top of the pops so far as men were concerned. It had been her quietly eccentric period, dressed in as weird a medley of cast-offs as a stealthily active imagination could contrive. She had even worn glasses with plain lenses, round-rimmed things that were encouraged to slip forward to the tip of her nose and make her look prematurely senile.

She had come down with a decent two-one and a lofty comment from her tutor that she could have had a first with a bit more effort. Hot-faced and angry, she had demanded 'Why the hell didn't you tell me that when I could have done something about it?' And then instantly apologised.

After that, London, year of our Lord nineteen hundred and seventy-four; an ill-paid job as a junior researcher in an advertising agency. Ridiculously nervous, dolled up in her best Biba gear, keeping a date forced on her by someone who was absolutely not her type.

She had fallen for Nick like a chimneypot from a rooftop. The first time he came up to her room her clothes came off in a breathless minute.

> *Who has not seen their lover*
> *Walking at ease*

16

With usual feet that cover
A pavement under trees;
Not singular, apart,
But featured, footed, dressed
Approaching the rest,
In the same dapple of the sunlight caught,
And thought:
Here comes my heart.

That was how she had seen it at the time.

Marriage against her mother's wish; a registry office *fait accompli*. Only his money as a reporter with the South London Press, hers with the agency. Nick bullied her into asking for a raise which, to her surprise, she instantly got. He moved in to share her little room with its single bed-and-a-half, washbasin and the curtained alcove they called the kitchen. It had been a bit like taking in a wolf as a housepet.

It suited Nick, left him to apply his driving, wilful energy to what he called getting it made. Courts, police stations and hospitals, then doorstepping, while his agency linage and earnings climbed. He was good at his job; very good. A bit like being good at writing graffiti on the walls of public lavatories, thought priggish Sarah.

Anonymity to by-line, op-ed to front page and then – he stayed drunk for an entire weekend and still managed to make love – a job in Fleet Street when the Street still housed all the big names.

Okay, it was the *Globe*. And the *Globe* was junk press. A rag. But every good journalist had to start somewhere, Nick said. If you took all the good journalists away from all the lousy newspapers, Nick said, the power of the press lords would be broken at a stroke. Anyway, the *Globe* sold four mill plus.

She remembered the first time he made the streamer; huge headlines, by-lined *Globe* man-on-the-spot Nick Brooke. She'd been secretly impressed, his first big break. A few more like that and he would be away to a real newspaper.

He had laughed. 'Hardly wrote a word of it, did I? Got it all wrong, Ess, bloody chief sub, that's who really wrote it, Tim Bryce breathing down the back of his neck.

'Know what sort of editor Tim is? A genius! No, seriously, a genius. Not a writing editor, probably can't spell, but the best production man in the game, make up an issue from rumours and sticky tape.

'News? News is what the *Globe* says is news. Buy it, steal it, kick-start it from nowhere. So long as it fills the spaces between the ads and fools the punter, you're in business.'

It had shocked her, the former fogeyish, intellectually snobby Sarah Purdy. The way you might feel about someone who'd got himself into the *Guinness Book of Records* for the number of times he'd played Russian roulette and won, when all the time the cartridges were blanks.

Yet she couldn't shake off the fascination. Even a grudging admiration, his will to succeed impressive in its total dedication. Anyway, Emma arrived, she gave up her job and they moved into a fourth-floor Bayswater walk-up; two bedrooms, a proper kitchen and all on Nick's money.

'Nick, you can't stay with that rag,' she used to say, feeling guilty, thinking that she could do part-time work as soon as Emma reached school age.

'Don't fret.' He had meant it. 'Enough exposure to give me a name, then bye-bye *Globe*.'

Well, he'd had plenty of splashes since then; even wrote them himself sometimes, though there was apparently a splash sub who could write more like Nick Brooke than Nick Brooke himself.

But between his rapidly fattening pay cheques and the expense accounts that gave him the high life he enjoyed, the inevitable happened.

'Of course I'd like to go to a quality, but they can't afford me. Or if they could now, they couldn't for much longer. The big money's where I'm already at, until I shift to TV. You're the last one to kick, Ess. You're the one that wanted to move out to the country.'

So now he was Nick Brooke, the *Globe* man-on-the-spot; the thrill of high living, a certain dubious fame, a job that was less a way of life than a blood sport. And it was true, she was the one who had talked him into a house in the country.

Swinging the car off the road she found herself, even after three months, doing the usual silent gloat.

Originally there had been a mansion, the Victorian Gothic dream of a City speculator with ambitions even more preposterous than Nick's. His grandson, too, had speculated, but once too often, tumbling into bankruptcy just as the house had tumbled into decay.

Now a different form of speculation had come to the rescue, developers buying up and demolishing the pretentious monster for the sake of a sliver of unwooded land and planning permission, rare in this part of south Surrey, for four executive dwellings.

A onetime servants' lodge, tucked into a corner too small for a fifth house and satisfactorily inconspicuous, had been refurbished and put on the market on the very Saturday that Nick, finally yielding, had agreed to come house-hunting in Dorking.

The house was plain but not ugly, and relatively cheap in an area full of properties that were anything but. Its postage-stamp scrap of territory precluded any future extensions that might have tempted higher bids, yet it was one of the few they had seen that he couldn't dismiss as either workman's primitive or sore-thumb tickytacky.

More than that, the general area was thick with the famous and well-heeled. Let Nick call it the only one hundred per cent mortgage with hot and cold running shivers, he saw it as a good temporary address, even if by his wildly ambitious standards it was only a stepping stone to far grander things.

For herself, she hadn't Nick's restless, almost angry drive to go high, high, high. It was a house, a nice house, their first house. Small and restricted it might be, but at the back it looked over a low hedge on to a genuine farm lane. All around them, some of the most beautiful woodlands and hill country between London and the south coast.

For once a bit of decent winter weather coincided both with the weekend and the fact that Nick was home to share it. She had been up early because of Emma, out early to get the shopping done while Nick had a lie-in. This afternoon, if Nick was willing, they would have a good walk.

Looking up at the closed curtains, Emma said, 'Daddy's *still* in bed. I'm going to wake him up.'

'Emma, no!' Sarah caught her just in time. Emma didn't see enough of Nick because of his job. She hated it when he stayed in bed late after a week of chasing whatever the *Globe* chose to call news. Emma also loved the chimes.

Three-note chimes. Privately, Sarah thought them a bit yuck, but in Nick's concept of the high life, chimes were posher. 'Just you see, Sarah,' her mother had said. 'Either he'll end up with a Rolls and a butler or you'll all be on supplementary benefit or whatever they call it.' Nick thought Mum was the kind of woman who gave the sex a bad name.

Emma wriggled, trying to escape. 'Let me! I want to! Daddy won't mind. I expect he doesn't know the time.'

'He won't know the time if he's asleep, and if he's asleep, it's because he's tired. Poor daddy! It would be horrid to wake him. Help me get the shopping out of the car. Then we'll go up tippy-toe to see if he's really asleep.'

'All right.' Emma gave in. 'And if he's still asleep, I'll tickle his nose with my feather.'

A jay's feather, her current treasure. Little by little, Sarah thought, she'll get used to it: new house, new school, living in the country.

Getting the shopping out of the car, she wondered how to distract Emma from waking Nick immediately. He *was* tired, no doubt of that. This week, to use one of his mid-Atlantic clichés, everything had come up in spades. First the Lincoln rape trial, then Nethercott Stoney. Nethercott Stoney was her number one bet for his behaviour over the past two days. He'd been proud of being the first media man on the scene, but she fancied it had affected him more than he was willing to admit.

Just as Emma was beginning to get restless again, the prospect of waking daddy by tickling his nose with a feather far more attractive than carrying potatoes as far as the front porch, Peggy Morcambe came out to collect her milk. She was another late riser though her husband, who ran a car showroom in Dorking, was out of the house by eight-thirty every day except Sundays.

Frilly in a pink housecoat and slippers with fur trimmings, she waved. 'Super day! I mean, for the time of year. Smashing! Hello, Emma.'

She had introduced herself as Peggy but she and Sarah weren't really on that sort of terms yet, even though the Morcambes had the house next door.

You could say that: the house next door. There was only one executive residence so far. The others were still being built. The only other neighbours were the Crabtrees, the old couple who had lived in the cottage on the corner for umpteen years. Sarah thought they were remarkably relaxed about the prospect of being hemmed in by four new houses, not to mention the loss of their view over the lane to Holmbury Hill. But Mrs Crabtree just shrugged and said it would be nice to have neighbours after thirty years on their own.

Though she had taken at once to Mrs Crabtree, who had a kind heart behind a brusque manner, usually wore trousers over her broad beam and knew everything about country things, Emma was altogether more cautious about the Morcambes.

Emma, Sarah thought guiltily, showed good sense.

'Getting to feel like home, is it?' They had been there three months now, she and Nick, but it suited Peggy Morcambe to play the pioneer on the strength of moving into the first completed house all of two months earlier. Anyway, the Brookes lived in converted servants' quarters, not a superior executive residence.

She was tall, blonde, fiftyish; a bony face, poor skin and a talent for choosing clothes that invariably managed to be neither cheap nor elegant. There was a daughter who worked in London as a secretary – the managing director's secretary; Peggy Morcambe always managed to work that in – and came home most weekends.

The Morcambes did a lot of entertaining at weekends. Sarah and Nick, they had said more than once, really must come over some Saturday night, when they had the right kind of people. Up to now, although there was a good deal of noise most Saturday nights, they had apparently not had the right kind of people.

Sarah told herself she was a snob, but it wasn't really that. It was just that Peggy Morcambe, the Morcambes as a family, come to that, were definitely not her type, though Nick liked to do his gay deceiver bit with what he called the bony blonde. Privately, he mocked her: 'My daughter the managing director's secretary.'

He'd have made a play for the daughter, too, but Tracey, even stringier than her mother and cautiously punk within an hour of arriving home for the weekend, always came with a boy in tow. The boys changed regularly but Nick insisted it was always the same one, a transvestite with a large wardrobe.

Sarah went reluctantly across to the wire mesh boundary fence. The Morcambes had planted it with beech within a month of Sarah's and Nick's arrival. Nothing personal, they said, just a question of waiting for the right time of year, but they also put up woven fencing six feet high along the back boundary, taking away a lot of light as well as the view of Holmbury Hill, the church and the village green.

Small price, Nick said, for dodging monologues on the weather, who'd got money, who hadn't, and the shocking state of the car business. Arthur Morcambe sold Japanese imports and drove one himself, a sort of Nip Porsche. His wife drove one too; nothing wrong with the state of the car business so far as the Morcambes were concerned.

'Just a few years, Ess, and they can shove it. We'll be up the hill with our two acres and a Jag. And a nice little runabout for you.'

He meant it. He might well do it. The prospect filled her with unease.

'Is Nick home this weekend?' Peggy Morcambe had a blue, popeyed stare which she reinforced by thrusting her head far forward as she talked. Every so often she would look away, her stare focused rigidly on infinity. Just as you thought she had forgotten all about you she would give a quick jerk of the head and come back. Nick said she was remote-controlled, her brain reprogrammed every five minutes.

'Still in bed,' Sarah said. 'He's been pushed a bit this week. I wish he didn't have to work so hard.'

Damn, why had she said that? The last thing she wanted was to discuss personal matters with Peggy Morcambe.

'That awful crash thing,' Peggy Morcambe said. 'My husband said he was on the front page, Nick, I mean.' She did her popeyed thing and added, 'They have all the papers in the showroom, of course.'

Just like my daughter the managing director's secretary; the umpteenth reminder that they didn't actually take a vulgar paper like the *Globe* themselves.

'Yes,' Sarah said. 'He didn't get back until after midnight.'

Why hadn't she just let it drop?

Emma spotted her skipping rope, ran to pick it up and began her usual unco-ordinated jumps and trippings. Sensible Emma!

'It must have been awful.' Peggy Morcambe's head performed another little jerk as if releasing some internal pressure. 'I mean, well, everything. Was it? Awful, I mean?'

What you mean, Sarah thought, is did he see all the bodies? Kids looking like hedgehogs run over by cars. Women screaming, the school smashed to rubble, something to talk about at your Saturday night rave-ups.

No, not fair, she wasn't like that. Just stupid, no imagination, obliged to batten vicariously on the experiences of people like Nick. Nick said Peggy Morcambe was the archetypal shock-horror-sex-probe-vampire.

She was hopeless, ought to say she had things to do. Ought to say they'd nothing in common, still nothing in common if they were marooned together on a desert island for the rest of their lives.

As usual, guilt made her garrulous. 'The police handled things very well, apparently. By the time Nick got there, the rescue services had things more or less under control. Except, of course . . .'

Except that children had been killed, maimed. How did you get that under control? Emma, trying to sing as she skipped, could be stiff on a slab, waiting to be cut up like meat at the butcher's shop so they could decide which bit of her had died first.

But those endlessly staring pop-eyes had finally found something to concentrate on. Head thrust forward, dainty furrows in that rarely troubled brow, Peggy Morcambe was saying, 'After midnight! Goodness! The crash was at about three-thirty, wasn't it? I mean, whatever time those poor children were leaving school. What did he do? I mean, did he have to talk to any of those poor women?'

No, she said, he didn't interview any of the mothers, just eyewitnesses. A lot of questions to the police and the fire brigade and the local hospital and oh, yes, he interviewed the top cop, only it had been cut by the rewrite sub. Nick said the *Globe* was the personal property of the rewrite subs.

And it took him from about four in the afternoon until . . . yes, well, I don't exactly know until when, or why, except that he wasn't back until after midnight. He often gets home after midnight, or not at all, and I often don't know why. Not really; just what he tells me.

Only she didn't say the last bit aloud. It wasn't the sort of thing you said aloud. Particularly to people like Peggy Morcambe.

Bitch! she told herself. Snob bitch! They were neighbours, going to be neighbours for years. You couldn't say what you'd like to say, that you really didn't give a damn what the Morcambes thought about Nick's job. Most of all you couldn't bring conversations like this to a quick, neat end without worrying whether the other person would brood on it, get steamed up, be hurt or whatever. Not if you were Sarah Brooke, you couldn't.

Inadequate snob bitch! That was about it. Little Sarah Purdy, Nick used to tease: good at exams, bad at people. Though he nearly always kissed her after he'd said it.

It was Peggy Morcambe who said, 'Well, can't stop here nattering all day. I mean, some of us have things to do. Ooops, sorry! Not you, sweetie, me, anything to dodge getting on with it, know what I mean?'

And she undulated off, a bottle of milk in each hand, fur-trimmed slippers with high heels, pastoral *à la* Marie Antoinette.

You should have said, Sarah told herself as she went back to the car, *you* should have said, 'Sorry, can't stop, things to do.' Should have gone on saying it until she got the message. If messages ever got past that smooth, pale, empty forehead.

She carried the last load from the car. Damn nuisance not having the door open, but if it had been open, Emma would have been upstairs like a shot. She went back to close the lid of the boot, then remembered the spade.

In the winter Nick always carried a spade in case he was snowed up, a tip he'd got from one of the old school. 'Shovel, set o' chains, bag of bleedin' grit, boy, way we used to do it in the days when you could be sent out at five minutes' notice and never mind the bleedin' weather.'

The spade was mucky, she had noticed, bunging in the shopping in Sainsbury's car-park. Got himself stuck in the mud? Not Nick. Fancied his driving, Nick did, not so daft as to park off the road without leaving at least one of the drive wheels on a good firm surface. A plastic bag of grit, too, pinched from one of the bins the local council had on roads with a tricky gradient. A bad winter could be quite an experience among these small, steep hills, according to the Crabtrees, though they said the council were quick to get the ploughs out.

Something else, now she came to notice; the plastic bag, ex-garden fertiliser, wasn't there. Bits of grit on the flooring but no bag, just the spade and the belt things you could fasten around the drive wheels to give them a better purchase.

No mud on the belts, hadn't been used since he got himself out of the snow in Shropshire – MAD AXEMAN'S REIGN OF TERROR – during the big fall, February before last. So what was all this about spades and grit?

Emma was still singing her skipping song: *The teachers are the brainy ones, the boys know how to fight. The girls have got the sexy legs, so* that's *all right.*

Eight years old.

She stopped to call plaintively, 'Mum, when can we go in? Can we go in, mum? I'm thirsty.'

'God, you look awful.' Sarah took Nick's dirty plate. 'Had a bad night, didn't you?'

'*I* had a bad night!' Emma looked up from colouring a picture. 'I was awake *all* night!'

'Didn't have a good one.' Nick hunched over the table like a down-and-out in a soup kitchen.

'What's on your conscience?' She bit her lip, slipped up there.

'Does it have to be my conscience? Anyway' – his laugh false – 'haven't got one, right? First thing the *Globe* checks when they hire you.'

She came to stroke the back of his neck. 'Is it those poor kids?'

'Oh, honestly, Ess! Just another job.'

It was Nethercott Stoney all right. Scoop of a lifetime and the *Globe* wouldn't touch it with a bargepole. Tim Bryce would throw a fit. So would everyone else. World exclusive, no way of cashing in, like pulling a big stroke and finding it was Mafia money. If they got the smallest inkling!

Ess was giving him her Samaritan look: There, tell mummy all about it and you'll feel *much* better. She said, 'Emma, be a pet and fetch me the tray, please.' Emma went off in slow motion.

'I'm sorry,' Sarah said. 'It's just that . . .' She lost her nerve; press him and he would flip. Why did men insist on keeping these things bottled up?

He sighed. 'Just what? It's nothing. I'm just tired.'

He had an urge to be angry, to take out on her what he daren't inflict on anyone else. He felt shame. He always did. And a kind of self-pity: the lousy, dirty job.

He had two wives. One, slim, dark, attractive; still a knockout on the special occasion. Sudden joyous enthusiasms, a soft, gentle wit in the right company, open and honest as daylight.

The other slummocked around in jeans or dungarees, thin, dark face almost scowling under the pressure of her feelings. Starving blacks. Emma. Radioactive pollution. Emma. Whales, seals, bloody dolphins. Emma.

The flip side of the girl he had married. Every so often, when he'd been taking too much heat and the going was rough he found himself tempted to put on his own flip side and beat the verbal hell out of her. She'd come up the easy way, he'd climbed the hard.

But he usually got over it because for the past nine years he'd made it hard for her too and she'd stuck it without complaining. If he sometimes felt that she'd taken him on with the whales, the dolphins and ban the bomb, it made no odds because her feelings were all of a piece. Nothing, least of all him, got short measure.

Married for nine years and the show still on the road when almost every other marriage he knew was either clapped out or headed for the rocks. Never have thought he'd be proud of a thing like that, but he was, even if the fact made it easier to forgive himself on the odd occasion when he behaved like a shit.

Well, he was going places and he was taking her with him. The time would come when he wouldn't have to behave like a shit because he'd no longer be in a shitty job. In the meantime, though it was nothing compared with what he had in mind for the future, she had what she'd always wanted, a house in the country. It was a start.

At least, that was how he had seen it until Nethercott Stoney.

Emma was back with the tray. Sarah said, 'Do you think you could clear daddy's things, sweetie?'

'Are we going out?' Emma picked up a teaspoon. 'It's Saturday. Are we going out, daddy? Can we do something nice? Can we' – her face lit up – 'go out and then talk to someone on your pocketphone? Can we ring Nanna? Or Tamsin? Can I talk to Tamsin?'

His Excell fascinated her. Belonged to the *Globe*, of course, but the odd call to Sarah's mother in Wells while they were on the top of Holmbury Hill or, better still from Emma's point of view, to one of her friends, was a treat he occasionally allowed, partly because he was away so much, partly for the sake of a little peace. Anything wrong with that?

No peace, not this morning, not for him, but although his stomach was acid with frustration he mustn't let it show.

He pushed his chair back, tousled, unshaven. 'Got to shower and get dressed first, honeybunch.' He looked toward Sarah. 'Any post?'

'I know where it is, dad.' Unresentful, Emma was off to fetch it.

If you can't avoid something unpleasant, Sarah told herself, go to meet it: positive is always better than negative. The gospel according to Penelope, who had run the assertiveness and self-awareness groups.

'One of them's a bill,' not looking at him as she cleared.

Not another row over bills! All paid, sooner or later, even if he did tend to leave them until the final notices arrived. When you earned big money you had big debts. Except that what he earned was other people's idea of big money, not his.

Watching her fuss around the table he grabbed her, surprising himself with the strength of his feelings.

'Not going to be like this for ever, Ess. We're going places. Promise.' He *had* to find a way.

'It's us that matter, not bloody money.' She could never swear convincingly.

'No,' he said, 'not just money. Going places is being someone. Not on the *Globe*. On a decent paper. Doing things that matter.'

'I won't care whether they matter' – she hugged him fiercely – 'so long as they aren't cheap. Hypocritical. Sensationalism pretending to be pity and moral indignation. So long as they don't make me want to puke.'

Emma was back with the post. 'This one's for you, dad.' He freed himself to take it. It was the telephone bill, a final notice.

'Oh God, Ess, I thought I'd paid it. I really did!' He could say that kind of thing even when they both knew it was untrue. In some ways he was more of a child than Emma.

He refused to look at her. 'I'd better get dressed.' Emma had gone again.

'Wait. In a minute. Nick, talk about it. It helps, honestly.'

'Talk about what, for God's sake?' He knew what.

'It's nothing to be ashamed of, being upset by something really awful.' She took his hands. 'If you want to know, I'm relieved. I hate to think of you as a sort of junkie, no feelings, nothing to live for except the next fix of misery or violence.'

'Ess, stop talking like a third-rate soap. I was inoculated against things like Nethercott Stoney when I was still ambulance chasing.'

'Ambulance chasing, doorstepping,' she said. 'I still cringe for you when I think what you've had to do.' But she kissed him.

He kissed her back. 'Look, give me time to sort myself out and we'll go into Dorking.' Anything to get his mind away from the subject.

Emma came back in time to hear.

'The library! Please! Then the Grotto. Can I have a coke and a doughnut? It's Saturday.'

'I'll take her to the library,' Sarah said. 'If we go now we can just catch the bus. You can come in the car and meet us at the Grotto. By the way, did you get yourself stuck in the mud up there?'

He looked genuinely puzzled. 'Mud? What mud? Where?'

'The spade's all muddy. And you used that grit stuff.' She went to help Emma on with her coat.

'Oh.' He found his heart thumping astoundingly. 'No, not me. The photographer, new guy from Oxford. Parked off the road, and slid into a sort of shallow ditch. We had to do a bit of digging, chuck the grit in to give him a purchase.'

'Under some trees.' She gave him a glance, saw his surprise. 'Leaf mould. Sandy soil and leaf mould, same sort of stuff as round here.' She grinned. 'You know my methods, Watson.'

She zipped up Emma's anorak. 'You'd better get yourself some more grit, hadn't you? Not that I like you pinching it from those bins. Look good, wouldn't it, the *Globe*'s man-on-the-spot caught stealing dirt instead of digging it up.'

'Cheap,' he said. 'Pretty cheap, my girl.' He watched them leave. If only she knew what he'd dug up.

He'd done his share of dirt-digging all right. Hanging around, hot and parched, cold and wet, by day, by night. Besieging closed doors, drawn curtains, shouting questions and offers of money through letterboxes. Sudden wild stampedes when the word went round that the mark, sometimes angry, often tearful or frightened, had sneaked out by a back door and could be caught, surrounded, bombarded with shouts and questions, all as brutal as a public stoning.

He'd been surprised how quickly he had learned to suppress such things as pity, embarrassment, decency. Devil take the hindmost. You didn't stand on ceremony, you stood on hands, shoulders, faces whose owners, given half a chance, would sure as hell stand on yours.

It was the beginning of the way to the top. He'd left it behind.

Play his present hand right and he need never come down. He owed it to Sarah.

Damp from the shower, still only half-dressed, he found himself peering across the narrow fields of the valley bottom toward the December trees. The mist would barely clear today. The trees marked the beginning of the woods that ran toward the top of Holmbury Hill. They reminded him of other woods, not far from Nethercott Stoney.

Push aside all thoughts of dead and maimed kids, of having to deal with Sarah if Emma had been one of the limp and bloody bundles he had seen hauled from the rubble. Two things had dropped out of the teatime sky over Nethercott Stoney. One was pure horror, the other pure luck.

Hadn't asked for it, wish it away if he could, bloody fool to ignore it now that it had happened.

On his way home he'd taken a minor road, its signpost all but lost in an overgrown, leafless hedgerow where red berries gave the illusion of winter blossom. The road started to climb almost at once, though the view was restricted, mostly by woodland that was probably someone's government-subsidised tax fiddle. That was when he realised he hadn't had a pee since Christ knew when.

If they only knew, all the berks with their glib talk of how the press boys – like blacks in the old Deep South, you were a 'boy' to the end – couldn't function away from bars and five-star hotels. When you were out on a job, the job came first. You could go for hours without seeing a sandwich or a cup of tea, hang on to your water till your bladder was fit to burst. Living on hard shit, old Ernie Mount used to call it. The punters thought it only happened to war correspondents.

Oh yes, he'd thought, pulling in on a muddy verge with the woodland bare, dark and impersonally menacing, he'd done all that and been good at it. No use moaning. It was the reporter's equivalent of square-bashing, just one more other-motivated squaddie sweating it out for a news editor who'd started that way himself and didn't see why the next generation should have it any easier.

But he wasn't going to be another bloody news editor. Not even an editor, last month's circulation figures popping up in imaginary 96-point every time the proprietor came on the phone. He was going to be the kind of god, he had told himself, killing the engine, that editors, even editors, only called rude names behind their famous backs. And not just for himself: for Ess.

He slid out of the car, the rural silence instantly enveloping. For the first time in hours he was aware of such things as the smell of damp earth, rotting leaves, a world free from pervasive tragedy that had to be cooked, sliced and packaged for readers who liked it served up with big pictures, small words, great pukey dollops of emotion.

That was all there was, silence and smells. No traffic sounds. Not even a cow or barking dog. The kind of silence that Emma still hadn't adapted to after the endless background growl of central London. The kind of silence that Sarah professed to love, yet grew uneasy under when she was alone at night with nothing but a farm track at the end of the garden and Dorking eight miles away down the hill.

Convention took him a pace or two into the wood before he pulled down his zip and stood there, his water, steaming and almost indecently noisy, spattering over rank grass, briars, a compost of fallen leaves.

Look around idly, as you did, zip himself up, look again as something penetrated his abstraction. Ahead, where the shadows thickened with the thickening trees and the late light was broken into innumerable fragments, a chunk of sky gleamed coldly where no such chunk should be.

The wood was wholly artificial, conifers, a rigorously drilled cash crop as alien to this outlying spur of the Cotswolds as new, raw brick in a country of weathered stone. Nothing to do with nature, everything to do with money; a precise geometry of profit.

Something had ripped through the ranks like chain shot on a Napoleonic battlefield. Instinct told him what it was before the words came to describe it. He went to investigate, treading gingerly over the kind of thing London didn't train you for.

A sizeable piece of helicopter, part of the nose, ripped away by the double force of collision and explosion. Mangled, blackened, skeletal. Eerie, even when you knew that its two former occupants were miles away in the Oxford city mortuary.

Back in the present, he towelled himself furiously, his eyes once again drawn back to the hill.

Bits of dried mud and leaf mould, Ess was right. Observant,

that girl, said less than she thought but didn't miss much. She must have assumed that he'd just abandoned the plastic sack he'd kept the grit in. Well, you had to get up early to think faster than Nick Brooke. A South London upbringing plus six years on the *Globe*: what you might call on-the-job training for keeping one step ahead.

Dressed and downstairs, he washed the spade, rubbed it dry. As an afterthought he vacced out the back of the car. A moment later he was thinking that there were times when you could be too careful. Ess had brought all kinds of things back from the top of Holmbury Hill. Chunks of stone for her new rockery, bits of wild flower she hoped might take root in the odd corner. The bloody car was probably full of bits of sand and leaf mould. He replaced the spade, grinning a little.

A new thought erased the grin. Why was he covering his tracks unless, subconsciously, he was expecting them to be looking for him?

Them? Who? Hell, he'd already thought it through a hundred times. No one could possibly know. No one, car or foot, had passed by while he was in the wood. No one . . .

A new thought. He backed the car into the drive, walked carefully around it, looking at the wheels. Muddy, yes; what cars weren't muddy in December? All the same, into the High Street carwash before he met up with Ess and Emma. Another thing he'd learned early in life: you bloody well couldn't be too careful.

On the way to Dorking the real problem returned. It had wrecked his sleep, would go on wrecking everything until he found an answer. All right, he had the thing hidden away safely enough, but he still hadn't a clue how he was going to use it. He only knew that, somehow, he would.

Had to, didn't he? Scoop of a lifetime!

Arriving back late, Nick threw himself into a chair, eyes closed.

Emma said, 'Daddy's sloshed.'

'Not sloshed.' He threw a cushion. 'Tired, my girl.' And to Sarah, 'Had a barney with next door, didn't I?'

'You're not serious?' Patronising, irritating, the Morcambes were still neighbours.

'Ran into them in town, the whole shower. Even oozy Arthur, flushed with success, flogged six Nissans since breakfast or something. All drinking unspeakable things in the White Horse.'

'Not really a row?' Sarah glanced at Emma, but she was back in her book. 'Anyway, you always say you don't like the White Horse.'

'Felt like a change.' Too restless to find anywhere to his taste.

'Are we going to have to apologise or something?'

'Shouldn't think so. All too tanked up to notice. Incidentally, the great Hugh Rossiter was with them.'

Her face lit. 'You met Hugh Rossiter? Why didn't you say?'

'Actually, he was with some people who were with them, some bank manager and his wife. Pickled in brandy, sitting there' – he drawled, exaggeratedly high-pitched and languid – 'doing his silent "If you'd seen what I've seen, dear old boy" thing.

'You know' – always that awkward mixture of envy and professional respect when Nick talked about Hugh Rossiter – 'latter-day Christ, crucified in six continents.'

'You're only jealous.'

'No I'm not. I know, he's seen it all, but before half of us were born. Vietnam was more or less his swansong. Even half the sheets he worked for have been dead for years. What impresses people like the Morcambes, scarcely heard of him before, let alone read him, is seeing him on the tube last year.'

He hunched himself, defensive.

'Okay, a bloody good journalist in his day. Memorable phrases, high moral tone, wring your heart like a wet dishcloth. But always letting his feelings get between him and the hard facts. That's not journalism, Ess. That's preaching.'

He mimed again. 'Dear old Hugh, one of the old school, valiant for truth but never betrays a confidence, don't breed 'em like that any more.'

He shook his head, driven by his inner tension. 'Doesn't work, not any more. You've got to be like a surgeon these days, never mind the patient, where's the cancer? If I'd let myself get all emotional over dead kids in Nethercott Stoney I wouldn't have signed off while the rest of the mob was still falling about over coppers' feet.'

'You just bottled up your feelings,' she said carefully. 'You're still bottling them up. Do you think I can't tell?'

'Oh, Ess, that's just you talking. Women enjoy being emotional, which is why most of them don't make it in the real world. Rossiter wrote some great stuff but times have changed. He wouldn't last a minute today.'

He watched her bite down on her lip and let the subject drop. How could she know that it wasn't really Rossiter? The real cause was buried up there on the hill.

Though of course he was envious, why not? A dinosaur, ought to be nothing more than a bundle of old clippings waiting to be resurrected from the obit files, then staging a comeback on TV as a nostalgic talking head.

'One series on the telly,' he said wistfully, 'is worth a million words. A million quid too, if you know how to play it right.'

'Can I have the telly on?' The keyword drew Emma from her book. 'I'm allowed to watch more on a Saturday. Can I, daddy?'

That's right, Sarah thought, try daddy. Soft touch, especially at weekends, especially when he's feeling sorry for himself. Talk about women enjoying emotion! He could wallow in it when he was in the mood.

'Nothing on yet, darling. Just boring old sport and stuff.'

'I *like* sport.' Emma could play this game indefinitely. 'I like football. And golf. And darts and snooker and – '

'Oh, come on, let her watch, for heaven's sake.' Nick doing his indulgent father act. 'Must be something that won't corrupt her morals.'

Emma scurried into the next room. Moments later the house rattled with gunfire.

Sarah went after her. 'Not that, darling, too noisy, and anyway, you won't like it.'

Nick closed his eyes again, no peace on the job, no peace at home. Story of the decade and he couldn't use it. Not couldn't: daren't, he had no illusions. Lock him up and throw away the key; the very least that could happen.

Yet it would be fame: Hugh Rossiter had never filed a bigger story in all his years of humping himself around the globe wringing his hands over the inevitable.

In fact it was a story made for Rossiter. In his prime he would have found a way to –

No! World copyright NICK BROOKE: from pole to pole like sky-writing. The kind of thing they'd talk about in Groucho's and El Vino's long after he was as old as Rossiter and Rossiter dead and forgotten. All right, he worked for the *Globe*, but he wasn't stupid. He knew the score.

Plus it *ought* to be told! People *ought* to know what lay behind all the crap the politicians talked: special relationship, NATO shield, Western democracies standing firm under the threat of tyranny. Blah-blah, crappity-crap, *ad* bloody *nauseam.*

And there was money in it, big, big money. Not just for himself; for Sarah, who deserved it. He owed it to Sarah to show what he was really capable of.

Only they'd make sure he never got to first base.

Old Tyrran, during his periodic descents on the slave pen, never tired of saying to Tim Bryce, 'What the *Globe* thrives on is exclusives, Timothy. The job of the *Globe* is not just to report news. The job of the *Globe* is to make news.'

The minute Tyrran had been whisked into his white Rolls, en route to inspect his next megabuck piggy bank, Tim, the owner's footprints all over him like mud on a rug, would be going around telling everybody, 'The job of the *Globe* is not to scavenge for bleedin' news. The job of the *Globe* is to dynamite it out, 'n' don't you ever forget.'

But if Nick Brooke went into the shop on Monday morning and told him about the kilotons of dynamite hidden away in a plastic sack up there under the dead bracken, Tim would throw six kinds of fit out of sheer fright.

He sat there, eyes clenched shut, every muscle locked about a core of despairing impotence, listening to Ess coming back.

Why, she was wondering, hadn't she just said, 'When you can write as well as Hugh Rossiter used to write, and about things as worthwhile, you'll really be something'?

Because she was Sarah Brooke, lots of convictions, not much self-confidence. Because Nick was as touchy as Emma in a sulk. And because he needed his illusions, all the more because he was ashamed of his job.

She sat down quietly. 'The homelife of the Lesser Dingbat. That should keep her quiet for a bit. Tell me about the White Horse.'

Pure frustration had taken him into the White Horse, where, at the weekend, Hooray Henries and rusticating Sloanes tended to supplement the locals; Gs and Ts and Bloody Marys, the air thick with confident yahs, ghaaaastlies and oh *no*! How *aw*fuls. Money was what came into Dorking on Saturday mornings; City types, advertising whizzkids, Range Rover yahoos, all in from their wooded hill stations to do a quick shoparound, sink a few before lunch.

The Morcambes and Tracey's boyfriend had tucked themselves into a corner by the window, a flushed collective look, thickets of empty glasses, full ashtrays. Nick might not have seen them in the crowded bar but Arthur Morcambe was not a man to be ignored.

'Nick!' A furiously wagged hand backed by a battery of family smiles. The bony blonde, glass in hand, leaning forward with a more than usual eagerness. Tracey Morcambe, the managing director's secretary, home from London, daintily punk in stonewashed denim and hair spiked in funeral director's sable. This week's boy a fey drip called Beverley, leather pants, one swinging earring, head planed like the top of a fence post.

Two other people he didn't know and, right in the corner, Hugh Rossiter. That crumpled, quizzical look the small screen had made familiar to millions: vaguely apologetic, even self-deprecating if you took it at face value which, Nick told himself reluctantly, he supposed he should. And, of course, sad. No, melancholy; that was the right word for Hugh.

He had a house somewhere in the Holmbury area, a big one on the posh southern slope of the hill where it would look thirty miles across the Weald toward the sea. That, the Morcambes had implied, was how you lived if you were a real writer, rich, famous and not on the *Globe*.

Nick didn't much use the White Horse, but whenever he looked in, Rossiter seemed to be there. Favoured a pseudo-antique high-backed bench that could have held two at a pinch but allowed him to isolate himself with the glass of brandy that was part of the Rossiter legend.

He had a reputation for matiness in the right crowd, a select bunch of one-time media stars, but Nick's impression was that he preferred his own company down here. That might be why he looked resigned and rueful now, penned in his corner like a polite bishop at a Mothers' Union bunfight.

One step short of shabby; an old blazer, unfashionable, worn with a V-neck pullover that was probably Marks and Spencer *circa* 1970. Collar of his shirt frayed, open at the neck, stuffed with a heavy silk scarf the way you saw black-and-white film stars in thirties Hollywood movies.

Must be loaded, for all that: half his life abroad on heavy expenses, all those books, now the TV series. You didn't run a fancy house up the hill on an overdraft.

35

Arthur Morcambe – the kind of man you wouldn't even buy a first-hand car from – had a bar in the corner of his living room: gilt, glass and cream synthetic leather; a framed notice on the wall behind: PLEASE DO NOT ASK FOR CREDIT AS A PUNCH IN THE MOUTH MAY OFFEND. It said all there was to say about Arthur.

Sleek in a polo-neck sweater of pale blue nylon, navy blue trousers and loafers with gold bars, he insisted on buying Nick a drink. The remaining two members of the party turned out to be Arthur's bank manager and his wife. They had joined Rossiter, the Morcambes had joined them. Like Rossiter's, their smiles were wan from over-exposure.

Peggy Morcambe introduced Nick to Rossiter. 'Nick's a journalist too. On the *Globe*.' For a moment unmistakable malice showed behind her popeyed gaze, then she produced that sudden, convulsive jerk of the head and stared through Nick at some distant part of the universe. He knew now why she had looked so unexpectedly pleased to see him.

'Don't worry, dear old chap.' Rossiter produced his tired smile. 'Won't tell a soul.'

It was the sort of joke Nick had to put up with from people on the heavies: *Observer, Guardian, Independent*. So much for the famous Rossiter sensitivity.

Before he could reply he found himself caught up in one of Arthur Morcambe's endless attacks on the British car industry, where, apparently, even the robots had acquired bad habits.

'Best thing, old boy, let the Nips take us over, teach us how to produce Rollers at Datsun prices.'

Tracey and Beverley were licking each other with their eyes. Peggy was saying to the bank manager's wife, 'and there we all were, I mean, all wanting to say, "But we *do* think murderers should be hanged," and her, you know, rabbiting on as if we were a bunch of wet social workers. I mean, you know, what do you say?'

She laughed shrilly, popped her blue doll's eyes, booted her mind into a new cycle with that choreic jerk of the head.

'Excuse me,' Nick said to Arthur. 'Got to take a leak.' He pushed his way through the throng in a suppressed frenzy of frustration. What did they know? Rossiter could afford to be tolerant, already had his day.

Someone came in after him, took the next stall. 'Oh dear,' Hugh Rossiter said softly. 'Do you feel like me, not quite your cup of tea?' Before Nick could answer, he went on. 'I do most humbly beg your forgiveness, dear old chap. My cheap remark about your paper, inexcusable. We inky band of scribblers all have to start somewhere, and few of us on the *Times*. For myself, I began on a Lincolnshire weekly, long since forgotten, in which news was what one might term minimalist bucolic.'

He sketched a headline: 'SMALL BLAZE IN OUTHOUSE. FIRE BRIGADE NOT CALLED.

'Mea culpa,' he said. 'Those of us with the gift of words have a sacred obligation to watch our tongues, and not just in the public prints. Let me confess. Nick Brooke is known to me: the *Globe*'s man-on-the-spot.'

'He didn't mean to insult you.' Sarah was relieved. 'And you didn't insult the Morcambes.'

'Yes and no,' Nick said. 'Walked out, straight from the gents. I told you though, all too pissed to notice.'

'What about Hugh Rossiter?'

'Walked out on him, too.'

'But why? He apologised. Came out specially to apologise.'

'To patronise.' Not true, but his feelings needed a bone to gnaw on. Again he produced that languid, self-mocking tone. 'We inky band of scribblers! The public prints!'

'Nick, what happened?'

'Let's share a private corpse reviver at the bar, dear boy, and chat of this and that.'

'Well?'

'I said' – he wanted to dodge now, but his conscience drove him on – 'maybe there were some inky scribblers who'd be better off dead.'

Breaking a silence reinforced by hollow voice-over from the television in the next room, he said, 'All right, I shouldn't have said it. Anyway, I meant people like me. The junk press. I didn't mean – '

'Of course you meant it.' He was taken aback by her anger. 'I know you, speak first, think after. Anyway, you could have apologised, couldn't you?'

'I was late. Missed the bus if I hadn't gone.'

She hissed her disbelief, the other Ess, a sort of emotional iceberg, the greater part of her feelings submerged and unsuspected until you ran foul of her and found yourself doing a *Titanic*.

Awkwardly he said, 'Apologise next time, all right?'

She shook her head despairingly. 'What did he say?'

'Nothing. Just nodded, smiled. I said I'd got to go and I went.'

Not true. What Rossiter had said, with his wry, quizzical smile, was, '*Touché*,' then, as Nick had started to apologise, cut him short with, 'Oh, but it's true, dear old chap. Only too true.'

2

SHOCK TWIST TO
AIR CRASH COVER-UP

As a weekend, brilliant, absolutely bloody brill. Bad marks from
Sarah for the brush with Rossiter, though that wry '*Touché*' still
stung. And still no idea how to handle the biggest story he was
ever likely to have without getting himself run over by the state
steam-roller.

Then, just when he was ready for bed, a call from Bill Creedy,
the *Globe*'s news editor. Some poor sod of a Soviet seaman had
jumped ship at Immingham, handed himself over to the local fuzz
as a political refugee. Soviet embassy already kicking up hell,
claiming the guy was being held against his will. Local stringer
keeping it warm for the moment, but if it blew up, Nick might have
to go up to Humberside, just thought I'd tip you off, sunshine.

So instead of getting his head down, a quick look to find out
just where Immingham was, a bit of ringing around to check the
ins and outs of political asylum and so on. He knew the sort of
thing, could almost write the banner: SOV SALT SKIPS SHIP: IVAN
TO BE ALONESKI!

He was already committed to an interview for the Bangladeshi
child bride piece. Tim Bryce would expect a deadpan racist angle
to cater for National Front readers, otherwise it was a case of
whipping up moral indignation like so much synthetic cream.

It stretched out to lunchtime, a couple of quick calls to the news
desk to make sure the Immingham thing hadn't mushroomed. The
Bangladeshi kid, her mother and her two fat aunts – ten words of
English between them so he could practically invent his own story
– got a hell of a kick out of watching him talking on his Excell like
they had a phone right there in their overcrowded, curry-ponging

sitting room, when vandalising every callbox inside a two-mile radius was the local Youth Training Scheme.

Back to the Street for a few bevvies with a mate on Reuters – hadn't had to move to dockland with the mob, lucky bastards – then out to Poplar to see what the afternoon held in the way of surprises. It held one that shook him like tripping on a step that wasn't there.

Apart from Tyrran's seldom occupied suite and a box where the managing editor dispensed booze to important visitors, only the editor and deputy editor of the *Globe* boasted private territory: glassed-in cubicles, side by side, each with the ubiquitous visual display terminal.

Monkey Willett, the deputy editor, lived like an American vice-president with a guilty half-hope that someone would call to tell him the boss had dropped dead and he was running the show. But Tim Bryce wasn't the kind of editor who waited until early evening before making his presence felt. One of the old school, he claimed to view direct input with contempt but secretly relished the absolute power of the new-style back bench.

Once he took over his screen, the pace hotting up, VDUs swapping copy, pics and page spreads like robot merchants in a microchip bazaar, he scythed from features to sport, art desk to city desk, making and remaking pages, crackling with more high voltage than the mainframe computer. Until then he was everywhere, an all-day man whose raucous, withering gibes cut swathes with the indiscriminate lethality of nails in a terrorist bomb.

He and Monkey were closeted in Monkey's glass box like a pair of piranhas in an aquarium. Tim Bryce could stare at a VDU, think up a new angle, junk a layout and plot the individual movements of every senior member of his staff without spoiling his act as the only editor in the business whose demotic English could have had a quiz panel trying to guess his job until Doomsday.

'Nick!' The carrying power of a bullfrog.

Nick braked exaggeratedly. 'Sir.'

Tim Bryce preached first-name democracy but secretly yearned to be editor of the *Times*. Convinced that being called 'sir' by Nick was a form of disrespect, he had yet to find a way to handle it.

His face was a cartoonist's delight. As a newborn babe, someone had put a thumb to his button nose and pushed until the entire face became concave. He had sparse hair, a high, bulging forehead, a large, pugnacious chin. Everything else jostled for living space at the bottom of a red and shallow bowl.

Monkey, on the other hand, had the hollow cheeks of a minor aesthete, the spurious spirituality of a praying mantis. He had been Edward Monk Willett at Cambridge; long hair, long poems, long by-lines in short-lived literary magazines. Faced on graduation with a choice between art and Fleet Street, he had unhesitatingly made the great sacrifice. The money was much, much better at the bottom.

'Where you off, brother?' Tim in a temper had the sightless, head-down glare of a berserker. A phone rang. He grabbed it, said 'No!', slammed it down.

'Good weekend, Nick?' Monkey, who would have backed Tim for editor of the *Times* or *Beano* so long as it allowed him to move into the top slot, had the soft, treacherous purr of a frustrated intellectual.

'Crashed out, Monk. Two big stories same day, leaves you a bit limp even if you can do it. Not many who can.'

Thirty K a year plus exies might sound good to your average wage-slave, but he was ace and it was time he had another hike. The mortgage, bloody insurances, all the rest of it, he was not about to indicate any kind of satisfaction.

Normally, Tim would have risen to it like a crocodile happening upon Moses in the bulrushes. This time he blinked his little eyes, jutted his big chin, looked as if he might butt Nick with his bulging forehead.

'Crashed out? What's that supposed to mean, brother? Lookin' around for plane bits?'

Jesus! Like a kick in the balls! What did they know that he didn't?

'Plane bits?' Play it cool, wait and see.

'I suppose you think you did us all well on those poor kids that got clobbered.'

'Good copy,' Monkey said. 'As far as it went.'

'Thanks.' So they thought he'd missed out somewhere. Best to attack. 'I just said, two stories in a day. I'd already input my piece on the rape trial verdict.'

'That verdict,' Tim said, 'was an aforegone conclusion, brother. We could have pulled most of your stuff out of the files.'

'Could have.' Rancid old bugger! 'You didn't though, ran my stuff near enough unsubbed I could almost recognise it. Same with Nethercott Stoney. Look' – time to counterattack – 'if I hadn't happened to be on my way back, you'd have had to send someone out cold. As it was, I was first past the post.'

'First on the course,' Tim said, 'first bloody off, too. Told the missus you'd be home early, had you?' His secretary peered round the door. He waved her away brusquely.

'Think I didn't read the competition?' Nick was stung. 'Best coverage bar none. The cops were getting really heavy by the time the rest turned up. I'd already been in over an hour, input a rush, back to the car three times with snaps, nannied the photographer round, talked to the emergency services while he did a saturation, got something out of the headmistress and two parents. My rushful was away while the other guys were still trying to get past the fuzz.'

'Maybe,' Tim said, 'you didn't ought to have been so bleedin' slick, brother. Maybe done better if you'd been last on the scene. Maybe then've got the right story.'

'What do you mean, the right story? Start from this dump and they'd have been lucky to get near enough to see the smoke.'

Tim said, 'Show'm, Monkey.'

Nick's belly spasmed. A D-notice, crisp and pithy. The chopper had carried secret military equipment, not all of it yet recovered. An intensive search was taking place. Until it was concluded, the co-operation of the media was requested in avoiding any mention, since participation in the search by the general public could seriously hamper operations.

He pretended to read it again. Why show it to him when his part in the affair was over?

Common sense provided some comfort. If they – he still wasn't precisely sure what he meant by 'they' – knew anything, they would be here, waiting for him. No they wouldn't. Already have been down to Dorking, asking him very awkward questions.

It had to be something else. He looked up from the D. 'So? Don't get it.' Tim was poised to release the all-purpose disgust he ladled over anyone he saw as having let down the *Globe*.

'You were first in, brother.'

Monkey, back in the act. 'In first, and you deserve the credit. Bill was as happy as a sandboy when your stuff started coming through. And the pics were good. But you missed a trick. You were out before they clamped down on security. You might have got us under the bar.'

Nick was both relieved and professionally disgusted. They meant that if he had managed to learn anything extra about the chopper, it might have been run before the security clamp-down.

'Do you think I didn't try? I talked to whoever would talk, I told you that. The Yanks wouldn't talk, not even their bloody drivers. Then the fuzz clamped down. Anyway' – were they still holding out on him? – 'just what do you think I might have picked up?'

He knew what he had picked up. He knew what it was they would all be looking for back there in the fields and woods. He knew exactly why that D-notice had been issued.

The Yanks must be wetting their pants. The missing chunk of their chopper had been found, but not what had been inside it. Since they were in England they'd have had to go to the British for help in finding it, but if the British found it they might read it.

Or someone might already have found it, turned it over to the authorities. The British authorities. Who would hand it back to the Yanks. Or would they?

Since nothing further had happened – Yankee viewpoint again – the British, saying nothing, were secretly considering their options, none of them likely to do much for the NATO alliance.

He saw now, should have seen it before, that the Yanks would do anything, pay anything, to get it back intact.

So if he were to put out a feeler . . .

The next thought came even faster. They would snuff him. Knock him down so fast he would barely know what had happened. And so – Jesus, he should have seen that too! – might the British authorities. Too much at stake. He had the brief, exceedingly unpleasant sensation of someone walking over his grave.

'I hope,' Tim was saying, 'you're not goin' soft, brother. The cops came the heavy? The Yanks wouldn't talk? What are you, a bleedin' trainee?'

A new abyss opening up. 'What do you want me to do? Go back?'

D-notices were theoretically advisory. Though Whitehall could make life very difficult for anyone who failed to play ball they could, theoretically, be ignored. Theoretically, Tim Bryce was the kind of man to ignore them. It had been done before.

But there was something else. 'You're on the committee!'

Tim's disgust intensified. It was true. He had been appointed to the D-notice Committee under some kind of Buggins's turn, a representative not of the *Globe* but the media as a whole.

'Not just soft! Half-bleedin'-witted! 'Course I'm on the committee, whole bloody point, right? You hadn't been in such a hurry to get away, we could've been home and dry. I'd have been ever so sorry, wouldn't I? Member of the bleedin' committee and runnin' a story I obviously wouldn't have run *if* I'd known it was *verboten*. Hardly come down strong on me, could they? But you, you soft git – '

'What story, for God's sake?' They couldn't send him back now. They didn't have the remotest idea what they were playing with.

'The chopper.' Monkey's soft, well-bred voice made people blink when he admitted to being deputy editor of the *Globe*. 'Finding it, whoever did. If you'd still been around, you'd have seen the commotion.'

'*What* commotion?'

'Listen, cock.' Tim Bryce wagged a stubby finger. 'They get a message that a chunk of that chopper's been found in a wood, right? So they send a bleedin' army, damn near, that much I do know. And for why? I'll tell you for why, brother. Because they reckoned whatever all this is about might be in that bleedin' wood.

'Only it wasn't, which is why we get this' – he waved the D under Nick's nose – 'and likewise why I'm givin' you a roustin', cos if you'd stuck around, you'd just about've had the nous to chase off and see what you could pick up, an' – '

'You really think they'd have let anyone get within a mile?' Nick began to feel trapped. 'Anyway, all guesswork, isn't it? We don't really have the faintest idea what it's all about.' He hoped to God he was sounding convincing.

'Just listen.' Tim was getting rough. 'I was in this game before your balls dropped. Think I stay on that piss-awful committee just cos I'm flattered they picked me?'

He prodded Nick. 'Ought to know me by now, brother. Don't do a thing, make a friend, walk a bleedin' yard unless there's a story, got me? Can't tell me anythin' about contacts. Live to top the ton, won't know as much about contacts as I do now.'

'Old Pals Act?'

Tim made a rude noise. 'No pals in this game, not when it

comes to a story. Asked a few questions, got a few answers.' He tapped the side of his nose and winked, jovial as a warthog.

Someone came in with some pictures. He waved them aside. 'Art desk. That's what they're paid for.' He would probably rubbish them later.

'Once upon a time' – Tim could be very ponderous – 'some geezer – local, traveller, don't know yet, but they soon will – happens to be drivin' along this country lane. Pulls in by a wood. Pick flowers, strain the greens, dump the kitchen sink, who cares? Whatever it was, it takes him into the wood and what does he find? We know. Secret equipment. Does he just say "None of my business" and drive on? He does not.'

'He telephoned the police about the bit of chopper,' Nick said. 'We all know that.' Wish to God he hadn't; a perverted sense of duty after taking what he had taken from the wreckage.

'Telephoned the police, we all know that! Got it on the agency wire, *not* from the *Globe*'s bloody man-on-the-spot. Did something else first, didn't he? You're not thinkin', brother.'

'Timing,' Monkey said. 'All a question of timing, Nicholas.'

Tim aimed a kick at Nick's crotch. 'Wouldn't have wasted much time in that wood once he'd checked there was no bodies or anything, right? Back in his car, drive like crazy to the first house with a phone, right?'

'Didn't he?' He was chasing his own tail.

'He didn't.' The great, know-it-all editor of the great, spill-it-all *Globe*. 'There was a gap, my contacts tell me, between findin' the thing and makin' the call. On account' – Tim aimed another mock kick at Nick's groin – 'of there bein' a house with a phone no more than a quarter of a mile along that road. Drove on past it, see?'

Nick remembered the house. Large, very fancy, the kind of house owned by the kind of people who lived in that area because it was the kind of area for their kind of people; people with indecent amounts of loot. Money! It no longer seemed important.

He said, 'How on earth could they know that?'

Tim sneered. 'Not on that committee just cos I fancy the company, brother. On it so's I can hear people like you say, "How do you know that?" and not tell 'em. Still, you poor bastard, got to be told somethin', I s'pose, eh, Monkey?'

'Since he didn't find it out.' Monkey's was Star Wars malice, shoot down anything that moved.

'Tyre-marks.' Tim said it with relish. 'Fresh tyre-marks. When this geezer drove off, he put his foot down. Marks told 'em the direction he'd come from, direction he was goin'.'

He eyed Nick, top to toe. 'Somethin' to work on. Right, Monk?'

'Timing,' Monkey said again. 'All a question of timing, Nick old boy.' He reached for a print-out. Nick saw his name at the top. His input from Nethercott Stoney. He could feel everything closing in.

'What did you do,' Monkey asked, 'after you'd inputted your stuff? Go straight home?' He was pretending to check; time in, time off. 'Look around? Or what?'

'Drove around first. No special reason, just see what was what.'

Tim cut in. 'And what *was* what, brother? Not bits of bleedin' helicopter, that's for sure.'

'Didn't take the Lambourn road?' Monkey asked. 'Faringdon, Lambourn, that way?'

'No, I didn't. And I didn't drive past a chunk of chopper. Or any cars parked on the edge of a wood. Or any suspicious characters poking about for whatever it is everybody's worked up about. Christ Almighty, what do you take me for?'

Tim showed no signs of relenting. There was a story to be had, and he meant to have it. Or lost, and he would crunch bones to know why.

'They've lost somethin'. Bothers them so much they put out a D-notice to keep the wraps on it. But that's only the half, sunbeam. It isn't lyin' in some ditch waitin' to be found. Some person or persons unknown has got it. Means to keep it, maybe even use it, or the powers-that-be wouldn't all be at panic stations. Right, Monk? We are agreed on that one?'

'Right, Tim,' Monkey said. 'On that one we agree.'

'And on one thing more, am I right, Monkey?'

Monkey nodded his one-time-scholar's head. 'They know who it is. And so do we.' They both looked at Nick.

'We all know who it is.' Tim all but spat. 'The geezer who didn't stop until his wheels had put some miles between him and that hunk of chopper. We know that. They know that. There's no D-notice on that.'

Nick could see what was coming next. The editor of the *Globe* was going to tell the *Globe*'s man-on-the-spot to start looking for himself.

'Look at Nick.' More refined sadism from Monkey. 'You'd think he thought we thought it was him.'

'Bloody well should've been him.' Tim aimed a last emasculating kick at Nick's crotch. '*Globe* man-on-the-spot.' He heaved himself away from the table, rumpled, ruthless, implacable.

'D-notice says we can't write about the search. But only *that* search. Somebody's got a secret. A secret's a story. The *Globe* wants it. I'm puttin' the dirt squad on it. They'll want to start with you, so don't go anywhere without I say okay.'

The dirt squad. A posher newspaper would have called it a special investigation team. On the *Globe* they made up their minds what they wanted to prove, then sent out the dirt squad to threaten the facts into fitting. Two ruthless young men, an even more ruthless young woman: ingenious, persistent, all the makings of a dedicated torture team.

He was going to have to help the dirt squad track him down, how about that! A good many people must already be looking for him. They might well make the dirt squad look like amateurs. They didn't know that he had driven past the house with the phone because he'd had his own pocketphone in the car, could phone from wherever he chose, which had been twenty-five miles and thirty minutes later.

He had called the police, without giving his name, to say there was a piece of chopper in the wood. A kind of salve for the conscience *Globe* staffers weren't supposed to have. He'd used the Excell to make the call then called Sarah again to tell her not to wait up, so if anyone checked on the places and times of his Excell calls he'd be able to . . .

'Liz and the boys' – Tim looked happy for the first time – 'will help you to remember things you didn't know you knew. Have a word with Bill Creedy first, though. If he says you have to go to Immingham, that comes first.'

He remembered something. 'What about that pal of yours in Tass? I see he's in your diary. Help you on the Immingham one, will he?'

'Peter Glashin.' Nick dragged his mind back through a thicket of dangers. 'Hardly a pal, but I'm lunching him tomorrow as it happens. You know what they're like. He'll tell me whatever he's been told to say, and he'll want an arm and a leg in return.'

Not true, really. He got on well with Peter, but this wasn't the time or the place to say so. This was the time, but absolutely not the place, to do some serious thinking.

Tim had had enough. Ready to lumber out, he jostled Nick brutally in passing. 'Tell your Russian pal you're in dead lumber at the *Globe*, brother. Ask him what *Pravda*'d give you to defect.' He took his angry laughter out to lay waste the newsroom.

Not just good at his job; the best. So he knew how to handle people like Peter Glashin.

Peter – Pyotr, actually – was a Tass man. Quite a few guys on the nationals wouldn't deal with him, wouldn't even be decently sociable. It was a laugh, really, when you thought what shits some of the guys on the nationals were. He'd sooner lunch with Glashin than Tim Bryce or Monkey Willett, any day.

Russian or not, commie or not, some kind of a spy or not, Peter was genuinely likeable. Good company, rewardingly indiscreet about his own people, willing to pass on a tip, flesh out a story with a Sov angle, made no secret of the fact that he was pushing his quota of party line, seeking his quota of inside info.

'The West is corrupt,' Glashin would say with his big, warm smile, 'but I am a man who enjoys occasional tasteful corruption.' His English was good and he could be very witty.

'Oh no,' he had said when Nick rang him to check their date. 'The treat is on me. I am behind on hospitality quota and I am Stakhanovite for entertainment.'

So the date was in Chelsea: expensive, very, very classy. Nick walked in past dark glass windows that let diners look out but made it difficult for passers-by to see in. What success was all about, right? You on the inside, looking out.

Sarah wouldn't agree. She was right, he popped that kind of thing up without thinking.

Glashin was on his feet in a moment, his smile white as the walls with their green glass décor. He had a corner table. Just how often did he do his Stakhanovite stuff here to get such favoured treatment? Still, that was Glashin; all plush and tassels.

The place was busy, the high-pitched belling and braying of the local *dolce vita* a gilt-edged guarantee of privacy. Not that the Chelsea set wouldn't fall about at the idea of other people's conversation being more interesting than their own.

'Wotcher, Peter,' Nick said. 'Nice little place you've got here.'

Glashin fussed him into his seat. 'We Soviets must have our compensations for the hardships of service in decadent West. And in England, for the weather.'

He laughed uproariously. It drew a glance or two, some of them admiring. Peter Glashin was quite a looker: tall, broad shoulders, fair hair, blue eyes. And his clothes were definitely classy.

'Is that gear of yours English?'

Glashin looked down at himself in mock dismay. 'You are telling me you think this suit is made in Moscow?'

'Don't know anything about Moscow tailoring. Was it?'

Glashin laughed again. 'You know *nothing* about Moscow tailoring.'

'Good-looking guy like you, makes me jealous.'

Glashin made a small sound of dismissal. 'You, too, also a good-looking guy. Ah, but married, I remember. Your wife is Sarah, I think.'

'Right.' A hell of a memory. Only the third time they had met but Glashin could pop it all up like a printout. Perhaps that was what he did; some secret computer up there in Hampstead.

When he had it made, he would bring Sarah to places like this. Poor old Ess, didn't see anything like it from one year's end to the next. But then, women were supposed to be more interested in kids and home than high living. And this wasn't high living: this was work.

Glashin laid aside his menu. 'You and your Sarah, one day we must dine. But beware, my dear Nick. Perhaps I shall steal her from you if she is very beautiful.'

Sarah, very beautiful? The first time he had had her, before he'd surprised himself by proposing, all he could think, afterwards, was that this fantastic, beautiful girl, had given herself to him. To him: her, the most beautiful girl in the world!

'Ess?' he said. 'Better than beautiful. Ess is just . . . Ess.' He hadn't meant to say that. True, though. He felt a warm glow. When he moved over to a decent sheet, maybe only one piece a week to think up, he would have more time. Then he would make a fuss of her, show her the *Globe* hadn't turned his heart to ice.

Glashin nodded. 'Love makes its own beauty, a saying we have.' His voice, strong, deep, was full of those surprisingly caressing Russian vowels Nick had never really noticed before meeting him.

'You have chosen? If not, I recommend mousseline of mullet to begin. We share half bottle of white wine, then we have something special while you ask me about a defecting Soviet sailor and I tell you such things are impossibility, contradiction in terms.'

As they ate, Glashin gave him some useful unattributables on the Sov seaman. Yes, his main problem was that he owed money to half the ship's crew and couldn't pay them back. But now he was ashore he might, strictly off the record this, be tempted to stay.

He spotted Nick's scepticism. 'Why do I tell you such things? You are good contact. My editor thinks Western tabloids are pornographic. Worse, badly written. I tell him, in West good journalists must work where they can. "Some day," I say to this man, "Nick Brooke will write for a real newspaper. Some day be famous. Then you will be happy he is my friend."'

The big laugh.

For their main course he chose a wine that would set him back around thirty quid. Tim Bryce, clearing Nick's expenses after their last lunch, had snarled, 'Bloody hell! What did you eat, caviar and chips? Couldn't have cost much more to entertain the bleedin' Romanovs!'

Glashin was still talking.

'You are ambitious, my dear Nick. That is good. All press men should be ambitious. A press man should feel always he has not yet done best work, even when he is on front page. It is here, hand on heart, that I must envy you. For the Soviet press man abroad, best stories are often not permitted on front page.

'What is most important publication in the Soviet Union? *Pravda? Izvestia?*' Glashin shook his head. 'Service Tass. Yet its circulation is very smallest.' No longer laughing.

'Western newsman does story,' Glashin said, an apologetic wave of the hand for returning to his topic. 'Good story, page one lead. Later comes perhaps better story. So, he must go to second lead, another page even. Or, really bad thing, yes? his story is spiked.'

He shrugged massively. 'But when you are good at your job, as good as Nick Brooke – no, no, my friend, I don't flatter. You are good and you know it – when you are very good, tomorrow

puts things right. Another story, and again you have page one
lead. Not so with man from Tass.'

A genuine newspaperman, this Glashin: there were some
things you knew without being told.

'But I bore you?' Glashin said.

'Not a bit.'

'We all have frustrations.' Glashin smiled wistfully. 'I tell you
some frustrations of man from Tass. I am filing copy every day,
such an amount of copy, it is expected. And much of it lifted
straight from Western press. Yet from one hundred stories maybe
five appear in newspapers, ninety-five to Service Tass for desks
of party officials, Ministries, editors of Soviet press, allowed to
read what Soviet people do not see.

'Ordinary story, Green Tass. Special story, White Tass: more
exclusive. Most important stories of all, Red Tass: most select
readership. Better the story I file, more secret it becomes. Such
a system' – Glashin's china-blue eyes were rueful – 'makes it hard
for best among us to remain ambitious. No by-line. Just Tass,
from London.'

'Who gets Red Tass? The Kremlin?'

'Something like that. High and mighty, I think you would say.'
Sipping a little wine, Glashin peered mischievously, 'Now you
wonder, does he mean KGB?'

'Do you?'

'In my country' – Glashin pretended to look cautiously to left
and right – 'are not many more high or more mighty than KGB.'

'So you really are a spy. Well, sort of?'

'Well, sort of,' Glashin echoed mockingly. 'Except that I am
Tass. One day, perhaps, you become foreign correspondent and
come to Moscow. There you will find we consider you spy first,
press second. Here, other way about.'

'Spy in your spare time?' You could say stuff like that to Peter.

Glashin shook his head patiently. 'Here in West, you say, "In
Russia, nothing changes. Communism is Tsar under another
name." Not so. Things change. Sure, First Chief Directorate
must spy, as your secret service must spy. Sure, all Soviet citizens
who go to other countries are used by First Chief Directorate to
gather information. Sure, Service Tass is read by First Chief
Directorate.

'But Tass is still Tass, news agency employing newsmen. New
Moscow will not thank them if they do this thing inefficiently.

New Moscow – this surprises you? – will not take the excuse that they spy.'

He reached to pat Nick's hand in a fatherly way. 'One thing more. What goes into Red Tass for high and mighty is often little more than you would print as ordinary news in West. Since Gorbachov we have *glasnost* policy, more openness, but we come slowly to such ideas. It is the duty of Tass man to speed this process, so he must first be good journalist, not spy.'

'You're not selling me a line, is that it? Just two hacks out for a touch of the high life.'

'Selling a line? Ah! I understand. Listen, I tell you. Distrust me just a little. Perhaps I distrust you a little also.'

The big laugh, quickly cut off.

'In between, we are friends. In between, I tell you that what I have said about this Soviet seaman is bullshit. He owes nobody money. He is simple, foolish, frightened man, wife and children back in Riga, who cannot make up his mind to go or stay. Write your story, Nick my friend. If he stays, you say he is dissident who chooses freedom. If he goes, you say he is victim of oppressive Soviet system that uses wives and children as tools in the struggle for world domination. How old is your wife?'

'Thirty-five. Why?'

'Tell me about her.'

'Not much to tell.' More grist for that Hampstead computer? 'Thinnish. Darkish. Serious-minded, cares a lot about a lot of things. And a hell of a good mum. We've a little girl, Emma. Emma's eight.'

'Serious-minded? And wife of a *Globe* man?' Glashin was teasing.

'Very,' he said. 'Life is real! Life is earnest! You know?'

'This I find hard to believe,' Glashin said mockingly. 'You know what is most astonishing for citizens of socialist countries coming to West? Triviality of daily life, Nikita. Sheer, unceasing, mind-boggling – this is good English verb, boggle, yes? – triviality of average Western newspapers, television programmes, daily talk.

'So, *Pravda* is hypocritical, *Globe* is hypocritical. *Pravda* is biased, *Globe* is biased. *Pravda* tells only half truth, *Globe* tells only half truth. But *Pravda* tells half truths about things that matter very much. *Globe*, almost all the Western press, not even serious about trivia.'

He was Nikita now, was he? He didn't mind, not from a decent guy like Glashin.

'*Globe* readers,' he said, 'are born boggled. Deboggle them and they'd stop buying the *Globe*. We just give them an idiot's version of what's going on in the world. Why not? It's an idiot world.'

'Sex?' Glashin said. 'Bingo? Crime and cult of personality? This is all that goes on in the world?'

'Editorial policy, mustn't bore them out of their little skulls.'

'What is editorial policy?' Glashin said quite sharply. 'Policy of owner. What is policy of owner? No interference as long as the paper makes money. But be serious and you lose money. So, few words, many pictures of women's breasts. Accountants are not paid to read.'

Just when things might have been getting altogether too serious, that huge, infectious laugh. 'Come, I joke. I write a piece on your Sarah. Red Tass only, we must not let Soviet people know there is one serious-minded person in England. But what does she think of her husband?'

'She'd like me to move. So would I. I will. You'll see. But not to Tass. She wouldn't like that, either.'

'Because Tass would not make Nick Brooke famous as Tass man-on-the-spot?'

'Wouldn't, would they? Come on, Peter! Don't tell me you never think it would be great to have millions of people back home saying how ace you are?'

'Cult of personality is no longer permitted in my country.' Glashin sighed. 'Pity. Is perhaps pleasant to be a celebrity. I think you will be a celebrity one day. Then you mix with VIPs, hear many things of interest to Pyotr Alexeyevitch. So, I cultivate you.' He raised his glass in mock salute.

There was sense in that. Most hacks picked up a hell of a lot of inside stuff, sometimes very sensitive, not for publication. It came to him that he had very sensitive information now, the most sensitive bloody information it would be possible to think of.

Ought to be told, top of the tree for the guy who told it. And worth money. Big money. Except that it was Nick Brooke, not the story, who would end up on the spike. Impaled from arse to gullet.

Glashin would give an arm and a leg for it.

Forget it!

'I tell you one thing more,' Glashin was saying. 'When you reach the top, Glashin can be very useful to you. Not just trivia about foolish Soviet seamen. Sometimes our people in Moscow wish to leak real information to Western correspondent. You know this kind of thing?'

Nick frowned. 'Not sure I get it.'

'I give you example. Suppose' – Glashin leaned closer – 'KGB wishes hint to be dropped to very high Soviet official who has become too openly corrupt. What shall be done? Simple. Little anecdote, exclusive, of course, but complete with facts, to some Western correspondent who is only too happy to file it back in his home office, good anti-Soviet propaganda.

'*Times* of London, perhaps, or *Washington Post*, carries this story with banner headline and much moral comment. Now it becomes province of Tass man in London or Washington. The province, shall we say, of Peter Glashin? So, he sends it back home and it finds itself in Tass digest.

'Not, to be sure, in Green Tass. That is for the lowly placed. Perhaps not even in White Tass. No, Nikita – you don't mind that I call you Nikita? – it will go into Red Tass, for it is secret, delicate, maybe damaging to people in high places.

'In Red Tass it is seen by top *apparatchiki*: Politburo, members of Supreme Soviet, heads of Ministries, editors of leading papers. Now it is like a parrot that has escaped its cage. Parrot that knows a certain thing and will shout it as it flies. And this very high official, who is perhaps even a minister, takes the hint that he must mend his ways.'

He shared the last of the bottle between them.

'Are you a Party member, Peter?'

'So, your good friend Glashin invites you out for pleasure of your company and you come full of suspicion. This man is a Party member. This man is not a true friend, what is he after? Why does he pretend to be human when he is Party member and Party members are not human?'

He wagged his head. 'And only moments ago I am inviting you to be Tass stringer. Perhaps with such jokes you prefer to be *Krokodil* stringer?'

'How much would *Krokodil* pay?' Some sort of satirical magazine, wasn't it, kind of Soviet *Private Eye*?

Glashin pretended disapproval. 'You think *Krokodil* pays

foreigners to make jokes about Soviet Union? *Krokodil* does not have foreign stringers, Nikita, just Tass, which sends stories home for *Krokodil* to turn into jokes.'

He chuckled. 'Red Tass, of course. Only *natchalstvo* can be permitted to read foreign jokes. Alas, *natchalstvo* – you call them perhaps big wheels – have no sense of humour. That is why they are allowed to read these jokes.'

He did his party trick, peering around with exaggerated caution. The ambience was about as unlikely for informers as the members' pavilion at Lord's. 'You know good anti-British jokes, Nikita? For those' – he gestured expansively – 'Kremlin gold. Numbered Swiss bank account.'

He frowned. 'Something is wrong? I have offended you.'

Nick shook his head quickly. 'Of course not. I was just . . .'

He had had a thought. A crazy thought, bloody dangerous, he must stop thinking it.

'What is this thought,' Glashin said, 'that you just have? Free press in this country, nothing forbidden. No unattributable briefings by ministers. No Official Secrets Act, D-notices, pre-publication embargos. No suppression of comment by injunction and contempt of court?' He would have heard of the Nethercott D-notice. Things like that never stayed secret.

'At least,' Nick said lamely, still haunted by that glitteringly dangerous thought, 'we don't have to leak stories to Tass to broadcast to London on Radio Moscow because we daren't say them outright.'

He knew instantly that a part of his mind that was beyond his control had made the remark. He knew exactly why.

'This is truly what you think? Don't be so sure, Nikita.' Glashin was looking at him almost fondly. 'We order a little more wine?'

'No, thank you.' A sensation first experienced when he discovered exactly what it was he had hauled from that hunk of helicopter. 'Work,' he said hastily. 'Tricky piece to write later. Too much booze won't help.'

'Booze?' Glashin looked reproachful. 'Good wine is now booze? But let me tell you something. You think using Red Tass as – what shall we call it? Post office for anonymous letters, yes? – you think this is trick only of Soviet Union?'

He nodded toward a bunch of well-groomed American males, their deep, confident voices dominating the background conversation. 'They use it. And they are not the only ones.'

'The Yanks? Using Red Tass?' Now all his suspicions were alert.

'Sometimes' – Glashin was suddenly serious – 'if Americans want to say things to allies that would cause much unpleasantness if spoken face to face, they bounce – yes, good word – they bounce from Tass.'

Another confidential lowering of the voice.

'Sometimes things must be said between friends that it is not easy to say and remain friends. How can such things be said by Americans to European allies without much ill feeling?'

At one stage of his career Nick had done gossip column stuff. It had taught him a lot about human nature. And about the art of scoring off. He saw where Glashin was heading.

'You tell a third person, someone you can be sure will pass it on. The ricochet technique.' If he worked for a serious paper instead of the *Globe* there would have been a story in this. Glashin knew he didn't.

'Just so.' Glashin smiled. 'The ricochet technique. Americans wish to say something unpleasant to British, but one cannot be unpleasant to an ally. We have same problem in the Warsaw Pact.

'Very well, someone, American press man, perhaps, who has been briefed by State Department, hints this very unpleasant thing about the British to Tass man.' He winked again. 'Off record, of course. Calculated indiscretion, just as with you and me at this moment, Nikita.

'It goes in Red Tass. KGB, who read Red Tass, consider whether it is to advantage of Soviet Union to publicise this bad American opinion of British ally. If so, editor of *Pravda* – or *Izvestia*, or Radio Moscow, no matter – writes a story on the difference between what Americans are saying to British and what they really think.

'The British study all Soviet press at Foreign Office and Secret Service, listen to all Soviet radio news at Caversham. They find this thing Americans have leaked. It goes into their Soviet press digests. Just like Red Tass, yes?

'Of course, the Americans deny: is simply Moscow making mischief. But' – he laid a finger to his nose – 'in British Foreign Office, in British Secret Service, in Number Ten, Downing Street, they say, "Yes, yes, our American allies deny it, but no smoke without some fire."

56

'So, maybe the British make a policy adjustment, the Americans gain objective, and Moscow has spread suspicion between NATO allies.'

He aimed an imaginary rifle. 'Ricochet? For us, *dezinformatsiya*. Disinformation.' The genial Glashin was back. 'We take coffee, yes? And just one small cognac.'

'Quite a story.'

'Quite a story. Perhaps even a scoop. Only' – his booming laugh – 'I deny, of course. Oh well, one day when you are famous, Nikita, you maybe use Glashin for such a scoop.'

Nick grinned. 'Scoop rates?' A current was tingling his veins, exciting, uncomfortable.

'Moscow Narodny Bank,' Glashin said in answer as the cigars came, 'operates Western style in City of London.' He spread his palms. 'Tass also. When in Rome, we can be very Roman.'

He produced a gold pen, a small notebook. 'Now, you give me your address. Tass is going to send flowers to this wife you leave at home. You don't think this gesture of good will ricochets?'

Nick watched the waiter light Glashin's cigar expertly: these places didn't just sell food, they sold care and deference. But it was the life. By God, it was the life!

Back in the office he found himself with other things to think about. Liz Balcon of the dirt squad was hovering, waiting to grill him about Nethercott Stoney yet again.

She had this theory that he might actually have seen whoever it was that had whatever it was 'they' were still looking for. That it might be one of the people actually on the spot who had later found the chopper's nose section. The other two, Crispin and Roger, were up there ferreting around the village, Christ knew what for.

It didn't worry him. The *Globe* had taught him to be a hell of a good liar in the line of duty.

On what was still called the back bench though it looked more like the bridge of the starship *Enterprise*, Monkey and Snip Wilson, the art editor, were mocking up a feature spread while the art desk fed in pictures. Monkey liked the early sessions. It was the only time he could pretend that Tim had dropped dead and the noble lord had put everything into the capable hands of a man who spoke the Queen's English.

People shuffled to and fro over the antistatic carpeting like extras in a silent movie. Plastic coffee cups adorned every flat surface in spite of endlessly repeated warnings that one spill in the wrong place could take the *Globe* off the street for a week. Some said it would be an act of charity.

At his own desk – he refused to call it a work station – Nick keyed in his personal cipher. Letters emerged on his screen.

GOOD MORNING, NICK

It was afternoon, but to argue would be like trying to beat a Cray III at chess.

He typed: DROP DEAD

The screen produced a silent string of responses:

DROP?

DROP?

DROP?

He sighed, cancelled, conformed, typing in: MESSAGES?

NO MESSAGES

HAVE A GOOD DAY

Cancel. Keystroke: <Write>. Type: GOD ROT THIS RAG AND ALL WHO FAIL IN HER.

Delete his ID, keystroke to mainframe, leave it to pop up among the subs when someone pulled the file from the copy bank. They would know who had written it. He didn't care.

Then Liz Balcon was at him again. She pulled up a chair, notebook at the ready, porthole-sized glasses, auburn topknot and dark, neat two-piece making her look secretarial-drab when she was viper-deadly.

'Okay to talk?'

'No.'

Saying 'No' to Liz was like telling the work station to drop dead. 'This Oxford guy, the freelance pixie.' She checked her notebook. 'Don Beale. Which way would he go back?'

'Pixie?'

'The photographer, don't be bloody boring. Which way would he go back?'

'Why don't you ask him?'

'We did. I'm checking.'

'He went back the way he said he went back.'

'Which way was that?'

'Look, Liz, I didn't follow him. He was off to print and feed in. I was off home as soon as I could manage.'

She riffled through her notes. Her spatulate thumbs reminded him of those frogs that had suckers on the tips of their fingers. She reminded him of frogs herself; skinny body, all points and angles, even her breasts, and great goggling eyes behind great goggling goggles.

She found what she had been looking for. 'Bampton. Said he stopped off in Bampton on the way back. "Got this girl in Bampton, does me a quick job." Meaning his pics.'

He grinned. 'Sure?'

No sense of humour, Liz. He had a feeling she would go far. He hoped it would be in another direction. She said, 'Bampton's not on the road past where they found that bit of helicopter.'

'So there you go. Oxford's not on the road, either.'

'How long have we used him?'

'Didn't he tell you?'

She closed her notebook, but kept her thumb in. 'Do you know how long we've been using him?'

'No. First time I've worked with him. Not long. Look, he didn't go anywhere near the chopper.'

'Can you prove it?'

'Can you prove he did, Liz?'

'Someone did, didn't they?' The unruffled persistence of a precocious child. Bet she had once had pigtails and a brace on her teeth. Bet she'd been the most unpopular girl in the class.

'All right, someone did. Why pick on Don?'

'Flaming Norah!' she said, unruffled. 'Who's picking on him? Not picking on anyone. Eliminating. Crispin has this theory.'

It would be Crispin! Liz and Crispin were like a pair of half-tamed weasels. 'Are you going to tell me what theory?'

'That place was full of meeja, yes?' She was one of the new wave, posh education then talk like an East End scrubber.

'Was it?' he said. 'Didn't notice. Already done my piece.'

Why bother? She said, 'Press, telly, the lot. From all over. I mean, you know, points of the compass. So what kind of person would be most likely to find something newsworthy, hang on to it, but phone in about the wreckage from a safe distance?'

He still wasn't sure why he'd phoned in. Warped sense of duty? Ward off the evil eye? That bloody Excell, too easy!

He sat looking at her, a strong urge to laugh, a strong urge to run. She misinterpreted. 'Well, news sense but social conscience, sort of.'

'Is that how you see the media?'

No sense of humour, on a different wavelength from sarcasm. Mockery? Forget it.

'What we think, anyway,' she said, ignoring the question. 'So this Don wassisname matters. But what we also thought' – her thumb was prising open those scribbled pages – 'was, you could give us a list.'

'A list?'

'You must have recognised a lot of people. This Kevin Thingy from the *Oxford Mail*, you knew him. So who else? Everybody knows you' – he looked for irony, waste of time – 'you know everybody. So. You can give us a list.'

It *was* irony, though; pure, uncut. The dirt squad – Liz, Crispin and that dark horse, Roger Petherbridge – had come up with a theory that held about as much water as a coffee strainer. That wood probably had a dozen people stopping to pee in it every day.

But the luck of the game, and this game was fifty per cent luck, had seen a wild throw land smack in the bull's-eye. What would Liz say if she knew that the quarry was there before her very eyes? Probably interview him without turning one of those rust-red hairs.

'As a matter of interest,' he said, and was childishly pleased to find how disinterested he could sound, 'does your theory include some idea of what it might be?'

Her turn to be puzzled. 'It?'

'The thingy.' He could mock her so long as he kept a straight face: she absolutely wasn't into mockery. 'Whatever it is Tim's told you you're looking for.'

'Oh.' In that two-piece suit she could be a cross-dresser and you'd have to guess which direction she'd crossed from. Pointy breasts, these days, came built into pointy bras, no guarantee what you'd find when you undid the wrapping. 'No. Does it matter? It's the guy we're after, isn't it?'

Strangely reassuring that they had no idea what it might be. 'How do you know it's a guy? There were at least three birds on that story, not counting the dumb ones who stand around holding things for telly crews.'

'Don't be sexist.' Like Sarah reproving Emma for a minor fault: clinically calm and detached. 'Anyway, does it matter what it is? Even who it is? All about why, I'd have thought.'

'Why what?' She was sharp, Liz, sharp and ruthless. Perhaps you could train weasels.

'I mean,' she said with that maddeningly unruffled patience, 'if it was, say, a bit of military equipment, I don't know, a radio thingy, something like that, why telephone afterwards? Why not just sort of nick it and fade?'

'Don't get you.'

'Not some kid,' she said, and used the end of her ballpoint to push her glasses up the bridge of her pinched and pointy nose. 'Young or old, I mean. Got it all worked out, wouldn't you think? Crispin and me do. And Roger. Roger doesn't think it was equipment. Roger thinks it was plans, something like that.' Through those portholes a pair of eyes you would have said were totally incurious stared unwinkingly.

There was a terrible fascination in it. 'What do you mean, plans?'

'You know. Secret papers. He was an Air Force colonel, the passenger, wasn't he?'

'That's what they said.'

'We checked,' she said. 'We talked to a man at the morgue.'

He could imagine the three of them like characters in a cartoon, six places at once, off-screen left to on-screen right, crossing and recrossing, notebooks at the ready: questions, questions, questions.

'You don't believe what you read in the papers?'

You couldn't even drown her in sarcasm. She popped up like the plastic duck Emma liked to hold between her legs in the bath and then let go. She said, 'It would make sense, that, don't you reckon? Secret papers? We wondered about Russians.'

She had the capacity to astonish, after all.

'You wondered *what*?'

'Russians. Well, you know.'

'No,' he said. 'I don't. Honestly.'

'All these Yank bases. Do you remember, we tried to do a piece on that Yank who raped those women in Cambridgeshire.'

She riffled her pages. For a moment he thought she was going to turn up the story.

'Air Force sergeant or something, up in Cambridgeshire. Used to go out in civilian clothes and offer lifts to women, then rape them. Well, they hushed it up. It was before they took away anonymity. He ended up in American custody. We heard he was court martialled and sent back to the States, but someone told us

61

he was just fined. His defence said they were women of low moral character or something.'

She said it all as if it was just gossip over those plastic coffee cups.

'Anyway,' she said, 'we got the heave when we started asking questions in a pub near the base. Someone from the Ministry of Defence showed up, said it was something that had been blown up out of all proportion and there were enemy agents who went around all the time, round these bases, I mean, listening for that kind of anti-American story to use in propaganda broadcasts from Moscow. Tim said we'd better drop it.'

Tim would. Tim was a right-or-wrong patriot as long as it didn't get in the way of an exclusive.

She tapped her pen on her pad. 'So we had to drop it that time, but you see what I mean?'

He saw two things. One was that Tim had probably had his arm twisted over that rape story. Probably by the people – MI5 or whoever – who called the shots on the D-notice committee. The other was that the *Globe* dirt squad was not taking a parochial view of the present story.

With a growing sense of unreality, he said, 'Are you suggesting that whoever found that bit of chopper might be an enemy agent?'

'Well,' she said, 'as *such*, maybe not. But I mean, if they have these people, the Russians, I mean, have these people, well, the one in that part of the world might have dashed to the scene and . . . well. You never know, do you?'

But he did know, nobody better.

He knew something else. These special investigators – dirt-diggers, Tim had it right, there – were a breed. They knew their job. It was to produce a story where no story had previously existed. It was to use the telephone endlessly and follow up every conceivable lead. It was to get on the knockers and bells and ask questions until people started saying things practically in self-defence, then lean on them and go on leaning.

Sometimes veiled threats of unwanted publicity, sometimes promises: cash changing hands in sums big enough to tempt but not too large to snuff out the hope of more. But mostly promises.

Above all it was to produce theories. Theory upon theory, a kind of journalistic fiction that would make a whizz of a story if you could manage to nudge the truth down a dark alley and beat the hell out of it.

They had gone an impressively long way, these three. A wrecked chopper. Missing documents. All kinds of shadowy characters – the icicled void was back in his gut, yet it was really a hell of a laugh – scouring the countryside under the cover of a D-notice.

Why? Because the documents were Top Secret. Someone had found them without turning them over to the Proper Authorities. That someone was an Enemy Agent.

MOLE SPY AT KIDDY SLAUGHTER SCENE?
SHOCK TWIST TO AIR CRASH COVER-UP
A *Globe* exclusive

They knew what kind of story Tim Bryce wanted, these three hyperactive dung beetles. Now they were trying to put it together like so much Lego. Next thing you knew, they'd have those aircraft shot down by a SAM missile.

'Wow!' he said. 'That's brill, Liz! So where do you go from here?'

But something was happening. Tim Bryce was in the news-room. With him was the third member of the dirt squad; deep, dark Roger.

Liz followed Nick's glance. 'If Rodge is back this early, means he's on to something. Hang about. I'll be back.'

No need to go. Tim was on his way down. Roger Petherbridge, anchorman of the dirt squad, the dangerous advantage of looking like a long-haired, half-baked student, had tagged on behind.

'Where's Crispin?' Tim demanded. 'This hairy berk says you'd know.' He was having one of his hot flushes.

Liz looked frail enough to make you think she might shatter if you shouted. It was all illusion. 'No need to bark. Probably on his way in. We're going to compare notes, then he's off to – to – '

'Probly?' Tim's rage expanded. 'Don't give me any problies. He's goin' no bloody where. Neither are you.'

'Warned off,' Roger said in his vague mumble. 'Thought I'd better come back and say.'

'Warned off?' Liz flipped open her notebook as if to take it all down. 'Who by? Could mean we've got a lead, don't you reckon?'

'Bleedin' lead all right,' Tim said. 'Lead you right to the nearest nick before you're much older, my girl. Special Branch, that's who by. Anybody'd think – '

But Monkey Willett was calling his name, holding a telephone and pointing at it as if it were an *objet trouvé*. Tim bellowed, 'Later, for Christ's sake!'

Monkey shook his head, hand on the mouthpiece. 'Boss man.'

Tim grabbed Nick's phone. 'Bryce.' He was already standing to attention. 'Give me time to get back to my office, right, sweetheart?' but Tyrran's secretary must have transferred him at once. He looked at Nick, Liz and Roger, jerked his head. They moved away. Everyone nearby became very busy.

Tim's conversation with the proprietor was brief and one-sided. He came after them like an ape on the loose, glaring at Roger.

'You and your bleedin' dirt squad! Stirred up a hornet's nest this time.' Nick's stomach did its lightning imitation of a freezer.

'Oh dear.' Roger could do triple toe loops on the thinnest ice. 'You mean your whole Nethercott Stoney idea's dropped dead?'

'*My* idea?' Cornered, Tim snarled, 'Take a walk.'

'Where to?' Roger looked anxious to please, an amiable halfwit.

'Greenland. The whole ruddy pack of you. Don't stop when you get to the top.'

'That include me?' Nick asked.

Tim's bottled-up spleen found a vent. 'Not you, brother. You're off to Birmingham.'

'You mean Immingham.'

Tim turned on the run, face red, indiscriminately angry.

'I mean Birmingham. Immingham's dead. Ivan's returned to the arms of his lovin' shipmates, everythin' forgiven. Next stop, Siberia, poor daft sod. But Lily Holden's accepted the terms. Now you go and hold her hand while she tells all.'

He saw the look on Nick's face. 'One word about chequebook journalism and you're out. Think yourself lucky you'll only cop an earful from Lily instead of an upper-class bollockin' from the noble lord.'

As Nick, with his own reasons for being angry now, passed Monkey, he received a lascivious wink. 'Word to the wise, Nicholas, hold both her hands. Have 'em on your crotch in the first five minutes otherwise, good-looking fellow like you.'

'We're really going to pay that cow for her story?'

Monkey took Nick into his fishtank after making sure Tim had gone. 'Not quite what she asked, but nearly.'

'How much is nearly?'

Monkey hesitated, but chequebook journalism seldom keeps its figures secret.'

'Fifteen.'

'Fifteen K!'

Fifteen thousand pounds to a crooked ex-tart. He had a story that was worth ten times as much just for starters.

'She'll drink it,' Monkey said, 'in three months.'

'She won't. She'll use it to buy Mike a hit. Only takes a thou to buy a blade in the back where Mike is.'

The biggest heist in years. Seven million quid in gold, vanished without trace from a bullion store with more security than Number Ten. Mike Holden had slipped out of the country the same day. No hard evidence, but the heist had his hallmark on it. He was enjoying the sun and the lack of an extradition treaty.

Lily had been left behind. Lily, they said, had been ditched, and Lily was a hard case herself. 'She'll pay someone to tidy Mike away,' Nick said again. 'Giving her fifteen thou is like hiring the knife.'

'Lily won't have Mike tidied,' Monkey said, and he seemed extraordinarily confident. 'Lily will drink Dom Perignon until she's peeing it into a gold *pot de chambre*, all because someone told her the best champagne is the Dom. That's the sort of thing you'll have to listen to when she's sober. When she isn't . . .'

He wasn't smiling; Monkey almost never smiled; but there was a song in his heart. He despised his work, was inescapably trapped in it and, worse, just short of the top of the ladder. The way he saw it, Nick Brooke's generation, the one that was trying to climb over him, should get used to the feel of hobnailed boots on its greedy little fingers.

'You'd better watch out,' he said. 'Likes a bit of the other, does Lily. Specially from sexy young studs-about-town. Contract'll be initialled today, so it's you for the delights of downtown Brum. In the meantime, how about that child bride rewrite? Or shall we have some faceless sub do his Nick Brooke imitation?'

'Mike ditched her. She'll buy some guy to park a knife in him. They come in penny bundles out there.'

Nick was speaking mechanically. Fifteen K to a woman like that; the dubious legality resting on the fact that Lily Holden herself had never been convicted of anything worse than being on the game before Mike took her in tow.

Monkey came his closest to smiling. 'She hasn't been ditched.

Mike is biding his time. When the dust settles, Lily will be on a plane. In the meantime, she'll use the *Globe* to tell some juicy ones about her sex life and settle old scores with a lot of people who won't dare sue.'

He patted Nick's shoulder. 'Very tasty. *Bon appétit.*'

Three days with Lily Holden in godawful Birmingham!

In general appearance she gave – couldn't remember the source of the quote – promise of pneumatic bliss, but many times patched, not to say retreaded. Long legs, spoiled by bony knees and beginning to run to flab in the thighs. A face held together with collagens. Hair cast in one piece from solid brass. Voice like a sawmill on overtime. More glitz and less style than a club magician's assistant.

She called him 'Nick luv', right from the start. Ritual passes, endless innuendos. On the first night he and she stayed up until the small hours while she drank undiluted gin and told him raunchily unpublishable tales of her life and times.

But Monkey's prediction of Nick's fate remained unfulfilled. She talked sex. She played sex. She had it with someone else, probably one of her own musclebound studs-about-town.

He failed totally to draw her on Mike Holden or the bullion robbery. Every mention of Mike drew 'That bastard!' from her like a kneejerk reflex, followed by, 'He treated me right, mind. While we had something going, Nick, he treated me right. The bastard!'

Her friends, whose liquidity problems were those of Niagara Falls, patronised him as if he sold the *Globe* on the corner of Colmore Row instead of being one of its ace writers. Buying and selling seemed to be the sort of thing Lily's friends were in and out of. Jags, BMWs and Range Rovers were another. Nobody ever said exactly what it was they were selling. Or whose.

The spin-off, high-denomination banknotes in wads like paperbacks for the man who wants everything, was well in evidence. So were loud laughs, loud voices, ponced-up Brummie accents like crowbars ripping off car panels in backstreet wreckers' yards.

The people who had money these days, for Christ's sake! The amount of money they had!

It was tempting to use his wit as a pin to prick the bloated bladders of their self-confidence, but these people were puncture-

66

proof. Not only that: some of them were the kind who'd pull off your arms and legs just for laughs.

Most of them were former sidekicks of Mike's. On the second night one of them, done a ten-stretch for robbery with violence according to Lily, followed Nick into the bog at the Upsadayzee Club: laser light show, a comedian whose combination of obscenity and racism made everyone except Nick fall about, strip acts with the delicacy of a public flaying.

Big shoulders propped against the door to make sure no one came in – or went out – he hoped the *Globe* wouldn't say naughty things about Moike.

'Moike still stands for summat in this town, know what I moin, Nick? Say summat Moike don't loike and, well, there's some up here down't reckon you lot down there too much anyrowd. Somebody moight just pay you a call, know what I moin? I moin that wouldn't be noice, that, would it?'

Echoes of these adenoidal accents would haunt him for years.

All that plus the thought that Lily was going to get fifteen K for something that was half gaudy truth, half highly-coloured fiction and all a lawyer's delight.

It gave him one thought to gnaw on. Any deal he might manage to make on what he'd found under that chunk of chopper would be no more immoral than the pile Woodward and Bernstein had made out of Watergate.

On the last day, after a boozy supper in the glitziest if not the best restaurant in Birmingham – glitz, for Lily Holden, was the bearskin rug of life – they went back, just the two of them, to that great mock-Tudor house in Solihull. She and Mike might have split, yet he seemed to have made very generous provision for her. The bastard!

Nick had spent a lot of time there over the past two days, making notes or pretending to make them while she switched between Cinderella and a low budget imitation of some ritzy American TV series. He'd brought his tape machine with him, but she would have none of it.

'You're a nice boy, Nick, and I'm not saying you'd set me up. But when it starts coming out, it'll be your words, not mine, get me, luv? Anybody who doesn't, you know, reckon what I've said about 'em, cross my heart and tell 'em I never said it, won't I? Wouldn't want you pulling out your little whatsit to make a liar of me, would I? Know what I'm saying?'

He knew what she meant: she would talk, but the *Globe* was stuck with the consequences. Exactly the sort of deal he wanted for himself, tell the full story but have someone else, someone big enough to soak up any possible kind of threat and pressure, standing between him and the heat.

Pull out his little whatsit. When Lily said that, she batted her artificial eyelashes so that he almost felt the draught. Lily was full of that kind of double meaning.

They were sitting on one of her bed-sized sofas, plush velvet, more braid and tassels than a Ruritanian hussar. Halfway to legless after the best part of a bottle of gin, she'd edged him into a corner, knees touching his, her scent as overpowering as a Kew Gardens hothouse.

As always, she had a drink in her hand. She called them gee-gees: gin and gin. The lemon and tonic only went into the first one. The glasses were cut crystal that weighed around half a pound. Cost me fifteen apiece, them, she'd said, and she did mean quid, not pee.

He tried to bring things to a reasonably tidy end, but she wasn't very interested. Knees pressed against his, the glass with its ice cubes held to her cheek, she was looking at him with a glazed fixity of purpose.

Her voice thick and husky, she said, 'You could pull out your little whatsit now, luv. Shame not to use it just once before we part, know what I mean?'

She snuggled up. 'I've come to be a bit fond, know that? If you and me was off on our own like, say some little villa near Marbella? we could find more things to do than swim in the pool.'

She grabbed him by the neck, twisted his head round, kissed him hard on the mouth. At that range he could see the pores of her skin, the cracks in her makeup. Her breath had more gin than her glass.

Mouth poised over his, she said, 'Don't you put this in your write-up, mind. My Mike'd – '

He saw her brain cells send her some kind of signal from way, way down. She blinked, automatically said, 'The bastard!' made a drunkenly awkward move, spilled her drink in her lap.

'Ow Gawd!' She giggled, fished between those improbable breasts, shoved a wispy handkerchief at him. Next thing he knew she'd got her skirt hoisted to her thighs: stockings, not tights, fancy garters, too.

Her tongue passed over mauve lips. 'Let's see what you can do for me down there, lover boy.'

His mind still on that significant slip of her tongue, he went chicken. He took the handkerchief and began to dab, careful to steer clear of what she called the naughty bits. He knew her main aim, now, was to draw him away from the unintentional lead.

She chose to turn his clumsy rebuff into a reflection on his bloody manhood. 'Got you wrong, did I, darling? What's up, too knackered to rise to the occasion?'

The sort of thing he never told Ess about: the real cost of the job. He would do anything to get out if it weren't that it paid so well.

Dress disarranged, her flushed face a mixture of anger and contempt, she waved her glass at him, scattering what little it still held.

Voice thick with booze and rage, she said, 'Had better men than you for afters, diddums. Only play with your sort to keep in practice.'

She was semi-legless, nothing like booze for making them careless. He'd had a lot to drink himself, but not so much that he didn't get the drift. If he'd been sober, he would have taken it slower.

'Keep in practice for who, Lily? For Mike?'

Her face slowly clouded with menace.

'Me and Mike is through. The bastard!' The expletive came after a brief pause, as if she had momentarily forgotten her lines.

'Mind,' she said, 'you want to watch it, anyway. He's touchy, is Mike. You might find he's got a long bloody arm, so don't you forget.'

He felt a small exultation. Couldn't fool him on this one; too old a hand. Monkey had been right after all. No hit. No split.

They were all greedy, these villains. Pull a zillion quid stroke and take the first flight to wherever: they'd still be grieving over the few crumbs they'd had to leave behind. When the cops finally gave up on the bullion job he reckoned it was only a matter of time before Lily realised the Holdens' family assets and slipped out to join Mike in a better class of climate.

Smoothing down her soaked skirt she said roughly, 'Push off

back to your hotel, wonder boy. Got my reputation to think of, haven't I?'

Drunk as she was, it pleased her. 'Better men than you, Nick luv. Better men than you. Go on. Sod off and write your bloody story. Then me and my lawyers'll check the spelling, know what I mean?'

Before he was out of the pillared front entrance with its gaudy palette of Victorian stained glass, he could hear her calling someone on the telephone.

He belted down the M1 toward London dangerously fast, longing to be back in Ess's wholesome company. Even the smoking charnel house at Nethercott Stoney seemed preferable to the kind of scene he'd been in for the past too many days. Only at the Newport Pagnell service station did he stop for a slash, a wash, fill up the tank.

When he walked back to the car it was dark, chill under a press of cloud that smelled of snow and threw back the jaundiced glow of the parking area lights. Not many about where he'd parked: a group of oldies looking lost and bewildered, a young couple with whining kids, some guys and birds, leather and jeans, who could equally have been university students or tearaways.

A graveyard of glinting metal, oil-rainbowed pools of water, the clicks of hot metal cooling. Beyond the desert, the endless rumble and snarl of goods and humanity on the move.

He found his car, switched on the radio for company, slotted the key into the ignition. As he reversed out of his space another car came to life, its awkward attempt at a turn blocking his own exit.

He waited impatiently. Instead of changing lock and moving off, it stalled. Only it wasn't a stall. Two men got out, one large, one smaller but wide. The larger one, moving unexpectedly fast, had the offside door open before Nick had had time to react. The wide man leaned negligently against the other door.

The previous time it had been the large man who had done the leaning, blocking Nick's exit from the toilet at the Upsadayzee Club. He thrust his head in, his big shoulders blocking out light.

'Now then, Nick lad.'

The Birmingham accent, comical enough to the Nick Brooke of London Town; as funny now as the sound of a bottle-end being knocked off in a barroom brawl.

'Fancy meeting you here, then. Still, quoite cosmopolitan,

70

these ployces, don't you reckon? Everything from big shots to shitbags. Lil'll be pleased we met up, though. Quoite chuff, Lil'll be.'

One minute you were Nick Brooke, a bit of a celebrity, safe and warm, on your way back to civilisation. The next, raw menace. Its breath on your face, the world shrunk to a tight, dark box, the threat of imminent violence stopping your breath in your throat.

He said nothing, hadn't even words ready to say.

The close, dark bulk reached to lay a hand on his shoulder. He tried not to shrink. The pinched-nosed, rasping accent said, 'Lil was dead worried, know what I moin? Sort of afroid she'd said things you moight get wrong. Moight mess up that wroite-up of yours. Know what I'm on about?'

'Yes,' he said. Or someone said, a voice something like his own.

'Yes. Thing is, friend' – the hand momentarily squeezed his shoulder so hard that thumb and fingers practically met – 'it's not Lil, see? It's what Moike moight think. Sees all the English papers, does Moike. Has them flown out, loike. Well, Lil wouldn't want Moike's friends dropping in on you, give you a slagging down, all on account of you getting it wrong. Wouldn't want you ending up a wheelchair job. I moin, wouldn't be noice, wouldn't that.'

The squeeze again. 'Would it?'

No, the half-familiar voice agreed.

'No.' Finger and thumb gripped his cheek, a cruel vice. 'And that ain't the worst of it, Nick. Lil says you're a married man, kiddy as well. Bothers her, does that. Lil likes kiddies. Only there's them that moight think that left to yourself you'd chance a slagging for the sake of a good yarn. But the kiddy, now. Nasty old world, Nick. There's them that's not above a bit of choild mowlestation, know what I moin?'

The finger and thumb, still sunk deep in his cheek, forced him to nod his understanding, then released him. The hand patted his cheek briskly. ''Course you do, Nick, word to the woise, eh? Moind how you gow, roight? Nasty things can happen out there in the fast lane.'

Fifteen K for a pack of lies from a blowsy ex-pro whose husband had terrorised the Midlands underworld before taking off for the good life. As told to Nick Brooke, mortgaged for ever

71

and a day to pay for a three-up, three-down chunk of Victorian whimsy outside Dorking, when he had something that would buy him the life of Riley. And ought to be told.

He got on the Excell to Ess to tell her he was going to be very late. She was resigned but understanding. As usual. Sometimes, including now, he wished she would show a bit more fight, lose her temper, shout.

Ess wasn't like that. Mother and mate, that was her scene, just take the knocks and put on a brave smile when things didn't go her way.

Okay, so women enjoyed being martyrs. But what about a situation where she might not just have to say boo to a goose but wring its bloody neck before it pecked her eyes out? What if she came up against Lily Holden's heavies? What if she had to do his stinking job?

Wasn't going to happen, was it? Nick Brooke, the *Globe*'s number one hotshot, one scoop already worse than useless, was going to have to keep quiet about another to protect his wife and child from mowlestation.

Oh Jesus! Oh Christ all bloody mighty! Cold, tired, hung over and sorry for himself, he revved angrily, left like a racing driver after an unscheduled pit stop.

Cold night, crisp, a three-quarter moon hanging up there as remote and heartless as Dame bloody Fortune. He swept up the deserted Dorking High Street, took the Guildford road, put his foot down.

Holmbury was a settlement of the dead, moonlight glinting bone-white on the petrol pumps of the garage, most of the village asleep, only an occasional distant light among the trees. Frost and low-lying mist had spun a chill pall along the valley bottom.

No lights at the Crabtrees, early to bed, early to rise. Ess and Emma would be in bed too. Ess was used to his sliding in beside her in the middle of the night. He couldn't wait, but he'd have to; something more important to do first. You could do a lot of thinking on a long night drive.

On to the crossroads, take the narrow lane past the sub-post-office, the reflection of his lights briefly brilliant in its glass as he swept past. A minor road, crossing the hill just short of the summit before winding down to Ewhurst. Savage pleasure in hauling the car round tight bends, up empty, narrow slopes, sandstone orange in the white glare, dead bracken and almost leafless trees spectral in their winter melancholy.

Just short of the top there was a track through the scrub that shortcut to the summit. The horsy people used it, then sat staring at the view over the Weald toward the South Downs and the sea as if they owned it. One way or another, he thought bitterly, they probably did.

Tuck the car into a dark little glade out of sight, take the torch, get the spade from the back. Remember to put it back clean or Ess would be asking more questions. Begin the climb under a sky gravid with moonlight and silence.

The countryside in the daytime was one thing. A densely wooded hill in the small hours was another. And it wasn't all that still. Things squeaked, hooted, scuttered. Just short of the top something all but went over his feet, dead bracken snapping and hissing with the speed of its passage. A fox? None too sure. He was angry to find his heart beating fast. Okay, born and bred a townie, so what? This was what Ess had wanted. Mortgage or not, he'd been happy to see her happy.

He'd chosen the spot carefully, cause to remember it from one of their earliest visits, still in London, bringing Emma out on Sundays for fresh country air. A solitary, twisted pine: he'd had the idea of climbing it to look for a missed path. A branch had snapped on the way up, no harm done except to his dignity. Ess and Emma had laughed a lot once they saw he was okay, most of all because even in the act of falling he'd yelled to them to look out.

From the tree, a sandy ride marked by a gorse bush, then a minor track. He took the track, low-growing vegetation tangling his shoes. A little hollow. After his fall they'd rested there, often used it as a picnic spot afterwards. He brushed aside dead bracken with the spade, thrust the blade in, wincing at the noise.

Still there, inside a plastic bag with a rattling residue of grit. He took it back to the car, shielded the light from the torch under the rug from the back seat, began his homework. Just short of four in the morning, the early pages letter-perfect, he finally made up his mind.

Glashin tried to make a joke of it: 'Why so urgent? You want to defect, Nikita? I don't advise it. London is much warmer than

Moscow in December and I think Moscow rate for *Globe* staffer is not so hot.'

'No offence, Peter,' Nick said, 'but I'd sooner defect to the Channel Islands. Look, remember telling me about stories you couldn't get your own sheets to publish? Red Tass and that?'

Glashin still wouldn't take it seriously. 'Poor Nikita, you have a scoop but because it contains no sex, no crime, no violence, *Globe* thinks not fit to print? Or perhaps it says something good about Soviet Union.'

'It's a scoop,' he said doggedly. 'A hell of a scoop.' He was going for broke, so there was bargaining to be done, no showing his hand until they reached some kind of understanding.

Glashin changed his tune, but only a little. 'Scoop? Big word, Nikita. Remember, Soviet press is not used to scoops. Sometimes we sit on a story for weeks while we discuss whether to print. Then decide not to print. Where are you? The *Globe* newsroom has buses running down the middle?'

'Call box. No hurry. I'm on my pay card.' He was on his Excell.

'Ah. Talk now, pay later.'

'Let's say I'm more interested in pay now, talk later.' He hadn't meant to be flip, there was more to it than just money, but it did the trick.

'I see.' Glashin's voice became more thoughtful. 'You have a story to sell, and you come to Glashin.'

'When we talked – '

'That was talk, Nikita. Good wine, good food, such talk sometimes becomes extravagant. Now you are in public call box, so you say, but Tass is guest in your country. How do I know this is not a trick?'

'Where's the trick in talking?'

'Talk is no problem, Nikita, as you would know if you lived in my country. In my country problem is who listens.'

'Look, Peter, no one's listening. I've got a story I can't offer to anyone else, a story that ought to be published. If we met, I could explain.'

They wrestled for a long time, Glashin mostly in silences. Yet again Nick said, 'Just name a place and a time. Anywhere you like. If I can't convince you in five minutes, that's it.'

Another stretching silence before Glashin said, 'Tomorrow is my birthday, Nikita. If you are still of same mind you call me and say, "Happy birthday, Peter." Then maybe I name a place.'

3

'SPY' DEAL: WHO SET UP WHO?

He looked at Ess: thin, almost skinny; huge eyes and that big mouth with a tuck at each corner. She smiled a lot, even when there was nothing to smile about, though her smile was often nervous.

Seven in the morning: thick sweater, old jeans tucked into half-boots, glamorous as a bloody potato picker yet he wanted to hug her, tell her to stop trying to hide the fact that she was worried about him, tell her everything was going to be all right.

Just as he was ready to leave she almost visibly plucked up her courage. 'I wouldn't mind if you chucked it in, Nick. We'd manage until you got something else. You would soon enough, anyway. I hate it when you have to waste your talent on stuff like the Holden story.'

All because he'd been awake half the night, memorising his homework. Going to be examined on it today, wasn't he?

He did give her a hug, kissed her hard. 'I'm okay, Ess. Okay about Nethercott, okay about the Holden slag, just waiting for the right chance. Do a good job whatever it is, file it on time, that's what it's all about. Then when opportunity knocks, up and away.'

He kissed her again. 'I'm late. Got to go, or I'll miss that train. Give you a call when I know what time I'll be back.'

'Yes,' she said. 'Of course. Be careful. It's foggy and I hate it when you drive fast.'

He found himself shaking his head as he slid into the car. Self-assertiveness classes! No wonder she'd packed it in. Simply wasn't made of the right stuff, too soft-hearted and loving. That was his good luck. Hers was that he had enough of the right stuff for both of them.

It was amazingly easy to become a conspirator, the more so since, so far, there was barely a conspiracy.

Balls! He wouldn't be meeting Glashin at Kenwood House on a brass monkey day – outside, too, for God's sake! – unless it was for the kind of chat you couldn't have in a posh Chelsea restaurant.

So here he was, an embryo conspirator, tramping up Highgate Hill on a raw, grey morning after changing tube compartments three times on the way to Archway to make sure he wasn't being followed.

Pretty silly, really. Who knew what he was up to, or even where he was? Out on a story that fell through as he had known it would, since he'd set it up to go that way. Then a quick call to Glashin.

He didn't know whether it was Glashin's birthday or not, didn't much care. He was in with a chance when nothing else offered even so much as the tinkle of small change. And nobody's mug: one little whiff of funny stuff and up yours, pal!

He pretended to look in a bookshop window, took another glance. No one behind. No dawdling cars or whatever, nobody in any parked one, not surprising, considering how bloody cold it was.

Hampstead Lane was deserted. Classy houses up here. If Ess ever felt like coming back to London, what about Hampstead or Highgate? *The* place for hacks who'd made it; rich novelists, well-known columnists and chat show kings, drinking themselves to death and moaning about how boring it was to have money.

He turned in through the North Wood entrance. The grounds weren't exactly going to be crowded. The wind whining along the North London heights had come straight from the Murmansk peninsula. Suit the Sovs, maybe, they had Gulags up here. Junior embassy staff, Aeroflot, permanent trade delegates and the like living together in commie comradeship. Glashin said that it was a bit like the YMCA.

Kenwood House looked bloody marvellous among the bare trees. Ess would know all about the architecture: eighteenth century, something to do with Adam? No need to be an expert to appreciate that fancy Grecian portico, though; stylish, suit anyone from a pop star to an Arab multimillionaire, not that he aspired to that sort of thing.

It had the right effect on him just when he was beginning to feel twitchy. Do a deal with Glashin, expose something that bloody well ought to be exposed, get himself a head start while he shopped around for a real job on a real paper. A chance like that could make you feel you'd come a long way from a life that had started in a three-up, three-down semi in Kennington.

His old man got into debt the way other people got into buses. His brother's idea of the good life was a clapped out Suzuki and ten pints up the Elephant come Saturday night. As for his mum, no use worrying about her. The last time he'd gone to visit her at that creepy great place out at Epsom they'd patted his head and turned him away: she was so far gone that the only thing they could do was keep her clean and top up her dosage three times a day. Best forget all about her, the doctor had said. She'd never come back to the real world.

Ess said he was too hard. Ess said he ought to make an effort to keep in touch, though it was his family that had given her the chop, right from the start. Women really were masochists when it came to family ties. As if there was some sacred duty. Sometimes you just had to face the facts, cut your losses and get on with your own life.

Out on the terrace, taking the full blast of that wind, he looked down the slope toward the lake. No sign of Glashin. Sticking to the agreed procedure, the summerhouse among the rhododendrons. Or was he – you could get fanciful, playing this game – somewhere in the shrubbery, checking to make sure his dear Nikita didn't have a posse of Special Branch in tow?

Two press guys meeting in the grounds of Kenwood House to discuss a possible story? One of them a Tass man? So what? If you could lunch with a Tass man at Auntie Claire's, you could take Gorbachov to tea at the Ritz.

Glashin was there all right, perched on a seat. Swish coat, a collar of astrakhan, an astrakhan hat, all very Russian and cosy.

'Nikita! How good that you come for my birthday. In this weather I feel very much at home.'

Not surprised. Like Siberia, shrubbery clicking and rustling in the wind. Nothing else in sight but a piece of very modern sculpture: either that or someone had dumped a load of scrap metal.

He sat reluctantly, the chill already tunnelling into his bones. What a laugh, made to feel ill-dressed, positively bloody poor, by a Soviet *apparatchik*!

Glashin handed him a flask, silver, sheathed in pigskin. 'Drink. You are not used to such weather, you English.'

He didn't really like vodka. Still, better than nothing. He drank. Vodka my foot, it was brandy, very good brandy. He handed the flask back, feeling the glow glide from his throat to his guts like an angel on skis.

'Do yourself well, Peter.' He thought that each time they met. True, though. Anyway, Peter was a decent guy.

Glashin shrugged comically. 'Banished from my fatherland, I drink to drown my unhappiness. This is to do myself well?'

'Can we walk? I'm freezing.'

Glashin snuggled his neck luxuriously into his astrakhan collar. 'To the lake, yes? Perhaps some of these ducks are from Russia. Did you know our Grand Duke Michael lived in this house once upon a time?'

He seemed to be in particularly good spirits, swinging his arms as he walked, snorting air as if it was high grade coke. They reached the lake in silence. He suspected that Glashin was deliberately prolonging it.

'Is it really your birthday?'

Glashin looked solemn. 'In Old Russia, calendar is different. In Old Russia, this is my birthday.' His face split in that wide, white grin. 'You don't believe?'

'If you say so.' Nick tended to see himself as the sophisticated man-about-town, unaware that 'town' was an imaginary place, a few streets, a few bars, mostly populated by media people. Now, in this grey and green desolation, the lake scrawled aimlessly by the wind, the discord of ducks mingled incongruously with the bee-hum of invisible traffic, Glashin managed to make him feel like a boy in his teens.

'What I say,' Glashin said, 'is nonsense and of no importance. What you say decides whether we waste our time, Nikita.'

'How much do you pay for a good story?' It came with a rush, made him sound even more of a kid. He hadn't meant to blurt it out like that. After all, it wasn't just a question of cash.

Glashin watched the ducks as if he hadn't heard. 'We should have brought bread. Life is hard for them, yes?'

'Life is competition.' Damn it, he hadn't come here to swap

platitudes. He could walk away, just a few civil words and back to where the competition was at least in civilised surroundings. It would give him some sort of moral victory. Or would it? They wouldn't be here if he hadn't telephoned Glashin. He wouldn't have telephoned Glashin if he hadn't hoped to get something out of it. The something he had in mind included money, and Glashin knew it. That gave Glashin the moral victory, walk or stay.

He said, 'I like to win.'

'At what, Nikita? You have gambling debts?'

'Good God, is that what you think? No debts. I just happen to be ambitious. Good at my job and ambitious. For myself, for my wife and kid. If you're ambitious, you want to win.'

'In the West, for some to win, many must lose. In my country, no absolute losers. Some big prizes; many, many small. I think you call them booby prizes?' Glashin laughed loudly. 'Okay, what is this story that is so important?'

Something disturbed the ducks. They took off in a thresh of white water, a clatter of wings.

'A big story,' Nick said. 'Very big. The biggest.' What had startled the ducks? Nothing. No one in sight. He was just jumpy.

'Come.' Glashin began walking again.

The grass was crisp in the cold air, the ground beneath it hard. That wood had been spongy between the road and the wreckage of the chopper. Had he left footmarks? If he had, they would have been trampled into anonymity when the cops and military arrived. Wouldn't they?

Glashin was walking slowly now, hands clasped behind. They might have been discussing the weather, the political situation, a nice point in philosophy. Glashin probably knew all about philosophy.

Glashin said, 'Who knows this big story?'

'Just me.'

'This can't be so,' Glashin said eventually. 'News is always about people, yes?' He shot a glance. 'So, when you say no one knows, you mean these people are not aware that what they do is known. I am right?'

'Yes.'

'And this news is exclusive.'

'I told you. A scoop. Hard news, not rumour.'

Glashin made a small sound. Impatience? Disgust? 'The *Globe* speaks today about a scoop. A woman in Birmingham who will talk of her past life with a criminal. Rumour scoops your scoop with a story that this woman will live with him again.'

Monkey had heard that rumour too. Tim had jeered, 'Opposition tryin' to rubbish us, brother. We got the story, nothin' they can do.'

Nick, Lily's heavies still large in his memory, had said nothing at all.

The ducks, wheeling back, passed over them with a soft creak of wings, coming in to a landing. 'In my country,' Glashin said, 'such stories are unthinkable. But then, in my country, no crime.' His loud laugh swung the ducks away across the sullen, ruffled water.

Barely interested, he said, 'This story only you know. Also about crime?'

'No. Of course not.'

A chuckle. 'Of course not, or no problem in selling.'

But it was about crime. Why hadn't he seen that before?

Carefully planned, not yet committed. Conspiracy to commit a felony: he'd covered the courts long enough to know the jargon. And by classifying their conspiracy, those who had prepared and approved the plan had also made it a crime to reveal it. Nothing wrong with that reasoning, was there? He wasn't stupid.

He said, 'As a matter of fact it is about a crime.' He felt a kind of excitement. There was a moral justification for what he was trying to do. Even Sarah would have to agree with that.

The ducks were airborne once more, a sudden explosion of wings. Something must be disturbing them over on the far side of the lake. He couldn't see anyone. His damned imagination at work again.

He said, 'A crime against humanity. Well, a proposed crime against humanity. I think you could call it that.' Practically everything the military planned was a crime against humanity, wasn't it?

Glashin stopped. 'My dear Nick.' He stood looking into Nick's face. 'You expect me to believe this?'

'It's true.'

Glashin's gaze was uncomfortable but Nick faced him out. He had never seen the moral dimension so clearly. It made the whole thing much easier to handle.

'The uncovering of a proposed crime against humanity,' Glashin said. 'For which you would like to be paid.'

Nick flushed. 'It's not just a question of money. This is a terrific story. The biggest. But no British paper would touch it.'

'Terrific story that requires terrific money, I think.'

'I'm taking a risk. A big risk. I'm entitled to some kind of compensation.' So was Sarah, a payoff for all the hard years.

The blue eyes showed something at last. He chose not to recognise it. 'What do you expect from me?' Glashin said. 'What do you think I am?'

'I expect you to want to see some kind of proof. Then I expect you to say that you'll have to talk to your bosses.'

'You can produce such proof?'

The next step was irrevocable. 'Yes.'

'Here? Now?'

He'd foreseen that. It was why he had done his homework up there on the hill. He said, 'First things first.'

'Meaning money?' No contempt. No anything.

'Meaning some sort of agreement.'

Glashin seemed to have retreated into himself, no longer the warm extrovert. 'I think we waste our time. I am disappointed, Nikita.'

'Two stages,' Nick said. 'First I convince you that I've got something you want. And tell you what I want for it. Not just money,' he repeated, half aware that it was himself he was trying to convince. 'A quid pro quo, inside stories from the Soviet angle. Exclusives that would help to get me a name.'

Glashin said nothing.

'Second, I show you, and you decide.'

'My name,' Glashin said quietly, 'is Pyotr Alexeyevitch Glashin. I work for Tass. I don't buy. I don't sell. I simply report.' The double meaning was certainly intentional.

'All right, report this. A fancy stamp, red, white and blue: eagle, arrows, olive branch. "Office of the Secretary of Defense". Defense spelled with an S. You know the sort of thing.'

Glashin didn't bat an eyelid.

'Copy number 7 of ten,' Nick said, 'the "seven" handwritten. Twelve pages.'

From the lake a duck called loudly. The wind found a small pile of dry leaves, riffled them through its fingers, left them for dead.

'Across the first page,' Nick said, 'sans serif, about eighteen point caps: TOP SECRET IN PERPETUITY.'

Glashin produced a spotless handkerchief, unfolded it, blew his nose. He refolded it, tucked it away, looked deliberately about him. Very shiny shoes, very small feet: Nick had never noticed before.

'The pages,' Nick said. 'Marked consecutively "Page one of twelve, page two of twelve" . . . so on. Skeleton letters, diagonally across each page, bottom left to top right: TOP SECRET. TOP SECRET. TOP SECRET, in red.

'Text, single-spaced. Numbered paras, thirty-two paras all told, plus a recap headed "Sum and Substance". Fancy typeface, kind of thing you see in presentation material. Laser printer, at a guess.'

Nick grinned. Glashin's eyebrows had risen slightly. 'Cat got your tongue, Peter?' He was beginning to feel more confident. 'Something my mum used to say. I'll give you another saying. All this detail is to add an air of verisimilitude to an otherwise bald and unconvincing narrative.'

'William Schwenk Gilbert,' Glashin said. 'Also, "artistic verisimilitude". Good press men must always check references.' Dry, noncommittal.

'If you say so. Page two has a distribution list that starts with the top man. Then the Secretaries of Defense and State. After that, let's see.' He began ticking them off on his fingers.

'National Security Adviser. Chairman, Joint Chiefs of Staff. Director of the Politico-Military Bureau. Director, International Security Affairs. Chairman, High Level Group. Chairman, Special Consultative Group. Don't ask me what they all mean.'

He took a pause, every word clear in his memory.

'General Officer Commanding US Forces, Europe; that's whose copy it was, by the way. Oh, and Chairman, IDD Committee. I'm not sure what that means either, but the whole thing's subtitled "Annex 2, Revised Integrated Decision Document". That could be the meaning of IDD.'

Glashin took a deep, silent breath. 'You learn these things by heart, Nikita?'

'Another stamp: "Reclassification Sigma One. Return to Office of the Secretary of Defense by hand of ranking officer for witnessed destruction". Then a bunch of signatures.'

He nodded, suppressed excitement producing an almost physical pressure in his head. 'That's it. So far. How much further do you want to go?'

Glashin studied his little feet, lips pursed. His head coming up suddenly, he began walking toward the house. 'This would not be news, Nikita. This would be espionage.'

An instant later he said, 'If it is true.'

'You know I didn't invent all that stuff. Are we in business?'

'Impossible.' Glashin's voice was firm. 'This is espionage. Goodbye, Nikita.' He lengthened his pace.

A hot welling-up of disappointment, anger even. 'Wait.' He actually grabbed at Glashin's arm.

Glashin freed it with dignity. 'You will please leave me.' His voice was cold. 'Such talk gets me seven days to leave England. You think my superiors would be amused?'

It couldn't end like this, not after all the agonising, the sweaty hesitation. 'Would they be amused if they knew you'd had the chance of stuff like this and turned it down?'

Without turning, Glashin said, 'How will they know that?'

'This story's coming out, Peter.' No caution now; he didn't care any more. 'Nothing will stop me. It'd just add to the interest to say who turned it down first.'

Glashin came very close. 'Once it is known what you have, I think you are in jail before you say two words more. In jail or worse.'

'Then you don't think I invented it. You know it's for real. It *is* for real.'

'So it is you who finds the wreckage in the wood.' Glashin said it wearily. 'And whatever else you find.'

He studied Nick's discomfort dispassionately. 'Simple to guess. Everyone knows of D-notice. Everyone knows something is lost. The rest is simple. You also, you are simple that you should think – '

He gripped Nick's arms fiercely. 'How do you imagine to get away with it? How do you think to make money? How do you even know we . . .'

He let his hands drop. 'I will give you very good advice. Burn this document. As soon as possible. Maybe it is not too late. Otherwise, they find you and . . .' He drew the edge of his gloved palm across his throat.

He was serious, Nick realised, but that couldn't be his last word, or why was he still waiting?

'There's a way, Peter. What's in that thing damn well ought to be published, and there's a way to do it. Through Red Tass. The ricochet technique. Cost you nothing to listen.'

'And if I agree this thing,' Glashin said eventually. 'How much does it cost then?'

The next morning he found just how good Glashin's intelligence had been. The Holden story not even written, yet the *Globe* with a four-column box: LILY, MIKE AND THE GOLD.

A lot of puff, but what it came down to was simple enough. Did Lily Holden really know nothing about the bullion robbery, or would she soon slip away to join Big Mike where there was no treaty of extradition but cheap booze and plenty of sun?

For the TRUE FACTS read Lily Holden's own story, as told to Nick Brooke. Only in the *Globe*, from next Monday. When the *Globe* claimed its facts to be true, something had clearly gone wrong.

It was all in a time-honoured tradition of the Street: dog don't eat dog but misses no chance of cocking a leg on a rival.

The *Mirror*, bidding against the *Globe* for Lily's story, had lost out. Armed with the rumour Glashin had retailed to Nick, today's issue carried a front-page above-fold shout – LOVE SPLIT THAT NEVER WAS? – in the hope of taking the shine off a *Globe* scoop.

In true tabloid style it moralised piously on the willingness of another newspaper to pay a large sum of money to someone whose links with a major crime might be – the whole thing a masterpiece of unactionable innuendo – such as to violate the ethics of an honourable profession.

Finding the spoiler in the *Mirror*'s first edition, the *Globe*'s night editor had promptly remade the front page in an attempt to turn sour grapes opportunism into a come-on for the forthcoming special.

Nick had no doubt where he stood. Lily and Mike, used to simpler morals and less incestuous forms of competition, would see it as a reporter from smartarse London pulling a fast one in spite of the threat of a slagging off.

Nick Brooke, the *Globe*'s man-on-the-spot, had been pitched from the safety of entrenched silence straight into no-man's-land. No-man's-land bore an alarming resemblance to that bleak, starkly lit parking lot at the Newport Pagnell service station.

Tim Bryce was less than sympathetic.

'Got somethin' like that and goin' to keep it to yourself?'

'Listen, they were all set to break my arms. Find yourself in the same situation, you'd have done the same thing.'

Tim made one of his vulgar noises. 'Get out! Been in worse holes than that while kids like you were still gettin' their kicks from playin' with themselves. Bluff, brother. Nothin' but bluff. Right, when are you leavin'?'

'Leaving?'

'For Brum, you soft git. Put yourself straight with Lil by tellin' her she's got the chance to deny it all. Offer she can't refuse, right?'

Nick was appalled. 'You haven't seen the muscle she has hanging about. That guy in the car-park threatened Sarah and Emma. What do you think he'll do when he sees me turn up again?'

He wasn't having Ess and Emma put at risk. And he had his deal with Glashin to get through. Buggered if he was going to have it wrecked by another trip to Birmingham and get himself worked over into the bargain.

'All right for you,' he said. 'The days have gone when people horsewhipped editors. Nearest you come to tough times is a slap on the wrist from the Press Council.'

Tim flushed. 'Is that so? Haven't talked to you since I saw Tyrran, have I? Muscle comes in more than penny sizes, believe you me, brother.

'Bleedin' Special Branch.' Nick's problems were forgotten. 'Passed the word up on our dirt squad, would you believe? Some faceless bastard in Five has a word with his pals in the Home Office. Next thing, Tyrran's got some slimy Deputy Under Secretary tellin' him over sherry – word to the wise, Tyrran old man – that his bad lads at the *Globe* are bein' un-British, sneakin' round a D-notice.

'Did Tyrran get to be a lord by sayin' "Up yours!"? No way! Wants his next takeover bid referred to the Monopoly Commission? No way! And could he' – his hot flushes practically overrunning each other – 'pick up the blower and just say, "Word to the wise, Tim old brother"?

'No way again! Got to be able to pass the word up that he's hauled his editor over the coals and it won't happen again.'

He wagged a stubby finger. 'Same treatment for Lil, okay?

Miss the chance of gettin' four million *Globe* readers in her corner? Not when our legal boys have had a word in her shell-like. She wants to be clean. We'll help her stay clean. She won't want any more bother from the Yard.'

He stopped, glaring. Monkey Willett had materialised, stealthy as an assassin.

'Chap from Special Branch to see Nick.' Nick's guts tied themselves in a bow.

Detective Sergeant Hamlet. How did you learn to live with a name like that? Forties, quiet, just a trace of Cockney accent, about as alarming as a dead fish on a slab. And that name!

Funny thing was, it fitted. Vague, stumblebum, didn't really seem all that interested. Routine enquiry, sir, everybody who was down there at the time of that air crash, won't keep you long.

Left as alone as you could be in those bloody glass boxes, Nick waited for Hamlet to produce some kind of a notebook, a new experience to be on the receiving end. No notebook. Instead of pitching straight in with the 'Where were you on the night of the seventeenth' stuff, the guy seemed to have nothing better to do than chat.

'This it, then?' As if he expected to see copies of the *Globe* whipping through by the thousands. 'Never been to a newspaper before. Thought there'd be more, you know, going on.'

Nick knew all the tricks; used them himself. Get the other guy relaxed, all going to be a breeze, then catch him off balance with a few fast ones. Can't be too careful, not even with a man called Hamlet.

'The newsroom's through those doors. Take you around after, if you like, but we print in another building.'

Couldn't have been less interested. 'Guvnor'll have my guts if I get back later than it takes. Some other time, maybe.' He used a pinky to ream out his earhole, examined it, finally came to the point.

'Down there at the time then, were you?'

'Nethercott Stoney?'

'Yeh, course, if that's what it's called. Won't stick in my mind, somehow. Sort of, you know, Lower Toad-in-the-Hole. Still, stick in my mind if it was my kids, I reckon. How soon were you there?'

Nick told him about being diverted on his way back from Lincoln. Hamlet seemed to be more interested in the rape trial.

'In court, were you? Wouldn't be in his shoes, bloody animal. Give him a rough ride when he starts his bird, the other cons. Hates a raper, does your average villain.'

Nick sat there waiting for the real thing. Which way did you go when you left the scene of the crash? Anywhere near the wood where they found the chopper bits? What kind of car? What kind of tyres? So what? Half the world must ride on Goodyear.

But Detective Sergeant Hamlet couldn't have cared less.

'Fancied the newspaper game myself, once. You know, O-level English when I left school. Went to the local rag, lost my bottle right on the doorstep, walked away without even going in. Yeh, well, came to the same thing in a way, s'pose. Interviews, enquiries, that sort of stuff. Do much of it yourself, do you?'

It was a good ten minutes before he came back to the purpose of his visit.

'Yeh, well so . . . you were there, what, about an hour after it happened? First on the spot apart from this *Oxford Mail* bloke, right?'

'First press man, yes.' He was still waiting for the tricky ones. Hamlet had a characteristic copper's look; blank-faced, long, staring silences, a suggestion of well-honed cunning and then: 'You're nicked.'

It never happened. 'Bloody Yanks,' Hamlet said without any real feeling. 'Stirring it up. As if we hadn't got enough to keep us busy. Don't ask me why, mind. Nothing changes. Tell you sod-all. See any odd characters around? Nutters? Deathwatch beetles? You know.'

Yes, he did know. Every disaster brought the nutters, anything for a sight of blood and bodies. Necrophiles, some of them. The fuzz and the rescue services got to be able to spot them a mile off, pack them off sharpish.

'No, nothing like that. Locals, cops, rescue services, media. No outsiders at all, so far as I know. Your lot were right on the ball.'

'Just wondered,' Hamlet said uninterestedly. 'Not that it figures. I mean where do you start? Give you a car, do they?'

Alarm bells. 'Sorry?'

'This lot.' Hamlet jerked his head to indicate the surroundings. 'Give you a company car?'

'Got to, really, always on the move.'

But it still wasn't what he had thought. Hamlet was going through the slow flowering of a grudge. 'Police corruption! Tell you, sir, pigeons get more bloody perks in this town. Nice fat expense account, too?'

Nick shrugged.

'Stand a bloke a jar for some info in our game,' Hamlet said, 'guvnor looks at you like you'd treated yourself to a month in Majorca when you ask for it back. Got your own house, have you?'

Time to ask what business it was of a bloody plainclothes sergeant, but you had to play these things along. He didn't want Hamlet, a man with a grievance – could his name have something to do with it? Must have to take a lot of piss – asking more awkward questions.

Nick pulled a face. 'My own house? Depends how you look at it. Mortgaged from now till doomsday.'

Hamlet gave him one of his long, blank stares, but this copper's lot was not a happy one.

'Yeh,' he said. 'Still. I mean, plugs you into the system, a house, right? Better'n money in the bank, some ways, keep up with inflation and that. Where you live, then?'

'Dorking.'

More fuel to Detective Sergeant Hamlet's slow-burning fire.

'Dorking.' Just as he might have said Hackney, Lambeth, a dozen other inner city disaster areas, but there was a full orchestra of undertones. A small jerk of his bullet head, mock respect. 'Where the posh folk live. Got kids, have you?'

'One. A little girl, eight.'

'Nice for her. Fresh air. Country. Trees and that. Still, same at Little Sinking, s'pose. Then a couple of planes collide and what have you got? Bloody mincemeat. So you didn't really see anything, then?'

Not just aimless: erratic as a bored child. Nick said, 'Well, I didn't miss a hell of a lot,' and laughed. 'I mean I wasn't exactly walking around with my eyes shut. Anything you think might help you with – '

' – my enquiries,' Hamlet finished for him. Like Liz Balcon of the dirt squad, not a trace of irony. Except that Liz would have gutted the average punter by this time, stripped him of info and left him for dead. Nick toyed briefly with the smashing idea of persuading Liz to join the Special Branch.

Hamlet said, 'Like what?'

'Sorry?' Better not let his mind wander too much.

'Like' – Hamlet subjected him to another of those inscrutable stares, simultaneously trying to screw his pinky back in his ear – 'what that might help me with my enquiries?'

'Well, don't know, do I?' Gone on long enough, but how did you say that to a copper? 'What you're enquiring about, I mean. Not exactly.'

'No.' Detective Sergeant Hamlet seemed to find that gloomily amusing. ''s right. You don't. Tell the truth, neither do we. Reckon you saw that D?'

Nick nodded. Hamlet nodded too. 'Yeh. Reckon you would. Well, lost something, didn't they? So if people like you go poking around trying to find out what it was – '

'Not me.'

'People like you' – Hamlet continued as if Nick hadn't spoken – 'poking about where you've no business to be, we're inclined to sit up and take notice. I mean' – his look kept settling on Nick's face and taking off again, like a restless fly – 'everybody, and I do mean everybody, that was around that place, then or later, got to check 'em out. What colour's that car of yours?'

'Blue.'

'Ford? Vauxhall?'

'Ford. Sierra.'

A sour grin. 'One or the other, has to be, 'less they hand out Jags and Rollers at this place. So. Blue Ford Sierra. Fleet car. Bet Ford falls over backward every time some punter walks in off the street to buy one out of his own pocket. Newish?'

'Ten thou, give or take.'

'Flogged a bit, I dare say. You press boys.'

'I don't hang about.'

'Tyres still in good nick?'

So they were on to tyres after all. 'Haven't been changed yet, if that's what you mean.' A tautening of the nerves, but he'd known they'd be checking on tyres.

Hamlet took the pressure off. 'Goodyears. Doesn't mean a thing.'

'Should it?'

'Buy a Sierra,' Hamlet said, bypassing the question, 'you get Goodyears. Millions of Sierras, millions of Goodyears.' He popped his mouth vacantly. 'And that's just Sierras. Yours out there in the parking?'

'Not today. Sometimes I come in by train, leave it at the station in case my wife needs it.'

'There's a good boy.' Still no irony. 'What station's that then? Dorking North?' He shrugged. 'Doesn't matter. Call the missus when you're going to be late, do you?'

'Sometimes.'

'That time? Tell her you'd be a bit late?'

There they were in that little glass box, where Monkey had left his monitor on so that some layout he had been studying stared from the screen like a ghost page. Outside, people passed to and fro, mostly the girls who ran the outer office. Messengers came in and out, motorcycle guys smothered in leathers, some of them without bothering to take off their helmets. You could get to wondering whether there really was anything alive inside the gear.

Twice Monkey had glided swiftly across the background, never a glance but Nick knew he was keeping an eye. No Tim. Tim would have taken himself off somewhere to sulk, probably the financial editor's box on the next floor. Up there they all sat watching screens that showed the progress of the round-the-world rip-off. Up there they wrote about money: pounds, dollars, yen, bought and sold in billions by kids younger than Nick who could personally pull in a hundred K a year.

Detective Sergeant Hamlet was indifferent to all of it. Hadn't taken a single note, his conversation a bit like the scribbles Emma made when she was tired of drawing but couldn't think of anything else to do.

Nick brought himself back to the last scribble. 'You mean did I call her that particular night?' Good old pocketphone, no being spotted in a call box.

'Yeh, from Little Sinking. Doesn't matter. Forget it. Just that us,' jabbing himself with a thumb, 'hung, drawn and bloody quartered if we wasted time on the wife. You know? Just waiting to bollocks you when you say you couldn't have been quicker. Book you in and out here, do they?'

It led to an account of how copy was inputted, time in, time off. All Hamlet had to do was ask to see Nick's inputs from Nethercott Stoney to be able to time the exact progress of events.

After that, which way did he go home? What time did he get there? Why so long? What happened in between? Then it would be over to Ess, whose petals would curl at the very sight of Detective Sergeant Hamlet.

Instead, Hamlet yawned, mouth wide open, a glimpse of a grey and coated tongue.

'Yeh, well, like I said. Opened that bloody door at the local rag and asked 'em for a job, maybe they'd have given me one. Doing the same thing as now, maybe, only for real dough. Company car, house in Dorking, the lot. Maybe even working for the *Globe*, right? Sitting here like you, listening to some bloody copper banging on about sweet F.A. What do you think, honestly? What do you reckon?'

He reckoned, Nick said, that Detective Sergeant Hamlet was probably right, certainly do no worse than Liz, Crispin and Roger, stirring it all up, and was there anything else?

'Oh yes.' Hamlet produced a notebook at last, fattish, thick covers, signs of heavy use. From another pocket he took out a metal case. It yielded a pair of spectacles that turned him into a scholar.

'This bloke on the *Oxford Mail*' – a ballpoint, non-functional end chewed like asparagus – 'if you'd just give me his name, save us a bit of bother.'

He wrote, a surprisingly literate hand, sighed. 'Near a hundred of you lot at Little Sinking. Joe Soap here's s'posed to see 'em all.'

He put everything away, held out a warm, casual hand. 'Hamlet by name, Hamlet by nature. Just farted about, didn't he? Hamlet, I mean. Never got anything done for yakking about it? Take me forever, this will, and all for the bloody Yanks.'

God help us, Nick thought, watching him leave, if that was a typical sample of Special Branch.

To the hill again, the moon dodging in and out of scudding cloud as if on the run. He left the new car in the same place, collected the shovel, torch and camera he'd switched from his own car, set off up the same sandy ride. Out on the summit a body-snatcher of a wind that probed for the resting places of dead leaves slashed his face relentlessly.

He always had the camera in the car; grab what you could if a story was breaking fast and a photographer wasn't handy. A fresh spool, a portrait lens that could go to within a foot. The first three pages, enough to show them the thing was genuine. And big. Very big.

What he was absolutely not going to do was to part with the original, not yet. Something up-front first, plus an idea of the bottom line. Tough haggling, the Sovs would be no pushover, that was for sure. Well, he could haggle with the best. No point in having a winning hand if you weren't prepared to raise your bid high enough to show them you weren't bluffing. And he was bidding for Ess and Emma as well as himself.

Take each page three times, enough to cover any slip-ups. Nine flashes, but all over in a minute or two, nobody to see them but the man in the moon. Tomorrow he had to leave the spool at the drop Glashin had nominated. Funny, passed that litter basket many a time, never a thought that one day he might be playing games he'd only ever seen in films.

The Weald came into view eight hundred feet below. No mist tonight, not with this snapping wind. Just moon-washed darkness dotted with tiny sparks of habitation. Far to the east the harsh glare of London Gatwick, a plane coming in low, nose lights on, flasher winking, no sound at all with the wind from the north-west.

For the rest, looking across that vast stretch of nothing, just a nebulous glow from distant Horsham, all the little villages too cradled by trees to make much of a show. His breath, as the moon made one of its swift and furtive sallies, launched ghostly pennants of radiance that fluttered briefly and were gone.

The lookout tree, then the picnic hollow. He stood for a moment, sizing things up before positioning the spade for the first careful thrust.

What was that?

He strained. Nothing. Just the wind whistling through its teeth. Distantly, audible now, the howl of reverse thrust as the plane, safely down, shed its landing speed on the Gatwick runway. He took the first step to where the package was buried.

Wait!

Breath stopped, muscles locked, ears frozen to the point of pain, the night exerting a kind of silent pressure on the drums without conveying information.

There *was* something. Between him and the point at which the land fell away southerly towards all that stuffed velvet emptiness with its pinheads of light. He found himself crouching.

Far below, miles away, a car, crawling noiselessly along some country road, took a bend and a rise. Its headlights flared momentarily, then it was lost among trees and high hedges. Much nearer, about forty or fifty yards from where he stood, he heard the sound again.

Kept his wits about him: at least he would be able to say that. Stuff everything in his pockets. Grab the spade, shuffle his feet carefully to muddle any marks he might have made. Cautious backward steps, still half-crouched, head bent so that any sudden shaft from a torch in hostile hands would not blind him or give others a clear glimpse of his face. Half run, bent low, until the loose sand of the ride slowed his steps.

Lose himself on the hill, hundreds of semi-wooded acres to give him cover? Hundreds of acres in which to get lost, take a tumble, feet entangled by tough ling, snaring bracken, a sprained ankle or worse.

Behind him another sharp crackle of disturbed vegetation. He took off, running as he had not run for years, a desperate combination of speed and caution that could only be achieved by sticking to the ride. Halfway down, a fresh thought: what if they were waiting at the car?

Behind him someone shouted, a man's voice, distant but clear. 'Hey! Hey, don't run away, damn it. Let's talk. No tricks, just talk, okay?'

He'd stopped, without meaning to. The other man – more than one, he thought now – was encouraged.

'Hey, listen, you know we have to play it straight. Here, take a look, no sting, no nothing, just talk, right?'

A torch came on, powerful, held high to illuminate a figure muffled in outdoor gear.

They couldn't see him, weren't sure where he was. He crept, circling, helped by a spectral seepage of moonlight. These trees, slender-trunked, had been thinned by a heath fire some years back. He knew where he was. They – he was sure there were two of them – didn't.

Some thirty minutes later in another place, after watching for fifteen minutes or more, he made up his mind. No one. He stepped out, unlocked the door, slid into the car.

Ess would be getting supper ready, Emma having her last play before bath and bed. He had a sudden, overwhelming longing to be with them, warm, safe.

He released the brake, hands frozen, a rigor of cold and tension. Let the car roll gently forward, no lights, crunching dead nature until the front wheels lurched softly over the edge of the road. That accent had been American. It frightened him more than anything else he could think of.

Ignition on, ease in the clutch, wincing at the sound. In the same moment another shout, the sky behind him bright and loud with sudden revs. He took off downhill, wrenching at the wheel to correct a fierce tail-wag, the glare of a following car blinding in his rear view mirror.

Anywhere but home. Ess wasn't built to take anything like this. In his mind he had an image of her crumpling like one of her own dresses slipping from its hanger. He had to shake them off, had to have time to think.

PART TWO

4

'Mum,' Emma said. 'Why are you pulling that funny face?'

'Am I, darling? What funny face?'

'Like this.' Emma scowled comically.

'Oh dear. I don't know. I was thinking.'

'Thinking what?'

'Oh, nothing much. Just thinking. Wondering what time daddy will be home for supper. Things like that.'

'Do you want to know something?' Emma said. 'I'm best in the class at somersaults.' She rolled head over heels, landing with a thump. Various things in the kitchen clinked and rattled.

'Careful, Emma. We don't want supper to end up on the floor.'

One ear on the radio, the other on Emma, slicing oranges for a fresh fruit salad. Nick oscillated wildly between high living and hastily grabbed sandwiches in pubs, not to mention oceans of booze. When he was at home, she did her best to make sure he had a balanced diet.

In the early days the wife of his then editor had given her a piece of advice. 'If you're married to a newspaperman, never cook anything hot until you see the whites of his eyes.'

So when he'd called in the late afternoon to say he wouldn't be too late, she'd thought: see him by bedtime if I'm lucky.

Emma said, 'Mum.' Sarah knew the tone: something coming up.

'Yes, sweetheart?'

'Why does daddy have to come home so late?' She picked up a fork and used it to draw grooves on the table.

Sarah retrieved the fork.

'Daddy has to work very hard. And he has to go to all sorts of places to write about things.'

'Miss Idlesby,' Emma said, 'says the *Globe* isn't a proper newspaper.' Miss Idlesby was her class teacher.

'There are all kinds of newspapers. The *Globe* is one kind. I expect Miss Idlesby reads another kind.'

'Miss Idlesby reads the *Independent*,' Emma said. 'She says the *Independent*'s a real newspaper. Will daddy work for a real newspaper one day?'

Perhaps she should have a word with Miss Idlesby at the next parent–teacher meeting. Only Miss Idlesby was a confident, opinionated woman who tended to see parents as well-meaning but misguided people who interfered with the proper raising of children.

'I expect daddy will work for another paper one day,' she said carefully. 'Then perhaps he won't be away so much.'

'I think I'll go and get a book.' From the hall her voice came back. 'I don't think I want to work on a newspaper when I grow up. Not even a proper one. It makes you tired. And cross, sometimes.'

Sarah hastily dried her hands. 'Emma, come here, darling. I want to tell you something.'

Distant, moving upstairs, Emma said, 'In a minute.' She sounded quite normal now. Most of the time Emma thought Nick was wonderful. Just, Sarah thought, as I did. Damn it! *Do*. Sort of; if only he worked for a proper newspaper. Back to the supper, a glance at the time to see how late 'early' was going to be.

Having dealt with global and national news, the radio was down to trivia. Two children dead in a house fire in north London. Someone in intensive care in Redhill Hospital after a hundred-miles-an-hour police chase along the M25. An arrest in the Guildford mugging spate.

Emma came back, thumped herself down on the floor. 'We could have supper down here. We could pretend we were having a picnic.' The newsreader had reached the weather. The wind would drop. It would be less cold. There would be snow, especially over high ground. Sarah drew back a corner of the curtain. White moths floated toward the light.

'It's snowing, Emma.'

'Snow!' Emma rushed to the window to see. 'Do you think it'll snow for Christmas? Can I have a toboggan? Tamsin's father's promised her a toboggan.'

'Perhaps. But it's quite a while to Christmas.' Sarah turned her attention to bananas. 'You never know, we might have a heat-wave for Christmas. We might have to put on our bikinis.' She turned off the radio, partly because the news was over, partly because she thought she had heard the sound of Nick's car.

'A *heat*wave? For *Christ*mas? Whoever heard of a heatwave for *Christ*mas? Can I have a banana?'

'Shush a minute.' Sarah brushed Emma's hand away absently. 'I thought I heard daddy.' He usually gave a cheeky double blast on the horn. She suspected the Morcambes didn't like it. If she told Nick, he'd probably do it more.

'It can't be daddy,' Emma was saying. 'He didn't go toot-toot.'

But she could hear the faint purr of the engine, the muffled thump of a door. Another thump, not Nick after all: must be people calling on the Morcambes.

The motor stopped, then no more noise. The Morcambes' callers usually did a lot of cheerful shouting when the Morcambes opened the door.

Except that – surely? – there was someone round the back, where the Morcambes' drive ran past.

Emma said, 'What are you listening for, mummy? It isn't daddy.'

'No,' Sarah said. 'We'll have to start getting you ready for bed if he isn't here soon.'

The front door chimes sounded just in time to stop Emma's ritual objections to going to bed before Nick was home. 'It *is* daddy!' Emma was up and running, the kitchen door slamming back against the wall. 'He's forgotten his key again. He's *always* forgetting his key.'

It wasn't Nick. The man at the door, topcoated, hatless, nondescript except for dark, bats' wing eyebrows, walked straight past her. No force, just the irresistible momentum of surprise.

'Mrs Nicholas Brooke? Chief Superintendent Capstick, Special Branch. I have a warrant to search this house under the Official Secrets Act. Is there anywhere you can send the child for the night, madam?' He held up some kind of identification. Sarah stared at it uncomprehendingly.

There was another man, younger. He too pushed past, went

through to the kitchen, unlocked the back door. A draught of cold air seeped in. Capstick closed the front door. The kitchen door framed a third man, snowflakes drifting about him in the shafted light. He stepped inside, incongruously wiping his feet. 'Shut that back door, sonny,' Capstick said sharply. 'Heat costs money.'

He really was nondescript: tallish, medium build, medium colour except for his black hair and eyebrows. Harmless, she would have said elsewhere. Nondescript, harmless.

Her first reactions had been mixed: bewilderment, shock, the beginnings of alarm. A small hand stealing into hers brought her back. No longer bouncily confident, Emma said, 'Who are they, mummy? What do they want?'

The chief superintendent bent to pat Emma's head. He had the beginnings of a bald patch. 'Don't worry, sweetheart, nobody's going to hurt you.'

She shrank from him. He turned to his men, his voice brusque. 'Don't stand gawping. Get on with it. Roofspace and floorboards first.'

The man who had come in the back way went into the dining room, switching on lights. Still stunned, Sarah watched him move chairs, start to roll back the carpet. The other man went upstairs. Taking her by the elbow, Capstick steered her towards the living room. He too switched on lights. Her lights. *My* lights!

Capstick said again, 'Is there a neighbour who'd look after the little girl, madam? This could take some time.'

Emma pulled at Sarah's hand. Her eyes, huge, glittered. 'Mummy? What do they want?'

Sarah hugged her tightly. 'It's all right, darling. No one's going to hurt you. This is all a silly mistake.'

'I don't like them,' Emma said. 'What do they want in our house?'

True feelings flooded in at last. Outrage. At the same time, the beginnings of a familiar sensation: large, confident men; no one here to deal with them. Whatever she said they would brush aside as Capstick had brushed her aside when she opened the front door.

She resisted Capstick's guiding hand. 'You've made a mistake. You must have. Please get out of my house.'

Upstairs, bumps and scrapes. No idea what to say next. This

was England. This was her home. These men were public servants. Her servants.

Also utterly confident. Whatever she said, they would ignore it.

'Show me your identification again.' Her tone unnaturally shrill, a stranger's. 'And I want to see the warrant.'

Capstick unfolded a paper, gave it to her. Official-looking, details typed in. At the foot a sprawled signature, indecipherable. All that registered was the typed-in address of the house. Nick's and her house. Capstick said, 'For the little girl's sake – '

She cut in, 'Where does it say our name?'

'Covers the premises, madam.' Even Capstick's polite patience was a provocation. 'It's the premises we're authorised to search, even if you weren't here.' He held out his ID.

Weakly aware that it carried his photograph and looked all too genuine, she wrapped both arms tightly about Emma. 'It's all right, darling. They're policemen. They're not going to hurt us.'

Just what her own mother would have said to Sarah at Emma's age. Policemen, men in authority. Men like that wouldn't be in authority if they didn't know best, dear. Nick could be very rude about it.

Nick! What was she thinking of?

'My husband will be home any minute, then there'll be a hell of a row.'

Capstick gave that one short shrift. 'We'll come to Mr Brooke later, madam. In the meantime it'd be best all round if you could make arrangements for this young lady to be taken care of for a time.'

Two thoughts loomed. Nick, troubled by something he stubbornly refused to discuss. And Capstick's response to the mention of his name: we know all about him. He's not going to be home any minute.

No one accompanied them to the Crabtrees. Glancing back as she crossed the road, her own house aglow with lights while legalised intruders ransacked it, she felt a brief, primitive urge to pick Emma up and run.

Outrage returned. She was going nowhere so long as these people remained. She would persist with her questions until Capstick, deceitfully harmless-looking, hermetically unemotional, realised that it really was a mistake.

No mistake. She felt it in her bones. Nick had been up to something.

She rang the Crabtrees' bell. 'Keep it a secret, shall we, Emma? Just you and me? I'll fetch you back the minute they've gone.' Emma just nodded, pinched and pale in the light that came on in the Crabtrees' porch.

Mrs Crabtree, unemotional, deceptively stony-faced, accepted without comment the amorphous explanation that something a bit tricky had come up. 'Sure there's nothing else we can do, love?' Charlie Crabtree, not one for talking much, hovered benevolently.

Sarah shook her head quickly. 'Thank you.'

A quick, shrewd look. 'Emma had her supper, has she?'

Emma, more herself, said, 'Yes, but daddy hasn't. Daddy's late as usual.' Sarah thanked God that Emma and Mrs Crabtree had hit it off at first sight.

'It'd be best, don't you think,' Mrs Crabtree said, 'if I got Emma ready for bed and put her in Susan's room? You can fetch her back when it suits, but if it doesn't she'll be all right.'

Practical, Emma said, 'Could I have Susan's bear?' Susan Crabtree, married and in Australia, still had a room in readiness for her annual visits; still had, too, her old teddy bear and other souvenirs of childhood. Sarah suspected it was the phlegmatic Mrs Crabtree, no time for such nonsense, you'd think, who couldn't bring herself to throw them out.

'You shall have Teddy, my love,' Mrs Crabtree said, 'and Mary Jane, and a book to read until you're settled.'

'And if she's still here,' Mr Crabtree said from the rearguard, 'I expec' she'd like some of my honey for breakfas'.'

'No, thank you.' Emma was firm. 'Mummy's going to come and fetch me when she's got rid of the men.'

Then she bit her lip, glancing at Sarah with guilty eyes. Mrs Crabtree's own lips tightened but she pretended not to hear.

Back home – familiar and yet disquietingly different – Capstick was where she had left him, the carpet slightly wrinkled, none of the furniture precisely where it had been when she went out. Upstairs the sounds of discreet ransacking continued.

Someone was in their bedroom, drawers being opened and closed. The thought of all the intimate things they could come across filled her with ineffectual rage. Capstick read her thoughts.

'They'll make as little mess as possible, not as if you're experts.'
Was that supposed to be funny?

Suit dark, ordinary, definitely off-the-peg. Brown shoes. Why
was it somehow strange to see a policeman in brown shoes?
Candid-looking grey eyes and that disarming bald patch revealed
when he bent to pat Emma. Pale-complexioned, looks faintly
placatory, a hint of humour. He had cut himself shaving.

She recognised the book in his hand: Edward Bond's *War
Plays*. He had closed it as she came in, but made no attempt to
replace it.

'Bit political, are you, Mrs Brooke?' Almost offhand curiosity.
A light, neutral voice, some sort of London accent.

'Do you have any right to ask that question?' Did he? She'd
no idea. She only had hearsay for the fact that a sheet of paper
gave them the right to search the house.

Capstick smiled faintly. 'You're not obliged to answer, but
none of us wants to be here all night.' He tapped the book
against the palm of the other hand. 'Little bit left of centre,
would you say?'

'Where's centre?'

She was in the classical situation they used to discuss in the
assertiveness group: confrontation with someone professionally
occupied, self-confident, no time to spare, unused to being
challenged, least of all by a woman. Keep your temper. They
always won if you lost your temper.

'What's your idea of centre, madam?'

'What are you? Thought police?'

'This isn't your book?' He held it up like evidence in court.

He knew it was her book. It had her name in it. Most of the
books in the house were hers. Nick wasn't a great reader.

'Will you put it back, please? It's not your property.' Her
knees wanted her to sit. To hell with her knees. And don't let
him complicate things. Stick to a single point.

She said again, 'Will you please tell me why you're here?'

'Can we sit down, Mrs Brooke? You look tired and I know I
am.'

'I'm perfectly all right, thank you. Please tell me why you're
here. And I'd be grateful if you'd put that book back where you
found it.'

He put it back. The shelf below was full of Virago editions,
quite a few feminist tracts among them. He ran a finger along

them one by one: books by women, about women, from women's points of view. And there were the CND magazines and the Greenpeace stuff and Friends of the Earth and . . .

'Does your husband have any views on this stuff?'

It took her breath away. She'd worked until Emma came, meant to work again when Emma was a bit older. 'I read what I like. Nick doesn't claim to own me.'

'Mrs Brooke.' Gentle now, sympathetic even. 'This is a shock for you, I know that. But we're not playing games, madam. You'd like to be rid of us. We've no wish to be here. Why don't you sit down while we check a couple of things?'

Laughter wrinkles in the corners of his eyes. Meet him socially and she might have thought him avuncular, even paternal. Probably had a family. Probably loved it.

'This is my house. I don't feel like sitting. Why are you here?'

Things like this didn't happen to ordinary people. Ordinary people had nothing to fear from the police.

He sat down himself, carefully easing up his trouser knees. She resented the humanity of the action. What he was doing to her was inhuman.

He said, 'Won't you sit now? Please?'

She sat, outmanoeuvred. 'Why are you here?'

'Sorry, madam, not my position to tell you. Do you know your husband's present whereabouts?'

'You mean, where he is?'

Cheap of her. Never mind. As he'd said, this wasn't a game. 'On his way home. You'll know soon enough.' There was a heavy thump from upstairs, a subdued murmur of voices.

'No, madam. Not on his way home.'

She waited. He added no more.

'But you know where he is?' Her mouth very dry.

'He won't be coming home, madam.'

'Why? What's he supposed to have done?' She had known all along, hadn't she? that he wouldn't be coming home.

'He's quite safe, madam. No need to worry about that.'

'No need to worry?' Her voice far too high; squawky. He was winning, damn him.

'Helping us with enquiries, madam.' The actual, ludicrous cliché. 'Now, if I could just – '

'What has he *done*?' Furious with herself, she amended the question. 'What is he supposed to have done?'

A brief hesitation before Capstick said, 'Don't know myself, to be honest. Meaning not exactly. Suspected offences under the Act, all I can tell you, madam.'

'The Official Secrets Act? That's ridiculous!'

'That's as may be, madam. I wouldn't know. Ours not to reason why.' Another heavy bump from upstairs, a smothered oath.

'What are you looking for?'

'Sorry, madam.' Why did she have a feeling that he didn't really know? 'About your husband. Did he – '

'I'm not saying any more. I want to talk to my solicitor.'

The only solicitor they had, she and Nick, was the man who'd done the conveyancing when they bought the house. A Dorking firm, virtually picked out of a hat. He would do. Any solicitor would do.

He was gentle but adamant, just like her with Emma when Emma was being difficult but not wilful. 'Not just yet, madam, if you don't mind.'

'I do mind. You can't stop me. It's my right.' Damn keeping calm! Why had she taken so long to allow herself the release of a good, knock-down, flat-out, flaming bloody row?

Capstick was shaking his head patiently. How dare he bloody well patronise her? 'All in good time. Look, Mrs Brooke,' trying a quiet threat, though his face had not been designed to accommodate menace, 'I could take you down to Dorking police station, you wouldn't like that. Don't suppose the little girl would, either, you gone from home, I mean, but that's *my* right.

'So why,' instantly avuncular again, 'don't we just get on with it, soonest started, soonest done?'

She took a deep breath, ignoring another thud from upstairs. Long past Emma's bedtime. She had to decide what to do, what she would say to the Crabtrees later.

'I want it on record that I asked to see a solicitor. And' – she got up, went to the desk for paper and pen – 'I want your full name, rank and number. Let me see that identity thing again.'

This couldn't be her, acting like this when her entire system was tingling with apprehension.

He could, she supposed, have refused. She supposed he could refuse almost anything. He didn't, handing over his identity card in silence. She made a production out of writing everything down, even repeating his names – Arthur Bream Lloyd Capstick

– aloud as she copied them. The implied mockery produced no effect.

'Bream Lloyd,' he said. 'The two grannies. Shouldn't be allowed, should it? Doing things like that to defenceless babes, but there you are.'

'Thank you.' Coldly, giving him back the card with its staring-eyed picture that helped a little by relegating him to the class of Woolworth colour snaps, four for a pound.

'Thank *you*, madam.'

He took his time over sliding his wallet away, patting the inside pocket like a man with heartburn, staring at her with eyes that didn't pop like the photograph.

'Mrs Brooke, I know how you must feel. I've a daughter not – '

'No!' She could handle that one. 'You don't know how I feel! Walking straight into my house. Going through my rooms. My things. Frightening my daughter.' Frightening her too, come to that, though she would die rather than admit it. 'No,' she said again. 'You absolutely do not know how I feel, Chief Superintendent.'

It made her feel a little better; thirty-five, not some wide-eyed, ignorant girl. She pressed her sensed advantage. 'My husband should have been home by now. He isn't here. You know where he is, but you're not going to tell me. And you won't let me see a lawyer. I'm going to report all that as soon as I get a chance. Until then you can ask questions until you're blue in the face, but you won't get me to answer them. I don't care if you do take me to the police station.'

The most assertive kind of self-assertiveness, if only her voice hadn't quavered.

A new idea. 'If I can't speak to my solicitor, I want to call my mother. You can't stop me doing that.'

He wasn't to know that her mother would probably say of course she must do whatever she was asked to do by the police, the underlying assumption being that it was probably all Nick's fault anyway.

'You have the right to inform a near relative, Mrs Brooke. The sooner you answer some simple questions, the sooner you can telephone Mrs Purdy.'

Knowing her mother's name took the wind out of her sails. She guessed it had been meant to.

Capstick pressed his advantage. 'Been a shock for you, 'course it has. I don't enjoy harassing women, Mrs Brooke, but I've my job to do.'

He seemed to settle within himself, as if a hurdle had been cleared. 'Now, let's start all over again. Your husband's been picked up by Special Branch on a matter affecting the security of the realm.'

The security of the realm? Ridiculous!

'Has he been charged?' Didn't they have to let them go if they weren't charged? Why was it she knew so little about such things? Because such things weren't supposed to happen to people like her.

Capstick dealt briskly with that one. 'Not in my hands, madam. I dare say your solicitor will go into it for you.'

'He's a newspaper man. Special reporter, not even political. Nick's about as political as Emma. You're crazy, the whole pack of you.'

'Not saying you're wrong, madam. They don't tell us everything. I don't think you realise that.'

'They?'

'The' – he waved a hand – 'powers that be. We do their dogsbodying, Mrs Brooke. Don't tell us everything, not by a long chalk. Maybe' – she knew he was looking for some way of soothing her – 'they did get it wrong. Maybe when they've questioned him they'll let him go.'

'You don't believe that.' Someone had come downstairs to open and close cupboards, her cupboards, in her kitchen.

He didn't answer. She was right; he didn't believe it. The telephone started to ring, making her jump.

One of his men – she registered him for the first time; youngish, fresh-faced, eyes that were much too old – looked round the door.

'Nothing so far, guv. Answer the blower?'

Capstick's imperturbability had its limits. 'Get it, man!'

A moment later, he was back. 'For you, guv. Five.'

Five? MI5, she supposed. This was not happening. This was not real. Yes, this was real. It was happening.

'If you'll excuse me, madam.' Capstick left. The younger one stayed. He and she were careful not to look at each other.

She sat in the familiar room which was not really familiar since they had not owned or occupied it long enough for it to be really familiar. Even some of the furniture, including the chair in which she sat, was not yet familiar. 'All right, all right,' Nick had said. 'But keep the brakes on, Ess. We're not made of money, not yet.'

She could hear Capstick's voice, too low for her to pick anything out. Someone else was doing most of the talking. The call ended. For a moment the house was totally silent.

Then he was back, a quick, silent mover. He motioned his junior out, closed the door, stood looking at nothing, almost as if he'd forgotten where he was, or why.

Eventually he met her gaze. 'Sorry to have to tell you this, Mrs Brooke. Your husband's met with an accident.'

She sat rigid, breath lost between lungs and lips.

'Is he . . . ?' The other Sarah, the one that could watch dispassionately and even, on occasions, jeer at the public performance of its twin, noted the cliché. In a moment she would say, 'You don't mean . . . ?'

'Are you going to tell me he's dead?'

'No, Mrs Brooke, not dead. But badly hurt, I'm afraid. Seems he drove into a motorway bridge.'

'Where is he?'

You're doing well, her other self told her, really well. The calm, sensible type: get the facts, save the reactions for later. She wanted to scream.

'In intensive care.' Not so much watching as studying her. 'All I can tell you for the moment. All I know myself.'

Her calm was a stretched thread. 'I want to see him. You can't stop me. I'll be ready just as soon as I've made arrangements about Emma.'

'I'm sorry, Mrs Brooke, they won't let you see him. Not yet, anyway. In the meantime we'll do everything – '

He caught and held her, minimum force, while she kicked, fought, called him names she normally never used. The man who had answered the telephone appeared in the doorway. Capstick snarled, 'Get out!' The door closed rapidly.

Eventually she gave up the struggle. 'It's you!' She fought back tears. 'If he's hurt, it's because you did it, you *bastards*!'

He sat her down as gently as any woman. 'George!' The same man appeared for the third time.

'Make some tea,' Capstick said. 'See if there's any spirits in that cabinet first. Whisky, brandy.'

Voice distant, mind numb, she started to say she didn't want anything, but Capstick, a different Capstick, was firm.

'A little shot of something, madam, then a nice cup of tea, it'll be best. I'd like to use your phone, with your permission.' Even in her present state she could see that the news had disconcerted him.

She allowed herself to be given a stiff Scotch, listening while he got on to Dorking police station and asked them to send a squad car. Oh, and a WPC. From an infinitely distant past came a memory: the local radio news had had something about a police chase and car crash on the M25.

When Capstick came back he looked at her speculatively. 'Afraid we'll have to wait a bit, Mrs Brooke. Someone from London's got to sort this one out. I've asked for a woman police officer to keep you company.'

'Bugger the WPC!' she shouted. 'And bugger you, too!' According to Nick, swearing only made her sound ridiculous. They would have to let her see Nick now. They would simply have to. Wouldn't they?

She waited in the reception area of the solicitor's office, physically sick with worry, scarcely slept at all. She had telephoned Redhill again. This time the girl on the switchboard – sounded cautious, or was that imagination? – put her through to intensive care.

The nurse in the intensive care ward had distanced herself by light years. Everything that could be done was being done; they could tell her more if she called again later.

She had demanded to see him. They had no right to stop her. Couldn't even remember exactly what she had said, only the savage gist.

At that stage a man, a Dr Quilter, came on. Talked fast, sounded nervous: imagination? Her husband was in theatre at that very moment. If she came to see him it would do no good and might be harmful. Everything that could be done was being done. She must try not to worry.

She had lost control, shouted incoherently, probably swore though she couldn't be sure. He had said he was very sorry. She had put the phone down.

Well, now she was behaving rationally, doing what little she could without making a nuisance of herself, as a sensible woman should. Exactly the opposite of the way Nick would have behaved. Or most men.

The receptionist said, 'I'm afraid Mr Pickering's out, Mrs Brooke.'

'I'm sorry, I should have phoned. When will he be back?' Even if it was within the hour, it would be unendurable.

'Not until late afternoon, I'm afraid. He's gone to London for the day.' The woman looked concerned. 'Could someone else help, or is Mr Pickering already handling the matter?'

Must be showing her feelings. 'It's just that I need some advice rather urgently. Mr Pickering dealt with us when we were buying our house.'

'I thought I remembered you. Did you particularly want Mr Pickering, Mrs Brooke? I could see who else is free.'

'No,' she said. 'It doesn't have to be Mr Pickering. And it is rather urgent.'

The woman keyed her intercom. 'I have a Mrs Brooke in reception. She's dealt with Mr Pickering once before, but this is different and it's rather urgent. Do you think . . . ?'

'Thanks, Maggy. I'll send her up.' She gave Sarah a smile. 'If you'll go up to the first floor, Mrs Bentley will be waiting for you. Hope everything works out all right, Mrs Brooke.'

Yes, it was showing. She smiled back, feeling her lips resisting the lie. 'Thank you.'

At the top of the stairs another woman, coming to meet her. 'Will you come this way, Mrs Brooke? Miss Smith can see you right away.'

The office was small, a view across the High Street to the raised pavement and the entrance to Sainsbury's. Things buzzed and quivered each time heavy traffic went by. The woman getting up from her desk was scarcely older than Sarah. Fobbed off with the most junior partner or whatever they called them? She was transferring her own sense of inadequacy to the other simply because she was a woman and young.

'Hello, Mrs Brooke. I'm Heather Smith. Sit down and tell me what I can do to help.'

A neat maroon two-piece and cream shirt. No rings, only a silver brooch set with nothing more elaborate than polished stones.

Face square, complexion sallow, chestnut hair, short with a fringe. Eyes brown, brows dark, heavy and unplucked. Nose small and snub, mouth straight, wide and quick to smile. Sarah liked her at once.

'Oh dear, you do look bothered. Would you like some coffee?' Without waiting for an answer she phoned for it, then folded strong hands, nails polished but not lacquered.

'Now, Mrs Brooke, tell me what it's all about.'

All the way in, rehearsing innumerable variations on the single stark fact around which all the rest was so much elaborate embroidery. It came straight out, no embroidery.

'My husband's been arrested under the Official Secrets Act. He's been badly hurt in a car smash and they won't let me see him.'

A tiny lift of those dark eyebrows. Silence, broken by a knock at the door. Coffee on a tray; pot, cups and saucers all of a deep blue that brought cheer into this little room with its cream walls, dark desk and chairs, a high green filing cabinet on which the tips of pot hyacinths were beginning to peek.

Sarah waited until the door had closed. 'And they've searched the house. They had a warrant. It seemed' – she gestured helplessly – 'to be in order.'

Heather Smith picked up the coffee pot. 'Milk, sugar? Help yourself.' Outside, the top of a Green Line bus slid past, the window buzzing like a wasp. For the first time since the ring at the door the previous night, Sarah felt reality beginning to force its way in. She pressed a palm to her face.

'Sugar, I think,' Heather Smith said calmly. 'Don't see you putting on weight in the circumstances.'

She picked up the phone. 'No calls, no interruptions, please, Maggy.' She reached for a ballpoint and pad.

'Suppose you begin at the very beginning. When you're ready. Don't feel pushed.'

A neat script, square like the face, no hesitation: write or not write. Time had passed: how much time?

Heather Smith said, 'Arrested, but not charged. Hm.'

'I don't know. Don't know anything.'

'Can't charge him if he's still unconscious.' She looked at her watch, a man's watch? Large enough anyway. 'Not much left of the morning. And your little girl – Emma – she's at school till three-thirty.'

Sarah nodded. Heather Smith had kept emotion as far away as

if they had been talking about conveyancing, yet she still felt drained. And hopeless, though she'd tried not to let it show. For the moment, anything that could be done would have to be done by someone else.

Heather Smith said, 'How about a drink? We could go over to the White Horse.'

Another nod. She might well have nodded if suicide had been proposed as a simple way out. 'Earlyish,' Heather said. 'Won't be busy yet. Could you go and grab us a couple of seats? Quiet corner, for preference. Couple of phone calls I'd like to make.'

Too early to be crowded. As she came in, one or two people glanced as if they already knew what had happened. Absurd, but a feeling she might have to get used to. It seemed an age before Heather herself, socking great coach-hide bag over one shoulder, marched in, spotted her at a glance, settled herself down.

'Smoke?'

Sarah shook her head.

'Shouldn't myself, but what the hell, I say.' She lit the cigarette with a throwaway lighter, blew smoke at the ceiling.

She waved smoke away. 'Well, progress of a kind.' The way she looked across the room as she said it suggested the kind of progress that got nobody very far.

'Rang a pal of mine who's a barrister.'

God, the cost! Nick would blow his top. An instant later the grotesqueness of the thought almost made her giggle.

'Are you all right?' Heather was looking at her with some concern. Sarah shared the joke. Heather smiled. 'I told you, he's a mate. Hasn't cost you a penny so far. But of course, it'll come to that.'

'I suppose so.'

Heather ordered a gin and tonic. Sarah wanted to pay. Heather refused. 'As I said, it'll come to that. You'll hardly qualify for legal aid.'

'Hardly. Big earnings, just up to our ears in debt, the usual. Oh God! I haven't told the paper.'

'The *Globe*?' Heather's face had the look Sarah had learned to put up with when the *Globe* was mentioned.

She had misjudged. Heather said, 'Have you thought about that?'

'About what?'

'Press. The media. Not going to be nice. So here goes with the question I should have asked you for starters. The question m'learned friend asked me, straight off. So far as you know, did he do it?'

'Do what?' Then, as if some shift of space and time had left her with an entirely new perspective, she saw the point.

Even then, it was hard to deal with. 'But I said, it's absurd.'

'Is it? When you don't even know what it is?' Heather Smith might remind you of an amiable spaniel but she was considering possibilities that Sarah, incredibly, had not yet faced up to.

More loudly than she had intended, Sarah said, 'Married for nine years? Do you think I wouldn't know?' Heather Smith might be all sorts of things, but she wasn't married.

Heather was looking at her almost whimsically. 'Do you? Know him? Really know him?' Seeing Sarah about to interrupt, she said, 'Away from home a lot. Know everything he does? Really? Everyone he meets?'

She laid a hand briefly on Sarah's. 'Think, Mrs Brooke. Do you?'

'This is silly. And look, can't you call me Sarah? I mean, would it be unprofessional?'

Heather laughed. 'Fat lot I care! All right, Mrs Brooke when we're in company. Business company. Sarah in private. Now.' Her drink came. She ignored it. 'Let's rephrase the question. *Could* he have done it? Whatever it is. Not motive. Opportunity.'

She sat there in the steadily growing clink and chatter as the lunchtime crowd came in. Near the foot of the stairs stood an artificial Christmas tree, festooned with tinsel and lights. The shops in the High Street were equally garish. Someone at the bar was talking about the price of turkeys; diabolical, old boy.

What if they knew? What if they all, up and down the High Street, knew what kind of Christmas the Brookes were likely to have?

They would know. The only question was when.

Heather Smith watched her calmly.

Sarah nodded, one quick jerk. 'Yes. Put that way, opportunity, he *could* have. But – '

'Try my job. You learn fast. No matter how long they've been married, "Oh no!" they say. "He'd never do a thing like that!" Then they find that he would. And she would. They both bloody well would. And they did. After that, no holding 'em.'

He couldn't have done it. Opportunity, yes. But anything like that, absolutely not. Only – like what? And anyway, why?

Almost at once, the thought that Nick would do anything for a story. Most of all a secret story. So, motive.

'He could have done it,' she said. 'Not spying or anything like that. He's not very political. But if it was – '

' – a story,' Heather finished for her. 'Yes, I'd thought of that.' She finished her drink. 'Have another, then we'll grab a snack.' She signalled the bar.

'This bloke I know, the barrister. Never touched a Secrets thing, mind, not many people have. But he knows folk who know folk. Doing a bit of checking out. And he filled me in on a few things.'

'What about seeing him? Nick.' It was all she could think of.

'We'll come to it. You never actually saw the other man? The one from MI5.'

It was easy to go back. She had never really come forward. 'No. His name was Norton-Jones. At least, that's what I heard Capstick call him.

'They talked in another room. What you have to realise' – Sarah shook her head, anguished – 'is that I was – I mean, nothing was real, and yet it *was* real, all in an absolutely horrible way. Nick being in an accident. Badly hurt. In intensive care. All that was real. And wanting to see him was real. I could have screamed. Lashed out, run, only . . .'

Heather's hand briefly touched hers again. 'All very natural. Now you're being very good. Probably disappointed them.'

'Got their own back, didn't they? Put a brick wall between Nick and me.'

Heather passed her the bar menu. 'Can't use habeas corpus, I'm afraid. Least, we could, but it wouldn't work. Secrets gives them virtually unlimited powers, so long as they go through certain legal motions. Still, I doubt they can stop you seeing him when he recovers consciousness. Just breathe down your neck all the time.'

She considered. 'Of course, they might insist he isn't fit to be visited.' Another straight look. 'From what we know, could be true. We might have to try for an independent opinion. I'll check up.'

'You said something about legal motions? Don't they have to charge him or something?'

'If they're going to hold him, they have to charge him. But' – a rueful clicking noise – 'so long as he's properly remanded, they can hold him pretty well as long as they like. In pursuit of enquiries, you know the line. Ninety-six hours before they even have to charge him, so long as the beaks dance to their tune at the hearing.'

The briefest of hesitations. 'Yes. Think we'll have to push for a medical report.'

'What do you mean, a hearing?'

'Before the magistrates. To ask for a remand in custody. Which wouldn't be refused. Most lay magistrates do as they're told when it's Official Secrets. If it's a London job, of course, they'll put him in front of a stipendiary.' Heather pulled a face. 'Don't know anything, do we? Who, what, where, when, why?'

It took Sarah a little time to realise that the question was not rhetorical. Heather's cool, unflustered look could be reassuring. This time it disquieted. Not just waiting for an answer; watching Sarah to see if her words might belie her look.

'You suspect me?'

'Not really.' Calmer than ever. 'But they might. I mean, they do know you're an anti-nuker, for instance.'

'Not very active these days. Just get the magazine.'

'Doubt if they'll make the distinction. And you're definitely a member of Greenpeace and Friends of the Earth, aren't you?'

'It's not a crime, for heaven's sake!'

'Circumstantial evidence,' Heather said drily. 'Doesn't do to make assumptions, just because they let you go.'

'But they said . . .'

'They said you were free to take legal advice. Free to get in touch with your mother. Free to go out, free to do whatever you wanted, so long as you made no attempt to go to your husband. And as long as you held yourself available for further questioning.'

She pulled a face. 'Not much of a freedom really, is it? We can push them on it, mind, and we will. When does your mother arrive?'

'About four. By train. She doesn't drive, and she' – Sarah heard her mother's high, uncomprehending voice: 'Can't just walk out, dear, things to be done' – 'had to do things first. Milk, papers, friends to tell. You know. She isn't a terribly flexible person.'

She stopped. A man was standing over their table. She had seen him before. One of Chief Superintendent Capstick's men, the one who had answered the telephone the previous evening.

'Mrs Brooke, sorry to interrupt, madam.' A quick, comprehensive look at Heather Smith. 'Chief Super sent me. We've found your husband's car in the station car-park. He thought you might want to collect it.'

'My husband's car?' Sarah stared foolishly.

Heather said, 'I'm Mrs Brooke's solicitor. Who are you, please?'

'Sergeant Inchbold, madam.' He was already feeling for his ID.

She waved it away. 'Let's be discreet, shall we? Are you saying the car Mr Brooke was driving when he had the accident wasn't his own?'

He hesitated. Heather said, 'Seems pretty obvious, sergeant.'

'Hired in London, madam.' He settled on an attitude. 'Want to know any more, you'll have to talk to the Chief Superintendent.'

'Who told you we were here?'

'Your office. They – ' He stopped, his lips quickly compressed. 'Want to know any more, better ask the Chief Super, madam. He's working out of the local station. Afternoon, ladies.'

'See?' Heather said. 'A sort of freedom. You didn't know he'd hired a car?'

Last night the ground had given way. Now she had the feeling that the sky was due to fall in. 'He went off to work in his own car. He leaves it at the station sometimes, depends what he's doing. I assumed he . . .'

'Well, grub first, assumptions later. We'll go back to the office after. Our coffee's cheaper than theirs. By the way, I suppose I should tell you that my lot are inclined to wish you'd taken your business elsewhere.' Once again the calm candid stare.

'Your lot?'

'The firm. Had to tell the senior partner before I came out. Spoiled his lunch, I shouldn't wonder.'

Everything was suddenly desolation: the crowded, cheerfully noisy bar, the cold world outside where the skies were sullen although there had been no more snow. Above all, a future that seemed to stretch ahead like a bleak, featureless tunnel.

'Why?'

'Dorking, Sarah,' Heather said. 'Loud-voiced, thick-skinned, High Tory Dorking. Money, property, even breeding sometimes, though that's dying out. I was brought up here. I know. Won't go down well, old-established High Street law firm defending a spy. A traitor. Chap who works for the ghastly *Globe*, too, even if it does tell four million people to vote Tory every election.'

Her voice underlined her own class and background.

'But where else could I go?'

'Go? Nowhere. What do you mean?' Heather produced a chuckle. 'Had to say it. Won't be the last time you hear it. Don't fret, they'll huff and they'll puff, but only in private. In public, they may not grin, but they'll bloody well bear it. Here's our grub. Dig in. Bet you've scarcely eaten since it happened.'

Eating mechanically, Sarah grappled with unwelcome new facts.

Nick had hired a car. He sometimes did, but only rarely. Heather Smith thought it suspicious. Everyone, not just High Tory Dorking, would think it suspicious: used his own car if he hadn't been up to something, stands to reason.

No, said the *Globe*, Mr Bryce wasn't in yet: would Mr Willett do?

Monkey was always smarmy-sweet with Sarah, yet for something like this, she preferred him to Tim Bryce, whose rough manners never stopped at domestic frontiers. Only this time was different.

To begin with, Monkey wasn't surprised, let alone shocked.

'An accident? Yes, well, as a matter of fact, we . . . guessed.'

When Nick failed to turn up, they would normally have called within the hour. If you worked for the *Globe* and you didn't show, either you called them pronto or it was what the hell?

No one had called.

And Monkey was talking about a hired car. 'Been on three times already. Seems they were a bit pressed, everything out or booked. Told him they could let him have it overnight, but only if he guaranteed to return it by ten this morning. Now they – Sarah? Hello? Are you still there?'

'They won't get the car,' she said. 'Don't you understand? It's a write-off.'

What about all the questions that Monkey, twenty years in newspapers, should have been asking? What's it all about, for

God's sake? Where is he? What in God's name was he up to? God was invoked a good deal on the *Globe*.

If Monkey wasn't asking the right questions, a lot more had gone wrong since last night.

'You do understand? He's badly hurt. And' – she went into it at a rush – 'there's more to it than you realise. He's – '

That reached him. 'Sarah love, I think I ought to tell you, there's a D out. And . . .' Trying, like Sarah herself, to work himself up to a gallop, he balked at the last moment. 'Where are you?'

She glanced at Heather Smith through the archway into the bar. 'On a public phone, if that's what you mean.' Another D-notice? Must be; Nick had mentioned one about Nethercott Stoney as an excuse for refusing to discuss it. No wonder Monkey wasn't saying the right things.

He was off again, picking his words carefully as if he were afraid of being overheard. 'Understand what I'm saying, sweetheart? When people drive into bridges on the M25 doing the ton with the cops in hot pursuit, the word gets out. But they slapped a D on. Page eight, one par column-filler, no more. Get me, sweetheart?'

A motorway bridge at a hundred! Feeling her knees beginning to give, she hung grimly on. More than Capstick or the hospital had told her. Nick must have . . . it meant that he must be . . .

She said, 'It's all a mistake, you do know that. I mean, Nick couldn't possibly – '

'Tim wants us to talk to you, angel.' His voice pressing. 'Better not come here, though.'

'No.' What on earth was he thinking about? 'Not while Nick's . . . not until he's . . .'

Monkey galloped her down this time. ''Course, sweet, 'course. We'll be in touch. Not going anywhere, right? I mean, Nick apart, you'll be at home, right? 'Course you will, the kiddy.'

He waited, then, as her silence lengthened, said, false as Judas, 'All on your side, sweetie, want you to know that. But best not to call here, yes? Best let us get to you. Oh, and Tim says don't worry about cash if it comes to . . . well, legal costs and that. We can reach an arrangement. I mean, you wouldn't want to talk to anyone but the *Globe*, now would you?'

She put the phone down and went back into the bar.

Heather said, 'Well?'

A long wait, while Heather said nothing.

'Nick drove into a motorway bridge at a hundred miles an hour. They already knew. I suppose I should have realised, bloody press! Only they know more than they're saying. Probably had a visit from Special Branch. And there's a D-notice on it.'

She wrenched and twisted her fingers, saw her wedding ring, began to twist that, trying to stop her hands from trembling. 'All assistance short of help, but please can they have an exclusive when it's safe. You know' – now her voice was trembling too – '"My life with a traitor. *Globe* wife tells all." Scared to talk to me at the moment, even more scared I might talk to another bloody paper.'

'Would they pay?'

'Oh, they'd pay. Chequebook journalism's a *Globe* special. Nick's just done a fifteen thousand pound job on Mike Holden's wife, pretty well named her own price, of course. Nick's just . . .'

Realising how ugly her voice sounded, she bit her lip.

'The law makes no distinction between rich and poor,' Heather said. 'Except when it comes to feeing counsel. Beggars can't be choosers.'

She glanced at her watch. 'Best get back. My barrister pal's likely to ring. And I need a word with the right department at the Home Office. After that you've Emma and your mother to think of while I make contact with your Chief Superintendent Capstick, him and his questions!'

Sarah looked for her bag, ready to rise, but someone else was standing over them. Oh God! Another one.

He couldn't be a policeman. Too old, to begin with, sixty if he was a day. And he didn't have that policeman's look, still waters running shallow but hiding all kinds of garbage.

Added to which, he was smiling. Had she seen him somewhere . . .?

'I trust I don't interrupt. Heather, my dear, how are you?' His smile embraced Sarah too: don't know you yet but let's be friends at once.

A light voice, almost a drawl, and laced with amusement that took in himself, as if to say yes, life's an absurdness, but then, so am I. A note, too, of pleading: forgive me for my absurdness; for practically anything I might say or do, since almost all of it is likely to be foolish.

His eyes, set in a face moulded into wistful amiability, were dark, melancholic, but sharply perceptive.

Heather, already smiling back, glanced quickly at Sarah and seemed to come to a decision. 'Hugh! How nice! We're just off, so you can hardly interrupt, but we'll spare you a minute.'

He pulled a face, a child disappointed. 'Going? Must you? No remote chance of inveigling you into a modest bacchanal?' He sat facing them, glass in hand.

'This is Sarah Brooke,' Heather said. 'A client of mine.' She turned to Sarah. 'Hugh Rossiter. An old friend.'

Seen him often on the box and still hadn't made the connection. She wasn't fit to be out.

'Oops!' He started to get up. 'Business! Terribly sorry.'

'It's all right, Hugh, honestly. For a few minutes, anyway.'

'Sure I can't get you something?' He held up his glass. 'Brandy, the universal solvent, excellent pre- and postprandial anaesthetic? No?'

Casually dressed, a general unkemptness suggesting the vocational bachelor down on his luck. Only he was married, wasn't he?

Heather shook her head. 'Best not, lots to do.'

'Problems? Oh, sorry, I shouldn't enquire. That's the trouble with us wretched hacks, always on the pry.'

He knows, Sarah thought; seeing him looking at her quizzically. Knows I'm the wife of a man who was bloody rude to him. Well, won't be long before the laugh's on his side.

He stood up. 'Ladies, my apologies. I detain you.' His fly zip was three inches short of respectability.

On the way out, Sarah said, 'Thank you.'

'What for?' Heather looked surprised.

'For not saying I was married to a journalist. To someone on the *Globe*.'

He'd known, for all that.

'Don't worry. Hugh's a pet. I hope you get to know him better. Right, now let's have a go at a few people. We'll ring Redhill first.'

Nick was back from theatre but still unconscious; no point in seeing him just yet. Nothing gained from asking when there would be.

Nick's car collected from the station. The police, Heather said, would have gone over it with a fine-tooth comb. For what? No idea. No one was saying. The pocketphone was still there, tucked under the road maps and junk Nick habitually drove around with. But they'd taken the spade.

Back to the house before going to collect Emma, then her mother. She had to decide what to say to Mum, knowing that whatever she said her mother would fail to understand.

It was bad, all bad. Going to get worse, much worse.

Though the police had gone there were small souvenirs of their visit everywhere, coming to her attention so gradually that she knew the place must be a litter of psychological boobytraps.

'Consider yourself lucky, madam,' Capstick had said. 'If we'd had to call in the real pros they'd still be taking the place apart.'

If she were questioned again the only comfort lay in the hope that Heather Smith would be with her. Capstick, Heather had remarked, had seemed to be unduly interested in Nick's coverage of the Nethercott Stoney disaster. Why was that?

Well, why *was* that?

Though it was from then on that Nick had become moody. And still more twitchy after interviewing Lily Holden in Birmingham. They hadn't asked about Lily.

Mechanically, she picked up the *Globe*. Nothing by Nick. Either turned in no copy yesterday, or had it spiked. But there was something about Mike Holden and Lily, rubbishing a rumour that Mike hadn't really abandoned Lily, that she would join him in some extradition haven when things died down. Perhaps Lily Holden wouldn't get her fifteen thousand after all. Nick would be pleased about that.

It led her back to the offer Tim Bryce had relayed through Monkey. Tim would commit murder rather than lose a story on a *Globe* man to another paper. No question of charity, just ghoulish professionalism. Well, Heather Smith had been right. She must swallow her pride, make the toughest bargain possible.

That was when Monkey's time bomb went off.

Tim Bryce was prepared to pay big money for Nick's story. But Nick finally in the clear would be ready to write his own story. The *Globe* would expect no less.

If Tim Bryce, generous as a backstreet credit company, was making offers in advance, there was only one possible explanation. He didn't expect Nick to be in a position to write anything at all. If not because he was guilty, then because he was dead.

A chill paralysis of terror.

The telephone began to ring. She answered with dread.

'Yes?'

'Mrs Brooke?' An unknown voice; male, flat, nasal.

'Yes.'

'Nick Brooke's woife?'

'Yes. Who's that?'

'Sarah, roight? How's the kiddy, Sarah?' Cocksure, adenoidally insinuating.

'Who is that, please?'

'Friend o' Nick's, Sarah. Tell him I called, will you?'

The click of the disconnection, the rapid purr of the dialling tone. Outside, it was snowing again.

Emma. Time to collect Emma from school. That was all she could think of. Just as she was leaving a florist's van pulled up and a girl, the archetypal fluffy blonde, came up the path cradling a cellophane-wrapped armful.

'Mrs Brooke?'

Yes, she said.

Two dozen superb crimson roses, must have cost the earth at this time of the year. Interflora card, dictated Interflora hand-printing, probably the girl's: Next time *à trois*! – Peter G. She dropped them in water, no idea who had sent them. Nick might know. Nick!

Unable to sleep except in snatches. Up and about long before it was light. Christmas was coming, the goose was getting fat. Terrific!

The tea she had made had gone cold. Light oozed slowly around the curtains, cows mooed at the early milking. Darkness and silence dwindled until they were concentrated wholly and tenaciously in her mind.

Even two dozen red roses failed to lift her spirits. Not just that they had no scent; too much to expect in the last gasp of the year. Nor that she would never know who had sent them unless – until – Nick could tell her. They were unnatural, as meretricious in their way as the commercialised gaiety of illuminated Christmas trees or the carols that blared from the chain stores in the High Street.

Her mother thought they were lovely.

The milk came. The papers came. The postman came. All the

post was for Nick, chiefly mailing shots. From now on until he was . . . from now on she must get used to opening his mail.

Only one thing puzzled. An anonymous envelope, London postmark, blurred and unreadable. Inside, a single photograph, black and white, no accompanying letter. She thought dully how rare black-and-white pictures were becoming. She thought dully that she was living in one. The envelope had come open and been clumsily resealed.

A picture of Nick and another man, walking, deep in conversation, in semi-rural surroundings. At least, she would have thought them semi-rural if she hadn't recognised the background, part of the façade at Kenwood House.

Nick had his usual raring-to-go look, half eager, half impatient. The other man, tall, bulky, considerably older, wore some sort of fur hat and collar that, between them, boxed out most of his face. A slight distortion of the background, suggesting a special lens: telephoto, zoom, she didn't know the difference. Probably from the *Globe*, posted before Nick's smash-up. Nick probably knew all about it. Only Nick . . .

Normally, things like that went on Nick's desk in the guest room, but things weren't normal any more. Chief Superintendent bloody Capstick's men had taken practically everything Nick had kept up there. Given her an itemised receipt, but nobody said anything about bringing things back.

Anyway, her mother was in the guest room now.

Eventually she heard the bump and patter that meant Emma was up and heading for mummy's room. She shot upstairs, taking the photograph with her. If the *Globe* wanted it back, they'd have to ask.

Waiting to go to school, Emma subjected them to a further bout of heart rending.

'Is daddy going to die?' The tears had welled fatly.

'Emma! What a thing to say!' Normally, Mrs Purdy's conditioned reaction to disaster, everything for the best in the best of all possible worlds, was one of Sarah's crosses. In present circumstances it served very nicely.

She had drawn Emma to her in an abstract but suffocating hug. 'No, darling, of course daddy's not going to die. He's going to get better and come home and everything will be all right again. You'll see.'

Please God! Whatever that meant.

Emma's attitude towards her grandmother was dichotomous: too many hugs and kisses, but indulgence by the cartload. Ever the pragmatist, she settled for an excess of formal affection as a bearable price for the indulgence.

This time she had found it difficult. 'I want to see him. I want to see daddy.' The tears were barely stemmed.

'So you shall, darling. We all want to see him. We just have to wait a little while, until poor daddy's feeling better.' It was at that moment, seeing her give Emma a kiss and simultaneously fish around the back of the sofa for her crochet, that Sarah divined her mother's true feelings.

She had asked a minimum of questions since her arrival. She knew things were bad. She was settling for ignorance and bliss.

Long ago, with the ripe knowledge of her early twenties, Sarah had decided that clergyman's daughter and army wife said it all.

Oh yes, clever Sarah Purdy had worked it all out; a certain belated sympathy for the colonel's sudden widow forced for the first time to make her own decisions, choose her own way through life.

Her own smug sense of superiority at the time; the intellectual certainty of those not necessarily so very clever at living but terribly brilliant at explaining the psychological whys and wherefores of other people's lives.

Poor mum, victim of hierarchical determinism. Poor Sarah: ditto.

Perhaps family history was on the verge of repeating itself.

As for her father; faded almost to nothing. A tower of strength? According to her mother, yes, yet her mother's memories must be almost as faded as her own. No matter. God the father, God the regiment, God the colonel's ghost: no woman, in Mrs Purdy's view, was the equal of a man.

Not just different; inferior. Her own father's Bible had said so. So had King's Regulations and the Army List.

Naturally, Sarah rejected the gospel, but she had had her own conditioning. Fight as she might, and she did her best, the concept of the strong, all-knowing male haunted her like guilt in a lapsed Catholic.

But the past had its spinoff. By the time the fuss bus, Linda Harper's turn today, arrived to pick up Emma, mum had reassured herself by reassuring Emma. Nick was a man, so everything would be all right. All was peace again in the best of all possible worlds.

For lack of anything more positive, people tended to settle on elegant as the word to describe Sarah's mother. Fine bones, graceful carriage, a smile that sometimes froze but seldom faltered. What had actually kept her going was an unwavering concentration on self.

'Poor Nick,' she said in her high, untroubled voice. 'I simply couldn't sleep for worrying about him. But you know, men do love to drive terribly fast, dear. Young married men with families ought to remember how much depends on them.'

'Yes, Mum.' Patience with both of them, Emma because she didn't know how to handle it, her mother because she did. Got to keep a hold, she thought. If I let go, everything will fall apart.

They had talked the previous evening after Emma had gone to bed.

Nick had had an accident. The police were involved. It was all a stupid misunderstanding, but nothing could be done until Nick was well enough to talk. Then everything would be sorted out.

Her mother had listened, or appeared to listen, but had asked few questions. Now she had decided on her attitude. The words came out like an often repeated party piece, alternating with the careful interplay of thread and crochet hook and every bit as mechanical.

'Poor Nick. The fault of the job, of course. Though after all, dear, he isn't forty yet, and already earning far, far more than your poor father could ever have hoped for. Even if he had lived to become a general as everyone said he would.

'Of course, your father – my own father, too – had a different attitude. Things *were* different in those days. The job mattered more than the reward. The job *was* the reward. But then, it was a job worth doing.

'Oh, I know we need newspapers. And I suppose any paper is better than none. But I do find it hard to believe that there's any sense of dedication, dear. More a matter of how much one earns, no question of whether one's making a worthwhile contribution to society.'

Sarah made her own small, mechanical noises, got on with her small mechanical tasks. Mum's own contribution to society began and ended on a scatter of untaxing and socially rewarding committees. If anyone brought up the subject of what her son-in-law did for a living she would run a verbal mile.

The telephone brought Mrs Purdy's monologue to a halt. It was Heather Smith. 'You sound upset. Is everything all right?'

'Yes. No.' Sarah laughed nervously. 'What am I supposed to say?'

'Bit difficult, isn't it? Listen, I don't know whether you're going to call this good news . . .'

'Doesn't have to be great to be good.' Her mother, laying down her crochet, glided out. Sarah heard her going upstairs, less out of consideration for Sarah than herself. Bad news upset her.

'You can see him,' Heather said, and then, after a second or two, 'Still there, are you? Sorry. Didn't know how else to put it.'

'It's all right.' Spoken in a kind of gasp. 'Is he . . . ?'

'Comatose seems to be the vogue word. Oh gosh, perhaps I should have come myself, only . . .'

'Only I might have panicked if I'd seen you walking up the path.' She took the plunge. 'He's not worse or anything?'

'No change. But you can see him. And you can talk to the doctor who's looking after him.'

'Will you come? I mean . . .' What did she mean?

'Not on, I'm afraid. Just you. And you have to accept that it's just for a look.'

'No scenes. Brave little woman, that sort of thing.'

'That sort of thing.' Another pause. 'They'll be there, of course.'

'The police?'

'They've orders to be unobtrusive, so long as you keep your side of the bargain.' Heather chuckled unexpectedly. 'Might be listening to us now, had you thought of that?'

'Listening?' At this moment? The phone, tapped? No, she hadn't thought of it. She said, 'Oh. Yes. See what you mean.'

Not really, not yet; hadn't had time to sink in.

Heather said, 'The doctor – Quilter, remember? – wants a word before you go in.'

'To soften me up?'

'Toughen you up. That was the other thing.' This time the pause was undoubtedly deliberate.

'Meaning he's not a pretty sight. To coin a phrase.'

'You don't strike me as the squeamish sort, Sarah. Not if you put your mind to it. I hope I'm not wrong.'

'No!' She came out quickly with that, less a response to the implied warning than to establish her own position. Up to now she had been swinging between extremes: Nick unconscious but more or less whole, Nick a bloody pulp that might live but would never again resemble the man she had married. Now she was going to find out, so she would not be squeamish.

'Good.' Whatever Heather was thinking, she had decided to keep it to herself. 'Right. What else? Oh, yes. How do I know all this? Because I've been there.'

The first shock had not prepared her for the second.

'There? The hospital?'

'The hospital,' Heather said, just a hint of apology. 'They sent a police car.'

'Why' – she must keep calm – 'couldn't they send a car for me?'

'Strictly police business. First things first.'

'Damn them!' Now she was like Emma, fighting back tears.

'I know.' That steady voice was a comfort. 'They wanted to charge him. I soon put a stop to that.'

'Charge him! But you said comatose. That means unconscious. Doesn't it?'

'He came to after the operation. Nodded his head when they asked him if he could understand. Of course, he couldn't, not really, and they knew it, wanted me there to cover themselves, little girl lawyer too green to tell them to get stuffed.'

'But you did?' Had she made a mistake? Did Heather really know enough about this kind of thing?

'I certainly did. Fortunately – don't misunderstand me – he'd passed out again before I got there. Wouldn't have made any difference. They knew they were trying it on and I made sure they knew I knew it. But they're obviously in a hell of a hurry to nail him down. Sorry, could have put that better.'

Sarah grasped at the first thought that stayed still long enough to be captured. 'But what could they charge him with?'

'Just offences under the Act, don't have to be specific at this stage.'

'And that's what they'll do? As soon as they can.'

'That's what they'll do.' For the first time, Heather let something like full-blooded emotion creep into her voice. 'Under the Act they can pretty well do what they like.'

'Yes, but . . .'

'Receiving information in contravention.' A sort of mocking gabble. 'Retaining information in contravention. Communicating information in contravention. Etcetera. *Ad nauseam*. Get it?'

'No, not really. What information? Who from? Who to?'

Another of Heather's grim little chuckles. 'It's like the old joke: go and see what Tommy's up to and tell him to stop it. Only they don't tell you. They just stop you.

'Look,' she said, 'to ease my conscience. They wouldn't have allowed you in when they charged him. So I reckoned the best thing – '

'It's all right. I understand. Just the shock. It's all shocks.'

'I know. So when will you go?'

'When can I go? That's when I'll go.'

'You can go now. Will you drop in on the way back, fill me in?'

'Promise.' She managed a joke, or was it defiance? 'At least if this phone's tapped they won't be surprised when I turn up.'

'Going to be upsetting for you, so mind what you say.'

'I'll do my best. I'm sorry you can't come.' Couldn't say she was sick with apprehension.

'Drop in on the way back,' Heather repeated. 'I'll show you the Act.' That unamused chuckle. 'Only just finished reading it myself. We had to get a copy from Guildford; not the sort of thing you'd find in the average solicitors' office. Tell you this, though. It's a marked deck, if you know anything about cards.'

She offered to take her mother with her 'for the run'.

Mum declined graciously. 'I'm sure it's best for Nick to have you to himself, dear. Anyway, don't you think someone should be here in case Emma's home before you're back? My experience of hospitals is that things always take longer than one expects.'

She didn't want to go. Didn't want to know, not yet.

On the way down the drive, Sarah saw Peggy Morcambe come round the side of their garage, so intent on not yet seeing her that it was almost funny. The next thing would be the sudden start of surprise, the wave. Then she would be trapped.

Not a single awkward question from the Crabtrees, though she had volunteered the information that Nick had had a bad smash-up and was in hospital.

Charlie Crabtree, not a talkative man at the best of times, had simply shaken his head and murmured, 'Murder, the roads, these days.' Mrs Crabtree produced one of her sharp glances. 'Don't have to say anything, say what you want anyway, just like me.' And that had been that.

Peggy Morcambe clearly knew something was up. She wouldn't rest until she had found out what it was. Sarah pretended to look the other way until she was out on the road. Then a quick smile and wave and away.

Guiding the car through the high-banked lanes, sufficient snow to wrap white scarves around the roots of trees and hedgerows, she had a crazy thought. The most direct way was straight through Dorking to Reigate. Instead, she took the narrow lane that wound up to Ranmore through naked beechwoods. From there it wasn't far to Leatherhead and the M25.

Though what Nick had been doing on the M25 . . . !

She took the Leatherhead slip road, eased herself into the fast mid-morning traffic, no clear idea of her purpose. Between Leatherhead and Reigate she came up with signs warning that the inside lane would be closed a quarter of a mile ahead. Plastic cones steered traffic into the two outer lanes. Even then she didn't make the connection.

The closed section was spanned by a bridge taking the road from Betchworth over the motorway to Walton-on-the-Hill. Inside the corridor made by the cones, fluorescent orange tapes marked off a smaller enclave around the northern support of the bridge. The tapes fluttered with the rush of the traffic. A motorway maintenance vehicle was parked just short of the bridge, amber flasher brilliant in the midwinter gloom. Three men in orange and white safety surcoats huddled against the chill.

A tiger had raked the buttress, the clawmarks jagged and cruel. The verge and hard shoulder were stained with the blood of the bridge. She stiffened convulsively, swerved a little, earned herself a reproving blast from a following car.

In her mind, as the car swept on, the clawmarks were as memorable as all that fluorescent orange.

But it couldn't be blood. She had imagined the blood. Had she? Or was she learning the trick of distancing herself from things too disturbing to be acceptable, just like an elegant, vitrified lady from Wells?

The hospital was a hospital, busy, the usual intermingling of the determinedly cheerful and the circumstantially bewildered. People sat waiting, chatting or listless. People limped. Someone was pushed past in a wheelchair that needed oil on its wheels. Ambulance men looked bored, young nurses tried not to look bored, a tall, harried man in a white coat swept past pursued by acolytes.

At reception her name produced a brief and rapidly suppressed reaction.

Not long after, the official reception. Quilter, unsure of his ground, was going to give her the treatment; a woman, best handled with brisk authority and impersonally patronising kindness.

'Mrs Brooke? Would you like to come with me, please?' No older than Nick, same dark good looks, same drawn and hungry look, possibly for the same general reasons.

A long corridor, its gleaming vinyl floor user-unfriendly. Through windows on either side single-storey buildings stretching away like architectural dominoes. An office where a nurse was shuffling through dog-eared files. She smiled uncertainly and, as if Sarah were a Boojum, softly and suddenly vanished away.

'Do sit down, Mrs Brooke.' Quilter divided his gaze between her and the door as if expecting a visitor at any moment. She realised that as well as being tired and overworked he was very nervous.

She said, 'I do know my husband's very ill.'

His mouth sprang open to produce the reflex assurance. He closed it again. 'Yes, Mrs Brooke. I'm afraid he is.' He sat himself uncomfortably on the edge of his desk, searching for genuine words.

'And I know he probably looks . . . a mess.'

If this had been another kind of doctor, loud-voiced and assured, she would have been another Sarah Brooke. The usual one, allowing herself, being a woman, to be treated as a creature of limited intelligence but an infinite capacity for suffering if it were presented with words of few syllables and a lofty sufficiency of compassion.

'And I know' – her voice suddenly much louder – 'I can't . . .'

She began again. 'I know all the circumstances.'

'Yes,' he said, and again, 'Yes. It's' – he too searched for words – 'difficult. I'm sorry.'

'How is he? Really?'

Didn't want to look at her: bad sign.

'I do want to know.'

That was what she would go on saying until someone told her: I do want to know. In assertiveness classes they called it the broken record technique.

He picked up a file from the table, glanced at it, closed it. She wasn't even convinced that it was Nick's file. 'Mr Impey, he's the surgeon, was going to have a word with you, but he was called away. He may be back by the time you've seen your husband.' He slid down from the desk.

'Is he going to die?' Just like Emma, only she hadn't meant to say it. She said, 'You may as well tell me.'

'No. I don't think so. But . . .' – a visible breath – 'quite a bit of damage, goes without saying. Femur – thighbone – fractured. Some broken ribs. Ruptured spleen and liver. Some brain swelling, we did a scan. Terrific oscillation in the skull at the moment of impact, of course. This is all impact damage.'

'We've operated to remove the spleen and done what we could to repair the liver. Pinned the femur.' He jerked clasped hands to emphasise his points. 'Had a general look around. He seems' – his fingers splayed tentatively – 'to have stood up to it all right.'

'So far?'

The fingers closed again. 'Let's face it, Mrs Brooke. A bit of a mess.'

Decided I'm not going to howl or faint, she thought. Decided I'm halfway sensible.

He began talking normally. 'He's comatose, came round for a bit but he's under sedation now. We don't want him shifting about, don't really want him doing anything until we've got a grip on things.'

'What else?' She was afraid to know. She had to.

'The liver may become a bit of a problem.'

'Yes.' Hanging on his words, supplicant.

'A bit of lung damage, and there's some brain swelling.' Wryly apologetic. 'Solid concrete, ninety plus to zero in a matter of seconds. He's lucky to be alive.'

He studied her for a moment. 'Look,' he said, genuine

sympathy that was almost her undoing, 'let me tell you what you're going to see.

'He's on a breathing machine, pumps the lungs, a tube' – he demonstrated with a forefinger – 'down his throat. Extra oxygen, the lung damage gave us some breathing problems. Oh, and myocardial contusion, destabilised the rhythm a bit.'

He saw her incomprehension. 'The heart took some punishment, rapid deceleration, probably. Well, brain, heart and lung damage, it all adds up to bad news.'

God, she was saying to herself: God! God! God!

'Blood drip,' Dr Quilter was saying. 'He lost quite a lot, as you'd expect. You'll see a couple of plastic bags under the bed, a bit blood-tinged. Chest drainage and urine, doesn't look nice but nothing too awful. Oh, and there'll be pumps, monitors, things like that.'

God! God! Oh God!

'He won't be able to talk to you, of course,' Quilter said. 'Just possible he might recognise your voice, though, if you speak to him. Later on, if everything goes well, he'll be able to communicate by moving his head, squeezing your hand, that sort of thing. But that's later on.'

He was watching her closely. 'Okay? Feel like a look?'

She communicated by moving her head.

It was at the end of another long corridor. With the cheerful tactlessness Nature sometimes displays, the sun had come out. Everything glinted and shone. The man sitting outside the door of the room, on a small, uncomfortable-looking chair of plastic and tubular steel, had been revelling in the sunlight as they turned the corner. He stood when he saw them. No need to wonder who he was: police written all over him.

'This is Mrs Brooke.' Quilter sounded stiff, disapproving.

A nurse sat at a desk that commanded the room. There were four beds, two of them unoccupied. One held a woman. Plumbed and wired like a washing machine, she appeared to be unconscious. The far corner, partially curtained, looked more like a repair shop than a bedspace.

'Over here, Mrs Brooke.' From the semi-curtained corner she could hear the soft, rhythmic sigh of some machine. The foot of the bed, the only part visible, had a pair of gas cylinders mounted on it. Sarah found herself – no, not herself, a stranger squatting in her mind – thinking idiotically: just like on TV.

The nurse – or is she a sister? Dark blue uniform: don't know – eased back the curtain. The lodger in her brain said – or perhaps the words were actually spoken – 'Oh my God! Nick! Oh . . . my . . . God!'

Someone's arm about her shoulders. Someone pressing her gently into a chair.

'Oh dear.' Heather was watchful. 'You wouldn't believe how guilty I've been feeling. Was it worse than you'd expected?'

'Don't say anything kind, or I shall howl.'

'Can I get you anything?'

A shake of the head.

'You're only just back?' Heather glanced at her mannish watch. 'Long time.'

'Yes. I'm all right now. At least . . .'

'Meaning you're not. Don't talk till you feel like it.'

'On the way back I kept thinking: got to go and see Heather. By the time you're there you'll have sorted yourself out. Haven't, have I?'

Heather made a little sign of contrition. 'On my conscience, horribly. Couldn't see much point in going into detail in advance. Bad enough when you found out. You saw Impey, I expect, as well as Dr Quilter?'

'The surgeon? Yes, I saw him. Consoled the poor helpless female. And very determined not to get too involved.'

'Cold-blooded gent, Mr Impey,' Heather said. 'Not to mention his guilty-until-proved-innocent attitude towards Nick. You don't mind if I call him Nick? I mean, if I'm calling you Sarah . . .'

Lucky day, Sarah thought, when Mr Whatsit who did our house stuff went to London and I got her.

'Please. Don't want to go banging on about "my husband", do we?'

'What did Impey tell you?'

'Lucky to be alive. Going to have more operations over more time than the entire population of Dorking. If he survives.'

She shook her head. 'No, got to be fair. He didn't say that. That's the way I heard it.'

'He'll survive,' Heather said. 'I grilled your Mr Impey. He twisted and turned, but I pinned him down. Your Nick will survive. A lot of what you saw is surface decoration. Once they get that lung and a few loose bits sorted out, it's a Lego job, slow but sure.'

She pulled a face herself. 'Sorry, sorry. That's what he said, the very detached and slippery Mr Impey. Who's also as conceited as hell. Not just your Nick who's at stake. Impey's reputation. That's why Nick'll be all right.'

'Yes,' Sarah said quickly. 'He'll be all right. I told Emma so, this morning, so it's got to be true. Only . . .'

'Go on.'

'Only when it's all over, they'll still be waiting for him. Just as they were waiting for me. And I still don't know why. Not really.'

'Waiting for you? Who?' For a fleeting moment Heather's normally stolid face showed ferocity.

'Capstick. And someone else.' She shuddered involuntarily. 'Someone who gave me the creeps. Norton-Jones. The MI5 man. I know it was Norton-Jones.'

She saw Heather's expression. 'Don't say it. All I had to do was sit tight and refuse to say anything until they'd let me call you.'

'After what you'd just been through? That's what they were counting on, of course.'

'They were right.'

Heather banged her fist hard on the desk, looked up, a faint smile. 'Lawyers are like doctors. Cool. Calm. Detached. The law has no feelings.'

She gave the desk another thump. 'Bastards! Okay. Tell.'

After her audience with Mr Impey, Quilter was waiting for her. 'How about a nice – '

' – cup of tea? No. Thanks. I'm all right.'

'Yes,' he said. 'Of course. Only . . .'

'Honestly. That man. Impey. What is he exactly?'

'Surgeon.' Referring to him simply as Impey clearly bothered Quilter. 'He's very good,' he said. 'Honestly. Brilliant. If anyone – '

' – can save him, he will. And that form I signed lets him do what he likes, right?' Down the interminable corridors, her heels clopping like a racehorse, Quilter doing little skips to keep in step.

'If you won't have any tea I think you should sit quietly in your car for a bit before you do any driving,' he said. 'I'll take you out.'

And there, standing by her car in the crowded car-park, was Capstick with one of the two men who had searched the house.

Quilter unexpectedly went on the attack.

'I think I ought to tell you' – words rattling out like nuts and bolts from a box – 'that Mrs Brooke is in a state of shock. Mrs Brooke is in no condition to be harassed. The best thing for Mrs Brooke is to be left alone until she's in a fit state to go home. Mrs Brooke – '

Capstick, twenty years his senior, was more than a match.

'I quite understand, doctor. Don't you worry yourself about that. Don't want any more accidents, do we now, madam? I'll drive you home myself.' He had seen young Quilter off in no time.

She had already been torn apart: anguish, helplessness, despair. Now rage, but it was a weak, childish sort of rage. By pushing his way into her house, male, assured, impregnable, Capstick had permanently captured the dominant role.

She tried, all the same. 'Look, I've got my own car, thank you very much. I'll be perfectly all right if you'll just leave me alone.' Even to herself she sounded feeble; a silly, semi-distracted girl.

'Sergeant Verity here,' Capstick said with implacable compassion, 'will drive your car for you. You and I will just go nice and gently in mine, right?'

Prizes for gentleness, compassion, whatever things coppers saved for Sundays. He and his sergeant eased her through closely parked cars to where their own was waiting in a space marked AMBULANCES ONLY.

Time for the broken record. 'I'd rather not, if you don't mind.' She stiffened herself like Emma when Emma didn't want to do something.

'Of course you'd rather not. We'd all rather not have had any of this happen.' Capstick opened the door of his car.

'I'd rather *not*, thank you very much.'

'Take it from me, madam, I know best.' Just as she would have done with Emma, gently forcing her in.

'I don't want to, do you understand?' In a moment she would crack, scream, throw an Emma-ish tantrum. There were people about. It would bring them running.

'Don't want a fuss, do we, madam? Don't want to have to tell people we're police officers acting in the course of our duty?'

It was a winning card, and he knew it. Her will said no. Her body slid meekly into the seat. The door closed on her. Capstick got in on the other side. Sergeant Verity said, 'Have your keys, please, madam?'

She handed them over.

'Now.' Capstick started up. 'Just – safety belt on? That's a good girl – just you sit back and relax. These things catch up on you, take it from me.'

Do as you're told, there's a good girl. She was not a good girl, didn't want to be a good girl, but she did as she was told.

As Capstick drove off she had a fleeting glimpse of someone in another parked car, though he turned his head away at once. A large-nosed, rusty-haired, flat-faced man, high colour in his cheeks, an air of unquestionability, a small, fixed twist of the mouth that could be mistaken for a smile.

Norton-Jones. She had never seen him, just heard his soft, toneless voice in another room that terrible night, but she knew. Norton-Jones of undiscussable Five.

Instead of taking the direct road, Capstick cut across country. Minor roads through the flat fields of the Weald; trees, hedgerows, the occasional house, all wraithlike in the December field-mist, the line of the North Downs a sullen, dark green wall to the west. A jumbo jet, trailing the whisper of its engines far behind it, seemed to hang motionless on the approach to Gatwick airport.

Capstick didn't speak until they had threaded the lanes for some little time.

'He'll be all right, madam, never you fear.' The words tiptoed their way into her numbed consciousness like visitors to a sickbed.

'Can't think what made him take off like that,' Capstick said, 'and that's a fact.'

He came to a tiny crossroads – old-fashioned wooden sign-posts, Leigh, Charlwood – waited a long time before crossing, although the roads were empty. 'Wasn't us, Mrs Brooke. I'd like you to know that.'

She took a long time to make the connection. 'Are you saying he wasn't being chased?'

'Just saying it wasn't us.' Capstick concentrated on driving.

'But the radio . . .' She relived it. The kitchen, preparing supper, the local radio news: a car crash following a police chase on the M25.

Careful driver, Capstick was a careful talker, too. 'Nobody's denying there was a police chase. All on the record. People doing the ton down a motorway are liable to get themselves chased if there happens to be a patrol car about.'

He braked for a tractor crossing the road. 'And if he puts on speed after he's been flagged down, he's going to get himself chased that bit harder. Law of the land, madam.'

'People? You mean Nick?'

'Drive fast,' Capstick said, 'that's one thing. Any eleven-year-old kid that's nicked a car from the street can drive fast. Drive well, something else, that is.'

They entered a straight stretch of road, open fields to one side, a straggling coppice on the other. There was a deserted lay-by ahead; puddles frozen over, the ice crushed and starred by previously parked vehicles, a dismal sprinkling of paper and abandoned cans. He pulled in, left the engine running. The car was fuggy-warm, a hint of stale tobacco smoke.

Capstick continued to look straight ahead at the empty road, the misty countryside.

'Piled himself up, madam, no one else to blame. No patrol car there to radio for help and he could have been dead on arrival.'

'I'm supposed to say thank you, is that it?' Her voice sounding distant, nothing but the purr of the engine.

'Mrs Brooke.' His voice was soft, patient. 'We don't play games. Not with the Act, we don't. But let's suppose, just let's suppose, somebody's got it all wrong.

'Let's suppose your husband was just doing his job. For the *Globe*, that is. Not necessarily wise. Not necessarily legal. Still, doing his job. They tell me he's good. Top of the heap.'

He waited. She said nothing. They'd talked to the *Globe*.

He was unruffled. 'Something's gone missing. Didn't need to tell you that, did I? Didn't turn your house over for fun. The idea is that whatever it is, your husband's got it. No, don't say anything, madam. Let me go on.'

A small act of defiance. 'You didn't find it, did you? Or I wouldn't be here.'

He didn't seem to mind. 'No, we didn't find it. So they tell me.

I did say, if you remember, that I didn't know what it was, not exactly.'

'But they do.'

'Don't know that either. All I know is, your husband's still under suspicion. When that patrol car caught up with him, driving like a raving loony, they said, he didn't behave like an innocent man. An innocent man would have stopped when they flagged him down.'

He gave her just long enough to let it sink in.

'Now, you're an intelligent girl. You can put two and two together.'

'Woman,' she said. 'Intelligent woman.'

'Of course. I beg your pardon, madam.' His meek capitulation helped to steady her nerves.

She said, 'I have a girl. A little girl. You're stopping me from getting back to her.'

'My very point, madam. You want to get back to the little one. You want your husband back with you. But nothing's going to be right until he's right, isn't that so? And I don't just mean well. I mean in the clear.'

Knowing he was looking at her, she stared straight ahead.

'Nothing's going to change for the better' – he rapped the steering wheel for emphasis – 'until I start getting some answers.'

He had turned further toward her. 'You've seen him, madam. Heard what Mr Impey had to say. Shan't be able to ask him anything of importance for at least . . .' His hands sketched out a shapeless period of time. 'Two weeks? Four? That solicitor of yours, Miss Smith, she'll try all the tricks, that's what she's there for.

'So . . . going to hang over him, you, everybody, isn't it? Sort of great black cloud. Not going to help him get better any quicker, is it? Not going to make life any easier? Not that it'll be easy at best.'

Doesn't look very much. Sounds nothing very much, either. Might not even take him for a policeman. But clever. Except for one mistake.

'Unless I help?'

Those fingers, pink nails, neat cuticles, strummed briefly on the wheel. 'No pressure, madam. Don't want you going back to that little Smith girl and telling her I leaned on you.' He'd made the mistake again. A moment later he said, 'Woman. The lady who's looking after your interests. Miss Smith.'

A car materialised in the distance, a Volvo, sidelights bright in the greyness. At first it was silent, a ghost car bearing down. The hum of the engine reached them only seconds before it was past, the driver's head barely distinguishable from the squat geometry of the headrest.

It was a long time before she asked how she was supposed to help.

'All right,' Heather said. 'What did he want to know?'

'All kinds of things. Starting' – taking it from her bag – 'with this.'

Watching Heather study the photograph, she said, 'It's Kenwood. Sorry. I expect you know.'

'Is the younger one Nick?' Heather looked up apologetically. 'I know I've seen him, but . . .'

'Yes, that's what Nick looked like. I don't know the other man. It came through the post this morning, addressed to Nick. Just the photograph, no letter or anything.'

'You showed it to Capstick?' It was the first time she had seen Heather at a loss.

'Capstick showed it to me. A copy. Oh, I should have said. Mine, the one that *did* come in the post, had been opened and resealed. I didn't give it a thought at the time.'

'Intercepting your mail. I think' – Heather looked grim – 'we'll take it for granted from now on that your phone's being tapped too. All right, he showed you this.' She tapped the photograph. 'What then?'

'Well, he'd been asking me a lot of questions about Nick's work. Obviously been talking to Nick's boss, Tim Bryce.'

Heather made a note. 'Go on.'

'He asked me if I ever met people Nick knew from his work. I mean, apart from people on the paper.'

'Anyone in particular?'

'A man called' – Sarah hesitated – 'Glashin. I think I've got it right. Peter Glashin.'

'Do you? Know him?'

'Never heard of him.' In this small office with its window on to normality, the world had shrunk. The feeling was comforting, but a bigger world still lay in wait.

'Go on, Sarah.'

'Well' – she found herself clenching her fists – 'he pressed me. Over and over. Was I sure? Never heard the name? Sure? Think. Never?'

'And?' Very matter-of-fact now, Heather.

'Just when I thought he believed me, he said, "What about this, Mrs Brooke?" That's when he gave me that picture.'

Heather stopped tapping her teeth with her pen and scribbled. 'Interception of Communications Act. Worth a try, anyway.'

She saw Sarah's puzzlement. 'If you think your phone's being tapped or your mail intercepted, there's an independent tribunal. They can request proof of need, slap on an embargo until they get it.'

She gave her short, dry chuckle. 'Spoiling tactics, that's all. Force them to show their hand. Not to us, of course, but at least it'll tell us whether they've really got a case.'

'I'm beginning to think they have.'

'Oh well!' Heather was suddenly brisk. 'Don't feel too badly about it. You're at your lowest ebb and he produces proof positive that Nick's been dealing with a man called Glashin. Only you don't know who Glashin is.'

A brief, quizzical glance before she went on. 'Trouble is, neither do we. Except' – she tapped the photograph – 'that this is what he looks like.'

She pursed her lips, reluctantly respectful. 'No witness, no official caution, so he knows what you said isn't evidence. At this stage he's not interested in evidence. Just information, that's what he's after.'

'I don't think he believed me when I said I'd never heard of Glashin. *You* believe me? I haven't the foggiest idea who he is.'

'Not an English name, shouldn't think so, anyway. And we might as well admit it, this' – another tap of Heather's pen on the photograph – 'looks like a clandestine shot. Of a clandestine meeting?'

'Just what Capstick said. No! He didn't!' Sarah clenched her fists again. 'That's the trouble. He hinted at all sorts of things, but he didn't *say* anything. All innuendo. Questions in the air.'

'Good at his job. Question, who took the photo?'

Sarah stared. 'Them. Didn't they? Capstick's people? Norton-Jones's people, the same, isn't it? Capstick said they'd had Nick under surveillance.' She shook her fists. 'Why? Why?'

'Why indeed?' Heather said. 'If they took it, why send a copy to Nick? Or make a copy for themselves. If they've had him under surveillance, why doesn't Capstick know what it is he's supposed to have, or what he's supposed to have done with it?'

'Don't know. Not a thing. Least of all what they're looking for. I only know Nick hasn't got it.' She waited for Heather to be reassuring.

Instead Heather said, 'Perhaps they think *you* know where it is,' and when Sarah stared, simply stared back.

'My mate in Guildford,' Heather said at last, 'the one who's a barrister, knows this man who knows a man who juniored in a treason trial. I think a word, don't you?' She made another note.

The door opened, a token knock. The man who looked in was sleek in a dark suit, sleek hair brushed sleekly back. Naturally high-coloured, his cheeks had an additional flush. He was talking as he came through the door, a folded newspaper borne ahead like a weapon.

It was the *Standard*. Lunchtime edition, just reached Dorking, Sarah found herself thinking, well-trained by Nick.

'Heather, have you seen this? It'll be all – '

He stopped abruptly at the sight of Sarah.

Heather said, 'This is Mrs Brooke, Dad,' and to Sarah, 'This is my father. He's the senior partner.'

Mr Smith made a visible effort. 'Mrs Brooke. I beg your pardon. I didn't know you were here. Please forgive me.' He started to withdraw, stiff and formal as an old-fashioned dress-shirt front.

'Don't go, Daddy.' Heather smiled quickly at Sarah. 'I'm not even a junior partner, not yet, but what's the use of having your father running the show if you can't twist his arm a bit?' She held out a hand for the newspaper.

Mr Smith went very professional.

'Mrs Brooke, please forgive me for any abruptness. It's just that we're a family firm, meaning, of course, that most of our practice is in wills, probate, conveyancing, that sort of thing. Your own unfortunate affair is . . .'

He took a deep breath. 'Of course, we're only too anxious – and happy – to be of whatever assistance we can. But I do wonder whether you've considered – '

Heather completed a quick glance at the paper. 'Dad, I accepted Mrs Brooke as a client. Of course' – transferring her gaze to Sarah – 'if she feels, the way things are developing, she'd rather go somewhere else?'

Sarah shook her head quickly. Heather, even quicker, stopped her before she could say a word. 'In that case, better see this.' She passed over the paper.

A single paragraph, dropped in the fudge box just before the edition went to press. Nicholas Edward Brooke, 38, journalist, Holmbury St Mary, Surrey, arrested in connection with offences under the Official Secrets Act, remanded in custody while the police pursued their enquiries.

Sarah gripped her lip between her teeth, fighting to calm herself. Now it would all come out. Idiotically, the first people she thought of were the Morcambes.

Mr Smith, stricken with something, perhaps even remorse, said, 'Of course, we shall do everything in our power, Mrs Brooke.'

'It's all right, Dad. Leave Mrs Brooke to me. I'll pop in to see you later.'

When her father had left, she said, 'Men! If they want you to look up to them, why do they make it so bloody difficult? You look awful. What about a brandy? No? No, it would be best if you went home, really. Have to tell your mother, won't you?

'I mean, there's bound to be talk now. And of course, there's Emma. Other kids can be very cruel. I know I was. At school, I mean. And there's the press . . .'

It was the nearest she had come to babbling.

She came round her desk, put both hands on Sarah's shoulders, looking as if she would like to give her a hug.

'Dad's right in a way, of course. One of the big London firms, stacks of experience with cases that stir up publicity. Better think it over. I wouldn't be offended. I could make some recommendations when I've talked to my bloke in Guildford.'

Sarah was shaking her head slowly, obstinately.

Heather said, 'I mean, haven't done much to protect you so far, have I?'

Sarah put up her hands to take Heather's from their resting place on her shoulders. She pressed them to her forehead, went on shaking her head.

'Can you take it?' Heather said quietly. 'Stand up for yourself? I mean, you'll have to, of course. But can you?'

Faintly smiling, Sarah said, 'I used to go to assertiveness

classes. That and self-awareness, it was the same woman who ran them.'

'Used to?'

'I gave it up.'

'Oh? Why?'

'We were doing this painting thing. Oh, I remember, that was self-awareness, actually. You all did a painting. Then you all talked about what it meant to you, and the woman who ran the classes, her name was Penelope, commented on what everybody said. Everybody commented on what everybody said. Well, that was when I gave it all up.'

'What sort of painting?'

'A staircase.' Sarah's smile lingered wanly. 'We all had to paint this picture of a staircase. Any staircase. Theirs all looked like staircases. Mine looked like . . . mine was all swirls and colours. Just swirls and colours. Super.'

'What did she say, the woman in charge? Penelope.'

'She said, "Sarah's going to tell us why she hasn't painted a proper staircase." I said, "Oh, I have. That's a proper staircase." She said, "But it doesn't look a bit like a staircase, Sarah. Everybody else's looks like a staircase. Yours looks like nothing on earth."'

Heather's hands folded in front of her, Sarah's in her lap, they looked at each other as gravely as if this, in due course, would be vital evidence.

'I said,' Sarah went on, '"That's right. It's a heavenly staircase." She said' – unconsciously, Sarah mimicked patient incomprehension – '"You *must* take this more *seriously*, Sarah. Self-awareness goes with self-assertiveness. We have to know all about ourselves if we're ever going to learn how to stand up for ourselves."

'I said, "Oh, I do take it seriously, Penelope. My staircase is a very serious staircase."'

Now it was Heather who was biting her lip.

Sarah said, 'She said, "How are you ever going to learn to be assertive if you turn everything into a joke?" I said, "I *do* want to be self-assertive. Honestly, Penelope, I really do."

'"Not if you turn everything into a joke. Where are you going, Sarah?"

'"Home. I don't think I'll come any more."

'"Sarah, I think you're making a big mistake. You're running away, Sarah. You'll never be able to assert yourself if you run away from challenges."

' "I'm not running away, Penelope. I'm just going home."

' "You're setting a bad example for the others, Sarah, by running away. You have to learn to stick things out. You have to learn to take a stand."

' "I'm not running away, Penelope. I'm just going home."

' "Please, Sarah, don't you see it's important for you to learn how to take a stand?"

' "I *am* taking a stand, Penelope. I'm going home."

' "I'm disappointed in you, Sarah, giving in like this."

' "I'm not giving in, Penelope. I'm just going home." '

Sarah stopped, her voice quivering. Heather's teeth were buried deep in her lower lip. Heather said shakily, 'So you never did learn to be assertive?'

'No.' Sarah's voice wobbled. 'I never did. I just went home.' She lost control. Heather's hands came back on her shoulders. Heather's head came down upon Sarah's. Eventually their joint shrieks of glee brought Heather's father's head round the door.

'It's all right, dad,' Heather said shakily. 'I'm just telling Mrs Brooke she's going to have to learn how to stick up for herself.' It started them off all over again.

'You'll be all right,' Heather said as they parted. 'Just think of Capstick as Penelope.'

On the way back to the West Street car-park, where Sergeant Verity had left her own car, she halted. She still hadn't told Heather about the anonymous telephone call. After a moment's hesitation she decided that it could wait.

'Tell him I called, will you?' the voice – Birmingham? West Midlands, anyway – had said, so it was some contact of Nick's, someone who didn't know what had happened to Nick in the meantime.

That someone would know soon enough, now. London by lunchtime, provincials, radio, TV following on, nationals tomorrow. For years Nick had been set on turning himself into a celebrity. Well, now he had made it.

Walking blindly along, she bumped into someone who steadied her, holding her briefly before releasing her.

It was Hugh Rossiter. In spite of the temperature he wore no coat. There was a CND badge on his lapel, a small, neat, chrome and enamel affair, much superior to the one she had worn during

her own feeble spell of anti-bomb zealotry. He was, she remembered, one of those people whose name was always appearing in
press advertisements protesting against this and denouncing that.

'Hello,' he said. 'Mrs Brooke, isn't it? You look fraught, dear
lady. Anything wrong?'

She stammered a denial, made her lame excuses, went on even
more quickly, conscious that he had turned to stare after her. It
was snowing again, fat flakes as big as ducks' feathers. The brief
laughter, like the nothing-on-earth staircase, had gone from
nowhere to nowhere. Everything was just as it was.

'I'm sorry, dear, but I think it would be for the best.' Faced with
the reality, Mrs Purdy had unexpectedly developed a tough
streak. But her toughness extended only so far. Not so much
crisis management as damage limitation.

'We have to think first of Emma,' mum was saying. 'If even
half of this awful business is true' – only told her half; not even
half – 'life might become very trying, Sarah. Very difficult for
everyone, now the newspapers have got hold of the story.'

Love that 'might'! she thought.

Her mother misinterpreted her hesitation.

'Yes, dear, I know. Emma will be upset at being away when
her daddy's ill. You must leave it to me to keep her amused.
She'll be even more upset if she hears other people talking, and
it won't be long before she will.'

Mum – you could call it a general rule – didn't like getting her
hands dirty. But she knew, veteran of the cloistered social life of
episcopal Wells, all about gossip.

She must lose Emma.

'So very fortunate,' her mother said, 'that it's getting near the
end of term. Emma won't miss very much. And after all, she
knows Wells better than she does Dorking.'

True; more friends of her own age down there than here,
where she had only just begun to settle in. And once over the
emotional hurdles, no great objection to finishing school early.
The fact that Emma, deprived of daddy, would miss mummy too
didn't seem to have entered into her mother's calculations.

'The news isn't going to stay in Dorking, Mum.'

'Surely,' Mrs Purdy said, 'there isn't much the papers can say
so long as poor Nick is in his present state?' Abandoning her

crochet she sat, hands in lap, staring at the flare and crackle of the pampered fire.

Sarah felt a pang. There was fixity in that stare. The thin hands stroked each other stealthily. She had listened silently to an expurgated version of disaster. It was clear that she put almost everything down to two facts: Nick's job and reckless driving. The police involvement she chose to see as some kind of retribution rather than anything to do with official secrets.

How could she expect to make her mother understand if she didn't understand herself?

Nick was in for a bad time, Capstick and the quietly disturbing Norton-Jones hovering about his bed like a pair of vultures, pick him to pieces while he was still alive.

'You don't know the press, Mum.' Whatever the *Globe* carried, its tabloid competitors would do their best to outrival.

She was surprised she hadn't heard any more from Monkey. Heather had still said nothing about legal costs. Her father certainly didn't look the type to run a private legal aid service.

Her mother, far from relaxing in the cheerful blaze from the fire, seemed tauter than ever under that oh so ladylike mask of composure. Why was she developing such hostility toward her own mother?

As if in answer, Mrs Purdy stirred. 'I do wish,' she said, 'that you and Nick and I . . . I do wish we were . . .' One well-groomed hand made a small movement of resignation.

She drew herself erect, head held high on that slim, still almost wrinkle-free neck. 'You'll stand by him, Sarah, of course. And so shall I, make no mistake. I know he finds me tiresome at times. I dare say I am, to someone like Nick. But in any case, there's Emma to think of.'

'Thanks, Mum. Don't worry. It'll work out.' Overwhelmed by guilt.

'As for Christmas,' Mrs Purdy said, all with the same apologetic determination, 'well, obviously Emma and I will come back. You certainly can't leave Nick and we must all be together. Still, it will probably have blown over by then. There's your Mrs Crabtree coming up the path with some flowers. And the fuss bus just arriving with Emma.'

As usual, Emma home from school was an elemental force, hardly time to say goodbye to the fuss bus mum and the two remaining children. No wave from the duty mum: did that mean anything, or nothing? How long before the word was round? How long before there was some kind of feedback?

Between Emma, explosive with energy – daddy temporarily forgotten, thank God – and Mrs Crabtree carrying a wonderful riot of colour from the Crabtree greenhouse, it was even possible, for a moment or two, to set Nick aside.

'Oh, they're gorgeous.' She took the flowers gratefully. 'Your husband's a genius, producing things like this in the middle of December. I don't know how he can bear to give them away.' She knew she was rabbiting, didn't give a damn.

Emma, running about like a rabbit herself, had a long and highly involved story about rehearsals for the school carol concert. She divided it impartially between Sarah and her mother while Sarah was pressing Mrs Crabtree to come inside and Mrs Crabtree saying in that sharp tone of hers that could deceive you into thinking she'd no time for you or your London nonsense, that Sarah had enough on her plate with Emma just home and such. Anyway, she certainly wasn't stepping inside in her mucky old wellies.

'I've got seven pounds to spend on Christmas presents,' Emma was telling Mrs Crabtree. 'And daddy promised me – '

Something in her chatter belatedly registered. 'What did you say about Miss Idlesby, Emma? She said what?'

Emma put her hands on her hips, what Nick called her little madam act. '*She* said, "Your mummy must take special care of you now, Emma." I said, "My mummy *always* takes special care of me, Miss Idlesby. So does my daddy." *She* said, "What a pity your daddy didn't take more care of you both." I don't think she thought I could hear that bit.'

A sudden switch of mood, doleful. 'When are we going to see him, Mum? I want to see him.'

'Soon, darling. When he's a bit better. We've just got to be patient.'

Amazingly, Emma took it well. 'Well, I hope it is soon. I hope he'll be better in time for the carol concert.' She went off singing 'Once in Royal David's City'. She was not a musical child.

Mrs Crabtree's eyes were understanding in her tell-nothing face. 'Take no notice of that ol' teacher, Sarah. Probably didn't mean any harm.'

She lowered her voice. 'My Charlie spotted it in the paper. "See this, Nell?" he said. "Got something wrong here, gal, I expec'. No wonder our Sarah's been bothered just lately." Not much he misses, my ol' boy.'

Sarah tried a smile. 'Yes, they've got something wrong all right, only . . .' What else had been said at school that might come out?

'Fond of you, love, me and Charlie,' Mrs Crabtree said grudgingly. 'You come on over any time you feel like it.' And then, with characteristic snappishness, 'Don't have to, mind.'

'Thank you. Thank you very much.' She was going to bawl if she wasn't careful. 'By the way, I think Emma and Mum will be going back to Wells for a bit. Up to Christmas, anyway. I'm all right, honestly.'

She could control herself most of the time. It was the sudden assaults of sympathy that were dangerous.

'Thanks for the flowers. And everything. It helps.' She watched Mrs Crabtree stump off. Almost easier to talk to than her mother. Except that her mother, too, was suffering; she realised that now.

Emma bounced back as she took the flowers into the kitchen. 'I know what they are. These are chrysanthemums. And those, those are . . .'

But anemones were too much for her. Instead, she said, 'I like them better than the other ones. The other ones have got big thorns.'

'What other ones?' Only half-listening.

'The ones you said came from the shop near the bus station. The shop where the woman's hair is all sticky-up and funny.'

Abstraction vanished. Still clutching Charlie Crabtree's pot plants, Sarah said, 'Oh Lord! Oh my God! The roses!'

When the door opened on moon-silvered darkness, frost already winking in dense constellations on the lawn, Heather gave a mock shudder.

'Hello. Brrrr! Cold as charity out there. Smashing night, though, all shiny bright. Wheeled my bike into the garden, is that okay?'

She slid off her crash helmet, shook her head to loosen her hair. Black leather from head to foot, she looked like a sanitised Hell's Angel.

It took Sarah a moment to grasp it. 'A motorbike? You mean

that was you? I heard it stop, but I thought it was someone going next door. How super! I'd no idea – '

' – that a respectable lady solicitor had the habit of whizzing around on two hundred and fifty cc of Japanese vrroom? Well, now you know.'

'You must be frozen. Oh dear, it makes me feel awful for making you turn out.'

'Glad of the excuse for a run. Usually it's just office in the morning, home in the evening, couple of hours at the weekend if I'm lucky.'

Heather unwound her scarf, her normally sallow face glowing. 'Anyway, I'm only at Shere, not exactly far.'

Sarah's mother came downstairs with her library book. Sarah said, 'This is Heather Smith, Mum. My solicitor.'

Mrs Purdy offered a patrician hand. 'Did I hear you'd come on a motor cycle?' making it sound immoral.

Heather confined her amusement to her eyes. 'Only a couple of miles. And a half-moon, all corny beautiful like a Christmas card.'

'One reads such dreadful things,' Mrs Purdy said. 'These awful stories of attacks on women. What *do* your parents say?'

'Mum! Heather isn't a child.'

'Don't live at home,' Heather said, 'so they can't say much. Anyway' – she looked down at herself: leathers, high boots, thick, high-neck sweater underneath – 'hard luck, any feller who tried it on. Cool his ardour, trying to get through my long johns.'

Mrs Purdy went faintly pink. 'Well, I suppose you know best, but I *do* think . . .'

Sarah said, 'I've a couple of things to discuss with Heather, Mum. Mind if we go in the kitchen? Then we'll all have a cup of coffee.'

From upstairs, Emma called, 'Who is it, Mummy?'

'No one you know, darling. You can read for a few more minutes, then I'm coming to put the light out.' She took Heather into the kitchen, closed the door behind them. 'That'll keep her quiet. Read all night if I let her.' Her attempt at casualness was cutting no ice.

Heather unzipped her bomber jacket, put it over the back of the chair. 'Okay, what's up that you didn't want to talk about on the phone?'

'This morning I couldn't sleep. I sat here for about three hours, waiting for the dawn. About the only thing I didn't go over a million times was the roses you saw in the hall. They just didn't seem important.'

'The roses.' Heather smiled politely. 'Ah.'

'I think Peter Glashin sent them. The man with Nick in the photograph.'

That made Heather sit up.

'Go on, say it. How could I possibly forget? If that man Capstick finds out – '

'How about me finding out first? The rest, I mean.'

'Sorry, sorry! Well, this great bunch of flowers turned up, fantastic red roses. Plus a card that just said, "Next time *à trois* – Peter G." I thought, probably some friend of Nick's who thought Nick would explain.' She shrugged helplessly. 'Or something.'

'Just that. Peter G. And you've only just remembered?'

Sarah explained.

Heather looked noncommittal. 'Even Capstick, talking about Peter Glashin, even that didn't remind you? When did you say this was?'

'The day I first saw you. The day after Nick's pile-up. I mean a lot of things had been happening. I was a bit steamed up. Just on the way to collect Emma from school, my turn for the fuss bus run and – '

'The what?'

'Sorry. We take it in turns, four of us, to pick up our kids from school. We found out we all live round here and someone said what a lot of fuss it would save. So, you know? The fuss bus.'

'Logical,' Heather said. 'Sort of. You were just on your way when the flowers came. After that . . . too many other things to think about. Seeing me. Seeing Nick. Not to mention seeing Capstick. Still got the card?'

'No. I kept it to ask Nick, but when he . . . No, I chucked it.'

'Pity.' Heather considered, chin propped on her hands. 'Not that it makes much odds really. Unless you want to change your testimony.'

'What do you mean?'

'That you'd never heard of Peter Glashin.'

A small shock, realising that Heather was waiting for an answer.

'No!' She heard her voice rise comically. 'It's true. I haven't heard of him. Never. And I've no idea why he should send me flowers. Peter Glashin, Peter G; didn't put them together. Just didn't give it a thought.'

'I believe you. Capstick wouldn't. So what? We won't tell him. After all, he pressed you hard enough over the photo. If he'd known about the flowers, he'd have socked you with that, too. Isn't likely to find out now. Anyway' – that dry little chuckle – 'can't be *sure* Peter G is Peter Glashin.'

'I think we can. So do you. And I think it's obvious that he and Nick had . . . dealings. But why? When? Don't know. Nick knows a lot of pretty weird people. One of them telephoned me, just before the flowers came, never even said who he was. You wouldn't believe some of the calls I've had from Nick's contacts. Weird? Wow!'

Heather grinned crookedly. 'Don't know much about the law, do you? My father and his respectable family firm, nothing but wills and conveyancing! If you want to listen to some real nutters, be a fly on the wall when some of them are talking about – say – their wills.'

She looked at Sarah curiously. 'Nick doesn't tell you everything he's been up to? Just the broad picture.'

'Oh, I get snippets. Sometimes the whole bit. Only not lately.'

'Particularly not lately?'

'Particularly not lately. He's been, well, tricky, this last week or two.'

'How, tricky? Unless you'd rather not.'

'Who am I going to tell, if I don't tell you? Mum's well-meaning. I mean, she does her best, but . . .'

'Nick's outside her experience?' Heather's chuckle, that tough, conspiratorial sound that made Sarah glad they were allies. 'Outside mine, too, chum. What do you mean, tricky?'

'Edgy. Mind' – a sudden rush of confidence – 'he's not always easy anyway. So single-minded. Ambitious. He's . . .'

Heather waited.

'I go around this house and practically everything I look at reminds me of him. As if he's dead already.' Her face was pale, her eyes as if she had rubbed them with grubby fists. 'Ever since – '

'Don't stop.'

'Remember that awful thing up in the Cotswolds? Those two planes colliding and falling on that school?'

'Nethercott Stoney. Got an aunt in that part.'

'Nick was there. Practically the first press man to get there.'

The dam burst. 'He likes to think he's tough. Sceptical, cynical, seen it all. You know? But he's not, not really. He hates working for that rag. Ashamed, even if he'd never say so. He's done all kinds of things that really made him puke. Pestering people, offering them money, digging out stuff they don't want to talk about. Dirt. He makes jokes about it sometimes, but I know how he really feels.'

'You were going to say about Nethercott Stoney.'

'Sorry, sorry, sorry. Yes. So he was there, wasn't he? It upset him. Those kids. Having to persuade mums to talk, all that stuff. Didn't say much, got all uptight when I tried to make him talk about it, but I could tell. He's been jumpy ever since. And then . . .'

'Yes.'

'Oh, he had to go up to Birmingham for a few days: I think I told you about that. Then all this happened.' Sarah jumped up. 'Why don't I make us that coffee? We'll have to look in on Mum for a few minutes before you go. You don't mind?'

'I don't mind. I'll make the coffee. You go on talking.'

'In that corner cupboard, then. And the crocks are to the left, over the cooker.' Sarah sat down again, elbows on the table, fists pushed into the hollows of her cheeks. 'I feel for him, that's the point, Heather. It's a sort of trap. He'd love to get out, but the money . . .'

'Money' – Heather was going methodically about her task – 'is *the* trap,' and then, 'I can see why he'd get fed up. Just like me.'

Another chuckle at Sarah's stare. 'Like having to act for people who're lying through their teeth, going to get away with murder, figuratively, because they can afford to buy me and a classy brief. Don't take any notice of my father. We do some police work too.'

Setting china on a tray she said, 'Whereabouts did Glashin come in, I wonder? I mean, the roses suggest something fairly recent, wouldn't you say?'

'Sort of thing a man might do if he and Nick had been lunching together. It happens. Not often. Only he doesn't know me.'

'You don't know who Nick's been lunching with lately?'

Sarah did sums on her fingers. 'The day after he came back from Nethercott was the weekend. Then he went off to Brum, only a couple of days in between. Oh, that probably explains the anonymous phone call. This man had a real Brummie accent.'

'Didn't he ask for Nick?'

'No. Mrs Brooke? Mrs Sarah Brooke?' She produced a fair attempt at adenoidal Brum. 'Then – click. No, he called me Sarah first. And he asked about Emma – I know all about you sort of thing. Cheeky, really.'

She shook her head. 'Probably something to do with the Holden thing but I haven't the foggiest what. Just like Glashin.'

'Get a few more anonymous calls now, shouldn't be surprised. Guilt by association, a few sturdy patriots calling to ask why you don't go to Russia.'

Seeing Sarah's expression, her own softened. 'That's why I asked you if you could take it. Best thing is just to put the phone down. Leave it off the hook if it gets bad.'

That tough chuckle. 'At least you won't have to tell the police, not if your line really is tapped. I bunged in an appeal under the Interception Act, by the way. Might decide them to leave you alone, though I doubt it. Right, coffee up.'

'We ought to go in to Mum. And Emma ought to go down.'

'And I ought to go, period. How do *you* feel about the way Nick earns his money?'

'Hate it. What did you think? What I hate even more is seeing what it does to him.' She laid her head on her folded arms, her voice muffled. 'It makes him a bit of a pig sometimes, but I still love him. Does that sound awful?'

''Course not.' Head down, Sarah missed the brief wistfulness of Heather's look. Heather said, 'Reason I asked, I had the *Globe* on the phone, just as I was leaving the office.'

Sarah looked up. 'Who was it? Tim Bryce? A man called Willett?'

'A girl called Liz Balcon, voice like a cut-throat razor. She wants to talk. Sooner the better, that's what she said.'

Liz Balcon, the Madam Mao of what Nick called the Gang of Three. The wolves were running. 'But why you?' An instant later she saw the real point. 'How did they know about you?'

'I asked her that. She laughed. She said, "Finding things out is what we're about."'

'They've no business to bother you.'

'No bother.' Heather's chuckle. 'The point is, Sarah, this thing is going to cost. They say they'll pay. Only if finding things out is what they're about . . .'

She picked up the tray. 'If I'm going to say hello to your mother before I leave, best do it now. Don't think your mum approves of my bike, mind. Or my attitude toward threats to my virtue.'

'Saying no to the *Globe*,' Sarah said reluctantly, 'won't stop them running the story. And running up debts is a way of life with us.'

'This Liz person didn't want to talk to you direct at this stage. Place crawling with fuzz: I quote. She asked if I would consent to act as go-between. For a proper consideration. Or as the lady put it, "We'd see you right, natch." Contracts aren't my strong thing, mind. If you did decide to go along with them, I could probably put you on to someone.'

Another chuckle, grimmer. 'Thing is, are you prepared to meet *their* price?'

She stood aside as Sarah went to open the door. 'The reason I ask – I can tell you this now – is that your Peter Glashin's a Soviet citizen. He works for Tass. And he and Nick are pals.'

Sarah's hand dropped away from the doorknob.

'She said,' Heather went on as if nothing untoward had happened, 'this Liz person, "I suppose they've linked Nick with Glashin? Anything you can tell us?" Well, finding out is what I'm about, too. Played stupid, didn't I? Didn't take me long to find out who Glashin was.'

She nodded respectfully. 'Didn't take her long to realise I was stringing her along, either.'

'They say all Tass men are spies, don't they?' Why wasn't she more surprised?

'I'm afraid they're going to say much worse things before this is all over. That's why I quizzed you before I let the cat out of the bag. I don't insist that my clients be innocent, but it does help no end.'

She motioned at the door. 'Let's go and make our peace.'

'Heather.'

Heather waited.

'Looks bad, doesn't it?'

'They obviously know a lot that we don't.'

'I think . . .' Sarah made a huge effort, pulled herself together. 'I think Nick must have been doing a deal of some sort. He's done all sorts of deals in his time. That doesn't make him a spy or something.'

Heather balanced the tray against the wall. 'Look, time to be frank. The press is going to give you a rough ride when it all starts seeping out. I said sleep on the *Globe* thing. I've changed my mind, might as well pick your friends in advance.'

'Better the devil you know.' They said it simultaneously. It eased the tension. They both laughed. As she opened the door, Sarah called, a new, brighter voice, 'Emma? Coming up to put your light out, darling. Time for little girls to go down.'

Heather thought: She's got guts. She'll need them.

Emma and Mrs Purdy were both in bed. Sarah had tried watching television. Tried listening to music. Tried to read; poetry – she used to write poetry until Nick teased her out of it – then a book about a man trying to make pottery and another man's wife in Provence. No use: none of it of the smallest use. Her mind kept returning to Nick, never really left him.

To begin with it had been the accident. Then, after seeing him, it had been his injuries; the question of whether he was ever going to recover. Unable to do his job. Unable to do anything. Faced with the prospect of being crippled, perhaps bedridden for life.

Now even that had receded a little, as if, in the theatre of her mind, the twists and turns of the plot were thrusting the central character deeper and deeper into tribulation. Crippled, perhaps bedridden, but still required to play out his part in something beginning to look unpleasantly like a treason trial.

The kind of story that tabloids like the *Globe* rated second only to a good juicy rape or murder as the very stuff of headlines; a jingoistic leader of at least six sentences.

No mistakes. No misunderstandings. And absolutely no warning of what happened next. The whole thing was over in seconds, except that it seemed to go on and on.

The big window on to the garden at the rear of the house shattered with paralysing violence. Someone ripped the curtain to one side. Something phallic and thrusting gleamed dully as it swept a short arc toward her. In that confined space the double explosion was like the end of the world. Small flying creatures, supersonic, stung her face, hands, every exposed area of flesh, with the voracity of hornets.

She was lying on the floor, hands to her face. Someone was screaming. She could barely hear the screaming because the inside of her head had exploded too. The intolerable pressure in her ears carried with it a diapason of sounds. She was stone deaf but she could hear screams and behind them the whole mad howl of the universe.

5

The snow had finally come. With it the Crabtrees and Mor-cambes, followed by the police in steadily growing numbers. Then the swift transfer of all of them – Emma, her mother, herself – to the Dorking General Hospital. Mum and Emma had been treated for shock, Sarah herself for more than a score of tiny flesh wounds caused by fragments of flying plaster.

No damage to the eardrums. The deafness would gradually go. She suspected they were shouting when they said it.

The wall facing the window had taken the brunt. Recollections fragmented; a jumble of disconnected sensations. Lying there, both ears simultaneously boxed by a vicious giant. Trickles of what turned out to be blood on her face and arms. Choking with dust and fright. And the screams, remote because of her deafness yet part of her personal chaos because it was she who was screaming in the violent release of shock and hysteria.

They broke gingerly through the shattered window after a deal of hammering on doors. Then through the doors themselves, faces grotesque in the light of torches that carved the darkness until someone found a light that had escaped the devastating double blast. Charlie Crabtree on his knees beside her amid the crunch of plaster. His wife with scalding tea of a strength and sweetness that would have brought Lazarus back from the dead. A series of crude, barely related vignettes in an infinity of meaninglessness.

No idea how long it was before the police turned up. No idea of the time between their first ponderous presence and the gradual restoring of order. The sight of Emma crying uncontrollably yet inaudibly had heightened her own panic. She had clutched her, hugged her, left her face and nightie speckled with blood she only dimly came to realise was her own.

Events had rolled on like three-dimensional cinema, superimposed, disjointed, endless baffling flashbacks, hour after hour until morning. Now she was back in a house transformed by snow, clumsy but well-meaning hands and the immanent aftermath of violence.

The Crabtrees had been in and out, endless errands of kindness. Peggy Morcambe put in appearances for the same nominal reason but her avid curiosity had been impossible to conceal. Sarah had finally expelled her under a semi-hysterical avalanche of excuses; putting an enemy on ice.

There were still police in the garden, staring morosely at a welter of footprints half-obliterated by a continuing snowfall. Indoors, their presence had dwindled to a single PC who hovered with the clumsy deference of a trainee butler. A reporter from the local newspaper had been dealt with brusquely.

The worst thing, the loss of Emma, but there had been no choice. Her mother, torn between daughter, granddaughter and her own inadequacy, had dithered. Sarah had been necessarily brutal in making up her own and her mother's mind.

It was an accident. Everything would be all right. Mummy was all right. The house would be all right. Emma should come back the moment everything had been sorted out. Now they had gone. One of the police cars that came and went endlessly had taken them to the station.

She made yet another attempt to persuade the young PC to let her into the shambles of the living room.

'More'n my life's worth, madam. Got to wait till forensic says it's okay.' He was happy to have her diverted by someone she had been expecting for hours.

Capstick on the doorstep was a model of decorum.

'Good morning, madam. Sorry to hear about this. Came down from London quick as I could.' He had developed a cold, voice a little hoarse, nose a little red. She felt a petty pleasure.

He looked at her critically. 'Bad business. Still, could have been worse. Those flesh wounds won't show at all in a day or so. How about your hearing? Coming back?'

Still beset with the hissing of serpents, she heard Heather's voice very clearly: *Think of him as Penelope.*

'Getting better. So long as I'm not pushed around.'

He did what he was good at, ignoring her latent hostility while he opened the door of the living room to look at the damage. Persons unknown had boarded up the window. The curtains, taken down and folded, lay across a chair. Otherwise things were much as on the previous night.

Capstick looked for a short time in silence, closed the door. 'They'll be through as fast as they can, not much to look for, really, not indoors.'

'Is that all you've got to say?' A moment before she had been working herself up to be unresponsive.

'No, madam. But what I want to say is best said sitting.'

He went to the seat he had pre-empted on the night of his first visit. She pointed at another, less comfortable. 'You'd better sit down. There.' He took it obediently. A childish triumph, the more so since the brief twitch of his lips told her that he understood.

She said, 'Before you ask, I've no idea who did it.'

More than her match, of course; just looked out of the window at the snowy garden. 'Played hob with any evidence, that has.' The men who had been searching had vanished.

He said, 'Don't suppose you've had time for the other hospital this morning. Your husband's as well as can be expected, so they tell me.'

That was below the belt. Her own problems had made her forget to call Redhill. Of course, Capstick would have known that. She had better remember, this Penelope was nobody's fool.

'Is that all you came for?' Unfair, even stupid.

'First things first, madam. Cross each bridge as we come to it, shall we?' He was good at that kind of ambiguity.

He pressed down on his thighs, arms akimbo. 'Well, it seems your problems aren't over. No idea at all who might be responsible?'

'None. I thought that would be your department.'

Challenging male authority in one of its exemplary forms. No. Challenging Penelope.

'Flesh and blood, madam, just like you.' He blew his nose discreetly.

'Drest in a little brief authority.' Sarah Purdy, bad at people, good at exams. She forced her hands to lie still in her lap.

'Shakespeare.' He gave her a quizzical look. 'Not going to

compete with you on that. Aren't you going to call that solicitor of yours before I ask any questions?'

'Because someone tried to kill me? Or do you think I did it myself?'

'Sawn-off double-barrel, at that range? Meant to have killed you, you'd be dead, madam.'

'Is that supposed to make me feel better?' The local police had said something similar. 'Anyway, how do you know I haven't called her?'

Another challenge, if the phone was tapped. But another sign that she'd gone to pieces: no Nick, no Heather.

'I think we'd have heard, madam.' He kept a straight face but he knew they were playing with double meanings.

'Should I call her? What are the rules when you've been shot at?' Sarcasm wasn't her normal thing, but she had a need to lash out.

Capstick was looking at her almost benevolently, damn him. 'Hasn't she warned you we're good at working round the rules? Just like lawyers. The world would be a harder place to live in if the rules couldn't be bent, madam, and I don't mean just for people like us.'

'I can stand on my rights but you'll still do as you please?'

'Your words, madam.'

Out there, beyond a window that still had glass in it, another world; clean, white. In it a robin sang jauntily.

He dabbed his nose with his handkerchief, tucked it away. 'Mrs Brooke, someone gave you a fright last night. I want to know why.'

'A fright! Like saying boo or something?'

'Better frightened than dead, madam. But better neither, wouldn't you say? So' – before she could answer – 'sooner we get to the bottom of things, the better for you. And your husband.'

'Me,' she said. 'Nick wasn't here. Nick doesn't come into it.' If she were wrong things would be that much more serious for Nick, even if she didn't know why.

'I thought the only thing my husband had to worry about was you. Apart from being half dead.'

'If that was true' – Capstick doled out the words – 'he wouldn't be half dead.'

Once again he helped her over the pause. 'I did tell you. He wasn't driving like that just because our lads were chasing him. I did tell you that, madam.'

She nodded reluctantly. Penelope? It wasn't working. 'Do you mind telling me what this has to do with last night?'

'Stick to your husband for the moment, shall we? You didn't know he'd hired a car that day?'

'No. I did tell *you* that, Chief Superintendent.'

Water off a duck's back. 'Left his own car at the station,' he said impassively. 'Did he tell you he would?'

'He didn't tell me he wasn't going to. That's the way we've always done it.'

'Told you when it wouldn't be there, is that it?'

'That's it.'

Outside, the young PC was talking to someone at the front door.

Sarah called, 'Let Mrs Crabtree in, please.' Capstick sat back.

From the hall Mrs Crabtree said, 'I hope that chap isn't going to stop me giving you some coffee, Sarah. Will it be two cups?'

Sarah caught Capstick's look, just a gleam in the eye. He knew she was going to say one cup. He knew why. He held no grudge.

'Two cups, please, Mrs Crabtree. It'll do if you just plonk them by the hatch. You're an angel.'

Smiling to himself, Capstick blew his nose again. A rattle of crockery, an aggressive thump on the hatch and Mrs Crabtree was gone.

'Before we come to last night,' Capstick said, 'I'd like your permission to have your car examined, please, madam.'

'Again?' Let him see she knew they must have searched it at the station.

He vaulted the question effortlessly. 'Mechanical examination, in a garage. We'd rather you didn't drive it again until it's been checked.'

'It's only just been serviced. What on earth does it have to do with last night?'

'Just like to examine it, madam. With your permission.'

She shrugged. He must have his reasons. Then she made the mental jump.

'That rented car he was driving, have you examined that?'

He laughed; not humour. 'Totalled it, didn't he? Good a write-off as you'd want to see.'

He got up, opened the hatch, reached in for the coffee. All neat and tidy, even a tray cloth. Smashing Mrs Crabtree, everything proper, even for bloody coppers.

'Yes,' he said over his shoulder. 'We examined the hire car.' He set the tray down at her side, resumed his seat.

'Pity to let your coffee go cold, madam.'

He watched her pour the first cup, held up his hand in refusal when she offered it to him. Damn him, won hands down on that one.

'Well?' She set the coffee aside. If he wouldn't, neither would she. So there!

'Possible steering fault.' He was watching her. 'Well, call it a fault.' What do you make of that, smarty-boots?

She was back to chewing her lip. 'Try not to do that, Sarah,' the other Penelope had always said in assertiveness classes. 'It's bad body language. It signals uncertainty.' Bugger Penelope! Both of them!

'You said he was chased. But not by the police.'

'Not at first, madam.' Back to the old *politesse*, was he? 'Only when they spotted him exceeding the limit.'

'Nick's a good driver. He likes to drive fast. He's done some rallying. He knows how to handle a car.' His quick nod told her he knew that too. It also invited her to draw a conclusion.

'You think he didn't lose control. Something in the car, the steering, whatever you said, went wrong. But why should our own car . . .'

She put a hand to a face that was a mess from flying plaster. 'It wasn't an accident at all?'

'Driving into a bridge support? On a straight stretch?' He let it register. 'The patrol car's report says he lost control.'

Tiger's claws raking raw concrete. The robin again, singing in the snow. Children's voices going down the lane past the Morcambes' house, three of them, tugging a sledge toward the slopes. Then, for a second or two, she was stone deaf again.

'Mrs Brooke?' Capstick's voice, distant. 'Are you all right, madam?'

'Yes,' she said. 'Yes, I'm quite all right.'

'Mrs Brooke, do you know if your husband had any enemies?' Again the brief deafness.

Capstick said, 'I don't think Miss Smith would object to that.'

If someone tried to kill Nick or fired a gun at her the police should be on her side, shouldn't they? But they weren't. They were part of the threat. She was confused. She had an idea he meant her to be.

She said, 'You don't do his kind of thing without ruffling a few feathers.'

But that was crazy. If someone had tried to kill Nick – wasn't that what Capstick had implied? – it had gone a bit further than ruffled feathers. Nick himself was under arrest, suspected of treason.

Capstick said, 'What about your kind of thing?'

'*My* kind of thing?'

'Campaign for Nuclear Disarmament,' he said, switching his gaze to the ceiling. 'Member for the past six years, direct debit authority to your bank. Been on six demos, two of them at the Greenham missile base. Greenpeace and Friends of the Earth; they're direct debits too. And three years, give or take, in women's groups that are supposed to boost your ego or something. Some of the members women's lib, some with social extremist connections. Antivivisection, vegetarian, anti almost everything in the real world.'

She was outraged. 'Since when are women's groups extremist organisations? Just because a woman belongs to an assertiveness group or whatever, does that make her a freak? A pervert, whatever bloody silly words people like you use?' Di-da-di-da!

When she ran out of steam he said, 'No, Mrs Brooke. Of course not. Any more than a woman who goes to judo classes. Please sit down, madam. I'm not feeling too clever with this cold and looking up at you makes my head ache.'

He reached for the abandoned cup of coffee. 'Do you mind if I change my mind about this?' He gulped half of it, sighed, sniffed, felt for his handkerchief.

'And yes,' he said, dabbing his reddened nose, 'I know you only went to judo because it was supposed to give you the confidence to stand up to people like me. Pity you only stuck it for a year.'

'Oh!' she said. 'Oh, you – you *sod*!' Once again she heard Nick telling her she shouldn't swear unless she wanted to make people laugh.

'Sorry, madam. No offence. Carrying out an investigation is rather like writing a guide book, got to check all the boring bits as well as the interesting ones, or how do you know what to leave out?'

'You must have talked to a lot of people. Wasted a lot of time.'

'What about enemies, madam? Meaning your husband's.'

Did Nick have enemies? When the mood was on him he could be like champagne, the life and soul of the party. But sometimes it was the kind that left sore heads. He saw no malice in it. His quick wit was a product of his background, the aggressive self-esteem of a man up from nowhere.

And so, enemies? Well, yes, almost certainly. Was there anyone in his trade who hadn't? But enemies who would murder? That was what Capstick was talking about. Wasn't it? *Don't chew your lip, Sarah: bad body language.*

'I don't believe it.'

'Believe what, Mrs Brooke?' Was he always so patient? Was there a wife at home who knew another side?

'That anyone would try to kill him. Anyone in his line, I mean.'

Almost instantly a name came into her mind: someone in his line. Glashin. A Soviet citizen. A Tass man. A spy?

Capstick folded his hands under his chin, briefly silent. She was getting to know his tricks. The next would be to look up and produce an apparent non sequitur.

Out of the blue, perhaps because he might say that name, Glashin, she produced a non sequitur of her own.

'Isn't chief superintendent quite a high rank?'

'Highish, madam.' He couldn't quite prevent tiny double lines above the bridge of his nose. One to me, she thought, not quite sure why.

'Highish for harassing housewives in their homes?' Was that all she was, a housewife? 'And collecting people's cars?'

'State security's a serious business, madam. We don't call it highish treason.'

So he could be witty as well as evasive. Fumbling in the dark, she said, 'Are you going to crawl under our car yourself? Or do you have minions for that sort of thing?'

A twitch of the lips. Amusement? Irritation? She had a dangerous urge to irritate him.

He went back to his coffee, sipped, suppressed a grimace. Gone cold. Hard luck, Penelope! He set down the cup. 'What about the joker who rang the other day? The one who didn't tell you his name.' He didn't even look up.

She recovered quickly. 'So you really are tapping our phone.'

Capstick shifted his chair to face her at close quarters.

'You've been doing all right, Mrs Brooke. Sticking up for your husband, sticking up for yourself. I admire you for that. Can we go back to your husband? He covered that bad business at Nethercott Stoney, didn't he? What time did he get back?'

She managed not to flinch, though his closeness and the question combined, as he had intended, to fluster her. Oh yes, he knew his stuff.

'Late. He had a meal on the way back. I think I'd like to see Miss Smith before I talk any more.'

'Do you know where he ate?'

'Did you hear what I said?'

'I heard, madam.' He held out his hands. 'No notes. No witnesses. No caution. Nothing you say is evidence, didn't Miss Smith tell you that?'

As she left the previous evening, Heather had said, 'He'll be back, the Chief Super. Go along with him. We might learn something. Just don't say anything about Glashin or the roses.' What Heather hadn't known then was what would bring him back.

'He eats all over the place when he's on a job. You've obviously been talking to the paper. Why don't you ask them? He'd put it down in his expenses.'

'He didn't, not for that night. You didn't ask him?'

'I told you. He was tired. Upset.'

Capstick's new silence made her even more defensive. 'He has his moods. It's natural. His job's not exactly – '

' – a bed of roses?' He turned very deliberately to look. Someone had moved Glashin's roses from the hall to a place in the window. Capstick had shifted his chair just to enable him to perform his little trick.

'Sometimes,' he said, 'luck turns against you. Happens often enough to me, believe me. But this time . . .' He looked almost sympathetic. 'That florist's shop up near the bus station. The girl who does the deliveries is engaged to a sergeant in the Dorking force. She saw the bit about your husband in the paper so, naturally enough – '

' – she told him about the flowers.' Sarah nodded fatalistically. '"Guess where I was, day before yesterday" sort of thing.'

He quirked his lips. 'Peter G. Of course, you could still say – '

'I could still say I'd never heard of him, but you obviously wouldn't believe me. In any case, it wouldn't be true, not any more.'

He wasn't going to help her, so she went on. When she stopped, he said, 'Clever lady, your Miss Smith. Yes, he's a Tass man.'

'And he sent me flowers, so I suppose Nick must have met him recently. Obvious, isn't it? And anyway, you knew. That photograph.' She looked at him helplessly. 'Which you didn't take, did you?'

He shook his head.

'So who did?'

'Tell me about Nethercott Stoney, madam.'

It was all coming together. 'When we were in your car,' she said, 'after I'd been to see Nick, you said something was missing. Was it from . . .?'

'Could be. I don't know. They think your husband does. Or you.'

'Me!' Of all the new shocks that was the greatest.

'They think he might have told you.'

'Because I'm against the bomb or something?'

'I'm against the bomb myself, Mrs Brooke. A daughter, two grandchildren. I'd like them to have a future. It's not what we're talking about.' Feeling for his handkerchief again, cold coming on apace. 'We're talking about top reporters. And pillow talk.' He blew his nose.

He said, 'We have reason to believe – '

'Oh no!' She couldn't help it: another standard police cliché.

'We have reason to believe,' he said patiently, 'that your husband may have found something from that air crash on his way home. We have reason to believe that he may have appropriated it for an illegal purpose. Private, personal, professional, we don't know. But illegal.

'We also know that he later had dealings with a citizen of a foreign country. We believe it may have been for purposes which could endanger the security of this country. Purposes that contravene Sections One and Two of the Act.'

It was like Emma's magic painting books. Things taking on

depth, relationships unsuspected until hidden chemicals began to work.

'And we have reason to believe,' Capstick concluded, 'that you, madam, may be fully informed both as to his intentions and the whereabouts of the missing item.' Folding his handkerchief neatly, he put it away.

'You can't be serious!'

'What happened to your husband on the M25 was serious,' he said. 'What happened to you last night, that was serious. What happens next might be more serious still.'

'What do you mean, next?'

'Somebody took that picture of your husband out at Kenwood. Somebody put the fear of God into him three days ago. Somebody scared the life out of you last night. Now why would they do all that, if it wasn't to put pressure on? And why wouldn't they do it again?'

It had ceased to be a needle match between her and a male chauvinist Penelope. Why had she ever thought it was?

'But I know nothing.' She was all but shouting. 'Absolutely nothing. The longer this goes on, the less I know. If I'm in danger I've a right to . . . It's the duty of the police . . .'

'I'm police, Mrs Brooke, and I'm trying to do my duty.' He went back to being patient. 'It's your husband we'd like to talk to. But we can't, not until he's on the mend. So, they think I should concentrate on you, madam.'

'What do you mean, "they"? Who are they? MI5? That man Norton-Jones, is he "them"? What on earth do they think I can tell them anyway?'

'As to that, madam, up to you to tell me, wouldn't you say? I doubt Miss Smith can help you on this one, but I can't stop you asking her, can I?' She fancied naming Norton-Jones had bothered him.

Someone rang the chimes at the front door. She heard it opened by the duty constable. A few moments later he was leaning over Capstick's chair, murmuring.

'For you, madam.' Capstick got up, started buttoning his coat. She went through in a dream, vaguely aware that he was following.

A young man in a sheepskin coat and a rather absurd fur hat. 'Mrs Brooke? Pete Turvey, *Dispatch*. Here to do you a bit of good, madam. All right if we come inside?'

Behind him, another young man – they could both give Nick about ten years – stuck up a battered-looking camera and took three or four shots. Beyond the hedge a glimpse of movement, Peggy Morcambe on the prowl.

Turvey was pressing forward – history repeating itself – as if to drive her back in. Capstick appeared.

Turvey, a salesman's gift of the gab, an accent suggesting that he had begun life quite a few miles north of London, said, 'Don't grab the first deal that comes along, Mrs Brooke, your old man'd be the first to tell you that. Need all the brass you can raise, right? Okay, we'll top anything this feller's offered, but we'd talk better inside.'

His photographer was shooting the house and surroundings. Unlike Turvey, he wore nothing but jeans, a bomber jacket, sneakers. The big lens swung back toward her. Instinctively, she put up a hand. He took two or three shots of her like that.

'Big, big money,' Turvey was saying. 'First come always bids low. Ask him if he's authorised to deal straight off the deck, Mrs Brooke. Don't fall for the sign now, pay later con.' He was talking about Capstick.

Capstick's arm came past her, ID displayed. 'Push off, sonny.'

'Oh, Jesus!' Over his shoulder, disgusted, contemptuous, Turvey said, 'Fuzz, Giles. Lay off a tick.'

Capstick beckoned to Giles. 'Film, sonny boy, or I'll be having a word with your editor.'

Giles hesitated. Suddenly nasty, Turvey said, 'What are you pulling, sergeant? Contempt of bloody Court Act?'

'Chief Superintendent,' Capstick said. 'Official Secrets do you for starters?' Giles crunched over the snow, silently gave him the film.

Turvey edged back. 'Know who tried to kill you, Mrs Brooke?'

Automatically she said, 'No.'

'Anything to do with your husband's arrest?'

She looked helplessly at Capstick. Another car took the corner into the drive in a splatter of flying snow and gravel. A man and a girl scrambled out.

'What about the car smash?' Turvey said quickly. 'Got anything more to tell us about that?'

Capstick drew her back inside, closed the door. Through the reeded glass she could see figures clustering at the foot of the drive.

'Better get on to Miss Smith, tell her the wolves have arrived. And pass the word to your mother to watch herself and the child. Won't take them long to track her down.' His eyes were peculiarly opaque.

'They wouldn't . . .' She was appalled.

'They would. They will.' It was as if he wished it.

She was at a loss, and yet she should have known. Nick had cut his teeth on doorstepping.

'Won't the Secrets Act . . . can't it . . .?'

'Hasn't gone that far yet, has it? Not for you. Mysterious shots in the night, that's what they'll go for.'

'What about police protection?' She looked wildly for the PC. He was nowhere in sight.

'Freedom of the press, madam.' Not a trace of irony. There was a soft scurry outside. Something dropped through the mailbox. A shadow departed. Capstick handed the note to Sarah.

'First bid. They'll raise the stakes, specially when more opposition shows up. They'd take over your life, mind, but it would buy a good defence for your husband. Lot of family, have you, apart from Emma and your mother? Your husband has, of course, sort of people who'll spin 'em a fine tale for a pound or two. Of course, your husband knows the game backwards.'

No need to be told. 'Drop 'em a few quid,' Nick used to say, 'and they'll shop their own mothers.'

'You don't have to talk to them, madam,' Capstick said, 'but it won't stop them trying to talk to you. Or anyone they can get their teeth into. Keep them off the actual premises, if you're lucky, but once you're outside . . .'

Winding me up, Sarah thought savagely, but once again Capstick's timing beat her.

'There's a way out. If I can go to my superiors and tell them Mrs Brooke has provided us with important information relating to an alleged offence under the Act, we can keep that lot well out of your way. Till then, someone blew a piece out of your sitting room. That's news.'

'You want to make me testify against Nick,' she said bitterly. 'Only you can't, can you? It isn't allowed.'

'Used not to be allowed. All that's changed now, Police and Criminal Evidence Act. Not only allowed, an offence to refuse in certain circumstances. Sensible co-operation though, that's what I'm talking about, madam. In any case, the deliberate withholding of evidence isn't likely to help him, not in the long run.'

'But I'm withholding nothing. I don't *know* anything. Haven't I made that plain?'

'So you tell me, madam. That's what I'll tell my superiors. Now, that car of yours.' He jingled car keys at her. They were not her own. 'Better let me into the garage from the inside, don't want them to have another go at you, do we?'

He slid the garage door up, slipped into the driving seat of the car. Turvey, the ill-clad Giles and the two newcomers were still in the lane. She saw with dismay that they were talking to Peggy Morcambe.

Capstick wound down the window. 'Talk it over with whoever you like, but you and I are the ones who have to talk it over in the end. Now, take my advice, Mrs Brooke. Go and ring Miss Smith.'

He reversed out swiftly, a neat three-pointer in the road, watched by the three men, the girl and Peggy Morcambe. Then he was gone, swerving neatly to avoid more arrivals with press written all over them. The car he had come in had gone. So had the amateur butler in blue.

She lowered the garage door hastily, leaned against it, her heart thumping. Eventually, she found herself thinking an old thought afresh. Wasn't it odd that all her dealings were with a chief superintendent? Odd that he had come in person to collect the car?

She went to ring Heather but Heather was out. She left a message.

Quick footsteps. Something else through the letterbox. Another car arriving. Someone shouted, 'Mrs Brooke? Spare us a minute, Mrs Brooke? We won't bite.'

The knot of reporters had become a small crowd that seemed to double when a TV crew appeared. They spent some thirty minutes in loud argument, another thirty minutes taking footage of the house and trying to get her to come to the front door, then importuned her on the telephone, terribly pressing, frighteningly insincere.

After checking on Nick – he had made some small improvement, she could visit him; but how? – she had talked to her mother and Emma again. No sign of the press. People, Mrs

Purdy told her with a febrile mixture of reassurance and suppressed hysteria, had been *most* tactful, *most* understanding, considering that it had been mentioned on the radio. Sarah had forgotten to listen, or had her subconscious steered her away?

All Emma had wanted to know was when she could come back? Outwardly extrovert, she had always harboured a menagerie of anxieties. Torturingly hard to say not yet, sweetheart, mummy would fetch her as soon as she could. This *couldn't* be happening! Not to her! How many times had she told herself that?

She kept answering calls in the hope that it might be Heather. Each time, some fast-talking press man anxious to ask questions or make a deal, any deal, name her figure so long as they could come inside. After she found herself talking to the local radio station at Guildford she took Heather's advice and left the phone off the hook. It cut her off from the world, including Heather.

She had drawn all the downstairs curtains. Someone with a pair of binoculars had been following her as she wandered aimlessly from room to room. The drawn drapes and accompanying gloom reminded her of an old-fashioned aunt who used to do the same thing whenever there was a death in the road. She herself was buried alive, occasionally peeking out like a wistful ghost.

She retreated upstairs. It encouraged them to tap on windows, call more questions. She had never had a clearer idea of the kind of path Nick had taken to the top.

Hunched miserably on the bed, wondering how to get in touch with Heather, she heard a subdued scuffling. Two of them, a man in a grubby sheepskin, a girl straight from the ski slopes of Chamonix or Saint Moritz, emptying the contents of the refuse bin into a large plastic sack.

'You haven't run out of luck,' Nick used to say in the early days, 'until you've scraped the bottom of the barrel.' They weren't scraping it. They were taking it with them.

They spotted her. The girl, face like a blonde waif, voice like a hacksaw, pounced.

'Mrs Brooke, save you a lot of grief and offer some very fancy money. Let us in and we'll lose the mob for you.'

The man was more of a psychologist. 'Sorry madam' – here we go again – 'but we can't go back without a story. We'd like something better than this.' He held up a back number of *Sanity*, the CND magazine, part of the fruit of the bin.

'Drop all this like a shot if you'll let us slip in,' he said. 'We don't smell, we don't bite, we'll put you over to our readers as someone they can really identify with.'

'The way Nick'd like to see it,' the girl said. 'Nick knows me, Mrs Brooke. Nick and me've been on a lot of jobs together.'

'They don't ask questions,' Nick used to say in the old days. 'They ask answers. They don't quote what people say, they quote what they ought to say if they had any bloody news sense. Then they swear blind they said it.'

'A thou in your hand straight off,' the girl was saying. 'Come in useful for this and that, all in crispies, don't even have to declare it.'

'And we'll get the pack off your back.' The psychologist. 'You let us in, we call up reinforcements and you're living it up in a swish hotel before the other guys can – '

She went back to sit on the bed until she heard Mrs Crabtree calling outside.

'Sarah? Are you there? It's me, Nell Crabtree.'

Mrs Crabtree, grim-faced in her old mac and gumboots. At the gate Charlie Crabtree, like Horatio at the bridge, all the hordes of Tuscany peppering him with questions that brought as much response as if he were some old scarecrow. Someone with a directional microphone poked it hopefully toward the house.

Once inside, she let rip. 'Bunch of rubbish they are and no mistake. Been to our house offering money and that, making a proper ol' nuisance of theirselves with their nosey questions. Even that Mrs Morcambe shut the door on 'em in the end though Lorda'mighty knows what she been saying to 'em first. Oh, gal, you're as pale as bread pudding.'

'I don't care about them,' Sarah said angrily. 'All I want is to be able to get over to Redhill to see Nick.'

'And so you shall, my pet. So you shall. Now you listen to me. That lady lawyer of yours've been on the phone and this is what she and my Charlie've cooked up together.'

Not long after, Charlie Crabtree went back home, reappearing shortly after in his battered old Land Rover. With many a clumsy manoeuvre that scattered the crowd he backed it into the drive. Leaving the engine running he leaned against it, his breath dense in the raw air. The drivers among the shuffling, foot-stamping throng edged towards their cars. Soon a watery fog of exhaust fumes made the scene Turneresque, expectant.

Everyone waited. Nothing happened. Much later, a motorbike came down the lane behind the house, a briskly moving blur of metal heading for the main road and scarcely visible through the dense, pleached hazel and thorn of the hedgerow. Riding pillion after sneaking through the hedge and over the field, Sarah hugged Heather like Eurydice claimed by Orpheus.

If Dr Quilter was surprised to see Sarah peeling off layers of thick clothing, he was too polite to comment.

'Don't worry about me.' Heather looked very butch in her leathers. 'I'll just hang about and play bongos on the crash helmets.'

Dr Quilter smiled doubtfully as he took Sarah in tow, yet it was clear where his sympathies lay. 'Maybe I shouldn't tell you this, Mrs Brooke, but your husband's had visitors.'

He had stopped where a window looked on to a small square of imprisoned ground. Someone had taken the decision to plant a small weeping willow, its skeletal dejection making it hard to believe another spring would come. Even the snow looked disheartened.

'Chief Superintendent Capstick?'

'No, not Capstick. Capstick was here yesterday. These chaps showed up today.'

'Was one of them Norton-Jones?'

'You know him?' Quilter was looking at her a little strangely.

'Not really. Just the name.'

'Yes,' he said. 'Norton-Jones. The other one was an American. An American accent, anyway. A big man, shiny red face?'

'American?' It meant nothing to her.

'I think so. I'm not sure of his name, something like Wise. He didn't say anything, just listened.'

'You probably shouldn't be telling me.'

'Probably not. But nobody told me not to.'

They began walking again. 'The thing is,' he said hesitantly, 'when your husband's made sufficient improvement I gather they might move him.'

A stomach-blow. 'Move him? Where? He's not fit, surely?'

'He's making some progress. Out of the coma, that's good, of course, and no sign of permanent brain damage.'

Don't chew your lip, Dr Quilter, bad body language.

'I want to know,' she said, inwardly terrified.

He tried a positive approach to bad news. 'Can't possibly move him anywhere in his present state, far too dangerous.'

'Go on.'

He took the plunge. 'We're a bit bothered about the possibility of infection in the abdomen. His temperature's jumping about a lot and the white cell count is high.'

He went back to being Pollyanna. 'Can't be certain. Look at it this way; means they'll have to leave him with us for the time being.'

How much of this could she take, and for how long?

Their slow progress recommenced. 'Of course,' Quilter said, 'we're looking at worse cases. It doesn't have to come to that.'

'No. Of course not. I suppose he can't talk yet?'

'We've got him sedated. And he still has the tube down his windpipe. But he's conscious. He can communicate. Up to a point.'

They arrived in the corridor leading to the intensive care unit. 'He can nod and shake his head,' Dr Quilter said. 'To the extent that he's with things, of course.'

Embarrassed? Feels sorry for a poor female creature?

'What it comes down to,' he said in a rush, 'is how long for us to get him fit enough to be moved.' A quick, apologetic glance. 'Into some high security place, this chap Norton-Jones didn't say where. Thought I ought to tell you.'

Outside intensive care he said, 'Afraid you'll have company.'

They had raised the head of the bed, propped Nick up. The facial dressings had been removed. A purple marbling of bruises down the right side of his face gave it its only colour. His eyes closed, he looked waxy, distant.

Still plumbed and wired up, every mod. con. The screen on the wall still producing its steadily advancing trace that never actually got anywhere. The oxygen cylinders had gone. The only new feature occupied a chair at the foot of the bed.

Not the one whose inappropriate civility had reminded her of a hotel doorman last time. This one was older, features rubbed down like medieval church brass until all that registered was his maleness, his stillness, the fact that he didn't belong.

'Detective Sergeant Hamlet,' Quilter said coldly.

'Afternoon, madam.' Pasty, tired-looking, resigned. Sarah waited for Hamlet to leave them. He retreated a few feet.

'Since your husband began to take notice' – Quilter's hostility to Hamlet was overt – 'Chief Superintendent Capstick has had a man at the bedside twenty-four hours a day. Our objections don't count.'

Expelling Hamlet from her thoughts, she stretched out her hand to touch Nick's. Limp, warm, no response.

'Can I . . . ?'

'Speak to him? I wish you would. Any response would be a good sign.'

She leaned forward. 'Nick? Nick, darling, it's Sarah.' Couldn't hear his breathing.

Quilter said, 'He may be able to hear you, Mrs Brooke, but don't expect too much.'

Nothing but tenderness, pity, a longing to cherish.

'Nick? It's Sarah, darling. Can you hear me?'

Nothing. She brought his hand to her lips, kissed it gently.

The smallest detectable tightening of his fingers? Or had she imagined it?

Still holding his hand she put her lips close to his head. 'Nick? Darling? It's Sarah.'

The hum of electrical equipment. A shrill, regular bleep, linked to that vital and yet intimidating monitor over the bed. The brisk, purposeful exchanges of two nurses.

Outside, echoes from another planet. A man's voice, robustly cheerful: 'Leave it here then, shall I?' and the heavy thud of a package. The throb of a vehicle in the distance. Brisk heels along one of those endless corridors, approaching, arriving, passing into silence.

The stertorous breathing of Detective Sergeant Hamlet.

She said, 'I don't care what Chief Superintendent Capstick says. You can see my husband's condition. Would you please go outside.'

Hamlet sucked in his lips, bent his head, gave it one quick jerk. 'Up to me, madam, do it with pleasure. Isn't up to me.'

She looked at Quilter. 'Are they here all the time? Day, night, all the time?'

'We've protested. Didn't get anywhere. They insist.'

He gave Hamlet an icy glare. 'In case he talks, that's what they say. He won't talk, not with them around.'

She went back to Hamlet. 'It's inhuman!' Sarah Brooke, outraged, pompous citizen.

'Sorry, madam.' The policeman's art of stripping an apology of all value. 'Orders.'

She would have to lump it. She put Hamlet, Quilter, everything out of her mind.

'Nick?' A whisper, lips so close that she could feel the warmth of her own deflected breath. 'Nick, darling? It's Sarah.'

His eyes fluttered.

Lips all but touching that blemished flesh, her head screened Nick from Hamlet. 'Nick?'

This time his head moved a little toward her. She kissed the ear gently. 'Nick? I'm here, darling.'

His head turned a little more. His eyes opened, defocused. He blinked, the slow irregular winking of someone only tenuously linked with externality. A tremor of the lips. A frown, perhaps puzzled by the tracheal tube in the corner of his mouth.

She looked into vacant eyes, only inches from her own, sensing the mind behind them struggling to draw together tangled threads. His lips moved again. No sound, but nine years of marriage had developed telepathy.

Ess.

As quietly as she dare. 'Nick?'

The blinking was less random. Mind back from elsewhere, though not yet to her.

Lips quivering, the tip of his tongue exploring the tube. Lips parting again. She was sure this time.

'Ess,' she said. 'That's right, darling. It's me. Ess.'

His eyes found her.

Hamlet cleared his throat. Quilter found his authority. 'Quiet!' She was proud of him.

'How are you, darling?'

She could see the question sinking, level below level, until it grounded in understanding.

Hamlet came up behind her to look directly down. She heard Quilter's angry intake of breath. Moving silently, he grasped Hamlet by the arm. 'He mustn't see you. Nobody but his wife. That's an order, sergeant.'

The conflict between duty and common humanity plainly visible, Hamlet retreated. She could hear Quilter whispering scoldingly.

But Nick had seen Hamlet. His eyes widened. His lips quivered. Fear. Unmistakable fear.

'It's all right, darling.' The way she would have dealt with a frightened Emma. 'Nothing to be afraid of.'

His eyes rolled, searching the space where Hamlet had stood. They came back to her. He was struggling to speak.

'Try not to worry,' she whispered. 'Everything's going to be all right.' Please God!

But everything was not all right. His eyes, dilated, were imploring now. His throat worked desperately. She propped herself over him, ear close to his mouth to catch any sound.

Dr Quilter said, 'Mrs Brooke, I think perhaps – '

Nick's hand, fumbling blindly, grasped hers with surprising strength. A strangled sound, little more than a scrape of the throat but no words. He was trying desperately to say something, and as desperately failing.

His other hand joined the first, clumsy, a blind man feeling. The forefinger found her palm, his nail digging into her in the intensity of his effort. Then it began to move and she understood what, with agonising clumsiness, he was trying to do: write, one awkward letter at a time.

L . . . O . . . O . . . K.

A pause, so long that she thought he had abandoned the effort. But no, he began again.

O . . . U . . . T.

Look out.

It was his final act. Eyes closed – no, clenched – he seemed to sink into the pillows. Dr Quilter took his wrist.

'Sister!'

He turned to Sarah. 'He's all right, Mrs Brooke, but I think we should leave him now. We don't want to exhaust him.' He had recognised an attempt to communicate, but failed to realise that it had succeeded.

She waited outside rather than stay near Hamlet, but Hamlet, a quandary of his own, passed her to walk very quickly down the corridor. There was a public telephone. He ducked inside its acoustic hood.

It was some time before Quilter came out. 'Well, he knew you were there all right, even if he couldn't respond. With a bit of luck there'll be some improvement tomorrow.'

'I shouldn't have pushed him.'

'He obviously wanted to speak. It's a good sign. Are you sure you're all right, Mrs Brooke?' He parted briefly from her to let two orderlies pushing a patient on a trolley get past. Detective Sergeant Hamlet had vanished.

Look out. Why should she look out?

He took her back to reception, the usual slow-motion turmoil, the usual muted babble. Hell was an eternal waiting-room. Corny! Sartre had worked that seam out. No sign of Heather.

Quilter halted, started to speak, stopped, said something different. 'People who've had violent accidents often find things a bit bewildering when they come round afterwards. Try not to let it worry you, Mrs Brooke.'

He said, 'I mean, what really matters is to get him fit again. After that . . .'

'Yes,' she said. 'After that . . .' She held out her hand. 'Thanks. Thanks a lot. Did . . . Mr Norton-Jones . . . Did he say he'd be back?'

'I don't know. He and Mr Impey went off together.' He smiled to cheer her up. 'Nobody tells people like me anything important.'

Realising he was still holding her hand he hastily released it, but his look betrayed him. Sarah Brooke, she told herself, wondering at her slowness, you've made a conquest.

'It's natural for him to be upset,' he said awkwardly. 'Your job's to keep smiling. Come and see him tomorrow.'

After ten minutes, still no Heather. She went to look outside. They were waiting by the ambulances, much laughing and talking that stopped as soon as she appeared. She was surrounded in a moment. Someone grabbed her left arm, someone her right. There were women among them; no, girls, even by her standards.

'Mrs Brooke, we've a car waiting just over there. We could talk on the way.'

'Mrs Brooke, my paper's willing to pay a lot of money for exclusive rights and a full story after the trial.'

'Look this way, Mrs Brooke. This way, please!' Electronic flash, only feet away. More followed, a flickering wall of brilliance.

'Sarah! Over here, Sarah!' She felt a surge of anger at that, her natural dislike of strangers who instantly used first names.

'Did you see your husband, Mrs Brooke? How is he?'

'Over here, Sarah!'

She was being tugged, pushed, jostled. A cylinder on a long

pole descended inches from her face. Someone humping a video camera on his shoulder. Anything she looked, anything she said, they would steal.

The old Sarah wanted to turn tail, to run, to hide. She tightened her lips, tried to shake off grasping hands, tried to walk on. No sign at all of Heather.

'How is he, Mrs Brooke? Is he going to live?'

'What was the first thing he said, Sarah?'

'How do you feel about all this, Mrs Brooke?'

Oh, marvellous, she wanted to say: absolutely over the bloody moon! Nick used to say it was the only answer when they asked you how you felt after you'd just lost your legs, your arms and your entire family.

'This way, please, Sarah? Could you give us a smile?'

'We're talking five figures, Mrs Brooke. You'll need all that and more for a top class brief.'

'Don't listen to them, Sarah. Just get in the car and we'll go somewhere where we can talk things over sensibly.'

'Piss off, Alastair, she's our bunny. That car over there, Mrs Brooke.' Nearly pulled off her feet on a patch of packed snow.

She found her voice. She said, 'Get out of my way, please. Just get out of my way.' No, she hadn't found her voice. She'd found someone else's, ten times as loud, with an edge like a circular saw.

It would have made no difference if Chief Superintendent Capstick, Detective Sergeant Hamlet and a uniformed officer in support, had not materialised to do an imitation of Moses parting the Red Sea. The mob crowded about them, cameras still blitzing. In a daze of nervous rage she saw that Capstick was steering her in the direction of her own car.

'Car's been checked, madam, everything okay. They've returned your husband's things, too. Got your keys, have you?' She found herself looking meekly for them in her bag.

'Can't do this every time, Mrs Brooke,' Capstick said blandly. 'The press have their rights.'

'What about my rights?' She was shouting at him. 'What about my bloody rights? I haven't done anything!'

'Remains to be seen, doesn't it, madam?' He motioned her off while the wolfpack shouted and flickered like a sort of pop *son et lumière*.

All she could concentrate on was what Nick had been trying to say. Look out? What was she supposed to look out for?

'Well.' Heather Smith closed and locked the door of her office, parked her helmet on the top of the filing cabinet. 'Doesn't do to underestimate Chief Super Capstick.' She had appeared, crouched over her Kawasaki like a black, goggle-eyed Fury, to tuck in behind Sarah in Reigate High Street.

Unzipping her leathers to reveal herself in sweater and long johns, she peeled off the thermal underwear, took a jacket and skirt from a hanger behind the door, dressed swiftly and wiggled her feet into a pair of shoes. On the other side of the window the mundane racket of traffic was music after the past few hours.

'Take a pew.' She was once again Capstick's lady lawyer. 'Tea's on the way.' She smiled wryly. 'Nonstop supply of refreshments, all you ever seem to get from me.'

'I don't understand. Where were you when I came out?'

Heather took a long breath. 'Pleading not guilty for Nick.'

Sarah opened her mouth, closed her eyes, moved her head slowly from side to side.

'I know. I know. No point in pulling any punches, though. Capstick was waiting in the car-park. That man Hamlet – what a name to live with! – passed the word that Nick was conscious. Capstick scooped me up, going to charge him, like it or not, couldn't refuse, could I?'

Sarah lowered her face into her hands.

'You might as well,' Heather said, 'hear the lot. The press mob was out there too. Capstick went straight out and read them a prepared statement, bare facts, Nicholas whatever-he-is Brooke, charged with offences under the Act, to be held in custody while the police continue their investigations. Obviously been carrying it around with him.'

There was something more than compassion in her gaze but she turned her head away as Sarah looked up.

'But how' – it was becoming too complex to grasp – 'did they get there, all those press people? They were still outside the house when you picked me up in the lane.'

'As I said,' Heather repeated, 'it doesn't do to underestimate Capstick. Or perhaps I should say Norton-Jones.'

'He's been there. With some American, apparently.'

Heather pursed her lips. 'American. Makes it pretty certain

it's to do with that air crash, doesn't it? Something missing. Something American. And they think Nick knows all about it. Do we know the Yank's name?'

'Wise. Or something like Wise. Red, shiny face. That's all we know.'

'Doesn't matter.' Heather picked up a pencil, rat-tatted the point on the desk. 'I was telling you, I had a little trick up my own sleeve. Worked, too, for what it's worth.'

Sarah was too weary to solve more puzzles.

'Fixed it with your Mrs Crabtree,' Heather said, 'to ring my secretary and say we were on our way to Redhill. Poor old Sarah, you're too zonked to work it out.'

'No, I get it. The only ones who knew were you, me, Mrs Crabtree, your secretary and whoever's listening to my phone.'

Heather waited. Sarah completed the puzzle. 'So the only way all those press people could have known where I was – '

' – was if they were told.'

'Norton-Jones,' Sarah said fatalistically.

'Or someone. Putting the pressure on.'

Tea came. Sarah said, 'He's scared, Heather. I've never seen Nick scared before.'

'Something to be scared about, or they wouldn't be in such a hurry. We'll challenge, of course, charging him in that state. They must know we will, didn't stop them doing it though.'

'They think he took something from that plane crash. They want it. Badly. Capstick' – she corrected herself – 'Norton-Jones thinks I might know where it is. Oh!'

'Oh what?'

'He spoke. Well, tried to tell me something, anyway.'

Heather nodded. '*Compos mentis*. That's what decided them to charge him. What did he – '

'"Look out." I think he said, "Look out."' She explained.

Heather considered it. 'But you don't know why, right?'

'No.'

'For yourself, perhaps. Take care?'

'Perhaps. He was scared. Really scared, Heather.'

Another brisk nod. 'Natural enough. What are you going to do? Now, I mean.'

'Go home. What else? *I* can't push off to Wells or anywhere, can I? Anyway' – she remembered – 'Dr Quilter thinks they'll move him as soon as he's fit. Somewhere more secure.'

'My barrister pal in Guildford warned me they would. Didn't want to give you something else to worry about.'

'Are we talking about prison?'

'Have to be a lot better, first. Prison medical services can't cope with surgery and such.'

Her telephone rang. She listened for a fairly long time, said, 'Thank you. I'll tell her.'

She looked at Sarah. 'The *Globe*, a Mr Willett? They're not sure the deal's still on.'

Sarah had just discovered that she was dead on her feet.

'They were going to buy the exclusive story, remember? Seems the proprietor may be having second thoughts.'

'Lord Tyrran? Not like him to . . . Oh well, so what!' Didn't care, very little she cared about, only Nick and Emma.

'There is,' Heather said delicately, 'that tiny problem of fees. Not to mention the fact that you'd be thrown back to the wolves.' She tapped her pencil against her teeth. 'My advice still acceptable? Hasn't done you much good so far.'

'Who else has?'

'Will you come and talk to a friend of mine? You've already met him. Hugh Rossiter. Some people think he's an old woman. I think he's an old fox. He knows things. And he cares, a lot, about a lot of things.'

'Nice to know somebody does,' Sarah said indifferently.

Once again she failed to see Heather's quickly suppressed reaction.

PART THREE

6

Hugh Rossiter turned off the radio after the news round-up. 'So wags the world, Elly, old girl,' he said softly. 'Old habits die hard and old hacks with them.'

Sam sidled in, hugging first the side of the door, then the refrigerator, veteran campaigner keeping close cover and protecting his rear. Rossiter saw him. 'What do you think, you old devil? Could the Brooke thing be fun? Or much grief for one and all?'

Sam mewed in the tone he used when he was pleading not guilty, no specific crime, just general insurance. Tail fluffed and erect, he circled Rossiter's legs, producing his most seductive purr. Good things were known to have their home in the tall, white, cold place.

Nudging him aside to open the fridge, Rossiter took two eggs and a bottle of milk in his right hand, used the left to fish a glass from the shelf above. One of the eggs plunged to the quarry-tiled floor. Putting yards between himself and complicity in a neatly split second, Sam contemplated the splatter from a chair.

'Not just getting ancient, Elly,' Rossiter said. 'Getting clumsy. Remember the days when I could carry four double Scotches in each hand?'

He set the milk and the remaining egg on the table, found a knife and a saucer, went down on his knees.

'Waste not' – he slid the broken egg on to the saucer – 'want not.

'I know, I know.' Rossiter cracked the second egg in the glass, nudged in the remains of the first, added milk, whipped them with a fork. 'What's in it for you? That about it, my furry chum?' He poured milk in the saucer. Sam was there in an instant to separate it from shards of shell.

'What everyone asks' – he found a bottle of cognac, tipped a good inch in the glass – 'except us, and thus are we held in contempt. Right, Samuel?'

Sam pricked his ears but went on lapping. Rossiter sucked the top off his breakfast, picked up the glass, went slopping in his down-at-heel slippers to the wheelback chair.

The Sunday papers had sat on the warm top of the Aga long enough to comfort his fingers. The first he picked up, after taking another draught of nourishment, had an across-four double heading.

NEWSMAN ON SECRETS CHARGE

NIGHT SHOTS AT WIFE BAFFLE SURREY POLICE

He pulled his gawdelpus face, shuffled through the pack, winced at the tabloids, selected the qualities, settled down to read.

The Home Office had taken its usual vow of silence on matters connected with security. All questions concerning the shooting incident at Holmbury St Mary had been passed to the Surrey County Constabulary, who had pronounced themselves 'baffled'. The rest was all 'understandings'.

It was understood that there was no identifiable connection between the shooting and the secrets charge against Nick Brooke, the *Globe*'s 'man-on-the-spot'. It was understood that his serious injuries had prevented Special Branch from making earlier charges. It was understood that the nature of the charges would not be revealed until Special Branch had completed further enquiries. In the meantime the magistrates had granted a further remand in custody.

What Rossiter called minestrone, a hotchpotch of fact, gossip and rumour. He tore off a page here, a page there, dropping the remains on the floor for Sam to tunnel under and settle himself to snooze.

'Nice girl, Elly,' Rossiter told the empty air, looking at a picture of Sarah. 'Just what the trash sheets and big tough coppers eat for breakfast. So' – he tilted the glass high, draining the dregs – 'I *think* one has an obligation.'

He added the glass to an assortment of unwashed dishes. 'Oh yes,' he said, 'the freedom of the press and the power of the popular prints are as love to lust. What's the hour, friend Samuel?'

But Sam was in his own dark world. Rossiter sighed, cocked his head sideways as if listening, said, 'Just going to do them, old girl.' He rinsed dishes splashily under the cold tap.

'That,' Heather said with satisfaction, 'should have well and truly lost the bastards.'

They were somewhere near the summit of the hill, dead bracken and leafless trees seasonal with sugar icing. After the rumble of the engine the silence was stunning.

Heather chuckled. 'The ranger would go spare, motorbikes on his lovely hill. Are you warm enough?'

Taut and sick with the apprehension that had become part of her daily life, Sarah nodded under her borrowed crash helmet. 'No chance they might cut across and be waiting for us?'

'Not a hope. All city slickers. For all they know we might as well have gone to the moon.' Heather took off her helmet, perched it on the handlebars. 'Listen. Just what you need.'

'I know. Nothing. Not even planes for the moment.' Yet this vast, blanched stillness was part of the continuing nightmare. In a desperate change of subject she said, 'Nick fell out of a tree not far from here.'

'Literally?'

'Literally. He climbed up to look for a path and the branch snapped. Emma thought it was great. She wanted him to do it again. There's a hollow near it where we used to picnic.' She stopped abruptly.

'Nick's making progress. Emma's all right. Let's take one thing at a time.'

'Sorry. I am trying.'

'I know. If you love someone and they're in a hell of a mess and – '

Heather donned her helmet abruptly. 'Oh well, best get on. Doesn't matter if we're a bit early. Or a bit late. All the same to old Hugh.'

Sarah squeezed her waist. 'What would I do without you?'

A quick, almost angry shake of Heather's head as she started up, trundled them cautiously down the frozen slope.

They came out on the road, a former cart track that time and the sandy soil had sunk deep below the surrounding woodland.

The engine at minimum revs, they could talk above its mutter. 'When I'm filthy rich,' Heather said, 'I'm going to have a house up here. Facing south, all the sun that's going, clear view to the coast.'

'Is Hugh Rossiter rich?'

'The house was his wife's. My father handles his affairs. Hugh's got enough to rub along, but he's bad with money. And a soft touch.

'And the house eats up a lot. Ought to sell it and buy something smaller, especially as he keeps up a little pad in London. Won't hear of it. Full of his wife's things, you see. Poor old Hugh, getting on two years since she died but he still misses her dreadfully.'

Sarah had thought him scruffy, she remembered. Perhaps neglected might have been a better word.

'So he lives alone. I remember now, sort of.'

'Elly, that was his wife, always called him the cat who walked all alone. Only not so much a cat as a mouse in cat's clothing.' Heather chuckled, that comforting sound. 'She was a super person.'

'He gave up foreign corresponding, didn't he? Just the occasional telly.'

'Supposed to be writing his memoirs, but his publisher's always ringing up and nagging him. I know what that means.'

'Not doing much writing.'

'In his head, maybe. On paper, I doubt it. When he was away the job would drag him by the hair, that's how he puts it. When he was at home, Elly would nag him. Now . . .'

She shook her head. 'Poor old Hugh. Drinks a bit.' Heather's voice was high and clear above the rumble of the engine. 'Drinks a lot, actually. Doesn't stop him thinking, though that's why he drinks.'

'How much have you said?'

She pulled up under a larch that had stooped itself over the road. 'Everybody thinks he's had his day, I think he's a super person, sanest I know, drunk or sober. And I told him everything.'

'But what can he do?'

'I don't know. But he'll come up with something. Only man I know who'd either tell you to push off or see you right if it took him the rest of his life.'

Unexpectedly the larch sifted a silent drift of snow over them. The last grains seemed to hang endlessly before stillness returned.

'Angels' feathers,' Heather said, and then, 'Only man I really care for. Chaste, passionate love. What do you make of that, Sarah Brooke?'

Revving up, she took the steep slope as if they were late for something that only happened once in a lifetime.

Just over the summit of the hill a crumbling tarmac drive, at its end a brick-pillared entry among thickets of wild rhododendrons. The drive was horribly potholed. More rhododendrons and the winter bones of briars; through them, a glimpse of garden, a dilapidated summerhouse.

Heather brought the bike to a halt. 'Hugh's signed a pact with nature since Elly went; leaves it alone and hopes it'll do the same for him. It doesn't.'

The house was a *fin de siècle* beauty shabby under penury and neglect. 'Lutyens,' Heather said. 'Scheduled, of course, but practically all Hugh manages to do is keep the rain out.' She parked behind an old Peugeot, nearly a museum piece in itself.

No need to knock or ring. The heavy oak door, darkened and dulled by weather, opened at once. 'Ladies! Welcome. Be pleased to enter.' She remembered now; the light, self-mocking voice, he and the world to be taken seriously at your peril.

A womanless house: no gleam on floors or woodwork, no general neatness and order. A glimpse through the open door of the cloakroom showed the lavatory with its seat up, the very hallmark of the male solitary.

He shepherded them through, heavy-rimmed spectacles perched atop his head the way some women wore sun-glasses, whimsical touch to a whimsical face.

The room he took them to was long, light, the faded elegance of old lace. Books, pictures, furniture that ranged over a century or two but rubbed along as amiably as old friends at a family reunion. All in good taste, Elly's presumably, but a fond neglect that came from much use and little upkeep. A log fire shimmered invitingly.

One wall was mostly window. Across a wide lawn that mingled freely with dilapidated borders was a coppice, some tumbledown fencing. Eight hundred feet below, a vast sweep of storybook England; farms, woods, pale drifts of smoke that tagged hidden villages. It stretched mistily, a snowy chequerboard dominated by the successive ramparts of the Surrey hills; Hindhead stretching out a last finger toward the coast.

Sarah forgot her problems. 'What a fabulous view!'

'Nonstop moving picture show, dear girl. Action-packed, as they say.'

Turning back to Heather he planted a light kiss on her forehead. 'Marry me, child, and all this will be yours someday. Leaky roofs, draughty windows, the finest collection of dry rot in private hands.'

'Sorry, Hugh, you're too much of a responsibility.' Heather's glance flickered to Sarah, a small, enigmatic smile.

'Always turns me down,' Rossiter told Sarah. 'Saw what a trouble I was to Elly, not going to take it on, not nohow. So!' He examined Sarah, hand on hips. 'Wife of the *Globe*'s man-on-the-spot. No wonder you were looking glum when I bade you my bright good day.'

'Hugh,' Heather said, 'this thing's gone far beyond a joke.'

'Of course it has, my own, my sweet. The Street of Shame is far beyond a joke. So is Plod when he breathes heavily and walks on tippytoe.'

He pushed a heap of books to one end of a sagging sofa, waved them both to sit, went to a long sideboard.

Above it was a portrait in oils, a girl of the forties, that upswept, top-rolled hairstyle that went with backs to the wall and padded shoulders to the wheel. Painted by an artist who had clearly fallen in love with his subject, she was no great beauty but her personality came through like mellow stone radiating its warmth long after sunset.

Heather mouthed silently: *Elly*.

'Who' – Rossiter revealed a display of bottles – 'says yes to a touch of the universal solvent?'

They refused. Jerking his head to make his glasses fall from his thinning crown to the tip of his nose, he peered in mock dismay. 'Come! The old toper can't drink on his own.'

'The old toper,' Heather said, 'usually does. That's why he's an old toper. Are you going to give us the benefit of your advice or are you going to get quietly pissed?'

'Pissed!' He took out a bottle and glass. 'When that I was a little tiny boy, with hey, ho, the wind and the rain, a man was said to be in his cups.'

He gave himself a modest measure of brandy but left the bottle out. 'Words,' he said to Sarah. 'When that I was a little tiny boy, I fell in love with words. An infinity of sounds turned into an infinity of squiggles to yield an infinity of meanings. But now! Do I render sacrifice to Bacchus? Bend the elbow? Look on the wine when it's red? Do I even get tanked, over-bevvied, legless? Oh no, desecrating both the grape and the language, I get pissed.'

He came to sit. Behind him, the door inched open. A marmalade cat with a pure white mask sidled in, tail gently waving. Mincing over to Rossiter it levitated to his lap and began to purr.

'This,' he told Sarah, 'is Sam, a cat of infinite cunning and a distant connection of the great Johnson. I am tolerated as provider and Boswell. Since we were talking of words, what word of your husband?'

She told him, meaning to be brief but finding it coming in spate.

'Hm,' he said finally. 'Your Chief Superintendent Capstick, like friend Job, seems to be good at multiplying words without knowledge.' He raised one eyebrow at Heather.

Heather nodded. 'Lots of pressure, not much action. No case against Sarah, that's why. But it isn't Sarah he's interested in. Prepared to wait till Nick can talk.'

'And will he?' The eyebrow turned toward Sarah.

She could feel the old Sarah wilting under their joint gaze: Nick's lawyer and Nick's lawyer's chaste love both clearly convinced of Nick's guilt.

Once, long ago, when she had only just been learning to swim, the class had gone to the local pool. Somehow she found the other girls all clustered in the middle while she, barely past the stage of keeping herself afloat, was alone and out of her depth.

She had panicked. Not openly, not hysterically, simply lost all confidence in her ability and simultaneously thought what everyone would say if she made any kind of scene. Soppy old Sarah, no good at swimming, no good at anything except English and history and soppy, boring poems.

So she had found herself going under, breathing water, struggling in the silent, roaring certainty that the fight would be lost, going to drown because drowning was better than being laughed at. But the instructor was suddenly at her side.

'All right, Sarah?' A supporting hand. No more than one small failure of will away from the end, she managed to say, 'Yes, Miss

Jeames. I just swallowed some water.' Miss Jeames, peerlessly tactful, had seen her to the steps, swum tactfully away.

She wasn't going to drown again for lack of fuss. Louder than she had intended, she said, 'The *Globe* man-on-the-spot probably did something bloody silly. The *Globe* man-on-the-spot's done a lot of silly things in his time. So has his wife. But nobody's going to make me believe he's a traitor or something. He doesn't give a toss about politics. And I'm the one who got blown out of my seat by a bloody shotgun.'

Rossiter, a little smile, said, 'So there!' and they were all laughing.

Rossiter said, 'Anyway, not much doubt who took a potshot at your wallpaper, dear girl. Your Nick obviously did something to upset the Holdens. Capstick must know that well enough. He just wants to make you feel nobody loves you except Special Branch.'

She stared stupidly. A Brummy accent: why hadn't she thought of that?

'It was a job. He had to do it, so he'd do it well. He was up there three days. He didn't get home until early Saturday morning.'

'A week yesterday.' Rossiter stroked Sam mechanically.

'A week yesterday.' Life had lost its tempo, a series of rushes and jerks.

'And Plod didn't raid you until the Wednesday.' He made an apologetic gesture. 'Sorry. Got to see what I say to find out what I think. Well, what I think is that Nick obviously did something between the weekend and Wednesday that decided Plod it was time to act.'

'Nothing special, not between Monday and his smash-up. The last time I *know* he ate out was the Tuesday of the week before. Just poked at his food when he came home, had lunch with this guy, didn't say who, I didn't ask. He was very broody.' She frowned. 'Glashin?'

'Glashin.'

'More than a week before the roses?'

'A long time. Unless . . .'

'Unless,' Heather said, 'something else had happened in between.'

'Lily Holden happened in between,' Sarah said. 'But I don't see what that could have to do with the roses.'

Rossiter laughed. 'No indeed! Peter Glashin sent you roses. Lily sent you a threatening phone call followed by a bouquet of buckshot. After that, the deluge. Or should I say the shower? Meaning the press. I understand that the *Globe*, motivated by that heartwarming altruism for which it is universally honoured, has offered its services in the defence of your unfortunate mate.'

'Maybe,' Heather said, 'and maybe not. Tyrran's dithering.'

'Been got at,' he said, 'by what he doubtless thinks are his friends in high places.' He achieved a feat, a quick toss of the head that shot up his glasses to settle on his pate like a tiara. 'Did I hear twenty thousand?'

'It was mentioned. I took it as seriously as the offer of a seat on Tyrran's board.'

'Quite right, child. The two you could be sure of. The noughts might be promises writ on air.'

He sipped a little more brandy. 'It wasn't just the soldiers who diced at the foot of the Cross. The press was there too.' Heather shook her head at Sarah: let him go on.

'When I was young,' Rossiter said, 'people, by and large, believed what they read in the papers, because, by and large, what the papers printed bore a passing resemblance to the truth. By and large, when I was young, the yellow press printed pap but not poison.'

Just like a tutorial, Sarah thought; Rossiter on the freedom of the press.

'By and large,' he said, 'when I was a young man, a decent hack would rather work for a pittance than trade his self-respect for riches. The freedom of the press didn't mean the right to intrude anywhere, blackguard anyone, invent anything so long as it pushed up circulation. It didn't mean be damned and still publish.'

He looked at her. 'A good journalist's first duty is to his conscience, his second to his readers, only then to his employer and his expense account. How would your Nick score on that?'

'He's often talked of resigning.'

Rossiter smiled. 'All good journalists regularly contemplate resignation. Usually by storming unannounced into the editor's sanctum.'

'Is the state of the country due to the state of the press? Or do you hold Nick personally responsible?'

'Of course not, dear girl. So long as your average citizen gets his dose of moral indignation through the letter-box every morning, he doesn't have to work it up for himself. Old fools like me were happy to oblige him with his daily fix.'

He inverted his glass over his mouth to catch the last drop, stared solemnly at Sarah. 'Twenty thousand. Let me tell you how it goes.

'They make you sign first. That ties you down. They shell out a thousand or two on account, then take over your life. Give you a couple of minders, possibly move you into a second-rate hotel, pump you dry of things you never meant to tell anyone, make you over into someone different. Someone with a better story than yours because it's half fiction.

'The rest of the money they reserve for a tomorrow that may never come. They fill their pages with stories about someone who just happens to have your name, then, one morning, it's all over. You wake up to find you're no one, not even the person you started off as.'

'I don't care about me,' she said. 'What about Nick?'

'Nick's public property now. They're not interested in public property, that's why they're all interested in you. Until next week. Then they'll be interested in someone else. Evelyn Waugh got it right, that splendid chap Corker. "News is what a chap who doesn't care much about anything wants to read. And it's only news until he's read it. After that it's dead." You'll be dead, too.'

He looked at her quizzically. 'Will you take the risk?'

'Sarah needs money,' Heather said, 'not sermons.'

'All right, we make up Tyrran's mind. But on our terms, not his.'

Heather sighed. 'You make it all sound so simple.'

'What Tyrran hates most,' he said, 'is losing. I should know. I worked for him a thousand years ago, when he bought the sheet in which I had a platform and a free hand. He wanted me to stay, but his only argument was money, so I left.'

He smiled wearily. 'He can't bear being done down. Make him think we've done him down and he'll come a-running.'

'How?' Heather demanded. 'Hugh, *how*, for heaven's sake?'

'Give me sole rights, child. What else?' He turned to Sarah, 'How do you feel about a fiver down and the rest in IOUs?'

The minute crepitations of the fire, the ticking of a brass

carriage clock. Outside, snow and silence. Heather said, 'Hugh, are you being wicked? Or amazingly clever?'

'Given up wickedness, child. Nothing so tedious as wickedness wedded to impotence. One condition. She stays here. House guest, lock, stock, etcetera. They'll find out, of course, but by then we'll have drawn up an agreement. After that . . . Well, after that is another story, by-line: Hugh Rossiter.'

Sarah looked at Heather. Heather gave her a little nod. 'And how,' she asked Rossiter, 'will you get the news to Tyrran?'

'All good hacks,' Rossiter said blandly, 'use attack as a means of self-assurance. We call a press conference.'

'State secrets. They won't let you call a press conference.'

'My press conference,' he said, 'wouldn't be about state secrets. It would be about how the Holdens blew Sarah Brooke's window out to teach Nick Brooke a lesson, when all the time it was the sewer press handing out dud cheques and one-way tickets to Promise Land.'

He smiled. 'I'd invite my old friend Peter Glashin. He loves that kind of copy. Goes down well in Tass.'

She traced him by a tremendous clatter of dishes. He was in the kitchen, draining rack piled high with dripping china.

'Where's Heather?' Her sleep had made her stupid.

'Back this evening with your things. Feel better for your nap?'

'I shouldn't have had it. Could I possibly use your phone? I ought to ring the hospital. And Emma. My daughter.'

'Phone's in the hall. Then, if you can bear it, you might allow an old newshound to pose a few questions.'

After her calls she found herself slumped on the stairs in the high, softly lit hall, fighting despair. Eventually Rossiter came to steer her gently back to the comfort of the living room. Curtains drawn, the fire coruscating ruddily, the soft glow of lamps with shades of faded silk and braid-edged, age-cracked parchment; the homely reassurance she needed. Sam, moulded to the rug before the fire like a casually dropped fur tippet, stretched out one paw languidly, opened his mouth in a pink and white yawn.

Rossiter studied her. 'Things not good, dear girl?'

'No,' she said. 'Not good.'

'Emma? Nick?'

'Oh, me, as much as anyone. Bloody pathetic really!'

'I despair of the world twice daily,' he said, 'and thrice on Sundays. But the wheel still turns. How are they?'

'Emma's very good, but homesick. She wants to see her daddy.'

'Of course she does. And Nick?'

'I only spoke to the sister. Very cagey, something to do with a bowel infection. Dr Quilter did warn me. At least, I think he did. He will try not to worry me. More frankness, less well-meaning fuss, that's what I need.'

He made a mock bow to his wife's portrait. 'Hear that, Elly? Just what you used to say when I was off somewhere special. "I always know when it's going to be tricky," she would say. "It's the only time you make a fuss of me."'

'That's what I mean. Too nice makes me suspicious.'

'In the medical profession,' he said tactfully, 'frankness can be a two-edged sword. Dr Quilter may be influenced by his own personal feelings as well as yours.'

The smallest of smiles lifted the corners of her mouth.

'Ah,' he said. 'Another admirer?'

'Another?'

'Words, words, words. I am indeed your admirer, most devoted. And so,' in a rush, 'is Heather, but . . .' He was watching her closely.

'Not much to admire in me, far from it. Just one of life's – '

'Don't say natural victims.' He was almost sharp. 'Not you, dear girl, not if you're true to yourself.'

'Words, words, words,' she said, an attempt at lightness. 'Nothing easier than words.'

He found a glass, measured his dose, pointed. 'See that?'

It was an old black-and-white glossy in a cheap frame over a table at which she guessed he worked. A black boy, emaciated, only one leg, the other severed above the knee. Balanced on a crude crutch he stared at the camera with a face that fate had stripped bare of expression.

'There's one of the natural victims, dear girl. Victim of smooth, articulate folk in parliaments, congresses, supreme soviets. Quick, slick folk writing for newspapers. Smart, literate folk in publishers' offices. Victim of words.'

He turned to look at the painting of his wife. 'Elly hadn't the deadly gift. She just cared, the only antidote. Won't make legs grow again or raise the dead from the grave. But the two of them, Elly and the boy, make me think before I write. And often lay down the pen. Words can kill.'

She knew he was both bolstering her and trying to draw her out of herself.

She made the effort. 'Words can bring hope too. Change things for the better. You know. Images of thought refined. The sweet converse of an innocent mind. Once upon a time I used to wallow in Keats.'

He watched her compassionately; slim, fragile-looking, dark-browed, yet a light in her eyes whenever she managed to separate herself from her troubles. 'Who are you when you're just you?'

'Sarah Brooke. Bad at people, good at exams.'

'Is that Nick?'

'There's some truth in it.'

'What exams?'

'English and history, sort of.'

'Ah,' he said. 'English and history, sort of. Words and deeds. Me too; see the deeds, write the words. Only we never called it history. We called it news. Well, that's what you were. What are you now?'

'A bad case of the wobblies. Like a top when it begins to run out of steam.'

'Wrong image,' he said. 'A top only stays up if you whip it. Come on, what are you when you're just you.'

'I used to write poetry. Try to.'

'Poetry,' he said, 'is in the ear of the writer. Better than writing history as it happened, like me. Better than living it. Like now.'

She laughed, a sad sound. 'Now is history? This now? My now?'

'History is about climates as well as people. Climates of fear where ordinary people find coppers knocking at their door and don't know why. Climates of greed that make men who set out to be good journalists end up on the *Globe* because it pays better. Climates in which pretty young women who – '

'What's pretty got to do with it?'

'Ouch!' He winced. 'Young women who want nothing better than to write poetry – not that there is anything better – suddenly find themselves in very unpoetic situations.'

'Youngish women who'd like to write poetry, bad poetry, in their own homes with their family safe and sound. Nothing to worry about except whether the bills will be paid when they're due.'

That sceptical eyebrow. 'Your Nick can't exactly be ill paid.'

'Not the most careful with his money, either. That's why he's still on the *Globe*, better tabloid and rich than respected and poor.'

With a rush of guilt that took her by surprise she added, 'That's not entirely fair. I pushed him into moving out here. It hasn't exactly reduced the household expenses.'

'How rich? And how tabloid?'

'Anything for a story,' she said. 'And nothing for nothing.'

'Would he knowingly do something . . . dangerous?'

'You were going to say "something wrong".'

'Dangerous I understand.'

She considered before answering.

'I suppose that question's been swimming about in there somewhere. Nick would rush after a story without stopping to consider the risk. But it would be, well, sort of kneejerk.'

'What if he had time to think?'

'I suppose he'd weigh up the chances.'

'The gains?'

'That as well.'

'I met him, you know. Did he tell you?'

'He says things he doesn't mean. Things that seem clever when he says them.'

'I patronised him. And I was chichi, an incurable habit of mine. He was right to feel put down. And to put me down. After all' – a wry smile – 'he'd nothing to lose. The old has-been.'

'He respects you.'

'As a journalist, possibly. But as a man . . .' He swirled the brandy in his glass. 'Act first, think after. Yes?'

'Yes.'

'But this time, when he thought after, he thought of Glashin.'

'I suppose so. Yes. Obviously.'

'And he isn't political. Just ambitious.'

'Yes.'

He swirled his glass carefully.

She said, 'Money, that's what you mean, isn't it?'

'Not necessarily. Or maybe both, nothing wrong with that. Whatever he found in the vicinity of that crash, he thought it was a story, not much doubt about that. Not much doubt what he'd do normally, either.'

'Take it to the *Globe*.'

'But he didn't. And he didn't tell you about it, though you usually knew what he was working on. The Holdens, Bangladeshi child brides and such.'

'Knew the *Globe* wouldn't touch it,' she said, no revelation.

'Secret papers.' He gave a grunt of amusement. 'Well, life has a bit of an addiction to clichés. Anyway, Glashin didn't get them. I think we can assume that photograph of Nick and Glashin was taken by Glashin's pals to show Nick they'd got him sewn up. If anything had been handed over, the picture would have shown it. I've had dealings with Ivan. I know his ways.'

'Then why did he meet Glashin?'

'To discuss a deal. The photo was to make sure he didn't back out.'

'But the Branch must have been on to him by then.'

He nodded. 'Didn't pick him up then because what they were really after, he didn't have with him. So the real questions' – his long, slim fingers twining, untwining – 'are, what has he done with whatever he found? Where had he been when he piled up the car? And who was after him to make him drive like that?'

'Those shots,' she began dubiously.

'Forget them, dear girl. You don't imagine Glashin, anyone on the Soviet side, would play rough games like that over here? Nick goes up to do a cash deal with Lily Holden, has to be fairly sympathetic or she won't play. Next thing she knows, the trash sheets are rubbishing her, *Globe* included. Who can it be but Nick?'

'She and her pals are simple-minded criminals, innocent as the day compared with the sewer press. And they wouldn't know what happened to Nick until they read about it or heard it on the news. No, dearest girl, the gun shots were Lily saying, "Naughty boy, Nicholas," and totally irrelevant.'

In the fireplace a log slumped, a sudden swirl of sparks. Sam's claws sank reflexively through Sarah's skirt, making her jump. Settling again, Sam purred perversely.

'Logs,' Rossiter said. 'More logs for the fire.' The big wicker basket at the side of the hearth was empty. He got up. 'Not too much snow this winter, please God. Last year there was a time when I had to keep taking the shovel to dig 'em out.'

Sarah stopped stroking Sam. 'The spade!'

Rossiter turned absently at the door. 'Spade, child? What spade?' Out in the hall the phone began to ring.

He came back from answering it. 'Got to get you over to Redhill, dear girl. Your Nick's taken a tiny turn for the worse.'

That was when history repeated itself but not as farce. A paralysing dissonance of breaking glass, the ear-tearing thunder of a discharge. Sam streaked like a projectile under the farthest chair. Sarah threw herself to the floor. Still standing, Rossiter stared, not at the window but the wall above the fireplace.

Of the portrait of his wife little remained but the shot-blasted frame, through which wrecked plaster and bare, pitted brick were shockingly exposed. Her ears once again ringing intolerably, Sarah was aware of the diminishing sound of a car engine at high revs.

Clapping the palms of his hands to his ears several times as if to squeeze out the violence, Rossiter went on looking at the savaged portrait.

'Not such a joke after all, old girl.' The words were not addressed to Sarah. He turned toward her. 'Are you all right?'

'Yes. Are you?' In this much larger room the effect had not been quite so deafening.

'Been shot at before, dear girl.' His eyes returned to the headless portrait. 'That's what hurts. That hurts like hell.' Through the shattered pane of the window a breeze stirred the drapes, bringing night into the room like a chilly phantom.

He drew the drapes across the gap with a fresh tinkle of falling glass. 'I think we may assume the rogue has fled.'

This time she was less frightened than angry. 'Isn't there some way to let that woman know there's nothing she can do about Nick now?'

'I doubt it's Nick they're trying to frighten. I think it's you.'

'Me? Why on earth should Lily Holden want to frighten me?'

'Why on earth, dear girl, should you imagine I meant Lily?'

'Then who?'

'Someone who thinks you know something? Who thinks it might be easier to break a woman than a man? Lily doesn't even know you're here.'

'Norton-Jones!' She was instantly certain.

'Maybe. What matters at present is getting you to Redhill.'

'You call the police. If you'd let me have your car, I'd be all right.'

Watching him hesitate, she all but stamped her foot. 'The police! It's got to be stopped!'

He saw her to his old Peugeot, waited anxiously while she tried three times before the cold engine fired. After watching its tail lights vanish round the bend of the drive, he went to call the police. The telephone was dead.

Back in the room, cold draughts stirring the curtains, he looked yet again at what was left of the painting. '*Not* fun, old girl. Forty years chasing around the world after wickedness, you get to know the smell.'

The roar of Heather's motorbike was thunderous. When she cut the engine it seemed to die, refire, then die again. Going to greet her, Rossiter discovered why: not one but two bikes.

Heather dumped the bags she had packed for Sarah, snatched off her helmet angrily.

'The bloody *Globe*! Specialise in hanging about making bloody nuisances of themselves. As your solicitor I advise you to order them off the premises.'

Liz Balcon's red hair emerged from her casque. The cold had got at her sharp nose. Her green eyes pink-rimmed, there was something rodentlike about her. She recognised Rossiter instantly.

'Hugh Rossiter! Well, glad to meet the living legend. Anything goes, right? This is Roger Petherbridge.'

Rossiter glanced wryly at Heather. 'Waylaid you, stuck to you like glue, couldn't shake 'em off, is that about it?'

'Waylaid me my foot.' Heather was still inclined to be short. 'Been camping outside my place ever since Sarah and I lost the pack. Drove my father spare when he found out, prosecute the pair of them if they set one foot over the boundary. But they're too sharp. Caught me out with the bloody bike instead.'

Liz was unabashed. 'Gordon Bennett! Where's that crappity-crap going to get us? Okay, don't know whether we've got a deal yet, not my fault. Doesn't mean my editor's going to sit back while the rest of the mob carve up a *Globe* man. Don't worry, Mr Rossiter. We're on your side.'

'Going to see us right, are you?' Heather recaptured her professional calm if not her normal good nature.

201

'Might manage to drop you a pony or two, call it exies if you don't want it to go through the books. Don't expect anyone to do anything for nothing, not our style, is it, Rodge?'

Roger Petherbridge, tall, shaggy, deceptively lumpen, was the brains of the *Globe* trio according to Sarah. He picked the targets, Liz was the hit-girl, Crispin gnawed the remains.

'Look at it this way, sir. Whether or not the owner lets us buy Mrs Brooke's story, shots through her window, that's something else.'

'Shots?' Rossiter blinked, one eyebrow hoisted.

'The other night. The Holden mob, we reckon.'

'Do you now?' Rossiter said vaguely. 'Interesting thought. Come in and tell me about it.' He waved them past Heather's rigid disapproval then nudged her and put a quick finger to his lips. She followed meekly.

'Petherbridge.' He showed them into the big sitting room. 'I once knew a Petherbridge, dear boy. Colin of that ilk, good man to be with in a bar or a hole.'

'My old man. Dead. Cancer of the gut. They wouldn't admit any connection with the Aussie nuke tests. He reckoned they lied. Weren't you there too?'

'That's what *they* said, is it? Ah well, we all know about *them*. He must have been proud of you, carrying on the family tradition.'

Roger flushed.

'Blimey O'Reilly!' Something had shaken Liz Balcon at last.

Rossiter followed her gaze. 'Ah, that. My late wife. Lost her head to a dark stranger.'

Roger went closer. 'When'd it happen?'

'Oh, dust barely settled, dear boy.' Rossiter glanced blandly at a stunned Heather. 'Shots still echoing among the reverberate hills.'

'You've got to be kidding,' Liz said.

Unzipping a pocket of his padded jacket, Roger hauled out a pocketphone. Rossiter blinked. 'Are those things standard issue now?'

'Times change, Mr Rossiter. Cleft sticks are out.'

Rossiter laid a quick hand on it. 'Wait, dear boy. One word with my legal adviser.' He led Heather aside. 'She's gone to Redhill in my car. Nick's taken a turn for the worse.'

'Are you all right?'

'Cross my heart.'

'Then I'll go.' She edged toward the hall. The pair from the *Globe* were at the window, Liz pulling aside the drapes. From the doorway Heather blew Rossiter a kiss and slipped silently out.

'Before you report back to base,' Rossiter said, 'do you think we might perhaps first summon Plod?'

Liz Balcon invoked another of her subastral deities. 'Flaming Norah! You mean you haven't told them?'

'The perpetrators,' Rossiter said, 'took the precaution of putting the phone out of action. Not just an exclusive, children. News that has not yet officially happened. By the way, Mrs Brooke's story is mine, bought and paid for. Well, bought.'

Roger, a rare animation, said 'Jesus!'

Once again Rossiter prevented him from using the pocket-phone. 'One small favour, since you owe it to me that your little cup runneth over. Outside. Mustn't provoke the local force beyond endurance.'

Less on the horns than tossed and gored by their dilemma, they allowed themselves to be ushered out.

'Can't expect us to call the fuzz and not the news desk,' Roger said almost apologetically, and then, in a hasty mumble, 'Got to start somewhere in this game, Mr Rossiter. My dad would have understood that.'

'Oh, true, he would, dear boy, so let me give you a tip. It's not who you write for but what you write, so my advice is, move up or move on. Now, police first, if you please. And I do advise caution. Something tells me they won't rejoice at your presence.' He closed and locked the door in the moment that Liz yelled, 'Hang about, Mr Rossiter, you haven't told us a dicky about anything yet!'

Capstick turned up just before midnight. A hoarseness suggested he was not yet rid of his cold but he civilly declined the offer of something to take away the chill.

'Well, sir, you haven't exactly made things easy for us.'

'Things haven't *been* easy, Chief Superintendent.'

'Offence in itself, sir, failing to report an offence.' Capstick was curiously uncertain.

'I dare say Inspector Crabbe of the Dorking constabulary told you the culprits cut the telephone wires or something?'

Capstick's face went instantly blank, much rather that line wasn't pursued.

'And the possibility of an armed man in the shrubbery. Anyway, minutes before those shots were fired' – Rossiter aimed one of Sam's paws at the window – 'the hospital rang to say it would be best if Mrs Brooke were to go over, chop chop. You're a humane chap, Chief Superintendent. Which would you have done first? Called the police or sped her on her way?'

He smiled amiably. 'You did know Mrs Brooke was my house guest? Of course you did.'

Capstick was showing signs of stress: edge-of-seat posture, deeply cleft brow, thumbs and forefingers massaging each other fretfully.

'And the press, sir? Reporters waiting for our men on arrival?'

'Sheer coincidence. Couldn't have called your people without them.'

Capstick snapped, gently, like exhausted elastic. 'How did they know Mrs Brooke was here?'

'They followed Miss Smith, though she did her best to lose them.'

Capstick took a deep breath. 'Founder member of CND, right, sir?'

'And proud of it.'

'Not exactly supporters of the Branch, sir, CND.'

'For myself,' Rossiter said, 'I would have put it the other way round. Would you care to explain the relevance of the Campaign for Nuclear Disarmament to the fact that someone blew my wife's head off?'

Capstick's eyes went uneasily to the damaged portrait. 'Might have been your head, sir. Or Mrs Brooke's. Have you thought of that?'

It isn't, Rossiter thought, that he doesn't know what to make of it. He does, and that's what's bothering him.

'A present from Birmingham, Chief Superintendent? Or haven't your enquiries got that far?'

Capstick sighed, a melancholy sound. 'Sir, the Branch doesn't waste its time on things like that. The Branch is concerned with state security. Not to mince words, sir, I could bring charges against you for knowingly obstructing us in the pursuit of our duties.'

Rossiter deposited Sam by the fire. 'I think not. You ought to be pleased those two *Globe* scavengers turned up.'

'Did a fine job of trampling all over the footprints, sir. Not that it would have made much odds. Just like last time, nothing to go by.'

'Just like last time! To misquote dear Oscar, to be shot at once may be regarded as a misfortune. To be shot at twice begins to look dangerously like a habit.'

Capstick dissuaded Sam from taking up residence on his lap. 'Mr Rossiter, you don't need to be told the press are going to be down like a plague of locusts.'

'Oh, indeed! Though the locust only does what comes naturally to a locust. The press, with distinguished exceptions, does what comes naturally to a louse.'

'But sir!' Capstick began, but Rossiter knew what he was up to.

'A prostitute can sell her body and keep her scruples,' he said. 'Sewer press journalists sell their scruples to keep their bodies. Their opinions are like the wind that bloweth where it listeth. Thou hearest the sound thereof, but cannot tell whence it cometh save that it bringeth with it the rank stench of hypocrisy. Ask my old friend Peter Glashin, Chief Superintendent. He has sound views on the subject.'

The mention of Glashin made Capstick blink. 'With due respect, sir' – Rossiter grinned like a crocodile at that – 'I don't need lectures on the gutter press. But for the *Globe* I wouldn't be on this case. But for the *Globe* we wouldn't have had two lots of buckshot through two separate windows. And young Brooke wouldn't be in a very bad way over in Redhill.'

'Is he that bad?'

'Yes, sir, he is. And no one but himself to blame. Which is why it beats me that you're willing to make life hard for people trying to clear up the mess.'

'Ah well' – Rossiter looked unconvincingly contrite – 'as you said, founder member of CND, supporter of all manner of bleeding heart causes that people like you officially frown upon. In short' – he spread his arms – 'enemy of the state.'

For a moment Capstick's unease seemed to become acute. 'Those shots,' he began, then changed his mind. 'You and I have got to be straight with each other, sir. Within reason.'

'The human condition in a nutshell. Sam, extract your claws

from the gentleman's knee.' Rossiter looked at Capstick expectantly.

'If you and Miss Smith are advising Mrs Brooke – '

'Oh, we are indeed.'

'Yes, sir. Then you'll know something went missing from that Yank chopper. We've very good reason to think Mrs Brooke's husband knows all about it.'

'And Mrs Brooke?'

'Hasn't been charged with anything. Not yet.' Capstick appeared to wrestle with himself. 'Look, sir, you've been around. You know what's what. I fancy Whitehall's keener on recovering what's missing than making life difficult for the Brookes.'

'Hands across the sea?'

'Something like that, sir. The Yanks finding out a British junk journalist took a document case from the wreckage.'

'They'll know already, won't they? You've charged him.'

'Know he's mixed up in something. Don't know the extent, not yet. Wouldn't do if they learn he'd been going to sell whatever it was to – '

'Peter Glashin.'

'An old friend, I think you said, sir.'

'Professionally speaking.'

'Of course, sir.'

'And with a certain amount of journalistic licence.'

'Go easy on the licence if I were in your shoes,' Capstick said.

He shifted in his chair, took another look at the decapitated portrait. 'That's wicked. Downright wicked.'

For an instant their eyes met. It was Capstick's that slid away. 'Well, sir, as I said, that's a thing for the local force. Would you mind telling me how long Mrs Brooke will be with you?'

The telephone rang.

Rossiter's eyebrows rose. Capstick's didn't. 'Well, well, well!' Rossiter quirked his lips. 'Better answer, yes? While it's still working.'

On his return his smile was a little more open. 'Just testing. Apparently your chaps in the local force reported the disconnection. Apparently it was easily rectified. Even at' – he looked at his watch – 'forty minutes past the witching hour.'

Capstick stood. 'How long did you say Mrs Brooke will be staying, sir?'

'Didn't. Couldn't. Don't know. Chief Superintendent, you're

a tallish chap. Would you mind . . .' He indicated the ruined portrait. With notable reluctance Capstick crossed to lift it down.

'Thank you.' Rossiter folded it in a gentle embrace, what was left of it facing Capstick. 'If it were anyone but the Holdens one would be inclined to think it deliberate. But such subtlety from Lily Holden's hard men? Are you sure you won't have that drink?'

Capstick seemed to be hypnotised by the painting. 'Kind of you, but we all have our beds to get to. I'll see myself out, sir.'

Rossiter ambled after him, still holding the ruined portrait. 'You'll be at the press conference?'

'Sir?'

'Oh dear, didn't I say? Only one way to stop these media vultures making a nuisance of themselves. Press conference up in town. Connaught Rooms, somewhere like that. Umpteen birds with one stone.'

'Can't call a press conference on this, sir. Pure dynamite, that's why it's D'd. You so much as pick up that phone and they'd – '

He stopped. Rossiter was smiling. 'Have me reconnected, get "A" branch to wire me up for the listeners at the same time, yes? If this poor little Pobble so much as tinkly-binkly-winkles a bell it'll be more than his toes he'll lose. And if it was that easy to do, who but your South London mob disconnected me in the first place?'

'Not ours, sir. We – ' Capstick all but bit off his tongue.

'Of course, as you said, all these shots through unoffending windows are a matter for the local force. Nothing to do with you. Or your masters. Or South London or wherever.

'But the press simply adores shots, dear old chap, even when they don't hit anyone. No question of D-notices, since they've nothing to do with Nethercott. So long as we steer clear of areas covered by the Official Secrets Act, the Contempt of Court Act, the Police and Criminal Evidence Act, the Public – '

Capstick was finally galvanised. 'Put that girl in front of the press and they'll winkle out every last little – '

'Not to worry, Chief Superintendent. A total *démenti*, you have my word. She'll deny all knowledge of anything rumoured to be missing from Nethercott Stoney. Total ignorance of any link between her husband's arrest and his alleged dealings with a Tass representative. Sheer coincidence that she's twice been shot at since. And so on; itemised and categorical denial. Mrs Brooke is a very intelligent young woman.'

Elly's portrait still prominent, he all but patted Capstick. 'As I'm sure your Mr Norton-Jones already knows, though I suspect he's being less than frank with you.'

This time he was unable to delay Capstick's departure: a great slamming of doors, muffled snarls at members of the local force, a use of horsepower that played havoc with Rossiter's dilapidated drive.

Sarah knew at once that something was wrong. A different doctor, plainly disconcerted to find her there at all. She took a grip on herself; any loss of self-control and he would find some specious reason for getting rid of a potentially hysterical woman.

'How is he? Is he much worse?'

Young, rosy, with a floppy lock of hair, he reminded her of the White Rabbit. 'Well, we can't exactly say no to that question, Mrs Brooke. At the same time – '

'Just tell me, please. Worrying's worse than knowing.'

'He's basically fit.' Talking across her, anxious to get to some point or other. 'I mean he was, before the accident. But – '

'Is it pneumonia? Or something else?'

He made up his mind. 'Pneumonia, but our main worry now is that there's an infection in the blood stream. We've changed the antibiotics and we've done some cultures to see what shows up, but we haven't got on top of the septicaemia and the kidneys are giving us problems.'

'Not your problems,' she wanted to say. 'Nick's problems. My problems,' but he was rattling out uninterruptible technicalities in an attempt to smother bad news. Fever. High white blood cell count. Low blood pressure and septicaemic shock. The phrases rolled over her, a rising tide of threat.

Lungs . . . bowels . . . kidneys. She listened while he went round and round a central fact that both were unwilling to hear spelled out. Nick was a cause for concern.

She was taken to see him, little more, now, than an inert assemblage of parts driven and drained by pumps, tubes and electrical circuits. The White Rabbit talked in a voice that seemed much too loud: the white blood cells again, renal failure, the need to stimulate the heart to keep up a head of steam.

She could have a bed for the night as it was late, though things would probably be much the same in the morning. He still seemed to be surprised that she had come, but Dr Quilter had gone off early.

A small cubicle not even in the same wing as the intensive care unit. A dressing gown so that she could take off her outer clothing and lie on the stiff white bed. A little nurse the colour of polished mahogany brought her hot chocolate, kind words and smiles that made her want to cry. Before she could sip any chocolate, remove any clothes, a single brisk tap at the door.

'Mrs Brooke. Good evening. Time to talk. Let's begin with the spade.' Norton-Jones came in without waiting to be asked.

In the morning, the telephone still working, Rossiter rang the hospital again. No, they didn't know Mrs Brooke's present whereabouts, but he could leave a message. Mr Brooke was as well as could be expected. He left no message, nothing he dare tell her until she was back.

He fed Sam, ate two pieces of burnt toast, scalded his mouth with black coffee, no *grande fine*, went yet again to look at the place where the portrait had hung. He sighed, kissed his fingers to the ghost, went out for logs, thinking about the spade.

The snow, trampled in places by many large boots, was thawing. Through gaps among dripping rhododendrons he caught a glimpse of metal. One police car, full of water vapour and fug, two hunched and bulky figures dimly seen. A window descended at his approach.

'Morning, sir. Everything all right?'

He contemplated them. 'Bastards!'

'Sir?'

'People who discharge lethal weapons through the windows of premises to which they have no legal claim.'

The two traded the looks for which policemen are specially trained. The driver edged up the peak of his hat. 'Anything we can do for you, sir?'

'Some chap in Vincent Lane,' Rossiter said vaguely. 'A bit draughty, do you see?' The look was exchanged again like a game of Pass the Parcel. 'Imperial Caesar dead and turned to clay would serve as well to keep the wind away, but a sheet of glass would be easier to come by.'

He stopped. A growing *whop-whop-whop* and over the tree-tops came a helicopter, its racket preventing all further attempts at conversation. Passing above, the *whop* changing to an ear-drilling roar, it vanished only to reappear. The hatch on the nearside had been slid back. Someone muffled like a plastic Eskimo raked them with a shoulder-held video camera. The two policemen were both getting out.

'Cheeky bugger!' The driver pulled up his collar against the freezing downdraught, tracking the chopper with a gorgon stare. 'Bloody media git!'

His mate reached to grab the microphone, bawling inaudibly as the thing above them returned to hover. The driver took Rossiter by the arm. 'Get in the car, sir. Don't have to put up with that kind of cheek.'

Rossiter freed himself. The machine dropped lower. Icy air cataracted. Melting snow flew from the trees like machine-gun fire.

'Shit!' The driver gave up, flinging himself into the car. Soaked and incredulous, Rossiter watched while someone very bulky levered himself through the hatch to jump, camera held high, on to grass swept clear of slush by the cruel downdraught. Running clear of the blades he laughed, holding his arms wide.

'Hey! Hey, ratbag! How're you doing there?'

'Good God, Elly,' Rossiter said, teeth chattering. 'Fasten your chastity belt, old girl. It's Dickie Wise.'

Wise was a big man, with plump, red cheeks that shone as if painted with lip gloss. Black hair and a heavy tan helped him to cheat the years. Dumping his gear and stripping himself of windproof coveralls, he watched Rossiter change out of soaked clothes.

'What do you mean, you thought you'd drop by?' Rossiter demanded. 'And where did you get that offensive tan? It looks as out of place as warpaint.'

'This climate,' Wise said in his booming voice, 'would make penguins look out of place.' He radiated crude energy like a not too dormant volcano. 'The tan comes from twenty minutes a day under something that looks like it moonlights hardening off paint jobs on automobiles. You could use one, old buddy. And dropping by means dropping by, just like the old days when Charlie had you pinned down.'

'Charlie?' Rossiter towelled his thin hair. 'You mean Plod. The fuzz, in your barbarous tongue. Come and have something to provide your vulgar excess of red blood corpuscles with a modicum of excitement.'

'Now you're talking. Elly always said you were the only guy she knew that couldn't say yes without making a speech.' For all his weight he walked rangily, a bar room brawler retired but not reformed.

Downstairs, he lowered himself into a chair, missing the scar where Elly Rossiter's portrait had hung. Rossiter went to his store. 'The bottle? Or have you learned to use a glass?'

'Up yours, ratbag.' They both drank, sighed, sat in a silence of anticipation and alcohol at work.

'So,' Wise said finally. 'What's the cause of the week?'

'Peace on earth. Good will toward men.'

'Been tried. Didn't work. They tell me you're back in trouble.'

'They?'

'Folk. You know? People with their ear to the ground.'

'Dear old boy,' Rossiter said, 'how would I know which people? How would I know which ground?'

Wise let his stare drift away to the window, one pane crudely replaced by cardboard, and the black-and-white panorama that lay icily still beyond.

'Colder than Nam. Hey, Hugh, remember?'

'How do you forget?'

'That LZ near Happy Valley? That was one hot LZ.' Without warning, he burst into a tuneless baritone.

> *'He stood on the steeple*
> *And pissed on the people*
> *But the people couldn't*
> *Piss on him.'*
> *Amen.*

'Your voice,' Rossiter said, 'has not improved with time. Nor your repertoire.'

'Company song of the guys who flew us out of Ia Drang, remember?'

'Is that why you came? A singing messenger?'

Wise ignored the question. 'Yup, hot as the handles of Hades, Ia Drang. Hotter than Inchon, right? A whole heap hotter than Wonsan and Iwon. Though maybe not as hot, temperaturewise, as – '

'Did you come here to reminisce, or will you wait for the book?'

'The book? Oh, sure, your memoirs, yeah, I heard.' He rolled his liquor around his mouth. 'Sure, sure, sure. Well you just put me down for a copy, hear?'

'If I ever finish it.' Dick Wise had to be the first to show his hand if it took for ever.

'Hugh Rossiter fail to file his copy? That'll be the day.'

Rossiter took his brandy to the window. From a naked beech a crow gave its rasping cry before floating silently down to the slushy lawn. He said, 'Crow knows what.'

'Crow what? About what?'

'About memoirs. It's a poem. About me. I shall recite.'

'Oh no! You didn't grow out of that yet?'

'*So he just went and ate what he could,*' Rossiter recited, '*And did what he could And grabbed what he could And saw what he could Then sat down to write his autobiography.*'

'Godammit, Hugh!'

But somehow his arms were just bits of stick
Somehow his guts were an old watch-chain
Somehow his feet were two old postcards
Somehow his head was a broken windowpane.
'I give up,' he said. He gave up.
Creation failed again.

He turned his back on the window. 'Good stuff. They made him Poet Laureate. That fixed him.'

Wise surrendered. 'What's this crap I hear? Hugh Rossiter, buying exclusives for cash?'

'News travels fast. Did they tell you how much I paid?'

'You with your watch-chain guts and postcard feet! Are you sure what you maybe paid wasn't just on account, ratbag? Can you take your bible oath no one is fixing to settle that account without telling you?' He no longer looked jolly.

'When people drop in on me for a visit, I like them to come through the gate, Dick. Not courtesy of Air Cav.'

'Air Cav,' Wise said, 'that was not. The Cav would have dropped me from the treetops.'

'Who were they?'

'Oh.' Wise looked blank. 'Guys. Just guys. Like' – he fished in a pocket – 'maybe I'm carrying a press card.' He slid it back.

'You filed a lot of reports from a lot of places. I never saw any of them in print. And you left your camera in the hall.'

'Are you kidding? I don't even know how to use that thing. What brought me? Would you believe friendship? I often think of those nights. You, me and Elly.'

He saw pain flit across Rossiter's face. 'Hey, Hugh, I'm sorry. I think of Elly too, right back to when I first met her and she looked exactly like her picture and I would have stolen her if – '

He followed Rossiter's gaze to the wall immediately above him. 'Oh Jesus!' He got up, stiff-armed. 'They did that?'

'Didn't just happen, dear boy. And no, I wouldn't believe friendship, not that alone.'

'I can take the heat off,' Wise said abruptly. 'Hear me, ratbag? I can cool this whole thing. Where's the girl?'

At the Dorking junction, shortcutting towards the Guildford road, she watched her rear-view mirror. The other car also turned into the road to Westcott, where the double line of willows always provided the first green of spring. Up on Ranmore snow still streaked the slopes.

The other car had dropped behind a red coupé positioned to overtake her on the first clear stretch. She too pulled to the centre. It earned her a peremptory blast; how dare a mere woman challenge the genetic horsepower of the highpowered male? Don't care: anything to keep the car that had been following her all the way from Redhill a little further back.

The road into Westcott was clear. The sports car drew level. It was old, struggling; driven not by a man but a young girl with flying hair. Sarah let her go as they came into the village. Her pursuer closed the gap.

In her mind Norton-Jones had never stopped talking, that doubt-free monologue, crisply coercive.

'Why did your husband hire a car, Mrs Brooke? Why did he put the spade in the back?'

Another quick check in the rear mirror. Hamlet? *Look, where it comes again!* But no, it wasn't Detective Sergeant Hamlet and he neither came nor went; always the same distance behind.

'The spade was there when Capstick's men searched his own car in the station car-park, Mrs Brooke. Why did he switch it to a hired car? And his camera and torch.'

Smiling contempt in a small, bare room with a narrow bed and

213

a cup of chocolate going cold. A trick, endlessly repetitive, of massaging his right thumb with the first and second fingers, his hawk nose tilted up.

The steep hill towards Wotton, valley below, hills across, the White Downs truly white. A choice of narrow, winding lanes. Turn off to Leith Hill? The man behind would have to show his hand.

She didn't want him to show his hand. The thought made her afraid. On to Abinger Hammer, big truck ahead, spray on her windscreen. She wished Heather were with her. Why Heather? Why not Nick?

'What did he tell you, Mrs Brooke? A big story? The chance of a lifetime? Then why didn't he offer it to the *Globe*? Why Glashin? And why did Glashin send you flowers?' A zealot's face, if zealots always smiled.

Steep hill again, this one a tricky one, always a chance of ice in winter. The truck dropped a gear, growling. A loose rope, mindlessly sadistic, flogged its tarpaulined load. The man behind her an effigy, unidentifiable.

'We know a great deal about you, Mrs Brooke. We make it our business to know a great deal about people like you. Politics. Prejudices. Pressure points. You're well endowed with weaknesses, Mrs Brooke. Most women are. Most women make a virtue of them. Do you perhaps enjoy being dominated? Did your husband dominate you? Or was he too weak? What in particular – or should one say who? – have you been finding exciting of late?'

He had lost her on that one, though she had found it inexplicably repellent. But then, she found Norton-Jones repellent too.

The road to Abinger, left. The steep climb to Ranmore, right.

Look, mummy, it's raining golden pennies where the sun shines through. Green smoke in the spring, bronze fires in the autumn, the beechwoods black now against the snow.

'We have been tolerant so far, Mrs Brooke. We have every right to move your husband elsewhere. It would raise problems, of course, in his present condition, but the individual must take second place to the wellbeing of the majority, the wellbeing of the state.'

The silence of the night: the silence of the recuperant, the sick, the dying. A bellpush over that white, clenched hospital bed, press for succour. She had never moved, never once spoken. He had never ceased to massage his thumb.

'You are in a position to help us, Mrs Brooke. If you do, it may be that things could be – shall we say? – hushed up. Certain guarantees in return for certain information? Otherwise . . .'

The Hammer junction, left for Horsham, left for home. A gleam of sunlight, a ghostly wink of silver among the watercress beds.

Left. Only she couldn't go home. Home was out of bounds.

'Security must take priority over humanitarian principles, Mrs Brooke. Without security, principles are a luxury. Us or them. It always comes down to that in the end.'

Left anyway.

'You can talk. Or your husband can be pressed to talk. You do see what that would mean? Moved elsewhere. A degree of . . . stress.'

No more massaging; thumb squeezed between fingers as if he had trapped a living creature.

All she had said, had gone on saying, was, 'I know nothing. Nothing at all, Penelope.'

Only she hadn't actually said Penelope, hadn't actually said anything. The little black nurse, back for a final word, had smiled uncomprehendingly at Norton-Jones. He had smiled back, that permanent, unchangeably disbelieving smile. He had returned it to Sarah, murmured some meaningless civility, left.

She looked for her present pursuer. Gone. Nothing in the rear-view mirror but the wet, slush-bordered road unwinding in reverse.

'You can take the heat off?'

Wise looked his age now: over the hill. He leaned forward urgently. 'No more fooling, friend of my youth. You don't know what you just got yourself tangled in.'

'I have lived this long and seen what I have seen,' Rossiter asked mildly, 'to be accused of innocence?'

'Ignorance, old buddy. That and this cute trick you have of thinking you can walk through shit and come out squeaky clean.'

'Do I detect a Trojan horse?'

'Old friend of Hugh Rossiter, plus a situation that has certain folk back there in Washington popping like corn in a hot skillet.'

'A situation? Or a story?'

Wise made a cloacal sound. 'Situation, story, don't touch it, it's poison. Stay with it and you're a special operation, you and the girl both. Meaning like the special operations they ran back in Nam.'

'That's all you're going to tell me?'

Wise looked at the eyepatched window, the brutalised wall above the fireplace. 'Going to tell you to lay off. Got to trust me, Hugh.'

The telephone: intimacy collapsing like a soufflé in a draught. Rossiter smiled apologetically and went to take it.

A brusque voice. 'Hugh? Bernard Smith. I'm trying to track Heather down. Is she by any chance with you?'

'She was here last night,' Rossiter told her father. 'Haven't seen her since then.'

'You're a valued client, Hugh, but this Brooke business . . . Press! Radio! TV! Well, not my job to advise you unasked.'

'Good of you.'

'Look, I'm taking Heather off. Gunshots! Gangsters! She's too young. Too inexperienced. I'll make proper arrangements, of course. One of the senior partners will take over. Sorry to add to your problems but if she should happen – '

'I'm not expecting her,' Rossiter said, 'but if she makes contact I'll tell her you called.' He wondered where she and Sarah had got to since the previous evening. He could do nothing while Dick Wise was there.

He went back to Wise. 'Not planning to stay?'

Wise was struggling into his coveralls. 'Said what they wanted me to say. The rest is up to you.'

'What if Plod asks questions?'

Wise hoisted the last zip. 'You get it from her. You give it to me. I give it to them and' – he snapped his fingers – '*finito*. Okay?'

He grabbed, and brought his mouth close to Rossiter's ear.

'We lost it. We want it back. The Brits get it first, they hand it over, but not before they peek. We wouldn't want them to peek. Bad for everybody concerned. I mean everybody. I mean bad.'

'And if I tell you she hasn't got it?'

Wise released him from the bearhug. 'Don't hear you, Hugh. Already told you more than I should.'

He collected the video camera, took a last look at the savaged wall. 'Nobody blasted *your* head from your shoulders yet. Let's keep it that way. Elly would thank me.'

'Is that thing coming back for you?'

'That thing' – Wise shouldered his gear – 'has done its stuff. There'll be a cab out there.'

'What if Plod asks questions?'

Wise waved his press card. 'On the way out? What can they do? Just the fact I came is going to give more important people than the fuzz a whole bunch of worry.'

'Because you're press?'

'Because I'm American.'

'You carried a press card in Vietnam. It takes more than a card and an insatiable appetite for alcohol to make you a genuine hack.'

'I carry cards the way you carry the cares of the world. Time you let someone else shoulder the load.'

Rossiter followed him out. From the tree near the house the crow called, a pessimistic sound. Wise pulled up a hood against drips.

'Us on one side, them on the other, you're between a rock and a hard place, old buddy. Okay, you've always been tougher than you look, but girls? Soft and squashy, right? I'll be back, so be sure to have it.'

He trudged toward the gate.

She had steeled herself to accept the fact that press and police would be back in force but a solitary car waited at the entrance to the drive. It had followed her all the way from Redhill, to vanish somewhere near the Abinger junction. As she slowed instinctively, it drove off, not slow, not fast; over the hill to Ewhurst.

Rossiter was out instantly. 'How is he?'

'Not so good. Some kind of blood infection that seems to be causing problems.' She tried not to show her worry: so many worries, with that one the worst. She must not give way. Nick would pull through.

'But he's going to be all right?'

'Dr Quilter thinks so. Unless they move him. Quilter says not bloody likely.'

'You look all in.'

'When the hospital rang, did they say it was Quilter?'

'I don't remember. I suppose I thought so.'

'They don't seem to know exactly who it was.' A crow cawed. She shivered.

'Come inside.'

She slid out. 'Norton-Jones was there. And I was followed home. Don't ask me who by. He's gone now.' She held out his car keys.

'Hang on to them for the time being.' He steered her toward the house. 'I don't want you having to ask, if there's another – '

'Emergency?'

'Life's one long emergency, dear girl. We just have the trick of forgetting it until it becomes pressing. Are you saying it was Norton-Jones I spoke to last night?'

'Don't know. What's the difference?' She saw the two glasses. 'You've had company.'

'All kinds of people here since you left. Would you . . .?' He indicated the brandy.

She shook her head. 'The universal solvent. Only it doesn't, does it? Solve anything.'

'Did Norton-Jones bring up the spade?'

That startled her.

'Last night, just before you left,' he said, 'you remembered about a spade. No time to tell me, but I made a sort of guess.'

'He always has a spade in the car in the winter. And grit and stuff, in case he gets snowed up or whatever.'

'And Norton-Jones knew.'

'Norton-Jones knew. And he knew Nick had switched the spade over to the hire car on the night he piled it up. A car he hired to reduce the risk of being identified. What he didn't know is that Nick had used the spade while he was on the Nethercott Stoney thing. Nick said it was because his photographer got bogged down.'

'Not difficult, is it, dear girl?'

She shook her head, crouched to the fire. 'He buried something after Nethercott. And on the night he drove into the bridge he'd been to dig it up. No! They'd have found it. So he was on his way to dig it up.'

'On the M25?'

'He'd been chased.' She looked at him hopelessly. 'We don't know where from. Or for how long.'

'Or who was doing the chasing. I'm inclined to believe Capstick when he says it wasn't the police.'

He pulled a face. 'M25! Orbital, serves the entire London region. He could have been going almost anywhere. So it could be buried almost anywhere. Only it wasn't.'

'Norton-Jones offered me a deal, tell him where it is and they'll – '

'Take the heat off?' She had never seen him look so – what? – bleak? 'No more shots through windows, that sort of thing.'

'You really think. . .?'

'You can bet on it. They only do it to annoy, because they know it teases. Capstick knows; has a good idea anyway.'

'And the man who followed me?'

'All part of the heat. You really don't know where it is?'

'I wish you'd stop saying that. I don't know where it is.'

'Well, there you are,' he said.

'I think I ought to talk to Heather.'

'She'd left before you saw Norton-Jones, obviously.'

'Left? Where?'

'She brought your things then set off after you to Redhill. Could well have changed her mind, though. A couple of *Globe* types had been trailing her, Liz somebody and a hairy lump called – '

' – Roger Petherbridge. I'll call her now.'

Not the time to tell her that Heather wasn't her lawyer any more. 'She isn't in yet. Give it an hour. She's – ' He stopped. Something was coming, a cornflakes crunch of gravel. It proved to be a van.

'Damn,' Sarah said. 'I half-hoped it might be her.'

'A chap from the town.' Rossiter had recognised the van. 'Come to fix the window. We'll retire to the kitchen.'

Young and perky, the glazier concentrated on Sarah. 'You the one being shot at then? Why they doing it, you reckon?'

'Nobody told them it's the close season,' Rossiter said.

'Townies, betcha. Same with the deer, innit? Come out here and knock 'em off for the freezer, ruddy South Londoners, innit?'

He was still interested in Sarah. 'Done your other window, didn't I? Old Mr Crabtree asked for me personal, send that Wayne Cooper he told the gaffer, known me since I was a kid, see? Big job, that, had to measure up and go back. Do this 'un out of the van, though them small panes is tricky, mind.' He started measuring the window.

In the kitchen, the chatty Wayne back at his van to cut glass, Rossiter said, 'Cheer up, dear girl. All shall be well and all manner of thing shall be well.' Sam appeared, tail undulating, settling to eat as if tomorrow would not be another day. In the next room Wayne was doing something with a hammer, tappety-tap.

'Had it occurred to you,' Rossiter said. 'So' – he waggled his fingers – 'indeterminate. All heavy threats, no action. I speak, of course, of Norton-Jones.' She realised he had been making holes in the brandy.

Wayne appeared. 'Got a pan and brush, have you?'

'Try the cupboard in the corner, dear boy.'

'My mate Bob Tucker,' Wayne said, 'he saw it, reckoned it was a Westland but he don't know one from another.'

'A helicopter?' Sarah said when at last Wayne went. 'Here?'

'Another visitor. Yankee, my old friend, Dick Wise, known him – Lord, Lord, doesn't bear thinking about!' He reached for his brandy.

'Wise! Does he have a red face?'

Rossiter rapped his brow with his knuckles. 'I'm past it. Red as a shiny apple.'

'What is he?'

'He has friends,' Rossiter said, 'who live in holes not far from Washington, DC.'

'And he came here? In a helicopter?'

He topped up his glass then reached to take her hand.

'They,' he said, 'Norton-Jones's they, would like you to help them find what Nick took. For the nice Americans. But friend Dick Wise, who's also part of a "they", says they'd rather find it themselves, thank you kindly. With your help.'

Articulation exaggerated by alcohol, every word stiff as a guardsman, he said, 'Dick said you were between a rock and a hard place. And that girls were soft and squashy. Melodramatic chaps, these Americans.'

'This isn't happening to me,' she said. 'This absolutely isn't happening to me.' A brittle rage. 'I don't *know* where the bloody thing is.'

'Oh, but you do. Out there.' He swept an arm, almost knocking over his glass. 'Hundreds of acres of wild heath and woodland. Somewhere out there.'

Wayne took that moment to say he had finished. She said

nothing until they had watched his van head for civilisation and sanity.

'Yes,' she said then. 'I'd guessed. Now you know too. Doesn't help, does it? Somewhere out there.'

The sunlight glimpsed on the way back from Redhill had returned. Pale lemon streamers stretched between the trees. She had a sudden longing.

'I'm going for a walk. Not far, just to get away for a bit.'

'Dearest girl,' he began and she broke briefly, slamming the table.

'Don't try to stop me, or I may decide not to come back. A home down there. A daughter in Wells. A husband in Redhill. I had a life once.'

'You'll have a life again.'

She looked at him. If anyone was soft and squashy! She was sick of all of them. Capstick. Norton-Jones. Him.

'Men! Bloody men! I'm sorry, madam, but if you don't like it you'll bloody well have to lump it. Think it over, madam, we know a lot about you. Strong points. Weak points. Your weakest point, madam, is that you're a woman.'

Stop it. This is what they want. This is what they're trying to do. But she had taken her finger out of the crack in the dyke.

'I mean it's well known, isn't it? Women aren't just the weaker sex. They love it. Men on top! The more you hurt us the better we like it. Every woman her own masochist because nobody but a bloody masochist would put up with a woman's life. Babies and a home as well as a job, or running a home and a family and being told you're lucky you don't have to go out to work.

'Coping with men like babies with muscle and gripes and bloody foul tempers. Sacrificing yourself for them and loving it, because that's the way women are made. If you don't get your kicks out of being kicked and loving it you're either a bloody freak or a lesbie.'

Far beyond what was permissible, as she saw by his face, but it was jammed up inside; had to come out or she would throw the biggest all-singing, all-dancing wobbly since time began.

'My dearest girl,' he said mildly.

'*Your* dearest girl! Dearest *girl*! Where would *we* get if we went around saying "My dearest boy"? Patronising bitch! Or you're asking for it. I mean, if you don't look like the back of a bus you're asking for it anyway. All women are really, aren't they?'

He would say: 'There. Feeling better now?' She would apologise.

He said, 'You sound just like Elly.' Before she could speak, a rapidly growing *whop-whop-whop* that, syllable by syllable, spelled helicopter.

Rossiter pushed his chair back. 'If this is my old buddy again, I don't want him to see you. Would you care to go and unpack?'

She left, not in obedience but because the game and the rules of the game were changing again and she needed time to think. The only thing she knew was that she would not go on as she had gone on up to now.

Behind her, Rossiter said, 'False alarm.'

Not any old helicopter: POLICE. On the nearside, just above the skids, a large ball-shaped object that rotated, staring like the eye of some huge insect.

'Coppers,' Rossiter said. 'Could this, one wonders, be our noble Chief Superintendent like the dove descending?'

The racket increased. The rotors blurred. It swung away over the surrounding trees.

'I'm going home.' She had reached a decision at last.

'Isn't that a little unwise?'

'Don't know anything about wise. Never have. Why did you say I sounded just like your wife?'

He pulled his wry face. 'When I asked her to marry me she said she'd better things to do than cater to my Oedipus complex.'

'She changed her mind. Women do. Part of our stupid nature.'

'Change yours. 'Twixt a rock and a hard place there's no hiding.'

'According to Norton-Jones I'll enjoy that. Fulfilling my natural function. He seemed to have the same sort of idea about Heather, hurt one, hurt both. I'll call her as soon as I'm back.'

'What did he say? About Heather?' From pickled and vague he had become pickled and intent.

'I just got the idea he thinks threatening Heather's the same as threatening me.' Another vehicle coming up the drive. She yelped. 'Bloody Capstick! No difference, I'm not staying.'

Capstick came in thunderously and without ceremony, Detective Sergeant Hamlet behind. 'Mrs Brooke, I'm going to ask you to come with me. It'll be easier all round if you behave sensibly.'

She was stunned. 'What for? I've done nothing.'

Rossiter confronted him, swaying very slightly. 'Are you arresting Mrs Brooke? If so, kindly state the charge. I also insist that Mrs Brooke's solicitor is informed before she leaves this house.' The fact of his drinking was plain in his speech.

Capstick showed the semi-savage patience of a man whose task is being hampered by the yapping of a small dog.

'Nothing'd make me happier than to let you talk to Mrs Brooke's solicitor, sir. Only Mrs Brooke's solicitor happens to be dead. What matters to me at the moment is making sure the same thing doesn't happen to Mrs Brooke.'

Two plainclothes men had stayed with the car. From time to time unintelligible bursts from its radio reached them. Shortly after Capstick had tossed his stun grenade the police helicopter clattered by once more.

'Area search,' Capstick said. 'Waste of time,' and then, 'Be sensible, madam. I could take you in, refusal to help a police officer in pursuit of his enquiries. I'd prefer something more civilised.'

Rossiter had suffered a hammer blow but now his feelings were for Sarah. 'Since you've told us practically nothing, you can hardly expect her to see things your way.'

'Miss Smith was murdered, sir. I'd have thought that was enough to be going on with.'

'Isn't murder a matter for the local force?'

Capstick wanted action, not talk. 'Miss Smith was mixed up in things a bit above her head. We can't afford to ignore that.'

'Not the Holden gang again?'

'Birmingham CID's picked up some of the Holden lot, sir. They'll not be troubling you again. This is something else. My superiors – ' He veered ambiguously. 'Things tend to move up.'

Sarah spoke for the first time. 'I want to see.'

Hamlet, making small, silent movements with the toe of his shoe, stopped as if in a game of Statues.

Capstick said, 'See who, Mrs Brooke?'

'Heather.'

Rossiter started to say something. Capstick stopped him, a jerk of the hand. 'She's dead, madam.'

'I want to see her.'

'Meant a lot to you, did she, madam?'

223

Rossiter stirred, taut awareness.

'Yes,' she said, a high dangerous voice. 'She did. I want to go there.'

'They'll have removed her by now, madam.' Capstick was the more disturbed, Rossiter thought, though he had the tighter grip.

She raced through his pause like a cat through a gap in traffic. 'Where from?'

'She was found' – behind him, Hamlet produced a notebook, licked his thumb, pushed back the pages – 'roughly halfway between here and – '

'The Leith Hill road, sir,' Hamlet said.

' – on what I gather is called the Leith Hill road. That's – '

'I know where it is,' she said. 'Better than you.'

Again he ignored the interruption. 'Just outside a village called' – Hamlet turned a page but kept his silence – 'Abinger Common. There's an old well – '

'St James's Well.'

' – at a road junction, more or less opposite the entrance to a clearing. It seems there are some old World War Two camp sites in the woods, just the old footings, all overgrown.'

Her pallor was deathlike.

'That's where she was found. Her bike caught someone's eye, taking the dog for a walk. She'd put up a hell of a fight. Strong girl, I expect you knew that, Mrs Brooke.'

'No!' she said violently, contradicting not him but the event. Rossiter reached to touch her. Equally violently she shook him off.

Rossiter said, 'Had she been . . .?'

'Can't say, sir. Up to forensic. I'm sorry, Mrs Brooke. Sooner not have told you just now.'

An inward struggle before he said, 'Don't pretend to understand these things, madam, a married woman like you, but I accept it must be – '

'Don't!' Rossiter's turn for violence, but he was too late.

She said, 'What's being married got to do with it?'

Capstick made the mistake of trying to retreat.

'Look, madam, your feelings for Miss Smith are your own affair. My only concern is to give you protection.'

'What's being married got to do with it?'

'Misunderstood me, madam,' Capstick said quickly. 'Where are Mrs Brooke's personal effects, sir?'

She turned on Rossiter. 'Is that what you meant when you said Quilter wasn't my only devoted admirer?'

He looked at Capstick. 'Let me talk to her a minute.'

Capstick folded his lips, nodded, went to join Hamlet. A burst of garbled speech from the police car hacked into the silence.

'Fell in love with you,' Rossiter said. Capstick's news had marked his face cruelly. 'It happens. You're not a girl, isn't that what you told me? Not innocent. She was happy just to be helping. She knew it would never . . .'

He had a blind stare. 'How did Byron put it? Love without his wings.'

She raised her voice. 'I'll get my things.'

Capstick came back. 'Very wise, madam.'

'One thing,' she said. 'Who am I being protected from?'

Capstick puckered his lips, a man about to whistle and hesitating over a choice of tune. 'Who sent you flowers, Mrs Brooke? Who sent the photograph?'

Rossiter's eyebrow was still game. 'Glashin? Balls, Chief Superintendent.'

'Not Glashin personally, sir. Don't act on their own, do they?'

'KGB?' Rossiter's eyebrow reached a new limit.

'Quick as you can, please, madam,' Capstick said, unhappy about more things than one.

Rossiter said, 'Don't leave anything that matters, Sarah. Check the drawers.'

She was in shock, body on automatic pilot, but she went straight to the drawers. An envelope with her name on it; a London address and telephone number, two keys. Rossiter had anticipated an emergency.

When Heather had talked about him on their ride over the hill tracks she had mentioned that Rossiter had a pad up in town. *He's the only man I really care for. What do you make of that, Sarah Brooke?*

She whimpered under her breath.

A motorbike was not equipped for carrying heavy luggage. One small case, an overnight shoulder bag. She changed into trousers, sweater, sensible shoes. Coat, woolly hat, a modest change of clothes in the shoulder bag. From the window she could see the two men leaning against the police car. She tiptoed to the head of the stairs.

Ominous silence. At any moment Capstick might send Hamlet

to find out what was going on. She went back, flushed the lavatory. To her keyed-up senses the sound was thunderous. All in a swoop; down the stairs, along the passage to a door that opened on a terrace at the rear of the house. At the far end of the corridor she heard Capstick's voice, alarmingly loud.

She was out, the door eased shut behind her.

Shrubbery and fencing below the terrace, the police car hidden on the far side of the house, the land dropping sharply away through scrub and woodland.

Over a rotting fence, an ancient wheelbarrow as a stepping stone; into quick cover among the trees. One advantage, she knew the hill; which path would take her down to Holmbury or Peaslake, which dropped southward to the high-hedged lanes of Ewhurst, Cranleigh, Forest Green.

She would have to be careful, have to look out for –

It stopped her head in her tracks, Nick's painful efforts to speak audible at last. *Look out.*

The lookout tree.

The hill had been a natural place for Nick to come, the vicinity of the lookout tree a natural place to choose. The little hollow where they had picnicked so often, not ten minutes' walk from where she stood.

No time now. No spade. Capstick must have discovered her absence. What would he do? Warn that damned helicopter, warn the local force – you found yourself dropping into their terminology, those bloody coppers – that she was on the loose. Report to his superiors.

'Things tend to move up,' he had said, suppressed anger rather than resignation. Or something more than either?

The fact that his own powers were limited? Things not so much tending to move up as being plucked from his hands? Norton-Jones?

Why her gut feeling that Capstick's dislike of Norton-Jones almost equalled her own? That it had gone beyond dislike, that Capstick, outwardly calm and matter-of-fact, was being inwardly shredded by something impossibly beyond his control?

They want to find it for the Yanks, Rossiter had said, but the Yanks would rather they didn't.

Two secret forces, outwardly with a common purpose, that in this case were pitted one against the other, God help anything that happened to get in the way. Heather, on her way from

Rossiter's house to Redhill late on a winter evening, had got in the way.

She found herself on her knees, tilting toward wet, frost-scythed bracken, crusty remnants of snow. Blackness, nausea, a kind of drowning. She looked up in time to see terror stand up and lift a hand in greeting.

Tall, wide-shouldered, a coiled spring tension. Warmly clad: combat green weatherproofs, brown leather boots strapped below the calves. A cagoule, the hood pulled around knitted headgear that covered all but a fraction of the face. Eyes bright, nose straight, lips full and red. Black gloves that called attention to his strangler's hands.

He had been lying in a small thicket of gorse and scrub oak. The glasses about his neck made it plain he had been watching the house. The whole of her snapshot taken on the ultra-short exposure of extreme fear.

He was perhaps fifteen feet away, the sun low behind him giving him a golden aura. 'Take it easy, ma'am, no cause to be scared.' Even in her fear she recognised the accent.

He covered most of the ground between them in four or five strides, high-stepping through the dead undergrowth. The red lips smiled. 'Let's talk, Mrs Brooke. This could be a lucky day for both of us.'

She was up faster than she would have thought possible, a little gasp of fear. Her shoulder bag slipped to the crook of her arm. She caught the strap, then, pure reflex, swung it clumsily at his head.

All it did was to make him duck. 'Whoa now! Easy, ma'am!' Not really taking her seriously, one hand thrust out to shield his face.

She grabbed his hand and pulled with the strength of fear, fighting for balance on the uneven ground. One of the few things she had learned during that not very effective year of lessons in self-defence.

It took him by surprise. As he stumbled forward she found herself going through the same drill she had practised with varying, never confident skill in the small upstairs room at that fusty-smelling church hall with the faded banner saying GOD IS LOVE. She lashed out with one sensible shoe.

Clumsy again, finding the cleft of hip and belly, a little above where she had aimed. He lost his balance completely, on his back with a crunch and crackle of dead vegetation.

Shock after shock. Helplessness. Endless intimidation. Now, at last, she had a solid target.

Half grunt, half yell, the small voice of savagery, she kicked again, all the strength she could summon. A high-pitched yelp, an oath subsumed in unsuppressible agony. Hands clutching his groin, teeth bared, he threshed like a man in a death agony.

She was running, hauling her bag behind her, stumbling, almost falling, her only thought to get away. It was some time before she realised that the only sound was her own agonised breathing, the thud of her feet on wet earth that smelled of the grave. Far below lay the Weald; white, black, green; afternoon light laying long brushstrokes of shadow.

Forget the lookout tree. What had been there this long could wait that much longer. A fierce, primitive satisfaction lent power to her legs, anaesthetised the stitch in her side. Target identified, attacked, disabled.

She took a gully path that would come out on the south side of the hill, the old Roman road that dropped down to Ewhurst. Might be traffic; she would have to take her chance.

Chance accepted the challenge. She reached the tarmac precisely as a car, the sound muffled by the high banks on either side, came round the corner, narrowly missing her before stopping with a squeal of brakes.

Old Mr Crabtree in his Land Rover, red-faced with cold winter air and rude health, already reaching across to open the door on her side.

'Now then, young Sarah. Hop in, gal. Just coming back from seein' that nephew of mine at Dunsfold. The ol' heap' – he thumped the steering wheel – 'gets the bit 'tween her teeth when she knows she's off home.'

He started up with a series of jerks and grinding gears, headed for Peaslake.

She said, 'I don't want to go home.'

They were in the heart of the woodland, the road single-track. He pulled off, cut the engine.

'Them ol' Morcambes, been havin' a right old field day, specially her. My Nell, she got so cross, can't hardly bear to meet her in the road. "Tattle-tattle-tattle," she says, "that's all that

woman can do, no thought for poor Sarah and Nick and the little
one." Where's it goin' to be, gal?'

'Not sure,' she said, Rossiter's foresight and the keys in her
pocket more or less dictating her next step.

Until moments ago she had been savouring the flavour of
victory. Not merely over her waylayer, over the whole bloody
pack of them in that secret, dictatorial and exclusively male
world. Now her feeling of triumph had all but vanished. She had
answered them in their own language, the language of violence.
It was a victory for them.

Patiently waiting for her answer, Charlie hissed to draw her
attention. On the far side of the road a patch of drab colour,
rusty against a dwindled bank of snow. Pricked ears, a glint of
sharp eyes, the vixen emerged to trot over the road, barely a
glance at the car.

'Thin pickin's,' he said, 'weather like this, but she keep her
cover, tend her business, leave everybody else to theirs.'

He looked at her. 'Haven't seen you, gal, if that's what's
frettin'. Me and Nell don't know much about things but we know
who we like. That's good enough for us.' He switched on again.
'Just you say where and we're off.'

PART FOUR

7

Once Capstick realised that Sarah had bolted it should have been the end of the party but for some reason, after sending Hamlet out to give instructions that produced a non-stop stream of radio messages, he came back alone.

'No idea where she might have gone, sir.' It wasn't even a question.

Rossiter shook his head, torn agonisingly between Sarah and Heather. 'Timbuctoo, for all I know. Good God, who could blame her?'

'Doesn't it worry you, sir? In the circumstances?'

'Of course it does! Damn it, man' – a laterally transferred anger – 'doesn't it worry *you*?' He must get away, must get to London, quickly.

'Wells or London,' Capstick said, half answering the question. 'Wells because the child's there. Or London because she lived there. Look, sir, so long as she's on her own she could be at risk.'

'Who from?'

'From her friends, sir, if they don't take her situation seriously.' Capstick was in no doubt that Rossiter had played some part in Sarah's disappearance. 'The press, if they happen to find her.'

No mention of Norton-Jones. That was an evasion. No, not an evasion; a deliberate omission. He needed a drink, Rossiter thought. And a way of escape.

'Bloody press get their hands on her,' Capstick said, 'her life won't be worth living.' Which worried him more, Sarah or the press?

'You seem to have done a good job of muzzling them up to now. Or are they clamouring' – Rossiter jerked a thumb – 'out there somewhere?'

'Ways and means, sir, you know that. Can't use a blanket injunction and Ds aren't mandatory, but sometimes, just some-times, we can lean on them for a day or two. If someone's at risk, for instance, and publicity might increase it.'

'Someone? Or something?'

Just for a moment he thought he might have lured Capstick. Not quite. 'Did Dr Quilter ask Mrs Brooke to go over to Redhill, sir?'

'I rather think it was your chap Norton-Jones.' Straight between the eyes, and a palpable hit.

A tap at the door heralded Hamlet. 'Message from Dorking, sir. Forensic says interference but not rape.'

Even as he closed his own eyes in relief, Rossiter heard the smallest of sighs from the policeman . . .

'Interference?' He needed to know. He needed a drink.

'Muddying the waters,' Capstick said, not quite under his breath, and insight told Rossiter he had never seriously believed it was rape. But Capstick was more worried than ever.

He looked up. 'What I said to Mrs Brooke about Miss Smith being lesbian. Shouldn't have said that, sir. Heat of the moment.'

'I've known Heather Smith a long time,' Rossiter said. 'She's – She was' – a careful search for the right words – 'a wholly admirable sort of woman. So is Mrs Brooke.'

'They'll track him down, sir. Nail the bastard. That side'll be sorted out.' Capstick was disassociating the Branch. From whom?

'You say "that side". Heather was Nick Brooke's lawyer. The press will make the connection, even if you don't. Can't lean on us for ever, Chief Superintendent. Truth will out.'

He'd done it now. A direct challenge.

'"Us", sir? You and the gutter press?'

'Once a press man, always a press man. That should tell you where I stand.'

'Where you always stood. Where Miss Smith stood too, fair and square behind the little girl, sir.' Capstick shook his head exasperatedly. 'The young woman. Mrs Brooke.'

Rossiter found an acid pleasure. 'Got at you too, did she?'

Capstick gave a grim bark. 'Perhaps I'm too old to catch on. Told my daughter about it. Now she won't be called girl any more, not by her own father who works with a bunch of grown men he calls lads.'

He checked the empty room. 'What's happened to Miss Smith' – his face briefly ferocious – 'has nothing to do with us.'

'Us?'

'The Branch, sir. Have to pull some naughty ones, I won't deny it. Some of the people we're supposed to protect the public from – terrorists, nutters, dedicated subversives – they're not very nice people either. Sometimes you have to get down to their level.'

Rossiter nodded noncommittally.

'But manslaughter,' Capstick said. 'Unlawful killing, call it what you like.' Rossiter held his breath.

Another perfunctory knock. Hamlet again, just as murder most foul had been downgraded to manslaughter.

'What the devil is it now?' Not the normal, patient Capstick.

'Sorry, sir.' Taking it stoically, Hamlet once more bent to mutter in Capstick's ear.

Capstick's expression changed and Rossiter knew that any further revelation had gone with this crowing of the cock. 'Wait, please, sergeant.' He looked at Rossiter with a very different expression.

'The Minister would like to see you, sir.'

'Dimmock?'

'Yes, sir.' Capstick was very formal now. 'As soon as possible. We're to provide you with a car, sir.'

Rossiter forgot about the need for a drink; time for that later. 'Why can't he ask me himself?'

'I couldn't say, sir. The message came through on the car radio.'

'More private?' Rossiter frowned. 'I'm not up in these things but I'd have thought it was the other way round.'

Whatever thoughts Capstick might be having he was not going to reveal them. 'Could you go now, sir?'

'I think I'll take myself, if you don't mind.' London was where he wanted to go anyway, but not with a police escort.

'A lot easier if we provide the car, Mr Rossiter. Or a driver.' Capstick looked pointedly at Rossiter's glass.

Rossiter's lips twisted. 'Murder's a remarkably sobering experience, Chief Superintendent.' He glanced at the wooden-faced Hamlet.

Capstick said, 'That'll be all, sergeant.'

Hamlet gone, Rossiter said, 'Or if not murder, unlawful killing. Don't fret. I'll drive carefully, and only to the station. I fancy he'll see me whenever I arrive, don't you?'

At the door he offered Capstick a token of friendship. 'The old boy net, is that what you're thinking? Sorry to shatter your disillusions but I never went to a posh school.'

He held out a hand. 'Still bloody press, Chief Superintendent. And not above a little gentle blackmail, even of ministers. Especially ministers like Gordon Dimmock.'

Capstick grasped the hand and the nettle he had been shrinking from. 'Let him see you know about Norton-Jones, sir. And if you should happen to hear from Mrs Brooke' – he had never looked more poker-faced – 'try to make her believe she's safer with us.'

Victoria Station concourse: the start of the homeward rush.

If Heather had arrived at the hospital, Norton-Jones with his sharp voice, his meaningless smile and his sickeningly prurient concept of their relationship, would never have got off the ground.

It had been very much to Norton-Jones's advantage that Heather had not arrived.

Paranoia was the name of the country whose border she had crossed when she had first opened her door on Capstick. She felt terrifyingly vulnerable, the one person in all this bustle with no aim, no purpose, no destination: someone whose face had been in the papers. She was Rossiter's top, whipped and now wobbling out of control.

She bought a *Standard*. The story was page 2 below the fold: SEX KILLING IN SURREY BEAUTY SPOT. A picture of Heather, blurred, hardly recognisable. She couldn't bring herself to read, not yet.

Rossiter had been clever: keys to his car, keys to his London pad, somewhere to run to and hide. A logical, mannish thought, even for a man as atypical as Hugh Rossiter. But what one man could think of another would guess.

She didn't mean Capstick. She meant Norton-Jones, who knew all about women, hadn't he said as much? Foibles, weakness, pressure points; inferior creatures who secretly loved what they most pretended to fear. Timid Sarah Brooke, on the run but hoping to be caught, because the only true safety lay in captivity.

He knew too that the trick was to drive the quarry underground, where all normal rules ceased to apply. That was the way men thought, match deviousness with deviousness, fight things out in the dark.

Norton-Jones knew that women, afraid of violence, were also afraid of the dark.

She dropped Rossiter's keys in the nearest refuse bin, hurried across the concourse into the Grosvenor Hotel. The little vixen: keep her cover, tend her business, leave everyone else to theirs.

First things first; call Redhill. No Dr Quilter, a woman doctor whose name meant nothing.

'I'm terribly sorry, Mrs Brooke, didn't they tell you? He isn't here any more.'

Norton-Jones, passionless master, teaching a child chess. The penalty for an impulsive move was to lose her key piece.

The woman lowered her voice. 'It came through the district manager, just get the patient ready to be moved. Dr Quilter – '

'Is he there?'

'No. Sorry. He was livid but there you are, all fixed up miles over our heads.'

'Do you know where they've taken my husband?'

'London, I think. I really am terribly sorry.' She was, too.

'How was he?'

'Well . . . Stable. So long as he continues to get proper attention.' Dodging that one; sufficient unto the day.

'Was he conscious?'

'I'm awfully sorry,' this doctor was saying. 'Really.' Sympathy, embarrassment, time to end the call. 'I'm sure you'll be told where he is. By them, I mean.'

Yes, Sarah said, she was sure she would. Thank you all very much. Goodbye. Next call. She would go completely mad if she couldn't get back Emma.

'Sarah?' Her mother, as much alarmed as relieved. 'Where are you? Where are you calling from? I've been so worried. The papers – '

'Have they been bothering you, Mum?' Got to stay laid back, play it all by ear.

'Yes. No. Oh dear. They did. At least, they tried. But then it all stopped. That poor Smith girl! What did I tell her?'

'What do you mean, they tried?' Had they tapped her mother's phone? Were they listening now, waiting for her to give herself away?

'Some man tried to talk to Emma. They'd all been taught at school to scream if strange men talked to them. She screamed, very loudly. I ran, of course, and so did he. The police said he was a reporter. Sarah, where are you, dear? Emma's getting difficult to handle, it's hardly surprising. And of course, one has to be *dreadfully* careful about the radio and television.'

She would go mad. 'Is she there now?'

'Oh dear, she's gone to play with Mark and Virginia. She'll be so upset – '

'Don't tell her. I'll call back later, but I can't say when. Nick's been moved. Until I get that sorted out I'm not too sure of my own plans.'

'Are you still with Hugh Rossiter? I don't honestly think it's altogether a good idea, Sarah, especially now that poor girl's been . . .'

Her mother broke off, wavering between doubt and a full-scale wobbly. Any moment now things were going to get really difficult.

'Look, Mum, I've got to go. I'll call you back soon, promise.' Not many units left on her phonecard and one last call to make. If only she had Nick's pocketphone, sitting uselessly back at the house now Capstick had returned his things.

Except that they might have some way of listening in to that kind of thing.

'Good afternoon. Soviet News Agency Tass. Can I help you?' Good English, but not English. She knew the place, a small, depressing square just off Shoe Lane, a cluster of faceless modern office blocks housing a mini-Babel of press agencies. Perhaps this woman felt at home in such close and anonymous surroundings. Or perhaps she felt homesick for the wide boulevards of Moscow.

'I'd like to speak to Mr Peter Glashin, please.'

'Who is calling?'

Answer straight out and she could forget it. 'My name's Sarah Purdy. I want to thank Mr Glashin for some flowers he sent me.' Wouldn't work. Would it?

'I'm sorry.' It wouldn't work. 'Mr Glashin has returned to Soviet Union since one week. Mr Glashin's period of duty here is completed.'

She cut off without even saying thank you.

For a moment, the overwhelming temptation to give up. Wells, a sleepy little West Country cathedral town. Sit it all out; Sarah, Mum, Emma and some comfortingly stuffy local lawyer. After all, it wasn't Sarah Brooke who'd done something wrong, stirred up God knew how many bloody termites in London, Washington, Moscow.

Except that an item of knowledge had lodged itself in her brain like an unwanted parasite. Except that Norton-Jones, expert in her weaknesses, had every intention of extracting it from her.

She forced herself to reopen the *Standard*, trying to shut out Heather's face. The piece was an agency taster, long on geography, short on facts, not the smallest reference to Nick or herself.

That splendid chap Corker: *News is what a chap who doesn't care much about anything wants to read. And it's only news until he's read it. After that it's dead.*

Until whoever was conducting a very efficient news management operation decided it was time to throw them back to the wolves she and Nick were yesterday's news. Unpersons. Dead. She refused to die. She would raise both herself and Nick from the dead.

The doorman plucked a taxi from the slow-moving, short-tempered crawl-past in Buckingham Palace Road. 'Where to, madam?'

'Poplar,' she said. 'The *Globe* newspaper.'

Wise drove up just as Rossiter was about to get into his old Peugeot. The cherry gloss of Wise's Ford Granada went well with the cherry gloss of his face. He slid out, his crackling aura, part transatlantic genes, part Grecian 2000, enhanced by an expensive topcoat of dark blue vicuña, a pale blue mohair scarf and a hat Rossiter could only think of as American-looking.

He took in Rossiter's shabby Burberry. 'Going somewhere?'

'No helicopter, not even a chauffeur? Have you been demoted?'

'That chopper was kind of a polite way for a bunch of people in Washington to tell another bunch of people in Whitehall to keep their hands on the table or lay down their cards. But the game' – working himself between Rossiter and the Peugeot – 'does not, repeat not, include murder.'

'Perhaps,' Rossiter said, 'there's more than one game.'

'Only one game, Hugh.'

Rossiter sighed. 'I have spent the greater part of a worthless life careering around this planet describing matters of life and death, the gist of my plaint invariably being that killing people solves nothing. Yet I do believe that this moribund old fart, this inky-fingered bleeding heart, this prosy old soak who has moralised under more date-lines than a convention of missionaries would choke whoever killed Heather Smith with his bare hands.'

He nodded emptily at Dick Wise. 'And now, if you'll excuse me, old buddy.'

'Only one game,' Wise repeated. 'More than two players.'

'Peter Glashin?' Rossiter showed weary contempt. 'An honest newsman, dear old chap. Publish it not in the streets of Askelon but some commies are nice guys.'

'So I'm a nice guy,' Wise said, 'who happens to work with some people in Langley who would like to be nice guys. And not just back home with their kids. They tried nice guying Nick Brooke the night he drove into the bridge.'

For the first time he had Rossiter's attention.

'You mean they're the ones who were chasing him?'

'Never got close enough to chase him. Guilt is what chased him. Panic is what chased him. Glashin's been back in Moscow this past week.'

He took Rossiter's arm, edging him toward the Granada. 'Since this morning Nick Brooke is in a private clinic I wouldn't recommend to my friends. Since last night Nick Brooke's attorney is dead. I think you should start worrying about Nick Brooke's wife.'

'She's not here.'

Wise laughed, a laugh packed with vitamins and trace elements but deficient in humour. 'My friends know that. So where is she now?'

Rossiter freed his arm. 'Got to go, dear old boy.'

Wise grabbed him, no attempt at gentleness. 'Listen, friend of my youth, you're fooling with people who have only one thought when it comes to national security. They want to win. Not some of the time. All of the time. That's what being American is all about.'

'I've often wondered.' Rossiter stood as stiffly as an obstinate child in Wise's bearhug.

'But' – Wise gave him a shake – 'they do not want people dead.' Another shake. 'They have not gone crazy. They do not blow holes in a picture of a woman I would have done my best to steal if she hadn't rated me a poor second to a guy called Rossiter.'

He released Rossiter but kept a hold on his hands. 'All they want is what's theirs. Now' – he brought Rossiter's hands together inside his own and squeezed them as tenderly as any lover – 'got to trust me, Hugh. Does the little lady know where it is?'

'She does, and so do I.'

'So where is it?'

'Out there.' He gestured beyond his boundaries. The sun had gone.

'Out there,' Wise said, 'is where one of my friends tried to talk to Nick Brooke the night he ended up wrapping himself around that bridge. Out there is where that same friend tried to talk to Nick Brooke's wife when she took to the hills this afternoon. Don't worry,' forestalling questions, 'she got away. He may never smile again.'

He winced at the thought. 'Out there will go down in Langley as this year's Bay of Pigs. The question is, just where out there?'

'The only one who knows,' Rossiter said, 'is Nick Brooke.'

Wise stared hard. 'Okay, it's the truth. It still leaves the wild man. We have to move fast, Hugh.'

He saw Rossiter's incomprehension. 'You think Special Branch killed Heather Smith?'

'Of course not.'

'So the fact she's dead is just some weird coincidence, right?'

'Norton-Jones?'

'Norton-Jones is the wild man. We have them too. Every once in a while one of them sets out to win the war on his own, remember arms for Iran and the Contras? But Norton-Jones didn't kill anyone. Let's just say he used some guy who was accident prone.'

'Some man,' Rossiter said, 'followed Mrs Brooke back from Redhill this morning. One of your friends?'

'Some man,' Wise said, 'followed Heather Smith when she set off for Redhill. That wasn't one of my friends.'

He produced an object from his topcoat, something Rossiter had seen before. He touched a series of keys, a green arrow, then zero. A tiny light came on. He held it out to Rossiter. 'Go ahead. Call her. You know where she is.'

Rossiter looked at the pocketphone. 'Sometimes I have a feeling the world is leaving me behind. Sometimes I'm glad.'

'Listen.' Wise was urgent now. 'Norton-Jones just wanted to stop the Smith girl getting to the hospital, but something went wrong. With wild men things have a habit of going wrong. Call the number. Tell her, once we take her under our protection she's okay and we parley for her old man. After that they're both in the clear. I don't just say it. I guarantee it.'

Another thrust of the phone. 'Better believe me, Hugh.'

Rossiter took the thing gingerly, touched numbers without letting Wise see.

'Just wait,' Wise ordered. Some seconds later they heard the call go through. Wise had turned the volume full up. No reply for a further second or two, then a click, followed by Rossiter's own voice.

'Hugh Rossiter is not here at present but will be happy to call you back if you will leave your name and number. Please speak after this infernal machine has made its infernal noise.'

Wise reached to terminate the call. 'So she's in London. Goddammit, you could have told me, Hugh. Goddammit, I should have guessed.'

'Maybe she's changed her mind,' Rossiter said, but he didn't believe it.

'I sure as hell hope you're right,' Wise said. 'You think Norton-Jones isn't waiting for you to lead him to her?'

Somewhere among the trees a crow cawed. 'Guts like an old watch-chain,' Rossiter said. 'Head like a broken windowpane. I give up.'

Cramming his American hat down on his American head, full of an American determination to win, Wise drove Rossiter towards the Granada.

'Get in. I'm taking you to London.'

In Mammon's City the lights blazed, stacked under low cloud that threw back their glare in pallid small change. Across the Shadwell Basin the masts of a scatter of small boats poked bleached and rootless out of their watery beds. Beyond them a gulf of darkness marked the Thames, hemmed by the flattened constellations of the Surrey shore.

Normally when she walked into the foyer of the *Globe* she would smile at the guard, look toward the desk and wave. She smiled, looked, waved, walked on. The usual crush; messengers coming and going, staff hurrying from level to level. More than one startled glance, more than one comical double-take, but no one blocked her way.

She squeezed past a motor-cycle courier with one of the packages that shuttled endlessly between the *Globe* and its outstations. The cubicles used by Tim Bryce and Monkey were unoccupied. On the other side of the newsroom doors telephones warbled like an aviary of tropical birds.

Mark Hennicker, the sports editor's deputy, came out as she went in, automatically holding back the door.

'Sarah!' So surprised that his usually quick brain had stalled.

'Hello, Mark. How's Dora?' Dora was Mark's current live-in.

'Fine,' he said, reflex response. 'We're getting spliced, registry office do just before Christmas, but . . .'

His mind changed frequencies and received a situation report. 'Good God! Sarah! What are you – ?' but she was already through. The back bench had its usual early evening complement: Monkey, Peter French, the night editor and his deputy. Precious bonus, there was Tim Bryce himself.

Shirt-sleeved, sweating as he always did once the hands of the clocks moved toward the start line, it was still far too early for him to deign to take a seat. Screens flickered and shifted, tossing copy, pictures, layouts between work stations, a silently skilful juggling act that swapped tidings, tattle, titillation in a two-dimensional shuffle of shadows.

Features was shouting something to Peter about losing three inches from the lead op-ed and recropping the pic. Tim, one hand on Monkey's shoulder, watched with his usual blend of concentration and contempt as microchips waltzed through what he had spent half a lifetime learning to do by hand.

No one noticed her. She placed herself immediately behind Tim, still not totally sure what she would do. Just the thought that this was where it had all started and, day by day, been chased or suppressed in response to forces she didn't understand.

Hiding among the headlines.

Someone brushed past to drop a print-out in front of Peter French. He glanced at it, handed it to Tim, Tim read it, his pushed-in face stony, then became aware that the someone was apparently still there.'What's up then? World come to an end or have you – '

He stopped. 'Jesus Christ! Sarah! What the hell are you doin' here?' His voice reached other desks. Eyes turned. Hands reached, nudging to turn a neighbour's eyes.

'Hello, Tim. What's the front page lead going to be tonight?'

All this time she had been locked in an unnatural calm. Now, heart thumping wildly, mouth dry, she had a sudden griping pain.

More than one reason to feel increasingly taut and panic-stricken during the past twenty-four hours. Not just events but the time of the month. Always, before her periods, pains, sullen headaches, attacks of what Nick called her nameless dreads.

Back bench, features and sports desks all staring now, familiar faces running a gamut from shock to furtive curiosity. Fighting back the urge to bend, hands to belly while the spasm passed, she saw the stares multiply down the room, a sudden whispering hiatus punctuated by the shrilling of the telephonic aviary. In moments the unthinkable had happened. The dental chatter of keyboards ceased. On every screen blue analogues lost life. With only hours to go, work on the first edition of the *Globe* came to a stop.

Tim saw it too. Face red and glistening, he roared his fury. 'What's up with you lot? Gone on strike? Waitin' for inspiration? Get your bloody heads down or go and collect your bloody cards.'

The *Globe* went back to work.

Tim thrust the crumpled sheet at Monkey. 'Watch 'em, Monk. Back in a tick.' He already had Sarah's arm in an unintentionally rough grip. 'Come on, girl, this is no place for you.'

Behind him a monitor made one of its rapid switches. Op-ed vanished, replaced by the front page. Reverse splash, the kind of thing the *Globe* used for what Nick called late night sextras.

FAKE RAPE: DID KILLER KNOW?
THE GIRL WHO 'HATED MEN'

Top right, quarter page, Heather's picture, smiling out at Sarah, a blue electronic ghost.

She shook off Tim's arm so violently that he almost lost balance.

'What's the matter with you? Don't you know a scoop when you see one? Vanished key witness in beauty spot sex killing

244

turns up in *Globe* newsroom. Isn't that sensational enough for your bloody front page?'

Once again everything came to a halt.

'Sarah.' None of Tim's experience had prepared him for this. 'Sarah, love, you're upset. Come outside. Let's get things sorted out.'

He jabbed a finger at Monkey. 'We'll be in the proprietor's suite. Get these idle gits back to work.' He raised his voice. 'One word from anybody about this and I'll pull their bleedin' arms off.'

The talons in Sarah's stomach gripped again, making her wince. Tim put an arm about her shoulders. She drove at his chest, only Monkey's quick hand saving him from toppling.

'You're slipping. Why don't you call Special Branch? *Globe* editor in newsroom arrest drama!' Behind her something was clicking like a Geiger counter in a high radiation area. She guessed what was happening. Someone with quick wits was in-putting verbatim.

Mopping his face, a man lashed hand and foot to teams of wild horses, Tim made a fresh attempt. 'Sarah, Sarah, you're upset, girl.'

'*Don't* call me girl!'

Dodging his outstretched hand she used a chair to step on to the nearest monitor desk, making herself visible the full length of the room. Not one man or woman in it was even pretending to work.

'In an exclusive interview,' she heard herself shouting, 'Sarah Brooke, thirty-five, wife of Nick Brooke, *Globe's* in-house spy-on-the-spot, revealed how secret papers discovered near kiddy slaughter village resulted in death of close friend Heather Smith, victim of MI5 woodland killer.'

Aware that she had passed the point of no return, another cramping jab of pain, she felt everything slipping away from her.

'Write! Call yourself journalists? Write, damn you!'

She recognised the expression on more than one upturned face. The *Globe* had discovered pity.

The doors thumped open: Stan Farthing, a drinking pal of Nick's, came in, battered camera bag over his shoulder. Tim looked wildly at him. 'Stop anybody else comin' through those bloody doors.'

She made a last attempt. 'Stan! Pics! Quick, for Nick's sake.

245

You'll never have another chance like it.' He hesitated but training came first. His camera was out and levelled.

She turned back to Tim. 'Well? Do you want the story or am I going to give it to someone else?

'Oh yes I will!' as he opened his mouth. 'I don't give a damn who gets it but this time the real story's going on someone's bloody front page.'

Sensing a scoop even if he had no idea what it was about, Stan took a run of shots.

Foundering among an archipelago of staring faces she glared down on Tim. 'What are you waiting for, you stupid sod? *Globe* mother in lesbian spy drama!'

Don't ever swear, Ess, makes you sound like a girl guide being naughty.

'Murder!' she shouted. 'Rape! Treason! What's the matter with you? Don't you understand English?'

Stan had stopped taking pictures. In a stillness broken only by the shrilling of unanswered phones, Tim roared his anguish, belatedly aware of a new danger.

'Kill those phones, anybody who's on an outside line. Jesus Christ Almighty, we're runnin' a bleedin' broadcastin' service.'

People were beginning to stand. From the far end of the room she saw Liz Balcon coming toward her, her angular face a mixture of pity and rapacious excitement.

Six feet three, the shoulders of a wrestler, Stan grasped her gently from behind, lifted her down. Tim's voice, hoarse but unexpectedly gentle. 'Sarah, Sarah love, I know how you must feel, but this isn't going to help him.'

Wise pulled in alongside Green Park. Soiled clouds scooted over the Palace, fleeing some celestial cleanup. Traffic in the Mall was even brisker, treating the speed limit as some quirky whim. Across the grass a jogger pounded plosively through a landscape that existed only in his mind.

'Got to walk from here to the Home Office, Hugh. Figure you can manage that?'

Rossiter, who had listened to little more than radio music and his own thoughts on the way up, cocked an eyebrow. 'How do you know I want to go to the Home Office? Or is that a silly question?'

Wise pulled his pocketphone out.

'Remember how it works?'

'Dear old chap! I can boil an egg if I put my mind to it. Just about.'

Wise looked at him with something approaching affection. 'They say the Almighty looks after drunks and children. I guess you qualify on both counts. Who told you the Minister wanted to see you?'

'Is there anything you don't know?'

'Damn right. Like why you can be so smart and act so dumb.'

'The Minister issued his invitation courtesy of Special Branch.'

'The Minister, Hugh, issued his invitation courtesy of a Special Branch car radio.'

'Ah. Eavesdropping.'

'Not really. That thing went out by radio so we would pick it up. So we would know, without a word being passed, that your people are trying to square things with our people and no questions asked. Let's call it SIGINT.'

Rossiter pulled a face. 'Acronymic is a language I tend to class with Esperanto.' He looked at the pocketphone with distaste.

'Not far from Harrogate,' Wise said, 'Uncle Sam has an ear that can listen to damn near anything you can think of, plus a whole heap that you can't. How do you think we zeroed in on Nick Brooke after that head-on at Nethercott Stoney?'

'He had one of these things?'

'Standard issue at the *Globe*,' Wise said. 'Brooke used it for everything. Even used it to set up his meet with Glashin. We plotted him around like we had him on a radar screen.'

He looked at Rossiter fondly. 'Relax, Einstein, you don't have to solve any problems. Aren't so many of these radio phones around and every call on every one of them is logged: time, place, duration. Plus we run computerised random sampling, pulls out every last little thing of interest. We traced him right back to the scene of that plane crash.

'A guy who finds a missing piece of chopper and reports it anonymously, you can say that's of interest. You can also say, ain't no such thing as anonymous when Big Ear's on the ball.'

He chuckled. 'Special Branch told Mrs Brooke a tale about funnied-up steering on the car he totalled so they could check out the other. They thought somebody must have it bugged. The guy was carrying his own bug around all the time.'

'But you didn't chase him. Didn't try to kill him.'

Wise snorted. 'That guy was programmed to self-destruct.'

Rossiter opened his door. 'I have an appointment.'

'You have no appointment, ratbag. You're just invited to drop by.' Wise punched his arm gently. 'Now how come a busy guy like your Minister is prepared to make that kind of an arrangement?'

Rossiter looked at him with a kind of despair. 'Dick, you see before you a man who has witnessed so much catastrophe that he has become infected. No, contagious. Beware.'

Wise thumped his deep chest. 'Immune, Hugh. Like that big ear up near Harrogate. Like a whole raft of things you people let us Yanks set up in your country. We didn't ask. You invited. That kind of invitation carries its own guarantee of immunity. Listen' – he reached across Rossiter to close the door firmly – 'tell the Minister who chauffeured you up, why don't you?'

'Does he know you?'

'Doesn't want to.' Wise chuckled again. 'You'll see. Now, before you leave I have to teach you a couple of tricks. Here, take a hold of this dohicky.'

He forced the pocketphone into Rossiter's unwilling hand.

A few minutes later he watched Rossiter slip it reluctantly into his shabby Burberry. 'Going to remember?'

'No.'

'You'll remember, Hugh. You have to. I'm your only hope.'

Rossiter rolled his eyes. 'Hear that, Elly?'

'You've lost Elly,' Wise said, never more serious. 'Lost Heather Smith. All set to lose Sarah Brooke unless you play ball. Still time to save her, so you just fix that sequence in your mind against the day, old buddy. No matter where you are, when you need us we'll find you.'

Only in walking across the park toward Victoria Street did it occur to Rossiter that his old buddy Dick Wise had said nothing about saving Nick Brooke.

Stan walked her to the proprietor's suite. People plied her with what seemed to have become a Sarah Brooke special: neat spirit, strong tea. She let it go down, a human waste disposal unit, stomach cramps pinning her to reality like a butterfly to a specimen board.

A clear, loud whisper, nothing to do with the external bedlam, said 'Heather is dead. Heather is dead.' She sat looking at their silly faces while that harsh whisper told her, over and over, that Heather was dead. Sometimes, in her confusion, she thought it was Nick who was dead.

New people came and went, people she didn't know. They too brought whispered messages, were dispatched on whispered errands. Something had happened in a world of which she was barely a part. Must be important, judging by the way Tim, glossy with anxious sweat, appeared, vanished, reappeared with the unpredictability of a TV set on the blink.

He seemed to be battling with a new crisis, an angry, bull-voiced general marshalling his forces against some surprise attack. She was on the verge of giggling. The giggling, once started, would never stop.

Pull yourself together, Sarah. Hysteria is a dismissive label, a male myth invented to . . .

What?

Don't chew your lip, Sarah. Lip-chewing is bad body language.

A new distraction, Tim saying, 'Some bastard out there saw the chance of making himself a fast century or two. Got to get her out of here. Got to tuck her away. I don't give a shit about bloody Ds. Not even the bloody army can keep this one under wraps.'

Messenger by messenger, it dawned. Her verbal shots had been leaked outside the *Globe*. The world, or at any rate its media wolves, had beaten a path to her door. She had hazy images of siege: a hundred Nicks sprung from the ground like dragon seed to replace the one they had taken away. Heather? Not even Persephone.

Liz Balcon came back, with her deep, shaggy Roger, unscrupulous, calculating Crispin: the *Globe's* dirt squad. Tim put a hand on Sarah's shoulder, hastily removed it as if he might be accused of molestation.

'Sarah, I know how you must feel, lass, but – '

'No,' she said. 'You don't.'

'Quite right, girl, I don't, but I – '

'Don't call me girl. I'm a married woman. I want to go home.'

Liz came to sit with her; old pointy tits, Nick used to call her. Her huge glasses flashed under the lights. 'We're going to get you out, Sarah. Setting things up fast as we can.'

'What things?'

'Can't take you home yet, Sarah.' Tim was back in the game. 'Hell on wheels out in the street.'

'Call the police.' Once again wrestling with dangerous laughter.

He took her seriously. 'No need, believe me. Got to move before anybody important shows.'

He stood over her, an uneasy compound of concern and cold, professional calculation. 'Got to understand, Sarah, need my head examinin' if I didn't splash this one. Laughin' stock of the Street.'

A series of pictures, almost as if she, like big Stan, had spent the last weeks going clickety-click. Pushed, squeezed, bullied and hounded for what felt like years, her imbued respect for the forces of law and order hampering her like a hobble skirt.

For law read discipline, for order, obedience. Tossed into a quasi-legal oubliette that went under the name of state security, she had escaped like the djinn from the bottle. Like the djinn from the bottle, nothing in the world was going to force her back in.

Tim loomed again, a lumbering, hot-faced troll. 'Goin' to need friends now, Sarah. This time it's all goin' to hang out. The *Globe's* goin' to run it till it bleedin' drops.'

Her own private whisper died away. Her mind calmed, thoughts and intentions as clear as pictures in a gallery. What Heather would want.

'What if I don't want to talk?'

'Sarah!' Like a poleaxed ox. 'Talkin' serious money, darlin'. Not just protection. Very serious money.'

She said nothing, parading around her new gallery, looking at all the bright new pictures.

Tim pawed his face with one big hand. 'No use sayin' you won't talk, sweetheart. You talked. And they know it now, that mob outside. I told you, one of my lot, crucify him when I find out, leaked it all out. You don't talk, they'll say it for you. I know those bastards.'

Spin-off from a vestigial conscience. The *Globe*, too, would tell Sarah Brooke's story 'in her own words' if it took all night to invent them. She could see the type size lumbering gigantically toward her.

So perhaps she would talk, and perhaps she knew how: not word by word yet but, as Nick liked to put it, she had the general drift.

Liz Balcon, fallen recording angel, said, 'Get you into a hotel to start with, Sarah. Quiet and peaceful while we sort it all out. A cassette thingy and a mike and, well, you know, just sort of natter.'

Heard it all from Nick. 'Just let 'em yack, bit of a prod here, push there, get the drift then let your imagination rip. Time you've finished, they think it's what they said. Anyway, draw 'em a picture of a cheque with a few Ks on it and half of them are ready to sign anything.'

Oh yes, she knew all right.

She said, 'I want more than money.'

'Name it, darlin'.' Tim brightened visibly. The victim was baring her throat.

'I want Nick back.' She had nearly said Heather.

It made everyone uncomfortable except Liz Balcon. 'No problem.' She glanced at Tim Bryce. 'Wind them up with the justice-must-be-done bit, right? Umpty million outraged *Globe* readers?' Even her lies were pointy.

She patted Sarah's knee. 'We tell your story, exclusive, two hundred per cent on your side, right? Jerk the tears like you're a freshly peeled onion. Anything else?'

'And I want Emma back.'

'The kid,' Liz explained quickly. ''Course, Sarah. Leave it to us.' She signalled. Roger pushed his way out of the room. Someone else came in, visible only to Sarah behind her executioners.

'We know where she is,' Liz said. 'Emma, I mean. What about mum?'

'Just Emma. But someone's got to protect my mother, keep her out of all this until I've time to get in touch.'

She was watching the man who had just arrived, face gaunt and waxen, the melancholy eyes of a bloodhound, clothes that murmured of style without mentioning money.

She said, 'If that's all right with Lord Tyrran.' It galvanised them like shouting, 'Fire!'

Hands thrust in the pockets of his navy blue barathea, sparse pewter hair a little dishevelled as if, against all probability, he had been running, Tyrran came to sit behind the reproduction George III desk as naturally as if he owned everything and everyone, which of course he did. He reminded her of pale effigies on Tudor tombs.

'So this is the young lady who's been stirring things up.'

Not so long ago his presence would have dried up her mouth, turned her body language to gibberish.

'I thought it was other people who'd been stirring things up.'

His thin lips twitched. 'If you've done nothing, why am I paged in my club? Why do I have to have assistance to get inside my own premises?'

Hands still deep in his pockets, eyes unblinking, he said, 'I make it my business to hear things.'

'Stick around,' said someone pulling her strings. 'You ain't heard nothing yet.' Premenstrual tension or no, she wanted to laugh.

He took it almost indifferently. 'It takes very little, these days, to precipitate crises. National crises. International crises. Crises are bad for business.'

'Stuff business.'

She heard a sharp hiccup in Tim Bryce's heavy breathing.

'On the other hand,' voice as dry as mummy dust, 'crises sell newspapers. Exclusive crises sell my newspapers. What else do you want?'

'Hugh Rossiter.' What Heather would have wanted her to say.

'Bloody near forgot,' Tim said, alarm in his voice. 'Listen, sweet, did you sign anythin'?'

Brittle and light as spun sugar, but she would be spun steel. 'No Hugh, no deal. Take it or leave it.'

'Hugh Rossiter,' Tyrran said. 'Now there's a name to conjure with, Timothy. Worked for me once, young lady, did you know that?'

'Yes,' she said. 'He wouldn't work for you now.'

He smiled, more of a rictus. 'In that I fear you're right. Get him, Timothy. She didn't sign anything. He'll come like the knight errant he is.'

'How do you know I didn't sign anything?'

'Hugh?' Another rustle of amusement. 'He'd never produce anything for you to sign. And lose it in five minutes if you signed it. A damn good newsman, no nose for business, none.'

He studied her, curiosity, not benevolence. 'You're a very determined young lady. Do you realise what it's going to be like?'

'Going to be all right, darlin',' Tim said, anxious reassurance. 'Goin' to look after you, don't you fret.'

252

'While I,' Tyrran told him, 'may or may not look after you, Timothy. Botch it and you may end up in jail. I may end up in jail, but on the whole I doubt it.

'And now' – he rose, hands still stuck limply into his pockets – 'I suggest you muster your troops. You're going to have to take her out through that front entrance. I don't envy you. I don't propose to be with you. I bid you goodnight.'

He left as if no one was there.

It ended as it had begun: nightmare. They mustered a dozen of the heftiest male staff. She heard Liz say, 'We're taking her to the – ' and Tim snarl, 'Don't tell me, don't want to know.'

Folding money flowed through the entrance doors to dissipate mysteriously on its way through various policemen. A Jaguar had forced itself to the edge of the kerb. An onslaught of brute flesh drove a wedge through massed media ranks.

Flash flickering blindingly, a nonstop storm of light. Loud voices, male, female, bawling incomprehensibilities, thrusting microphones and cassette recorders at her.

A last push, someone pressing her head down just in time to stop it smashing against the roof of the car, they rammed her home like a cannon ball down the barrel of a gun. A ragged slam of doors; Liz Balcon and two giants, one of them Stan, still clutching his scruffy camera bag.

Then off. A screech of tyres. A barrage of slamming doors as other cars started up behind them. A brief, crooked view across the light-scrawled stillness of the Shadwell Basin.

'Gordon Bennett! Rough while it lasted.' Liz looked owl-like in the flickering semi-darkness. 'I know what we need. Socking great doubles of something fierce.'

'No,' she said. 'A hot water bottle.'

The big lenses flashed blankly.

'The curse. And I need some Tampax.'

'Oh! Gosh! You poor thing.' Liz looked almost human.

Pain and the sudden acceleration of the Jaguar as it broke clear drove her back, doubled up. Her eyes and nose filled with water. She did her best to stop it. It would have to wait. No hysteria, Sarah. Hysteria is a thing invented by sadistic men to justify their theory of masochistic women. Men have crack-ups, burn-out, battle fatigue.

* * *

253

The room was discreetly impressive and the pictures included portraits of past giants, but the windows looked over brown concrete bunkers suggesting the headquarters of an occupation force. Rossiter sighed inwardly, remembering the faded Victorian magnificence of the ministerial rooms in the old Home Office in Whitehall. That place had been built with a sturdy awareness of supremacy, this one in stubborn defence of decline.

'Hugh. Thank you for coming.' The Minister was a slight, sardonic man with a potentially wounding wit and a taste for gallows humour.

Rossiter allowed his hand to be wrung. 'How are you, Gordon? Or do you want me to call you Minister?'

'Known each other a long time, Hugh. Let's not be formal.' Saving the formality for if he should become Secretary of State, he waved Rossiter to a seat then circled the big room like a hound casting for a scent.

'They tell me you're writing your memoirs.'

'Who tells you?'

'Ah! Naughty! Everyone. Why not? Doyen of peripatetic scribes. Master of the well-turned phrase. Publishing event of the year, got to be.'

'You make it sound like an order.'

'I'd like to make it an order.'

He ignored his desk to take a chair facing Rossiter. 'Can we be civilised about this? I do like to be civilised.' His feral grin went strangely with his good clothes and soft voice, tending to give an almost sexual thrill to middle-aged matrons at constituency fund raisings and annual party conferences.

'Pretend to be good always, and even God will be fooled. How long can you go on being civilised about murder, Gordon?'

'What if I were to say, "A word to the wise"?'

'Oh, but I'm not, Gordon. Neither is Mrs Brooke. We're babes in the wood, not politicians, so wisdom we both disclaim.'

'Or that I feel I owe it to Elly to keep you out of trouble?'

'Hear that, Elly?' Rossiter cast his eyes toward the chandelier. 'An angel and minister of grace to defend us.'

'Can we call this a briefing?'

Rossiter's eyebrow rose sceptically. 'Unattributable?'

'Unpublishable.'

'You don't mean that. You mean highly publishable but you

hope to God it won't be. Or perhaps you've got something you'd
rather I published instead.'

'When we tell you how to write a story' – the Minister produced
the awful sincerity of a fundamentalist preacher – 'you can tell us
how to go about our business.'

Rossiter laughed aloud, even Heather briefly forgotten.
'You're always telling us how to write our stories, Gordon, you
and your like. The trouble is, they're hardly ever the stories we
want to write. That's why we're scavengers.'

'Not everyone is Hugh Rossiter. When the media as a whole
can be trusted to respect a secret – ' He stopped because Rossiter
was laughing again.

'If your average media man,' he said, 'published every secret
he ran across in the course of his working life, your average
politician would come out as a cross between a crook and a
certifiable loony. I think I'll call you Minister, Minister.'

Never openly showing resentment was one of the things that
made the Minister dangerous, just as never being abashed was
one of his incongruous attractions.

'You're too old a hand to be taken in by flattery, Hugh. I
asked you to come because you've a reputation for discretion.'

'You hope to persuade me to keep a secret.'

'I've every reason to know you keep secrets, or you wouldn't
be here. This young idiot Brooke, on the other hand – '

Rossiter interrupted. 'I've never retailed scandal. Or vicious
rumours. Never wittingly put anything about that might harm the
things all good men ought to believe in. But I've never been the
type to sit on a story that ought to be told, just because someone
didn't want me to tell it. Could we get to the point? I've other
fish to fry.'

The Minister's nod was almost approving. 'Mrs Brooke's not
there, Hugh, not at that little place of yours off Gower Street.
Our people can be clumsy, God knows, but they're not fools.
And they see no reason why they shouldn't take out a warrant
for your arrest.'

'Do go on.'

'Something is missing. You know that much. Not only is it
secret, the very fact of its existence is secret. If you know the
nature or content, in whole or in part, of the missing item, you're
indictable. If you know the whereabouts of the item, though not
necessarily its nature, and fail to communicate that information

to the proper authority, you're indictable. In sum or part, old boy, both major indictable offences.'

'Yes,' Rossiter said. 'That's more or less the way Dicky Wise saw it, though he used less fancy words.'

'Know him as Dicky, do you?'

'Known him for years.'

The Minister stroked the sharp chin the political cartoonists delighted to exploit. 'All right, time to come clean.'

'The incredible you do at once,' Rossiter said. 'The impossible may take a little longer. Sorry. And before you begin, old hacks never retire.'

That triangular grin, never baring the teeth yet hinting at more than the normal quota, all sharp. 'Ah, but Rossiter respects a confidence. Am I right? This isn't just a confidence. It's a secret. The kind of secret that demands silence.'

'The world,' Rossiter told him, 'is full of gossiping silence.'

The Minister crossed his legs. 'I'll take that chance. With you.'

'That means you've no choice.'

'Must be a bit schizoid, idealist and cynic. I expect you know Mildenhall's one of the bases we let the Americans use.'

'Really?' Rossiter said. 'We let them, do we?'

'It's become a clandestine Heathrow,' the Minister said. 'Come and go as they please, no questions asked, none answered. I'm reliably told there are US personnel on some of these bases who don't even know which country they're in. Mildenhall, Kyongsong, Rhein-Main, Guantanamo, the only thing that changes is the climate.'

'But the passenger in that crashed helicopter, one Colonel George Kowicki, knew he was in England all right. And so, old boy, did we. On the personal staff of General Wylie, US Third Air Force, HQ Mildenhall. Principal function, liaison between the US Third Air Force and General Abbott in Belgium.'

The Minister looked at Rossiter, no more grins. 'That's not the secret. Just fixes the level of what you've got yourself mixed up in.'

It was also the level, Rossiter reminded himself, of what Sarah Brooke and Heather Smith had got themselves mixed up in.

'General Abbott as Supreme Commander, NATO? Or as GOC American Forces in Europe?'

'Kowicki's duties,' the Minister said, 'were strictly American.

256

Kowicki was killed in the execution of his strictly American duties.'

'So what was he carrying in that chopper?'

'Our chaps across the river' – the Minister nodded in the general direction of Secret Intelligence headquarters in Lambeth – 'tell us that our American allies had a private get-together at Mildenhall the day before Nethercott Stoney. Top brass, chaired by George Abbott. According to the NATO Diary, mind, General Abbott was in Mons that day.'

He crossed his legs the other way. 'Not going to write anything about this one, Hugh. Not even in your memoirs. Right?'

'What sort of get-together?'

'United States European Command covert committee. Everyone in NATO knows it exists. Nobody asks questions. On that day General Abbott was said to have had a slight chill, confined to quarters. Mons is no distance at all from Mildenhall with a fast plane at your disposal and a policy of easy come, easy go.'

'Would I be right in thinking the committee is covert because it discusses things it's best the rest of NATO shouldn't know about?'

'Nobody,' the Minister said again, 'asks questions. Nobody would like to see our American friends pick up their marbles and go home. For the same reason we don't ask who comes in and out of Mildenhall.'

The fuzz, Wise had said, wouldn't stop him leaving Rossiter's house after that first spectacular visit. Not because he was supposed to be press. Because he was American.

'Is Dick Wise in this country officially, or not?'

'Am I supposed to know him?' Subtlety was not one of the Minister's strong points.

Rossiter nodded in acknowledgement of the answer. 'The Americans discussed their marbles. In secret. At Mildenhall. And after that came Nethercott Stoney.'

'Colonel Kowicki,' the Minister said, 'just *might* have been taking something very important back to Washington. It just *might* have been a copy of the minutes of that meeting. Personal delivery, too secret to go any other way. He only got as far as Nethercott Stoney.'

'I see now,' Rossiter said, 'what everybody means when they talk of the special relationship.'

The Minister's attitude to Rossiter had changed. It might almost have been called possessive.

'If our American allies simply tell us there were secret documents in that helicopter, something they wouldn't want to have lying around, we have to believe them. It's our duty to look for them. It's our duty to hand them back.'

'Unopened. Unread.'

'That goes without saying.' The Minister returned Rossiter's look without blinking.

Not just possessive; a challenge: upright Hugh Rossiter trapped between the moral high ground and his respect for a confidence.

Watching him, the Minister's own battered conscience briefly surfaced.

'Damn it, Hugh, that young fool knew what he was doing. We're interested in damage control now, not victimisation.'

'Then why,' Rossiter said bitterly, 'so many victims?'

A small, comfortable but hardly luxurious hotel out at Richmond, set back from the road, well screened by shrubbery, a bedroomed annexe for business conferences. The *Globe* had clearly used the place before; no booking in, no questions asked and instant privacy.

Stan and the minder had vanished. She was alone with Liz Balcon. It was of no importance. Nick was in danger. Heather was dead. She had forced herself on to the front pages at last. Now she would get even.

Liz was efficient, she had to say that. A packet of Tampax, some aspirin, a hot water bottle, an offer of food and drink. They had a small suite. There should have been a television set, of course, and a radio, but the TV had gone and the radio didn't work. Without even trying to make it sound convincing, Liz said she would get it fixed.

There was a telephone but Liz made a point of saying that it went through the desk. Best not, Liz said, speak to anyone just now, not Emma, not her mum, everything was being taken care of.

She herself, like Nick, had a pocketphone. She made several brief, guarded calls, the last one to do with Emma. 'Okay,' she kept saying. 'Yup. Tell them okay. Yup, fine, okeydoke.'

'She's coming here, isn't she?' Having Emma with her would ease the burden.

''Course. Where else? When we say we'll deliver' – Liz raised a thumb, clicked her tongue – 'we deliver. Agency in Bristol, private car, trained nanny to look after her. Not to worry.'

Not to worry! It brought back that frightening urge to laugh. If she let go now it would be a bottomless pit.

'I hope nobody says anything about Nick to Emma. She doesn't know how bad he is.'

'She doesn't?' Fiddling competently with a cassette recorder, Liz was unable to hide a fleeting emotion.

'IS MY DADDY DEAD?' HEARTBREAK. By Liz Balcon. A *Globe* exclusive.

Liz recovered quickly. 'Just as well we're collecting her, only a matter of time before she got it from somewhere. All right if we kick a few things around now?'

She put the recorder on a little table in front of the sofa, rummaged in an outsize shoulder bag, shut it with a snap like a mousetrap. Notebook and ballpoint at the ready, she patted the place at her side.

'Come and sit. How's the tum? Sure you don't want that drink? No? Bottle of plonk later, perhaps. We'll eat here in the room.'

How could she live the life she lived and keep that flawless, almost childlike complexion? How could she do what she did and preserve that totally wrinkle-free forehead? Was there, some-where, the picture of a female Dorian Gray?

One last matter before she set about getting her revenge. 'What about Hugh Rossiter?' The *Globe* might have the story: she needed Rossiter's support.

Liz took off her great lenses, breathed on each in turn, polished them. 'Crispin'll find him. Crispin could find ice lollies in hell.'

She wrinkled her nose to adjust her glasses, tranquil as a nun. 'Right? Right. If it's okay with you I'd like to start with the sex angle. I mean it's going to come out, we'd dug in already, only with Tim bowing and scraping to the Tyrant and D-notices fizzing about like farts in a bottle we . . .'

She stopped. 'What's up?'

'What sex angle?'

'Oh, come on.' Liz laughed. 'Don't go all coy, Sarah. You married a feller, you took up with a les, who cares? I'm broad-minded. No, she took up with you, that's the angle we'll take.

Don't worry. We're on your side. We'll be firstest with the mostest, that's how Roger – '

'Bugger Roger!'

Liz was not easily startled, but for a moment she sat mouth open, her pointy nose in her pointy face – Nick was right, she did have pointy tits; everything pointy; she was a female Struwwelpeter – lifted toward Sarah with the absurd effect of an arrow stopped in mid-flight.

'Look, Sarah, the *Globe* – '

'And bugger the *Globe*!' For the first time her swearing sounded real. Heather would have been proud. She didn't mean Heather. She meant Nick.

Liz went to the house phone. 'Bottle of vodka and some tomato splits, please. Oh, and a thingy of ice.'

She slapped down the phone. 'Nick must have told you.'

Heather was dead. Funny thing, she kept thinking Nick was dead, too, because she'd felt all along he would die, hadn't she? Or was it that she hadn't really loved him, not for a long time now? She *had* loved him, loved him a lot; wasn't that something?

Another bout of anarchy; they would come and go and come again, faster and faster until, in the end . . .

'Nick must have told me what?'

'What it's like,' Liz said. 'Big I-ams and nobodies. Nutters, creeps, crooks. Rich men, poor men, beggarmen and politicians. You start on the doorstep, hunting in packs – '

'Raking through dustbins.'

'Raking through dustbins. And blimey O'Reilly, the stuff in the dustbins is *clean*!'

She adjusted her glasses, big enough to let her eyes rove around behind them like fish in a bowl. 'Nick used to be the expert. Nick's really ace.'

She used both hands to push the lenses to the tip of that arrowhead nose. 'Like, you know, tripping up Lily Holden? One of the nice people who've been helping pay your mortgage and keep Emma and Mothercare happy?'

'Junk people, junk press!'

'Sure, junk press,' Liz said calmly. 'Tales of junk people, by junk people, for junk people. That's where it's all at, on the junk heap.'

'What are you trying to say?' Claws in her belly, dull aches in her back and head.

'What I'm trying to say' – was Liz, in her laconic, seen-it-all way, trying to be friendly? – 'you need money, need friends, got something to say, so if not us, who? At least we do it well.

'All the others'll be at it, right this minute, scissors and paste jobs. We're the only ones who might draw your kind of picture. No friends, no fistful of readies, you're in shtuck.' She patted the sofa.

Sarah shook her head dazedly. 'Don't you understand?' Couldn't go over there and sit down, not yet. 'What's been happening to me is nothing to do with sex. It's about what can happen to somebody ordinary, someone like me or you, if they decide you're not on their side. If you're telling the truth and they don't believe you.'

Liz checked her watch, patted her hair, smoothed down her dress, but she was listening.

Squeezing her hands so hard that it hurt, Sarah said, 'Nick did something stupid. Wrong if you like, no argument. But he did it because he's become what your kind of job turns people into. You said he was ace, and he was; ace at getting the best out of your kind of story. But ace at something else, ace at forgetting he was basically decent, basically kind, basically had feelings.'

Oh God, tears in her eyes, choking her nose.

'And what for, in the end? Money? Well, why not? But to *be* someone as well, only he couldn't see that the sort of person he wanted to be isn't worth being at all.'

'Power.' Liz nodded. 'You sort of get a taste for it. You know?'

'Other people's power, not yours! What makes people like you important, if you're important at all, isn't what *you* are, it's what *they* are, the people you write about. If you've got a sort of aura, it's the aura of other people's importance. And if you work for the *Globe*, half of them tend to be important for all the wrong reasons.'

'Gordon Bennett!' Liz said, no resentment. 'Don't care whose nose you get up, do you?' She came to take Sarah by the arm and this time there was no resistance.

She sat her on the sofa, pushing notepad and tape recorder away. A tap at the door. She waited until the room waiter had gone, poured herself tomato juice, added vodka and ice, stirred it with a finger.

'Listen, while I tell you how it is.' She sank half of her drink without blinking. 'Guess who's just down the corridor in this dump. Don't know, so I'll tell you.'

She counted them off on her fingers. 'Rodge, leave him out. Leave out another guy and old Stan, who've we got left? Your Nick's brother – '

She nodded, watching Sarah's face. 'Yup. Right little charmer, Nick's brother, sell his mum for fifty nicker only she's in the booby hatch. We won't use that, other rags will, want to bet?'

'That's in one room. Next door? Well, next door we've got next door, meaning next door to you. Peggy Morcambe?'

'No,' using surprising strength to hold Sarah down, 'listen. Not telling you this for fun, just to show you the way it's stacked. Here.'

She held out her glass. Sarah gulped obediently.

'More like it! How's the tum? Nothing like a Bloody Mary for showing a tum who's boss. Okay, so we're a bunch of shits, right? Only this was up and running before you put on your act for old Uncle Tim.

'Now' – another bony squeeze to stop Sarah interrupting – 'you decide you're not going to talk, you think we call off the parade? Not bloody likely! So take some advice from a junkie. Co-operate. I'm on your side, cross my heart and hope to die.'

She refilled her glass, her eyes never away from Sarah's face.

Sarah said, 'Heather Smith was our solicitor. Just that.'

Liz said, 'Not much sex in soliciting, not that kind. Do you want the punters to read your version or not?'

'Heather was murdered.'

'That story's still running. Killed. No rape. Somebody tried to make it look like rape. Well, attempted rape. The buzz, not official yet, is some private investigator is on the run, seen in your area the night Heather Smith died. The buzz is this guy's been known to do jobs for Five.'

She let it sink in, sank a second Bloody Mary herself. 'Given the job of keeping an eye on Rossiter's house, right. Sees you set off to see your Nick at Redhill. Sees Heather Smith set off after you. A few loose bits here, but Rodge and Crispin reckon this guy had the word to stall her, Heather. Spin her some yarn, right?

'Well.' She still had a hand on Sarah's arm. 'Big strong girl, your Heather. Chuck that Kawasaki of hers about like it was a kiddy bike, saw it ourselves, didn't we? Not going to take any crap from strangers, so it gets a bit physical, guy loses his cool and – '

'Don't!'

Heather's wiry arms about her, pressing her down. Bile in her throat, clenched fists in her guts, the roaring sound of darkness.

Eventually she had everything under control.

'He pulls off her drawers,' Liz said calmly, 'make it look like a sex thing only all he had in mind was to cover his tracks. Crispin says there's a lot of acid flying around between Five and the Branch, lot of tight lips, too. Have another Mary, do you good.'

She released Sarah.

'We're the dirt squad, right? Garbage collectors. Well, you'd be surprised.' A not unfriendly pat. 'Stick around, Sarah. All going to hang out when it's time.'

'But Nick – '

Liz was shaking her head, auburn ponytail swinging. 'Not Nick. Meaning not what you mean, not yet. Tyrran put the clamps on that, friends in high places. Tyrran wants pole position for the *Globe* when the big one breaks, but softly, softly, that's the Tyrant's style. Meantime it's like Crispin says, keep pissing a quart into a pint pot and it's bound to overflow.'

She took Sarah's hands. 'Play it our way. We'll see you right.'

'And Nick's brother? That woman, Peggy Morcambe?'

'Leave that to Rodge. They'll say what he wants them to say. All we want for now is Nick being conned by Glashin, then Glashin's pals trying to kill him in a rigged car smash. Plus a les being raped, only she wasn't, and out come more great dollops of muck on Five. Sexy stuff, undercover infighting, can't go wrong with that. Plus Nick is – '

The house phone shrilled. Liz answered, said, 'Right with you', dropped it back on the hook.

'Back in a tick. Give yourself another slug if you feel like it. Look, not even going to lock you in, we do sometimes, no kidding. But you and me are nose to tail in the same lane now, everything's going to be great. Anyway, Emma on the way? Got to stick around for that, right?'

The Minister was typically unrepentant. 'Victims? Self-made, old boy. But the whole purpose of this meeting, Hugh, is to make sure there aren't any more. That's why I'm going to take you into my confidence.'

'What if I don't want to know?'

'Forfeited your choice, my lad.' There were times when the Minister could smile and come close to being a villain.

'Scribblers like you,' he said, 'enjoy the luxury of choosing your facts. People like me sometimes have the dangerous option of burying them.'

'People like me,' Rossiter said, 'occasionally have the pleasure of digging them up.'

'Can't have it both ways.' The Minister fetched a plain folder from his desk.

'Take a look.' His eyes jeered at Rossiter's obvious hesitation. 'Easy to speak no evil if you keep your eyes and ears shut. Go on. Read it. Facts are sacred, isn't that your creed?'

It was a report from the River Police, Wapping Pier, on the retrieval of a male body from the Thames near Greenwich, provisionally identified as Walter James Exton, general manager of a South London debt collecting agency.

The original report had followed routine, but it had travelled far in a matter of hours, passing from an Assistant Commissioner at New Scotland Yard to the Secretary of State before reaching the Minister. It had also acquired a series of annotations.

A marginal scribble from the Secretary of State: *Please handle as agreed*. A restricted circulation authorisation, alphanumerical titles rather than names. Rossiter had a shrewd idea where the owners of the titles might be found but something else caught his eye, someone's handwritten instruction: *Let Capstick see this*.

Lighting a cigarette, the Minister temporarily vanished behind nimbocumulus. He waved it away. 'In it up to your halo now, Hugh.'

'Am I supposed to know the deceased?'

'Not unless you have the sight, as my Irish grandmother used to call it.' The Minister jetted smoke through his nostrils.

'But if I tell you' – the Minister reached to flick the file from Rossiter's unresisting fingers – 'that his professional activities kept him in your neck of the woods during the last few days.

'There are debts you owe,' he said, that extraordinary blend of raw insensitivity and candour, 'and debts you pay. Either way they can sometimes be called in a bit sharpish. Know anything about debt collecting?'

'Not much.'

'You would if you were a politician. A lot of ferreting around, sort of combination of psychology and animal cunning. Sort of low level private investigation.'

'Dicky Wise' – Rossiter was a man with a bad taste in his mouth – 'talked about a wild man. A chap' – he floated it out as a question – 'called Norton-Jones?'

The Minister was too hardened to be caught out. 'I've heard the expression used for the odd one who goes over the top. This chap' – he tapped the file – 'isn't Norton-Jones, of course. Just one of Norton-Jones's unofficial middlemen. Feel like a drink?'

'More like a mouthwash.'

The Minister had once again acquired a kind of perverse moral ascendancy. 'You with your conscience, me with all the dirty jobs your conscience and my Secretary of State's won't let you both take on. Elly once told me there had to be two kinds, yours and mine. She had a fancy word for it: symbiosis. Like the toff and the cloakroom attendant, clean towels for grubby hands.'

'Does it help,' Rossiter asked, 'if I agree?'

'Your Miss Smith,' the Minister said. 'Not actually murder, Hugh, not that it makes much difference.'

'Hardly any at all. It was in another country: and besides, the wench is dead.'

The Minister was not a man for other people's quotations. 'This chap Exton was ex-Security Service, did low level jobs for Five. Well, for Norton-Jones. Didn't know his own strength.'

'Killed her in a fit of absentmindedness, chucked himself into the Thames out of remorse?'

'Better than me with words, Hugh, but chucked we could agree on.'

The Minister went to sit behind his desk. 'Feel any better if I tell you the whole business has gone to the Attorney-General's office?'

'Nothing,' Rossiter said, 'is likely to make me feel any better. But if you're telling me this is the end of victimisation I might manage a faint *laudamus*.'

'The Attorney-General' – the Minister cuddled his file – 'has the right, the duty, even, to suppress sensitive information on the grounds – I quote – that making it public would not be in the interests of the community as a whole.'

'It's going to be covered up.'

'Cover up what? Some wretched little debt collector who's made a bit of a pig's ear of things chucks himself into the river.'

'And Norton-Jones?'

'We cannot' – the Minister's voice hardened – 'bring national security into disrepute because one man succumbs to the stresses of an exceptionally demanding job.'

'Have I got it right?' Rossiter asked. 'Some highly sensitive document goes missing after that plane crash. It's American, and you have to help them find it. A job for Five, with the help of the Branch, and the man in charge in Five is Norton-Jones.'

'Who took a matter of days,' the Minister said, 'to establish the fact that a grubby little muckraker, any story for a price, any price for a story, had not only found it but arranged to sell it to a Soviet agent masquerading as a Tass man. Don't tell me the great Hugh Rossiter's going to put his reputation on the line for a gutter press scavenger and a Soviet spy pretending to be a journalist?'

'Don't tell me,' Rossiter said, 'that a murderous attack upon one young woman and the systematic intimidation of another are to be kept under wraps to protect people like Norton-Jones. People whose chief aim in finding those documents for our American allies was to read them first.'

'Not them, Hugh.' The Minister was brazen. 'Norton-Jones. Just Norton-Jones. Call him a wild man if you like, the Yanks have had their fair share. Anyway, there's always one rotten apple in every barrel.'

'That's what they always say. And what I always say is, why is everyone always so sure it's only one?'

'Extended leave.' The Minister was still unruffled. 'And highly unlikely he'll be returning to duty. Security isn't a parlour game but we do draw the line, you know.'

'In the interests of the community as a whole? Or the interests of the alliance, the Yanks knowing all about young Brooke? Still, I dare say you've told them they'll just have to be patient until the boy's on the mend, no problem in persuading him to say where the missing whatsit is, once he's recovered.'

Upending the file the Minister used it to rap his desk with finicky precision. 'Yes, well, as to that, Hugh, we have something of a problem.'

Big Ben struck the quarter remotely, as if from far across the Thames. Rossiter became aware of the room's stillness, though it was barely a stone's throw from the bustle of Victoria Street, the whirligig of Parliament Square.

The Minister's self-assurance had taken on a certain brittleness.

'Norton-Jones decided Brooke had to be moved. Shocking security where he was, that sort of thing, absolutely his own decision. Damn it, Hugh, I don't check these things in person. We try to ensure the right men are in charge and let them get on with it.'

The truth crept up on Rossiter like a barefoot assassin.

'The fact is,' the Minister said, 'Brooke died about four hours ago, shouldn't have been moved, I suppose. Well, now you know.'

'And Mrs Brooke.' Nothing mild about Rossiter now. 'When will she know?'

'Did a bunk, didn't she?' A touch of the old aggression. 'When she's found, she'll be told. We're not barbarians. As I said, one rotten apple. My real reason for asking you to drop in – '

'Was because you hoped I might know where she was. Hoped I might be the one to give her the glad tidings? What do I say to her? Not to worry any more, all over and done with, everything back to normal, so sorry she was bothered?'

He rubbed his grey face. 'Old Hugh Rossiter, last of the old school, slowly drinking himself into his grave. Never breaks a confidence, past it now anyway, but a specialist in reporting bad news. Have I got it about right?'

'Over and done with?' The Minister stared at him incredulously. 'You know damn well she knows where that stuff is, Hugh. You know the consequences for our relations with the Yanks. She's got to talk to them, direct, or they're never going to believe we didn't find the bloody thing ourselves.'

'Got to talk? Tell her her husband's dead but she hasn't a thing in the world to worry about so long as she'll talk?'

Rossiter pushed back his chair. 'How do I get out of this damn place?' He started toward the big double doors, then came back.

'If I find her, and God knows where I'm supposed to start looking, I'll make bloody sure she talks. Did anyone tell you about my press conference? You're invited. He's bloody well invited, isn't he, Elly? Because we need each other, Gordon and me, the sot and the lavatory man.'

A sharp knock preceded a Private Secretary, dark-suited, white-shirted, a plump penguin with a sheaf of papers in one flipper.

'You rang, Minister?'

'Mr Rossiter's leaving.' Rossiter guessed from the quick exchange of looks that any attempt he might make to find Sarah Brooke would be in the nature of a guided tour for the Branch.

The Private Secretary, capable of a little drama, drew the evening papers from his hoard and spread them on the desk. Sarah's face leaped out beneath headlines heavy enough to crush her.

While they were looking together, Rossiter showed himself out.

Liz set her pad aside, turned off the recorder, slipped off her glasses to squeeze the bridge of her sharp nose with finger and thumb.

'God, Sarah, you're making it hard.' It was the first time she had shown signs of stress.

'I'm telling the truth.'

'Can't use it. Look' – she fixed herself another Bloody Mary, rather less vodka – 'you know the game. Bryce has been on three times already. If I don't phone something in he's going to go spare.'

'Where's Hugh?'

'If I knew, I'd tell you. Crispin'll find him. Anyway' – she sipped her drink, pulled a face, set it down – 'Rossiter's no good to you on this one, only be in the way.'

Something was terribly wrong. She could feel it hanging in the air. Nick would say it was the nameless dreads that usually came with her period. Heather would cheer her up; surprising if you didn't feel the strain after all this.

Only all this included the fact that Heather was dead.

'You can't make me say what I can't say.' She went to the window, parted the drapes to press her forehead to cold glass. Outside there was a paved path, a high wall, dancing specks of snow.

Liz stayed where she was, reflected in the glass of the window. She waited for Liz's next move. Liz Balcon, Nick used to say, could get a clam to tell its life story between one wave and the next.

'I'm sorry.' The chill from the windowpane drove into her skull like a nail. 'What happens if I don't talk?'

Skinny Liz had gone waiflike, an Auschwitz case in a two-piece.

268

'Dunno. Never happened before. Jesus, I must be slipping.' But she went on sitting.

She said, 'Track you down, won't they? Stands to reason.'

'Who?'

'Them.' Liz laughed, the right sound, Sarah thought, from the wrong person. 'The lot that've been making your life a misery. The lot our rag supports. Funny, don't you reckon? The five per cent who run the show, getting half their votes from the ten per cent who can't read.'

Sarah turned. 'Why do you do it? I used to ask Nick. He never could answer, not really.'

'It's a job. No, Christ, you could imagine some creepy South American torturer saying that. I reckon it's like all these scientists. You know? Decent, home-loving guys with wives and kids and that and they're into inventing deathrays. Got what it takes and a sort of challenge, so, forget what it's for and go for the challenge. Well, that's us, I reckon.'

She slashed through the notes on her pad. 'Well,' she said, 'some of us, anyway.' The house phone rang to say that Emma had arrived.

As they left the room Liz checked the empty corridor. 'By this time your face'll be about as well-known as the Queen's. Just telling you for your own good.'

The side entrance led to a drive. Small, gritty snowflakes danced like gnats in an icy wind. The car, black with tinted glass that gave it a sinister air, was just turning the corner. Its wheels crunched on gravel with the sound of bones being crushed.

'Get the kid inside fast,' Liz said. 'Where's that bloody Rodge? Supposed to be lending a hand. Bloody men!'

A woman got out first, reached inside. 'Come on, Emma.' Emma appeared, pale, only half awake.

'Mummy!' She threw herself at Sarah, hugging her, pressing her face into Sarah's belly like any small, nuzzling creature.

'Emma,' Sarah hugged her, unable to find words. 'Emma, my precious.'

'Save it,' Liz said. 'Get her inside before she freezes.'

'We could do with a drink,' the woman said, a West Country accent. 'And a bite of something. Lucky we made it before this lot started,' and to Emma, 'Been as good as gold, haven't you, my love?' She had a cold and a strong smell of eucalyptus.

They all bundled inside, including the driver, a man of no

words but ex-police written all over him. His brief nod at Sarah told her that he knew who she was.

'Where's bloody Rodge?' Liz demanded again. 'Look' – to Sarah – 'wait in the room. Back in a tick when I've fixed a few things.' She bent to Emma. 'Want something to eat, poppet? Nice hot drink of something?' The voice of a different Liz, old pointy tits gone soft.

Emma shook her head, still pressed tightly against Sarah. 'Get her a sandwich,' Sarah said. 'Marmite, Bovril, something like that. And a cup of hot chocolate.'

'Will do. Keep out of sight. Back soon as I can.' She shooed the others down the deserted corridor and was gone.

'Mummy,' Emma said again. 'I missed you. It was horrid. And I didn't like that woman. She smells funny.'

Sarah closed the door of the room, knelt to take Emma in her arms. 'Listen, sweetheart, do you trust me?'

Emma nodded. 'Of course. Are we going to see daddy?'

'Tomorrow, perhaps. We're going somewhere else first, only we've got to be quiet and ever so quick, before anyone comes back.'

Emma's colour was hectic now, excitement and the rosiness of a child back from deep sleep. 'Good!' she said. 'I didn't like those people, not really. That woman, she smells of cough sweets.'

Sarah shrugged on her coat, grabbed her shoulder bag, swept Emma into the bathroom, closed and bolted the door.

'Want to wee first?'

Emma shook her head. 'We went at a place where we stopped for petrol. Are those people going to come after us?'

'Not if we're quick.' Better have a wee herself; God knew when the next chance would come. 'And clever, we've got to be clever.'

She zipped up trousers and jacket, opened the window. Cold air and a flurry of stray flakes. 'I'll get out first, then I'll lift you.'

Emma was quicker. 'If we move that' – a bath stool – 'I could stand on it.' She relinquished it to Sarah and stood with her gloved hands clasped, hardly able to contain her eagerness.

It would take Liz, empty room, locked bathroom door, no time at all to guess what had happened.

'Quick. This way. Tippytoe.' She took Emma's hand, trying not to drag her, heading around the back of the building on the narrow paved path she had seen earlier through the window of the room.

Away. All she could think of for the time being; get away.

After that . . . well, that would come later and in another place, if only they could escape the attentions of all the people who, for a score of reasons, would throw everything into the task of tracking them down. For the first time in hours she thought of Norton-Jones and shivered from something deeper than the cold.

They turned the corner, Emma silent and intent upon this new development in a life that had been little else but shocks and surprises since the night – a million years ago? – that had brought Capstick to the front door. Sarah found herself thinking of him almost as a friend as she peered round the corner at the floodlit front of the hotel.

'Emma! Quick! Run!' She all but scooped Emma up.

'Taxi! Taxi!'

Just pulling away, its hire light on, one of those impossible turns with which London taxis perpetually astonish.

Young, the thin, potentially cheeky face of the professional London cabby, the driver already had the door open. 'Bit o' luck there, madam. No night for hanging about. Now then, young lady,' giving Emma a broad wink – 'and where might you want to go?'

By this time your face will be about as well known as the Queen's. Main line stations? Forget it. Where were they now? Richmond.

'Wimbledon station,' she said in a rush.

'Gateway to the South,' he said and was cut off as his controller came in with a crackle of static and 'Uh, yeh, Glenthorne Road and the Broadway. Bunch o' bloody wogs by the sound of 'em. Over.'

Outside the Home Office bunker Rossiter bought a *News* and was reading the front page as footsteps fell in with his own.

'Well, sir, cat among the pigeons and no mistake.'

He looked at the other man and thought that he might have been taken for anything but what he was, an agent of the secret state. Pater familias, that former favourite name for writers of moralising letters to the press.

'How old is your daughter, Chief Superintendent?'

'Thirty-one, sir. A bit younger than Mrs Brooke.' A few more steps, taking them into Broadway, before Capstick said, 'A bit smarter, too. Not so educated, perhaps, but a bit more in the way of things.'

Coming up on New Scotland Yard and the revolving sign that should have been selling something, hot-dogs or ice-cream, Rossiter said, 'I'd have thought it hard to be more in the way of things than Mrs Brooke at this moment. Where do you drink? Or do you?'

Capstick steered him into Victoria Street. 'The Albert's handy, sir, if it's a quick one.'

'Nothing quicker than a double brandy.'

Leaning against the bar, Capstick looked impassively at Rossiter. 'Your idea, sir, getting Mrs Brooke in the way of the press tonight?'

'At the *Globe*? Good God, no!' Rossiter looked wearily offended. 'The poison press isn't my cup of tea and I'm not theirs. The *Globe* once did me the honour of calling me Public Enemy Number One over a piece I did on CND.'

'You wouldn't have invited them to that press conference of yours?'

'Oh, I see. Yes, well I may not care for them, but a free press is like being pregnant, all or nothing.'

He swirled his brandy, tipped it down. 'The other half?'

Capstick shook his head. 'Where are you off to now, sir, if I might ask?'

'Ask what you like, can't you? The law's on your side. Anyway' – Rossiter looked at the other man almost affectionately – 'shouldn't you be in hot pursuit instead of tippling with passé prima donnas?'

Capstick was buttoning his coat. 'They know where I am, sir. And I've learned what I was after. You wouldn't be standing here boozing if you knew where she was.'

'Boozing, not getting pissed. I could find it in my heart to like you, Chief Super, were the times less brisk and giddy-paced. Do I gather you've lost her?'

'Tracked her out to Richmond, got there just in time to find she'd given the *Globe* the slip. Excuse me, sir. I think you're about to be solicited.'

Rossiter looked round.

'Mr Rossiter? Crispin Craig, the *Globe*. Mrs Brooke' – the fair, lank-haired Crispin, his pale eyes fathomless, his ears

practically key-hole shaped, looked doubtfully at Capstick –
'wants to see you. Get you there in a jiff, taxi waiting outside.'

Rossiter laid a hand on Crispin's shoulder. 'Let me introduce
you, dear old chap. My friend Chief Superintendent Capstick.
He's terribly anxious to get in touch with Mrs Brooke himself,
so . . .'

Capstick displayed his ID. 'Delmay's Hotel, Richmond, that
what you had in mind, lad?'

He patted Crispin's arm. 'Get in touch with your office. Things
have moved on a bit.'

'Or in *Globe* language,' Rossiter said with some relish, 'piss
off, dear boy.' His brief pleasure over with Crispin's departure,
he went back to being old. 'I take it you're trying to find her?'

'She had a flying start, sir. Could be anywhere.'

'Wells?'

'They fetched the little girl up. When Mrs Brooke flew the
coop she took the child with her.' Capstick decided to produce
his last card. 'Mr Norton-Jones's an old hand, sir. Not many
tricks he doesn't know.'

It startled Rossiter. 'But I understood from the Minister – '

'He was off this one?' Capstick looked briefly as Hamlet
appeared at the far corner of the bar, shook his head and then
jerked a thumb to indicate that he would wait outside. 'Officially,
yes. Officially, suspended from duty. But they have to find him
to tell him. In the meantime, well, he doesn't give up easily, Mr
Norton-Jones. Give you a lift to Victoria, sir?'

'What about my house?' Rossiter said. 'Have you put a man
there, too?'

Capstick set down his beer only half drunk. 'Got a whole
country to watch, sir. We're doing what we can. Mr Norton-
Jones isn't a killer, just' – he searched for the words – 'a patriot
gone wrong.'

'Tell you something, Chief Superintendent.' Rossiter looked
longingly at his empty glass before pushing it away. 'In a long life
spent watching the world go by, I've often found it hard to make
the distinction. I think I'll walk to Victoria.'

He knew why Nick was dead, the Minister embarrassed.
Norton-Jones had overdone the pressure. And Sarah Brooke
probably didn't even know.

* * *

Emma finally in bed and settled, Nell Crabtree looked at Sarah grimly. 'Now, Sarah, we can't leave things like this.' She and Mrs Crabtree were sharing an old sofa moulded over the years to the shape of ample bottoms. Charlie Crabtree, who had come all the way to Epsom to pick them up without asking a single question, sucked his empty pipe and stared at the fire, but he was listening.

She said, 'They weren't going to let me see Nick, Hugh Rossiter, anyone. They just wanted to use me.' No use trying to explain things to these two; decent, ordinary people so far as anybody was ordinary in a situation where it was an extraordinary feat just to be decent.

'It's a scandal,' Mrs Crabtree said. 'Say what you like, it's a scandal.' She would clearly have liked to say more but Charlie Crabtree, one of those trifling shifts of position that people who have lived with each other for fifty years use instead of telepathy, conveyed a gentle warning.

'It's good of you,' Sarah said. 'To have me, I mean, but I ought not to be here.' She knew, in the vaguest of terms, what she was going to do. She just had to pick her moment.

'You could call Mr Rossiter,' Charlie Crabtree said. 'Give him a bit of time, then see if he's back. Or I could run you up there in the ol' bus, wouldn't take – '

'No.' About that she could be decisive. 'I shouldn't have got you mixed up in this to begin with. I'm not letting you do any more.'

'But tomorrow,' Mrs Crabtree said, her concern making her look even more dour.

'Is another day.'

She was tired beyond imagining; the kind of tiredness that made time meaningless, where you went on because it was the only place to go. Perhaps she should tell Capstick what she knew. Perhaps then they would leave her in peace.

Only there was Nick.

'I've got to go home,' she said.

'Home?' That startled Mrs Crabtree. 'Not tonight you won't. Why, whatever could you do there tonight?'

'Cold,' Charlie Crabtree said. 'Cold an' dark, not bein' lived in, see what I mean, gal? You want somethin' particular, you just tell me where it is an' I'll nip across double quick.'

'That's right,' Nell Crabtree said. 'My ol' boy'll get it, whatever it is. Then tomorrow we'll all go over, put on a bit of warm and see what's what. All clean and tidy it is, glass back in the window, everything neat as a pin.'

'That young Wayne Cooper,' Charlie said. 'Me an' his boss's dad was at school together. Come on, gal, just say what it is you must have that can't wait. I'll be there an' back in two shakes of a lamb's tail.'

'No,' she said. 'I'll come with you. It'll be quicker. I know where everything is.' She knew what they were thinking: one sight of home and she would go to pieces.

'I need some things for Emma. Not just clothes: books, toys, things like that. I shan't make a scene or anything. Promise.'

Mrs Crabtree gave in. 'Go over with her then, Charlie. You wrap up warm then, gal. It's cold out there and we don't want you coming down with anything.'

Charlie was at the window. 'Stopped snowin', looks like. An' I see them Morcambes is back. Lights in the house, so I reckon we'd better be a bit careful, don't want that lot stickin' their noses into your business more than they have already.'

It reminded Sarah. She looked at her watch. 'I want' – it was almost on the hour – 'to hear the news. I want to know what they say.'

She sat down again. 'I want to. If you won't let me I'll go back home and listen there.'

Nell Crabtree took in that disturbing calm at a glance. 'No use, Charlie. Made up her mind, Sarah has. Turn the thing on.'

They listened to the radio news. At the very end, like a throwaway gag, the man arrested and charged with offences under the Act after crashing on the M25 had died of his injuries. An official statement would be made in the House the following day.

Other than that, nothing. Bedlam in the *Globe* newsroom, bedlam on the Street, nothing about it on the news. Sarah Brooke and her public tantrum had never taken place. She had a vision of the British media buried, cold and silent, under a chilly blizzard of injunctions.

Mrs Crabtree flung plump arms about her, her surface brusqueness gone. 'Oh, Sarah. Oh, my love, my love.'

Sarah freed herself. 'It's all right. Honestly. I think I've been expecting it and now it's happened. I'll howl, I know I will, but later, not yet. Can we go and get those things, please?'

It had stopped snowing. The air was a little warmer. The moon, high above the hill, wore thin cloud like a bridal veil. Through the trees and shrubbery she could see the Morcambes' house, a blaze of light.

She unlocked the door of her own house, switched on the light and for a terrifying instant thought she would break. Everything familiar in the yellow light: the little table they had bought second hand at the auction, the mirror her mother had given her, the row of pegs with Emma's anorak, her own anorak, and Nick's . . .

'Steady, gal.' Charlie's strong arm under her elbow.

It was enough. 'I'm all right. Honestly. I'm okay.'

'Now then,' he said, stolidly matter-of-fact. 'Can I do anythin' or will you be quicker on your own?'

'Upstairs,' she said quickly. 'That's where everything is. I won't be a tick.'

More lights, more blows to the guts where tension already lurked. She made herself into an automaton. That's what They thought: Sarah Brooke, robot, programmed to perform rudimentary tasks, circuits carefully mapped, fuses that would blow the moment the stress grew too great for a mere woman to bear.

Well, she thought, knowing that she was not in her perfect mind, stuff Them!

A few things from Emma's room, a few from her own. Then the spare room and there it was.

She remembered Nick bringing it home for the first time. 'Look at it. Doesn't weigh much more than a pound, stick it in your pocket, forget about it, always there when you need it. Call London, Australia, the man in the moon.' Then he'd pulled a face. 'And they can call you back.'

ROAM, CALL, MODEM, LOCK, STORE, SEND. Brief panic while she struggled to recall how the thing worked. A surge of relief as she realised she could remember. She slid it carefully among the clothes she had grabbed for Emma, closed the drawer, turned out the light, started downstairs just as someone rang Nick's chimes.

Charlie opening the door, Peggy Morcambe's voice, shrill with disappointment. 'Oh, it's you. I thought it might be Sarah.'

Arthur Morcambe. 'Saw the lights, old man, thought we'd better nip over and see what was what.'

'Sarah?' Charlie, innocent as a choirboy. 'She's not here. Just me doin' the rounds, make sure everythin's okay this cold weather.'

Lame, frustrated responses from the Morcambes; Charlie cutting them off. 'Expec' you're glad it's not a burglar, anyway.'

She tiptoed down, slipped through to the garage while Charlie saw the Morcambes off. He put out the lights, closed the door, had to, and set off down the drive, knowing that she could let herself out. She released the catch of the garage door from the inside, eased it up on moonlight boosted by virgin snow, started the car and drove out, stopping by him in the road.

'What you doin', gal? Where you off to?' In spite of his alarm he kept his voice down, no fool, Charlie Crabtree.

She thrust Emma's things at him. 'I'm not going to do anything awful, only see Hugh Rossiter. Don't worry. I'll be back.'

She let in the gear, headed east towards the minor road over Holmbury Hill. Only when a lone driver coming in the opposite direction flashed her did she realise she had no lights. Even then she was reluctant to put them on. Disappear into the darkness, exactly what she had in mind.

Paying off his taxi, Rossiter looked for signs of Capstick's men. There were none, though Sam materialised with a token rebuke for neglect. He let them both in then went about drawing curtains and putting on lights. It was more than the darkness he was shutting out.

He looked at the shot-blasted frame of the portrait propped against the wall. 'What will she do, Elly?'

He poured himself a generous measure of brandy, started to remove his Burberry, stopped with one arm still tangled as he felt the bulk of the pocketphone.

Sitting down and resisting Sam's attempts to join him, he contemplated the thing. 'Elly,' he said, 'you know my mechanical skills. Got to help me on this one.'

He ran his fingers gingerly over the keys several times, sighed, finished his brandy, set the glass in the hearth.

'Okay, old girl. Here goes.'

Nothing happened for so long that he was on the point of abandoning the experiment. In that instant a voice, tiny but clear, said, 'Kinsman? Come in, Kinsman.'

Before he could react another voice, stronger, said, 'Here,

277

gimme that thing,' and then, loud and clear, 'Hey, ratbag! What's the news?'

A statement in the House. She knew what that would mean; a darker, smoother, altogether more skilful version of the one where the drunk – or the black or the petty villain – resisted arrest, collected an amazing number of self-inflicted injuries and died in custody at the local police station. Nick had covered more than one of those in the early days.

A full enquiry after a long delay. A verdict of accidental death.

Nick's was an accidental death. He had had the misfortune to have an accident, and the greater misfortune to have had it with the wrong people.

So she drove, the country roads virtually deserted, and gradually became aware that she herself might well be an accident someone was looking for with a view to making it happen.

And the junk press – no, she preferred Hugh Rossiter's word, the sewer press – would have another run of one-day-wonder headlines on whatever made the most sexy story of the week: needn't even be about sex.

Except that she, cruising the eerie, empty lanes, their snowy verges fluorescent in the moonlight, was the only person in the world who knew where it was, the thing that would settle everything.

She passed a pub aglow with promised comfort, each window outlined with the multicoloured lights of Christmas. It made her want to cry; not the beauty, for they were garish, but the fact that in spite of the commercialism it was still a time when even the most unlikely people could briefly forget their own selfish wants and throw off sparks of warmth and good will. And Nick and Heather were dead.

Once again she found herself drowning, eyes and nose waterlogged. This time she let it rip, pulling in to the side of the road, switching off, putting her hands and head down on the wheel while she first tried to keep things within bounds, just a private, controllable grief, and then thought that her whole body would shake itself to pieces while her sobs climbed the register, turned animal and ended in exhausted but cathartic whimpers.

Cars went past at irregular intervals, momentarily flooding her with light that illuminated nothing and made the subsequent darkness more absolute. Only the moon remained tranquil above the black bulk of the hill.

She mopped herself up as best she could and turned the car toward the hill. Halfway there, she remembered. No spade. She stopped, fumbled for Nick's pocketphone and called Rossiter's number. Engaged.

'Listen,' Wise told Rossiter. 'Don't talk. Just listen. First thing you do, you find yourself a scratch pad and a pen. When you're ready just whistle.'

He found himself what was needed and whistled.

'Okay, you can whistle. Now, remember the song I favoured you with, first time I visited with you? Air Cav? Sure you do, you heard it often enough before those guys ran out of beer and let us go back to Saigon with the hooch run. So write it out, okay? Then whistle.'

Rossiter solemnly wrote:

> *He stood on the steeple*
> *And pissed on the people*
> *But the people couldn't*
> *Piss on him.*
> *Amen.*

He whistled.

'You and your watch-chain guts,' Wise said. 'Okay, now you mark the seventh letter of the first line, the first letter of the second line, the first letter of the third line . . .'

When he had written down and converted all the letters into numbers he had a call code.

'Now punch it up.' The pocketphone went dead.

When Wise's voice returned he was notably more cheerful. 'Okay, ratbag, at ease.'

'You mean I can talk?'

'You can talk, you can sing. Only thing you will not, repeat will not do is say any more poems.'

'Can I ask you what all that was about?'

'Never know who's listening. Now nobody's listening except you, me, and that place near Harrogate. Oh, and maybe a computer back at Fort Meade but who gives a shit about computers?'

'I share the sentiment if not the language.'

'So tell me what you know.'

'The wild man's still on the loose.'

'That we know. What we need to know is where he's heading.'

'My guess would be that he's heading for wherever whatever it is you want is hidden.'

'We know that too. He got it out of Nick Brooke, your people tell you that?'

'I guessed.'

'You guessed! He puts terminal pressure on a sick man to get a piece of information and you have to guess that's what happened because nobody up there is going to tell you. Because they're all set to cover it up the way they've covered up everything else, and they know that even if that old straight arrow Hugh Rossiter breaks a confidence they can gag the press and fool the judge and bury the whole thing six feet deep the way they always do. Good old national security.'

'They also know I wouldn't do anything to put Mrs Brooke in danger.'

'She *is* in danger.'

'I know that.'

'But not where she is right now?'

'If I knew that, I'd be a happier man.'

'I'll tell you where she is,' Wise said. 'Where she's always been, between a rock and a hard place. And I'll tell you where she's heading. For the same place as Norton-Jones.'

'For God's sake,' Rossiter said, 'does anyone else have to die for a lousy piece of paper?'

'Whoever reads it,' Wise said. 'That's why we have to find her. Listen, who else do you know that has one of these radio phones?'

'No one.' He remembered Roger Petherbridge. 'The *Globe* uses them.'

'Someone just tried to call you.'

'How do you know?'

'Somebody with a radiophone' – Wise skipped the question – 'just tried to call you on your home number. They'll try again pretty soon.'

'If someone was trying to get me on the ordinary phone it would have rung anyway.'

'No it wouldn't,' Wise said. 'We intercepted and gave them

the engaged signal, don't want to make anyone suspicious or why did I have you switch channels?'

Rossiter's non-technical mind finally made a connection. 'Your fancy place near Harrogate. The place that told you what Nick Brooke was doing from the time he left Nethercott Stoney right up to his accident. In that case, you must know who's trying to call me now. Or at least, where they are.'

He waited. He said, 'Dick?' There was no answer, but out in the hall the ordinary, old-fashioned telephone began to ring.

She had recovered. Fear, the chill of the night, behind it all the knowledge that someone called Nick, to whom she had given most of her adult years, who had shared her bed and seeded her with life, had gone as abruptly as Heather and for as unexplained a reason. Yet she had recovered. For now. For long enough. She willed it.

Then there was Rossiter's voice on the phone.

'Hello,' she said. 'It's me.'

'Don't use that thing again.' His normally drawling voice was urgent. 'Don't answer if anyone calls. Wait for me under the clock.' He was gone.

Under the clock. He was drunk again. Out of his mind. Or had she misheard? She sat in the moonlit night, the pocketphone she must not use on her lap. Another car coming round the bend, passing, slowing. Its reverse lights came on. It backed level. The driver's window came down.

'Everything all right?' A man's voice, loud, cheerful, had had a drink or two. He terrified her: so might they come out of the darkness to make everything all wrong.

She started up, let in the clutch, shot dangerously forward on the inside while his lights dwindled in her rear-view mirror. No pursuit. Crazy woman, scared of strange men even when they only wanted to help.

The next right fork, piling on the speed. The car clock said getting on for ten, awkward to see unless she bent her head.

In her mind's eye she saw the other clock, hanging up there over the road, just like that.

He was there first, waiting in the old Peugeot. She pulled in by the blacksmith's and he was out before she had switched off. She wound down her window. He put in his head and he smelled of brandy but his first question was eminently rational.

'Is Emma all right?'

'She's with the Crabtrees.'

'Get out. Leave it here. We'll go in mine.' It was as if they had discussed the whole thing before, were acting according to a prearranged plan.

'I haven't got a spade.'

'I have.' They were away, leaving behind the hanging clock that made Abinger Hammer modestly famous in these parts.

'Good girl. I was scared stiff you wouldn't understand. Then I was sure you would.'

He turned, as she had known he would, at the junction with the Holmbury road. 'You do know, don't you?'

'What? Where it is? Or that Nick's dead?'

'Oh dear God!'

'Don't say anything conventional. Or kind. Did they get you out to that place at Richmond?'

'No. A human ferret called Crispin found me but Capstick saw him off. A good man of his kind.'

Scrupulously avoiding the smallest reference to Nick, Heather, anything that might cause her to come apart, he said, 'How well do you know the hill? On foot.'

'Very.'

'In the dark?'

'It isn't, is it? Not really.'

'"And hand in hand,"' he said, '"on the edge of the sand, they danced by the light of the moon." Shall we dance, dear girl, you and I?'

'Oh yes,' she said, her voice taut enough to snap, 'and sing to a small guitar.'

He drove the car off the road and tucked it among the trees.

'It's quite a bit further from here,' she said.

'But far fewer folk know this way up.' He began to lock the car, changed his mind. 'What the hell! Keep an eye on it, Elly, old girl.' He checked his torch, opened the boot for the spade, produced a silver flask from his pocket and offered it to Sarah.

'What the hell!' She took it, swallowed, coughed.

'Not a cough in a carload,' he said, mock indignation. '*Grande champagne,* none of your cooking cognac.' He took a long swig. 'All right, lead on.'

'Up there.' She indicated a steep slope. 'Then we follow the ridge.'

'Are you scared?' He asked it meekly. 'Like me?'

'Petrified.' But her fear was temporarily overmastered by a cold determination to strike a last blow, successful this time, for herself, for Nick, for Heather.

She scrambled after him up the rutted slope. The rise in temperature had produced a slight fog which the moon made luminescent. Here in the scrubland the snow was uneven, a thick powdering on bracken and ling, patches of darkness where it had failed to penetrate sheltered pockets.

Once on the top a track ran ahead, crossed at one point by a crumbling row of concrete blocks, all that was left of World War Two tank traps. Dead bracken had bearded them and broom stretched skeletal fingers.

He stopped. 'Did you hear anything?'

'Gatwick,' she said. 'Coming and going for Christmas.'

'God bless us every one. Are we still of one mind, dear girl?'

'Oh yes,' she said. 'We hold your press conference.'

'Behold, I bring you good tidings.'

'Glory to God in the highest,' she said, a tremor in her voice, 'and on earth peace, good will toward men.'

'Dick Wise says it's been tried and it didn't work.'

'If at first you don't succeed . . .'

He held her back. 'Good tidings of great joy it is not, or there wouldn't be so many people doing their best to keep it quiet. Are you quite sure you understand?'

'The truth,' she said. 'The whole truth and nothing but the truth.'

'So we dig up the truth – '

' – and tell it to the world' – she held up her Excell – 'on these. Who shall we start with? Tass?'

He shouldered the spade, loping along in her small shadow while his own tagged on behind. 'I think I ought to tell you that once Nick found the thing and read it, he was – '

'Don't!'

'I have to, dearest girl, since you do appear to be in my care now.' They came to a single tree at a meeting of trails.

'If I'm in your care,' she said, 'I'm in Elly's care, seems to me. Do you think she minds? This is the lookout tree, by the way.'

It wasn't much of a tree, a spindly pine that, over the years, had lost most of its lower branches. The moon had developed a double ring. From where they stood the tree poised in front of it preposterously, a spindly Giacometti saint with a double halo.

'What I was going to say,' Rossiter told her, 'is that what Nick came upon, what we propose to dig up and broadcast, is something so secret that I doubt he'd have lived even if he hadn't died. I fear I make small sense.'

'They would have killed him anyway. To stop it getting out. Who are they?'

He shrugged helplessly. 'Don't ask me. If knowledge is power, secret knowledge is . . .'

The unspoken words trailed after his moonlit breath and vanished.

He said, 'As the great Book says, their name is Legion, for they are many.'

'Their name's Penelope. You have to learn to stand up to Penelope or you'll never be able to stand up to anyone.'

'Really?' he said. 'Then perhaps that's where Nick went wrong. Yes, well, the other thing is that as soon as we start telling the truth, they'll know. They have an ear in Harrogate.'

His pocketphone started to call, astonishingly loud in the night though it was in his pocket. 'See what I mean?' he said. 'I fancy it's best we should be away from home.'

They waited until it stopped. Almost at once her own began to clamour. They gave it the same treatment. 'If you want to know,' she said with a kind of gasp, 'I've never been so frightened in my life.' She pointed. 'Along that one, not very far. We might have to do quite a bit of digging.'

'American digging, yes? Not British digging.' He took the lead, aircraft noises from Gatwick the only sound in the night.

'What do you mean, British or American?'

'I am not,' Rossiter said, 'particularly pro-American or particularly anti-American. I am not, I trust I don't offend, particularly pro- or anti-British. In my circlings of the globe I have been witness to the civilising missions of both and I could see little difference. But when the Americans start to dig, everything tends to end up out in the open. When the British start to dig, it usually ends up six feet deep.'

'This time,' she said, another gasp, 'we dig American.'

'Are you all right?'

'More or less. Just started my period. Sorry to make you blush.'

'Dearest girl, when I last blushed I was old enough to be your brother. The news agencies first, then. I have their telephone numbers engraved on my heart as the sad queen had Calais engraved on hers.'

'Bloody Mary.' Sarah laughed shakily. 'Poor old Liz. I wonder if she's still digging dirt for the *Globe*? Down the path by that clump of gorse. You'll see the clearing as soon as we're past.'

Just past the gorse he stopped so suddenly that they collided.

'He that diggeth a pit,' he said, 'shall fall into it. Why should the devil have all the best quotes?'

The little clearing had been turned over, most of it lightly, some with an energy that suggested manic purpose. There could be little doubt that what had been dug for had been found. There was only one real hole. It was empty, and beside it lay a spade.

Sarah turned toward him without speaking. Tiny moons glittered in each eye before she brushed them away. Then her gaze shifted.

'There! Sticking out of the dirt. That's the sack he hid it in.'

Raking the sandy soil aside with her bare hands, she grabbed the corner of the plastic fertiliser bag. It resisted briefly then came free. It had concealed a man's head. He had been shot through the mouth. The effect was messy.

Reaching her, Rossiter tripped on a hand, half buried, its fingers wrapped about an automatic pistol. She was retching, producing nothing other than great gulps of air that were almost shrieks. He drew her away.

'Norton-Jones?'

She nodded, unable to speak.

He held her close. Heather had loved her. He could love her himself, but for his age. In his head he said: 'Sorry, Elly, old girl. Just another touch of Love without his wings.'

'I think we would do well to put some distance between us and Mr Norton-Jones.' He raised a hand, tipsily jaunty. 'Thou wretched, rash, intruding fool, farewell!'

Coming up almost noiselessly behind them Dick Wise, that big man with the feather tread, said, 'That's the trouble with you

British. Always living in the past. Now, which one of you two is going to let me talk to momma?'

He held out a hand for a pocketphone. He was back in his coveralls, one capacious pocket distorted by a rolled, plastic-bound document on which the Great Seal of the United States was partially visible.

They saw it almost as soon as they heard its unfriendly clatter, navigation lights winking as it came low over Leith Hill on a direct line from Gatwick. Rossiter pulled Sarah to him, cradling her face between his arms and his chest. Head bowed, eyes squinting, he heard the thing pass over, circle, return. A shaft of blinding light found them. When he looked up it was not at the moon but the sun, from which a harness was already being winched down.

Wise had hardly looked at the body. 'Feeling better now, honey?' His hand inserted itself gently under Sarah's chin. 'Take it easy. Everything's going to be downhill from now on.'

She resisted his hand, head still pressed into Rossiter's chest, eyes tight shut, face the colour of moonlight.

'We're not going in that thing,' Rossiter shouted above the racket. 'Elly told me never to fly with strange men. Especially to Mildenhall.'

'Just be glad,' Wise said, 'you didn't arrive in time to dig that thing up. Would have set me a problem.' He put his mouth close to Rossiter's ear. 'I keep telling you, got to trust me, Hugh. This isn't Nam.'

'Not for the moment, but the day might come.'

'Hey,' Wise said, and sounded hurt. 'Is that a nice thing to say?' He reached for the dangling harness, looped one arm through. 'I ride, you and the lady walk. Okay?' As he adjusted the harness about his big frame the unzipped top of his coveralls bulged to reveal an empty shoulder holster.

'Get the little lady home, Hugh. It's all over.'

'What about him?' Rossiter gestured toward the body. 'We can't just leave him.'

'Are you kidding?' In spite of the racket Wise seemed to have no problem in making himself heard. 'They need that suicide so they can hush everything up. Some poor guy serving his country, undercover hero, couldn't take the strain any longer, but still good for taking the blame.'

286

He buckled the harness casually.

'The British junk press will lap it up like it's the latest TV soap. The rest will hint and speculate but a few legalised threats from Whitehall and they'll start figuring the cost of injunctions and court actions.'

He gave Rossiter a last friendly squeeze. 'Kind of thing your people do in their sleep, right? Kind of thing they can bury six feet deep? Merry Christmas, old buddy.'

He signalled the winchman and floated gently up. Moments later there was nothing but diminishing noise and a single winking light that vanished over the hill. Far below, moonlight and fog covered the Weald in a ghostly pall of radiance.

Still cradled in Rossiter's arms, Sarah was racked with violent, silent spasms that shook his own body.

Rossiter tightened his hold on her, her hair soft against his face. 'Home,' he said softly. 'He's right. It's over now. And there's still Emma.' He drew her firmly away from the clearing.

Only as he saw her into the car did she speak. 'We'll never know,' she said. 'After all that, we'll never know.'

He switched on his lights. They seemed to thicken the darkness. Sarah found a handkerchief and blew her nose vigorously. 'But then,' she said, her voice suddenly harsh and unchallengeably assertive, 'we never do, do we? Not really.'